The King's Jewel

The King's Jewel

Sarena and Sasha Nanua

iUniverse LLC
Bloomington

The King's Jewel

iUniverse books may be ordered through booksellers or by contacting:

iUniverse LLC
1663 Liberty Drive
Bloomington, IN 47403
www.iuniverse.com
1-800-Authors (1-800-288-4677)

ISBN: 978-1-4759-9879-5 (sc)
ISBN: 978-1-4759-9880-1 (e)

Library of Congress Control Number: 2013912650

Printed in the United States of America

iUniverse rev. date: 09/11/2013

To Mom, Dad, and Aneil,
for your continuous support and love

Prologue

The Sorcerers Underworld
1915

The woman's feet pounded against the cool sand with urgency. She was heading toward an abandoned farmhouse which was located on the far end of the Sapphire Quarter. Night had already begun to fall, and with that, her hope had, too.

After a long and strenuous journey across the sandy beach, she had finally reached the house. The door was wide open, as if inviting her in, and she took a cautious step inside. The house was dark and vacant. The windows were boarded up, but a hint of moonlight would occasionally seep through the cracks.

The woman's mossy green eyes darted across the room before they landed on a lonely cabinet. She headed across the room toward it, hurriedly opened the cabinet door, and peered within it. A small, wooden block was attached to the back of the cabinet. She extended her arm and pulled the wooden block, turning it like a lever. A short *click* sounded from the back of the mysterious cabinet, and she pulled the block out. With curious eyes she peered inside the opening in the cabinet and pulled out the object hidden within it.

Her trembling hands caressed the object as she set it on the floor. It looked like a genie lamp, rusted with age. One hand rested on the golden lamp, the other clamped to the handle. Then she rubbed her hand against the lamp—once, twice, three times—before stepping backward and examining the lamp in front of her.

Tufts of white smoke began to trail from the spout of the lamp, extending to the top of the house, until the mist disappeared to reveal a genie. He wore a dark vest and puffy purple silk pants that reached his pointy shoes. A great lump of curly red hair sprouted from his head and he wore an expression of both sleepiness and excitement, as if he woke from a deep sleep.

"Ah, been trapped in that lamp for nearly two hundred years, I tell you!" he said with an accent that hinted on Irish.

The woman stared at him with a shocked expression. "Are—are you Arnold, the Great Genie?"

The genie's lips curved down in a frown. *"Ar . . . nold."* He stretched the word as if it was foreign to him. "Arnold. Yes, I suppose that's me. Been two hundred years, mind you, so my mind's a tad foggy. But that needn't stop me from doing my job!" He paused, as if pondering what to say next. "What is your name?"

"Vina," the woman stated. "My name is Vina."

"Very well, Vina. I am a genie, and thus I may grant you three wishes. But there are some restrictions on the types of wishes you can make: no wish can bring back a life, cause immortality, or true love. Otherwise, you are free to make any wish you like."

Vina laced her fingers in a pleading gesture. "I need you to keep my husband safe. Juan is fighting in the Great Sorcerer War and I can't risk his life! Please, you have to help me!" she cried worriedly.

Arnold swirled his fingers in an odd way before scratching the tiny tufts of red hair on the edge of his chin.

"I'm afraid that's too close to immortality, dearie. There is nothing I can do."

"Please!" Vina cried with urgency, tears springing to her green eyes. After such a long trip to find this genie, this was definitely not the news she wished to hear. "Maybe I can provide you some trinkets which you could use at the Blessing River! I would do it myself, but you are obviously much more powerful than I." She immediately began to pull many small trinkets from her pocket: a watch, a shiny bracelet, and even a half-nibbled piece of chocolate in a thin wrapper.

The genie stared at the trinkets, his mind spinning as he contemplated the objects. He quickly collected these items and stuffed them in the silk pockets inside his vest. "I will journey to the Blessing River and try to perform this wish. However, if I do not return within two hours' time, you must expect the worst. Your husband may already be dead."

Vina nodded her head. "Quickly, then."

Arnold nodded. His body began to shimmer, and soon he was shrouded by a thick, purple smoke. He'd disappeared, leaving Vina alone and anxious for his arrival that was yet to come.

* * *

Arnold stood on the edge of the sandy beach, contemplating the waves that receded toward the Blessing River. He had promised this woman—Vina—that he would use her trinkets in order to keep her husband safe. The purpose of the Blessing River was to provide sorcerers with a blessing of sorts. They could receive a blessing by throwing a keepsake into the Blessing River, which would then wash ashore and provide some form of blessing for the owner. This would most certainly help Arnold, the Great Genie, with performing Vina's wish.

Arnold reached into his pocket, pulled out the trinkets from beneath, and closed his eyes. He focused on the wish, the words pressed against his lips. Then he threw the trinkets into the ocean and waited for whatever fortune was to come.

But what had come was not fortune; it was misfortune.

Arnold peered around the Blessing River, his curly hair bouncing like ping-pong balls. Where were the trinkets? Weren't they supposed to return to shore?

Arnold turned his head toward the sand beneath his feet. He noticed a small piece of chocolate in a shiny wrapper set in front of his toes as it washed ashore. Then, as the chocolate just barely touched his feet, he felt an odd tingle in his fingers. He was about to reach out for the chocolate when he noticed something very odd about his feet. His skin seemed to be chipping off, replaced by a dark brown coating. He looked at his hands and noticed crinkles forming in his palms. His skin chipped away once again, revealing another mysterious brown coating.

What was going on?

The genie stared at his body, mouth agape as his silk clothing disappeared, replaced by another coat of the strange substance. He lifted his hands to his eyes and examined them. Then he lightly pressed his pointer finger to his tongue. The taste was distinctive: chocolate.

Chocolate?

The genie gently moved his hands across his face, feeling the dark substance swallow his skin and creep around his eyelids. Arnold was well aware of what had occurred—a wish gone awry. Surely he could wish away the chocolate coating, return himself to his normal form, but he soon realized it was far too late.

He was no longer Arnold, the Great Genie. He was Arnold, the chocolate man.

* * *

It wasn't long before Vina had left for the Blessing River. The genie had said he would return within two hours' time, but he had not returned. The genie had disappeared, nowhere to be found. Vina wondered if the trinkets had worked. If so, her husband would be safe. If not . . . Well, she didn't want to think about that at the moment.

Vina bent toward the sand and allowed the cool water to rush over her fingertips. From the corner of her left eye she could see something flashing silver. She looked over and saw a thin, silver wrapper that looked oddly familiar. It was the chocolate wrapper she'd given to Arnold earlier, but the chocolate inside had disappeared.

As she looked forward she slowly noticed small, dark brown footprints in the sand. Vina immediately gasped.

She remained kneeled against the cool sand and pressed her hands in a set of footprints. The realization of what had happened hit her sooner than she could comprehend.

If Arnold had indeed made these chocolate footprints, then the wish had gone awry. And that could only mean one thing.

The wish had not worked.

Her husband was dead.

Vina looked across the water in shock. Soon enough, warm tears had reached her eyes. She was sobbing heavily, her body heaving up and down. She quaked and convulsed as she cried, filled with such immense sorrow for her loss. She wanted to keep her husband safe during the War, but it was far too late for that. Her husband, who was now dead, was arguably in the middle of being transferred to the Death Field of the Sorcerers Underworld.

As waves of water surrounded her feet, she began to release her clammy hands from her face. A slow but surely dawning realization began to permeate her mind. It was a change—she no longer felt sorrow in the loss of her husband. What she felt was different, something she'd never think of feeling when her husband passed: happiness.

Her hands swooped down to her cloak, smoothing the ruffles. Her eyes were not puffy and red as they should have been. Instead, her eyes were black.

She wasn't crying at all. She was laughing.

ONE: AWAKENING

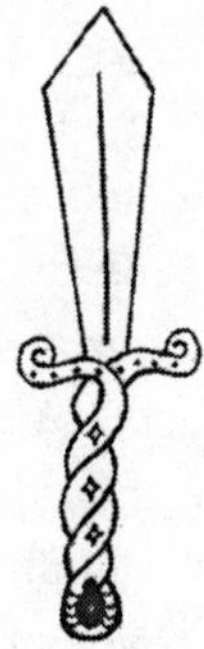

The Sorcerers Underworld
Present day

When the bag lifted off my head, the world was like a blurry painting. The air smelled strange and my surroundings were foreign to me. I struggled to move my hands and feet, but they were knotted. The darkness made everything look like a moving shadow, flickering here and there. I noticed a fire not too far away from me. It seemed to move closer to me, sauntering as the flames licked the air. But as it came closer, I noticed that it was not a fire at all. It was the flames of Ash's red hair, her eyes intensely burning into mine.

Ash's mouth peeled into a knowing smile, her teeth gleaming. *"You're in the Sorcerers Underworld."*

I jerked off my back, feeling cold sweat run down my spine. Ash's words still haunted me even hours, perhaps days after my relocation to the Sorcerers Underworld. I didn't have any recollection or memory as to how I'd gotten here. The floor beneath me was chalk white and nothing but an occasional ray of sunlight showed any sign of life. How there was sunlight in the Underworld was pretty much beyond me, but it was still a helpful indication of the passing days and nights.

I immediately pressed my hand against my neck, relieved to feel my gemstone necklace safely resting on my chest. Then I stood from my crouched position, arched my back so I could relieve my tense muscles, and stared at the wall in front me. As I examined the wall, the whiteness seemed to disappear, replaced by a wavering black door. I rubbed my sleep-crusted eyes and moved toward the door, then placed my hand on the knob hesitantly. Yes, this door was definitely real. I tried twisting the knob, but it would barely turn ninety degrees, leaving me locked in the white room.

I leaned down on my left knee and stared through the key hole. There was utter blackness for a moment, but I waited patiently. A sudden blue circle of light emerged and I felt a painful stab in my right eye.

"Ouch!" I veered backward, cupping my eye in pain. When the pain had finally subsided I removed my hand from my eye. The image in front of me was distorted, half clear and the other half blurry. After blinking repeatedly, I could finally make out the tiny, hovering blue figure in front of me.

"Three days."

"Huh?" I asked blearily. Then the figure moved toward the door, inched back through the keyhole, and disappeared from sight.

The door began to shake abruptly. I jumped back with surprise and found myself pressed against the opposite wall. Then, with a gentle creak, the door slid open and I found myself face-to-face with the blue figure once again. The minute creature hovered in the air, and then zoomed off suddenly. I forcefully removed myself from the wall, consumed by a million thoughts, but I knew this door wouldn't stay open for long. I felt the urge to follow the creature into the dark passageway beyond the door, so I moved with a slow and suspicious manner toward the hall. Once I'd finally made it into the hall, I turned and examined the white room. It looked like no more than a small children's room, and yet caused my stomach to stir uncomfortably.

I turned back, feeling both cautious and enticed, and followed the creature. It looked small, with wings that fluttered in the air like a nervous butterfly. As I ascended along the passage I noticed large, white pillars standing proudly in a vertical arrangement. Royal blue draperies hung from the ceiling, encoded with words I supposed were written in Latin. The creature was leading me to a vast door of some sort, located near the end of the hall. When I approached the many stairs that led to it, I noticed two angered gargoyles posted at opposite sides of the door. Their bodies were stone statues, but their eyes seemed to move, scanning the hall for passersby.

"Newcomer?" one asked.

"Hm. Smells interesting . . . like the Pro . . . the Pro . . ." The gargoyle stopped speaking abruptly, mouth agape, but that was pretty hard to tell since it was carved out of stone.

The other gargoyle decided to carry on for the other flabbergasted gargoyle: "The council has not yet ended. You must wait until the sentencing has been completed."

I cleared my throat. I didn't exactly picture being greeted by two stone gargoyles when I entered the Sorcerers Underworld. "And when will that be?"

The gargoyle gave a throaty laugh. "Ask your Time Sprite."

I turned and stared at the blue creature. *A Time Sprite?*

I opened my mouth to speak, but then the Time Sprite caught my attention. It moved toward the door and illuminated the words embedded within it: entrance to sc.

My eyebrows creased. The last time I'd seen this door was the night of the feast, when Adam had told me about the prophecy. Had he actually led me to a place in the Sorcerers Underworld?

"Fifteen seconds," the Time Sprite informed.

"What?" I asked. My mind was still processing this new information.

"Twelve seconds . . . Ten seconds . . ."

I turned toward the door, the gargoyles now immobile. The Time Sprite's voice sang in my ear: "Five, four . . ."

I counted the seconds down in my head: *Three . . . two . . . one.*

The door slammed open. A lady with short, black hair emerged and angrily stomped down the concrete stairs. A gray thundercloud erupted over her head, hovering over her as she trailed down the hall. Then she disappeared in a plume of gray and black smoke.

I turned my attention back to the open door. A circular railing was situated in the middle of the room, and the electric blue Sphere hovered in the centre; the Sphere looked like a giant ball of contained, visible electricity. There were many people all standing around the circular railing, chatting away without notice of myself or the Time Sprite.

All of a sudden a man with oily black hair—Ion—stepped from the crowd of murmuring people and silenced them. "Quiet!" he yelled.

The Sorcerer Line fell silent.

A lady ducked under the railing and appeared on the other side, nearing the blue Sphere. Her coal black eyes left me with no sympathy.

Lembrose.

My hands clenched, unclenched, and then I decided to step forward. Suddenly I felt as if I'd hit an invisible sheet of concrete and found myself falling backward. I landed hard on the dusty stairs, my elbows numb. After sucking in a breath between my gritted teeth, I lifted myself from the stairs and looked back through the invisible sheet to find Vina speaking as if she hadn't noticed me at all.

"Although unsuccessful in capturing the gemstones, yet another problem has arisen. We are all aware of the missing crown—the King's Jewel. It is only safe to say that one of our own has stolen it." She paused, scanning the crowd. "Mira."

The crowd gasped, murmurs sweeping around the room. "Mira took it!"

"It really was her!"

"In a tornado, too!"

"I said *quiet*!" Ion repeated.

"The only one who should be silencing anyone is me," came an unfamiliar and commanding voice. Everyone looked up to find a lady looking of my mother's age, perhaps older, with faint wrinkles that surrounded her bright blue eyes. Her hands were clasped together gracefully. She wore a shimmering blue cloak and her hair was long and wavy, gold as the sun. As she moved forward, her beautiful gemstone necklace sparkled as if it were alive. It was composed of an intricate web of sapphires and a rainbow-glinting diamond that seemed to disappear in the light every few seconds.

The lady turned toward the ring of sorcerers in front of her. The crowd gasped, colour draining from their faces.

"Queen Magestaria," Vina said, bowing down to her with some difficulty. "I was unaware—"

"Unaware?" the queen asked. "Unaware that you and many others had threatened the *Prophetic Child,* let alone abort my mission of peace in caring for her? Vina," she snapped suddenly, "you were given one task and one task only. And what had you done? You promised that your days of malice were over. Now a Sorcerer Field has been detected—an illegal use of magic—and you dare tell *me* that you were *unaware*? Oh, fellow sorcerers, you needn't worry about that." Her voice dripped with false sympathy. "Due to your evident violation of my wishes, all members of the Sorcerer Line are sentenced to indefinite time in the Dungeons."

Voices sprouted from the ring of sorcerers, all surprised or outraged. The queen silenced them once again. "I hereby announce the incarceration of the Sorcerer Line for the following actions: manipulation of a mortal and usage of a shape-shifting potion as a form of impersonation; threat to the Prophetic Child; and the misleading of the heir to the Sorcerers Underworld." Before the Sorcerer Line could utter a single word, the queen snapped her fingers and the sorcerers disappeared into a plume of ominous black smoke.

The railing was now deserted. The queen remained standing near a long podium, as if contemplating something. I saw the invisible sheet waver before me, and realized that the force field was disappearing. I walked forward cautiously, passing the familiar blue Sphere and circling the railing. The queen stepped forward, and then gestured toward a seat by the thrones. I moved carefully, but still found myself in awe of her presence, her beauty, her power.

"Cocoa, Arica?" she asked. A mug immediately appeared on the counter that divided the space between us. The mug began to fill itself with a hot substance until it brimmed with steaming cocoa.

"Er, yes, thank you," I said, bringing the cocoa to my dry lips. I took a satisfying sip and felt the warmth slide down my throat. I was so unaware of how hungry I'd been, especially after realizing I'd been in the Sorcerers Underworld for three days, unconscious for the most part.

"I feel as though I must apologize for what has been brought on to you over the past months. I apologize for the actions of my trusted . . . friend. Vina." She swallowed, the wrinkles around her eyes deepening. "I suspected you were the Prophetic Child for a long time now. Vina was sent to ensure your care as you lived your life in the mortal world."

"O-oh," I stammered. "I-I—"

"You must feel drained." She touched her icy hands to my burning forehead. "Would you care for another mug of hot cocoa?"

I looked down at my mug to realize I had already finished the entire cup. I quickly nodded my head and she waved me another.

"T-thanks, Your Highness."

She sighed, looking into my eyes hopefully. "Call me Magestaria, Queen of the Sorcerers Underworld." She stood from her throne and swiped the empty mugs away with a flick of her fingers. "I presume your arrival to the Sorcerers Underworld was . . . ?"

"Not exactly what I was expecting," I said with a slight chuckle.

Queen Magestaria beamed. "As I thought. I was lucky enough to hear word of the Sorcerer Line entering the Sorcerers Underworld not long after you'd arrived. When I captured the whole of the Sorcerer Line and their descendants, they were immediately questioned and ultimately taken to Sorcerer Council, as you just witnessed."

I struggled to digest this new information, but a question was still glued to my mind. "Um, Queen Magestaria, I don't really understand. Le-Vina said that the school wasn't *real.*" I knew the question wasn't associated to her previous comment, but I was still frazzled by that thought. Halloween night felt like it had only occurred minutes before I'd awoken to this place.

"Not real?" She pursed her lips, contemplating. "Here," she said, rising from her chair, "come with me, and perhaps I will clarify some of the questions I'm sure you've been meaning to ask."

She began to exit the room, and I turned to follow her with weak legs. I definitely had a lot of questions bouncing around in my head, but none of the others seemed to reach my limp tongue.

"Arica, what you've just witnessed here is a Sorcerer Council. This mansion is the official Head Quarters of the Sorcerers Underworld, where many Councils have taken place over the past centuries." She led me down the stairs, then toward a large window that was positioned between two massive pillars. "There are five separate sectors in the Sorcerers Underworld, which could either be referred to as Sectors or Quarters. We still call them Quarters even though there are five of them, because there were originally only four. European Quartz was added only centuries ago." She spoke as if *centuries* meant only a few years. "We are in the Sapphire Quarter. The five sections are—"

"Ruby, Quartz, Sapphire, Jade, and Topaz?" I finished.

The queen lifted her eyebrows.

"Lucky guess," I answered.

She laughed melodically. "I knew of Vina's creation of a new school, to look over you. Unfortunately, the Sorcerer Field was virtually undetectable."

"Sorcerer Field? What is that?" I questioned.

She pressed her lips together, and then began her explanation. "A Sorcerer Field is an illegal form of magic that allows one's imagination to create a solid object. For example, if I wished for a cup of cocoa, I could literally just wish it upon me now, just as I had in the Council room. Since I am the queen, I do have the exception to do that sort of thing."

"Then, Your Highness, why is it illegal?"

"Because this type of magic could go to extreme lengths. For example, someone could simply wish upon a weapon of mass destruction. That wouldn't be very good, would it?"

"I suppose not," I muttered.

"And Vina's Sorcerer Field allowed her to imagine a school, and bring it to life, making it practically undetectable to all mortals and sorcerers. I was aware that Vina was once involved in malevolence in the past, but we believed she had changed, long after her gemstones were taken. And this use of time-travel . . ." The queen stopped herself, clearly exasperated despite her noble stature.

"She said the school wasn't real. That she wouldn't take 'precious time' building one," I said, making air quotes, but then I stopped myself because it felt a bit inappropriately casual in front of the queen.

"The school is most certainly *real* in the sense that it is palpable, yes, but it was most certainly not *built* like most mortal buildings. Everyone attending and teaching at that school most certainly exists, as well," she explained. "But these Sorcerer Fields do not last forever. At some point or another, it will begin to disappear."

"The school will disappear?" I shivered, thinking of my old classmates, but mostly just Monika and Jake. "When will that happen?"

"That cannot be determined," the queen said sorrowfully. "It would depend on how strong the sorcerer or sorceress is. But you shouldn't worry about your friends. Vina is evidently very powerful. More powerful than I once believed." She pressed her pointer finger and thumb to the bridge of her nose, but then regained composure. Her eyes were aglow with wisdom and warmth. "I believed Vina had changed, but my son knew better of this."

"Your son?"

"Yes. He stayed at your school to ensure your safety, being the Prophetic Child, as we believed. It had become his one and only duty to protect you. I believe he acted as a janitor."

My heart thumped. "Janitor?"

"Why, yes, indeed." She glanced out the window, her pale reflection cast in the window, and then turned back to me with warm eyes. "I believe it is time for you to meet my son: Adam Collins, the prince."

TWO: A TOUR

I gasped. *Prince?*

The queen looked at me with fond, caring eyes. "I hope he has taken care of you over the past few months. It is only my dream that he will one day turn out to be someone as thoughtful and encouraging as his father, King Thoven." She stared dreamily out the window. "I'm sure you've probably heard of the surprising news pass lately . . . ?"

"Surprising news?" I asked.

"Indeed," she said in a sigh. "The king's crown, also known as the Jewel, is missing. I suspected Vina from the start—but now it seems that Mira, creator of weather, may be the one behind it."

A symphony of footsteps shuffled our way. I looked up to find Janine, Jess, and Joseph, all shakily walking toward me. Janine and Jess, by the looks of their hair and clothes, seemed as if they'd been playing an intense game of wrestling, and Joseph looked as if he just woke up from a long, dark sleep.

"Janine, Jess, Joseph!" I cried. I embraced each of them in a hug, feeling as if my chest had been lifted. Seeing my cousins had never felt so relieving.

"Arica, where've you been?" Jess asked. "Joseph, Janine and I have already toured the whole mansion—except the Dungeons, of course—no thanks to Joseph and his continuous rambles about wanting to visit the King's Library." Jess's face lit up. "Oh, and you won't believe who we met! Remember the janitor who walked in during the battle? He's actually the prince!"

"My son," the queen remarked. "How lovely to meet you all. I've heard much about you three from Adam."

Joseph hung his jaw in awe. "Queen Magestaria! I can't even begin to tell you how lucky I feel in your presence." Then Joseph began to scratch his neck like he had during the feast. "I haven't read a book in *three* days! This is disastrous!"

The queen gave a pleasant laugh. "I have heard much about you, Joseph. You seem like a bright, young man."

Joseph abruptly stopped scratching his neck and blushed. "Well, it is my passion to—"

"Ah, the twins!" the queen interrupted, gazing at the twins while cupping their faces. When the queen turned around they gave Joseph a wide smirk and stuck out their tongues.

Joseph turned bright red and stormed after the queen as soon as she left. Janine, Jessica, and I followed, grinning.

"Now, as you all may know, you have been in the Sorcerers Underworld for three days. Have your Time Sprites gotten to you in time?" The queen grabbed another mug of hot cocoa from the air and lifted her pinkie as she sipped.

"Why, of course," Joseph said, adjusting his tie from the Albert Einstein costume he'd been wearing since Halloween. "I named mine Bookworm. We love to read together."

Janine and Jessica snorted in reply while slapping their knees. "*Bookworm?* Get real, Joseph!" Their laughter echoed off the walls.

"*Ahem,*" the queen said.

Janine and Jess shut up.

"Well, then. It seems that I have to give a small explanation to you all. You see, time runs differently in the Sorcerers Underworld than it does in the mortal world. For instance, if I spent three days in the Sorcerers Underworld, that would only be about twenty minutes in the mortal world."

My eyes widened. "You mean . . . it's still *Halloween*?"

"Indeed it is. But no need to worry about that logic right now. We must be heading off on our tour—I'm sure Prince Adam will greet us along the way."

* * *

The tour of the mansion started with the Dungeons.

These were not just any Dungeons—these Dungeons were jail cells, filled with creatures and guarded by very powerful magic. The Dungeons' jail cells also spoke—yeah, I said *spoke*—giving routine reports on what the inmates were up to. It was a pretty well-thought out system, completed with full security down to the last drop of magic.

"Wow," I said as we reached the entrance to the Dungeons. The mouth of the cavern greeted us as we entered. Each jail cell was unique in some way, holding some sort of magical being: monstrous creatures and foreboding sorcerers, some of which I scarily recognized. As we passed the cells, the queen led us to a man who stood at the opposite end of the corridor. He wore a long, black cloak and had short brown hair and gray eyes that made him seem very young. The wrinkles lightly pressed against his forehead made it seem otherwise.

"Pedro, how are the Dungeons holding up thus far?" the queen asked the man.

He slightly turned his torso, letting his head dip as a sign of respect for the queen. "Very well. Cerberus hasn't escaped for three weeks now." He gestured toward a cell occupied by a giant dog with three heads mounted upon its great neck. One of its noses peeked between the cell bars and a ball of dog slobber slipped from its pointed teeth to Joseph's arm. Joseph recoiled in disgust.

The queen chuckled lightly. Joseph's mouth hung in a little O shape, aghast. "Cerberus?" He gulped. "The three-headed dog?"

Pedro laughed, but his dark eyes were slightly weary. "He's not harmful in the slightest," Pedro responded.

The queen gestured toward Pedro and then said, "Arica, Janine, Jessica, and Joseph, meet our Jail Guard, Pedro. He has the power to make one obey his commands, but of course, his powers are not directed toward humans. He uses his power to ensure the creatures or even sorcerers sentenced to this prison do not escape."

Pedro was gently padding one of the dog's giant noses when he abruptly stopped, turning toward us. Cerberus wagged all three of its tongues in delight.

"Did you say . . . Arica?" Pedro asked. Then he took my hand, shaking it vigorously. "The Prophetic Child herself!" He laughed in amazement. "This is unbelievable!"

The queen nodded in agreement. "Well, Pedro, as we must continue our tour, you must assure me no mischief will arise whilst I'm gone."

"Of course not, Your Highness," he said, averting his attention from me.

Suddenly a loud *bang* sounded from behind the Dungeons.

"What was that?" Janine asked with a quiver in her voice.

"A creature, maybe?" Jess asked with concern.

"No," I said in the silence. "It sounded more like a person."

"People, more like it," Joseph chimed in.

"Oh, that's probably the old Crigo in the back. I think he wants to return to the Crigo Pit," he said with a weary chuckle. He turned his head toward the back. As he turned I noticed something very odd about something on his neck, behind his ear. A bruise? No, it was a tattoo of some sort. A giant S engulfed in black flames.

"I'll be off, then," Pedro said, throwing his hood over his head and gliding out of sight.

I stood, perplexed, and found myself wondering about Pedro's tattoo and what it could possibly mean. Then the queen turned toward us and said, "That's it for the Dungeons. I suppose our next stop is the kitchen."

As we walked past the vast array of pillars toward the other end of the mansion, Joseph was still trying to get rid of the slobber from the dog's mouth. "Ugh, I just bought this robe!" he said sadly.

Janine and Jessica giggled uncontrollably. Their laughter faded as we turned down a dark, winding corridor to a dead end.

The queen contemplated the stone wall, allowing her hand to brush over the cool stone. Then she stepped backward and gave a concentrated stare to the wall, as if having a staring contest. "Kitchen," she announced suddenly, and then the wall dissolved to show yet another corridor, this time leading to a bright white room.

"Fascinating," Joseph murmured.

With haste, we followed Queen Magestaria to the room. Inside was a blond man who was busily speaking to a chef in the kitchen with an interrogating tone of voice. I immediately recognized the man's square features and golden hair. He was Adam Collins.

"Adam," the queen said, her voice holding a hint of surprise, "what brings you to the kitchen?"

Adam's gaze shifted abruptly. "Mother," he called, also surprised, the two syllables coming out clumsily. He straightened his back and clenched his hands, as if he hadn't even seen her walk in. "I've just been speaking to Lewis about the stolen Jewel situation. He's been told to be a primary suspect."

"Honestly, I don't know anything!" Lewis said with a frazzled voice. His white apron contrasted with his dark skin and gray eyes, and his curly black hair just barely slid past his ears. He looked to be the Head of the kitchen, though his comrades didn't seem very helpful during the interrogation.

"Rumours have slid around about Mira hiding the King's Jewel in a tornado somewhere in the mortal world," the queen informed. "I cannot pinpoint if this is true."

"Yeah, I heard that, too," Lewis said hurriedly, as though the queen's commentary were a sort of escape from his interrogation. "Salad, Your Highness?" He pulled out a wad of lettuce and began chopping at an inhuman speed. Before I knew it, he'd already made a brightly coloured salad in just seconds.

"No, thank you," Adam said sharply, and then he abruptly pulled the knife from Lewis's hand. "A knife—your knife—was found at the crime scene just days ago. Care to explain?" Adam said, and then jabbed the knife down into the cutting board and while giving a concentrated stare.

"I-I—" Lewis stuttered, mouth opening and closing as if he were a fish passing through water. "I was working late that night," he finally said, pressing his hands against the counter. "The king passed by, though he wasn't wearing his crown. I offered some food, but he said no. He seemed worried. I dunno what about. I guess the missing Jewel, now that I think about it. Anyway, I was getting ready to leave when I saw a shadow flicker by—someone was coming into the kitchen. A girl, by the looks of it. Her voice was snake-like, inhuman. She wanted something from me—she was threatening me. She wanted my knife. So I gave it to her, and then she disappeared. Just like that." His forehead was covered in beads of sweat.

"Vina?" I asked abruptly. There didn't seem to be any other possible answer.

"Maybe," Adam agreed, looking over to me. For some reason, I felt like my eyes were glued to his. It was strange to see him as someone other than the school janitor—as someone as important as the *prince* of the Sorcerers Underworld.

"Last I saw you I was about to be drowned in a torrent of water," he said with a laugh.

I was about to laugh, too, until I remembered what had happened that night—Halloween night. Vina threatened us with an ultimatum: give her the gemstones, or no Jessica. After a dangerous encounter with Scorzzards (a scorpion-lizard hybrid with a taste for flesh), we'd stumbled upon the drama room—the place I'd been dying to get into for the past two months. That was also the day I learned that the Sapphires were secretly working with Lembrose-Vina—behind my back and plotting against me.

They were all descendents of the Sorcerer Line, a sinister group of sorcerers whose goal was to retrieve our gemstones for their evil plans.

Adam had also made an unexpected appearance during our confrontation, appearing in a portal of water. He'd said something to Vina—something about telling his mother? Wait—the queen, of course! He told Vina he was going to tell his mother, the queen, about her malevolent plans, but she didn't seem shaken by his threat. Then he'd been whisked away by the pool of water, plunged behind the brick wall into darkness. Adam had gone through a portal of some sort, but where exactly did that portal lead to? The Sorcerers Underworld? And why had it taken him away? Perhaps Vina had created it as a sort of trap to ensure he wouldn't interrupt the battle and destroy her plans.

I turned my attention to the silvery bowl of salad. A bright light reflected off the bowl, sweeping across my vision. The flashing light reminded me of something—someone: Jane and her bright retainer. What had happened to Jane? She'd been tricked, forced under Sleeplock so that she could carry out Vina's requests and replace Jessica. But where was Jane now? The thoughts flooded through my mind as though it were a gateway to a dimension of unanswered questions.

"Aaaaaah!" Lewis screamed suddenly, ducking behind the counter.

"What? What is it?" Janine asked with concern.

Lewis's breath came in ragged pants, slowly returning to normal intervals. "It's her," he said, his finger pointing shakily. "She's the girl."

I followed his finger and stared at the girl he was pointing at. At first I didn't understand, but soon I realized what he was talking about: the girl who'd stolen his knife. He was pointing at Jess.

"Jessica?" Joseph asked with mild revelation. "No, it couldn't have been Jessica. She was captured by the Sorcerer Li—"

"No," I spoke up. "Not this Jess. The impersonator—that's who he saw, not *our* Jessica. I think Ash brought Jane here and she was told to take the knife from Lewis as a sort of set up."

"Then it's settled," Adam claimed. "If Ash was involved in this, then Vina must've stolen the crown."

"But she couldn't have," Joseph said in utter disagreement. "She was always at the school, preparing for the battle on Halloween night."

"No one can be sure," Adam said evenly.

"But I think I am," Joseph said coolly. His response was quick-witted, but the slobber on his robe was overtly not helping his tough image.

"Boys, we must address the matter at hand," the queen stated sternly. "If Vina *is* the thief, she could in no way be in possession of it. Not after she's just been sent to the Dungeons for indefinite time. Someone else must have it. An acquaintance."

"An acquaintance?" Jessica asked. "Such as . . . ?"

"Only time will tell," she responded. "I must arrange time to speak to Vina about this matter soon. Otherwise, I think we're done visiting the kitchen, yes, Adam?" the queen noted with the slightest parental severity. Adam nodded wordlessly.

"I suppose you're all getting tired of touring this mansion. How about you go outside, visit Majestorium Square?" the queen suggested.

"Majestorium Square!" Joseph cried with disbelief. "That was once the homeland of the Majestora, a species of sirens! They lived in a vast sea, home to countless Underworld creatures, but it was dried out centuries ago by the dense heat of the Sapphire Quarter. Now many novelty stores have been put in replacement as the greatest tourist attraction of the Sorcerers Underworld!"

The queen laughed, patting her son on the shoulder. "A very knowledgeable young sorcerer indeed," she noted. "Now, you five go on, I think I'll make a quick trip to the Dungeons to visit Vina. Thank you for your time, Lewis."

Lewis was still shakily standing by the counter, analyzing our conversation. He nodded his head with wide eyes.

Adam led the way out, Joseph close behind, and then we exited the mansion to the fresh air of the Sorcerers Underworld. The sky was tinged blue and the world looked like a miraculous replication of the mortal world, only more magical. The streets were ringed with shacks and houses of all shapes and sizes, and soon we found ourselves heading down an alleyway toward Majestorium Square. We walked out of the dark path and into the hustle and bustle of sorcerers, squirming our way through the many magical beings going about their day. The Square was tightly packed, like the streets of New York City but ten times the crowd. The Square was outlined with several stores, some more densely packed than others. Time Sprites eagerly followed their owners, giving updates with high-pitched voices.

I turned my head and examined the stores: Granny Goblins was closest to me, its slogan spoken through a short, wart-covered goblin as it said, *"Need a nanny? We've got a granny!"* in a throaty tone. Beside this was another store named Faun & Sons, which looked a little more run-down than the rest. The store was located farther back, down the alleyway, shrouded in a thick layer of cobwebs. Its green paint was peeling off in spiral curls; each curl ended in a jagged shape, as if they were claws from a wolf's paw.

"This looks promising," Jessica said sarcastically.

"Oh, perhaps I can get a new robe from here!" Joseph said, his voice hopeful.

Adam furrowed his eyebrows. "Of all the times I've passed through Majestorium Square, I've never seen this store. And besides, I don't think they sell robes, either. We should just move on . . . ."

"We'll never know if we don't try," Joseph concluded. Then he led the way with a march. A light ringing came from the doorway as we entered. The store was dark, rusted with age. The walls wept with sadness, the dry gray paint ending in globs of tears. Many shelves were set in disarray, holding glass antiquities and bronzed statues.

"Wow, look at this!" Joseph said in amazement as he held a glass ball in his hand. "What do you think it is?"

"Joseph, don't!" Adam cried, but it was already too late. The glass ball Joseph was holding had fallen out of his hands and shattered into minuscule pieces on the ground.

Adam gave an exasperated sigh. "Heato Spheres," he explained. "They hold pixie dust, but when touched by a being *other* than a fairy, they heat up and drop to the ground. Then the pixie dust moves elsewhere."

"Oh," Joseph said with a crestfallen expression. He stared down at the pixie dust that was now slowly seeping into the ground.

"What was that noise?" someone asked. I turned my head to see a man emerge from the back of the room, carrying a sort of stick or cane in one hand. His facial features were not exactly normal; in fact, his face looked almost wolf-like, his hands covered in tufts of curly brown-black hair. Two short, black horns peered over his dishevelled hair. His pants had shrunk to below his knees, revealing furry brown legs and polished hooves. Based on the name of the store, I predicted he was a faun.

The man looked down at the Heato Sphere, eyes wide. Then he looked up at Joseph, a look of fury pressed against his features and into the deepest recesses of his eyes.

"I—I'm so sorry, I'll—" Joseph began with a stutter.

"Oh, my dear boy, why apologize?" the faun interjected, a smile spreading across his face. "I've been trying to get rid of that thing for years!" His eyes lit up. He held out his arms as if to hug Joseph, but then stopped when he saw the slobber on his robe. "Ah, never mind that! Come in, all of you, have a look around!" He moved around the shelves, hurriedly sweeping away the cobwebs with his wooden stick.

"How long do you think it's been since he had customers?" Janine whispered in my ear.

"Twenty years!" the man cried happily.

The five of us exchanged uneasy glances.

The man continued to remove the cobwebs with his stick, trying to reach for a giant cobweb at the high corner of the room.

"Here, allow me," Adam said. He turned and picked up a light object that was fairly lofty, and then handed it to the faun. "This should be tall enough to reach—"

"No, no!" the man cried, batting him away.

"What's wrong?" Joseph asked.

"Keep that thing away from me!" he said, swiping the stick through the air as if he were trying to swat a fly. "I can't touch it!"

"Why not?" Jess asked.

The furry man lowered his stick cautiously. "It's the curse!" he cried. "I can't touch any object . . . except this cane. That's why no one comes," he said sorrowfully. "It's the curse."

"What curse?" I asked.

The man huffed and rested his weight on his cane. "Over twenty years ago, my eldest son had attained a job—an Underworld lawyer, you see—and my other son was heading off for college at the University of the Sorcerers Underworld. Anyway," he said, tears sparkling in his eyes, "my son, as talented as he was, had extraordinary powers. I was sure he was the Prophetic Child, so I took him to the Royal family to confirm this. When the king denied my beliefs, I decided to abandon my store and leave for another part of the Sorcerers Underworld, a place where people would be accepting of my son and in awe of his power. But the king stopped me before I could go; he cursed me, ensuring that I could never touch *anything* again, except for my cane. I couldn't even touch my own son. And the curse has not been lifted. If I do touch something, I will crumble to ashes."

"That seems a little harsh," Janine stated, looking over at Adam.

Adam cleared his throat, possibly offended by the remark against his family. "What he did was a crime. He falsely stated that his son was *the* Child of the Prophecy. His son is not the Prophetic Child—she is," he said, turning to me. I felt my cheeks burn, turning painfully red.

The faun faced me with pain in his reddening eyes, his pupils growing larger. "You!" he cried, holding his stick above his head. "You did this to me!" He took a deep breath and ran forward. His hooves clicked against the ground, and then he swept his cane in the air like a baseball bat.

The cane connected with the glass bottles on the shelves, and shatters rained to the floor. The faun grunted angrily and continued toward me. I ducked, crawling along the floor quickly and sweeping away the glass shatters. Then I rolled around the corner and rested behind a grand statue, holding my breath.

"Yoo-hoo . . ." the faun called tauntingly. "Where are you . . . ?"

"Psst," someone whispered. I turned my head and noticed the twins and Joseph hiding behind a tall bookshelf. Janine was pointing to a door at the back: an exit.

I nodded my head, and was about to silently travel to my cousins when something caught my eye. A small, square piece of glass outlined in a thick black frame lay beneath me. I picked it up and analyzed it, then held it to my eye. When I looked through it, the world looked slightly distorted; everything moved at odd angles. The objects around me swirled and bent, and the glass also seemed to fog up at moments, making it seem as if I was looking through a cloud.

When I turned my head, I noticed an odd figure wavering in front of me. The colours seemed to swarm, bouncing around like a kaleidoscope.

I slowly lowered the glass to see the faun before me, cane in hand.

"Arghhh!" he yelled, swatting his cane to the ground. A yelp escaped my mouth and I rolled out of the cane's path.

"Quick, the back exit!" Adam called from the doorway, the twins and Joseph not far behind. I heaved myself from the floor and followed my cousins, the five of us making a beeline to the exit.

"Hurry, he's right behind us!" I yelled.

I pushed my way across the store and toward the alleyway, and slammed the door behind me. The door directly whacked the faun right in the face, and with a resounding *thump* I assumed he had fallen backward. I was about to run down the alley when an idea formed in my mind. It was crazy, but seeing everything I'd gone through in the past two months, crazy would say the *least* of what the plan truly was.

With the idea still firmly pressed in my mind, I turned and ran back. The faun was, as I assumed, lying motionless on the floor. I headed for the front of the store and picked up a Heato Sphere from the shelves. A hot, searing pain enveloped my hands and I immediately turned to throw the Heato Sphere into the furnace located at the back of store. A flame began to set, licking the dreary paint set against the walls. I immediately ran out of the store, heading toward my cousins, their faces pale and weary.

"Arica, what were you thinking going back in there?" Jessica asked.

I took a moment to catch my breath. "I thought maybe I'd—"

"The faun!" Adam yelled suddenly. I shifted my gaze toward the back exit, finding the faun slowly limping his way out of the flaming store. Smoke began to shroud his form and he coughed continuously until he emerged from the thick plume.

"Look at what you did!" he said, eyes glazed. The smoke behind him crawled through the air and swallowed the sky, casting a gray gloominess over the store. "My store," he cried, waving the cane in the air, "my beautiful store!"

"Hey!" Adam called, moving toward the faun. He turned his torso, meeting Adam's eyes. "I think I know a way to end your suffering," Adam said kindly.

The faun held a glint of hope in his eyes. “How?” he asked eagerly.

“Here,” Adam said gently, and miraculously a baseball appeared in his palm out of wisps of nothingness. “Catch.” He threw the ball toward him, and the faun caught it in his two palms, the cane crashing against the ground.

A grin spread across the faun’s face, but his happiness was short-lived. In nanoseconds he’d disintegrated to a pile of ashes, and the store erupted into flames behind him.

THREE: THE FLOOD

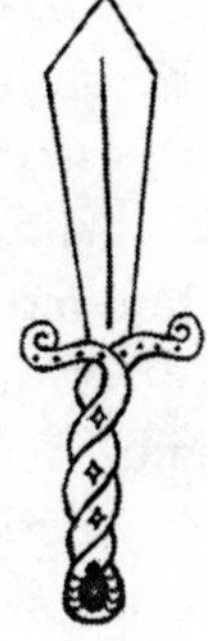

"Nice going, Joseph," Janine and Jessica chorused.

Five minutes had passed since the strange faun store had caught fire. We had all escaped in a mad dash to get as far as we could from the smoldering building, and a few people from the Square had noticed the fire. At first they seemed terrified, but then we explained the situation and the fire had quickly disappeared. I was still in shock from the faun's sudden disintegration, but I supposed I would have to get used to strange things like that in the future.

"What?" Joseph snapped, probably for the millionth time. "All I wanted was *one* robe. *One robe*!" he cried to his sisters. "Now my robe's covered in slobber *and* soot." He wiped at his clothing irritably. The particles of soot were like hands clinging to Joseph's robe, forbidden from letting go.

After we'd finally managed to scrape the soot off our faces, we were back in the pandemonium of Majestorium Square. No one seemed to have taken notice of the exploding novelty store, but the faun was the least of my problems. There were several sorcerers bustling about, waving newspapers in the air as they shouted, "Get the latest edition of *Sorcerers Spark*!" The title on the paper read: MISSING JEWEL THIEF RUMOURED TO BE AMONG US.

"Who would steal the king's crown, anyway? And why?" Joseph asked.

"I don't know. A way of gaining attention, I suppose," Adam surmised. "And my father's crown holds all his power—anyone who could obtain the Jewel would become one of the most powerful sorcerers of our generation."

"Where is your father now?" Joseph asked curiously.

"He hasn't left his chamber since the Jewel was stolen," he said. "He's in a great state of grief," he added sombrely.

After silently squeezing our way through the crowd, I remembered the odd piece of glass I'd found on the floor in Faun & Sons. I fished the object out of my pocket and observed the black frame that surrounded the glass. The glass was circular, roughly the same diameter of the human eye. I held it to my eye and noticed the same figures roaming Majestorium Square, except they looked distorted. I also noticed two other figures (one male and the other female), but their skin was translucent, reminiscent of a ghost.

The two figures were whispering something to one another. Their voices seemed to escalate as they drew closer. The man spoke in gentle, broken whispers: "I heard . . . Andrea, perhaps . . ."

"No, Filip . . ." the woman added.

When the two figures disappeared from sight, I lowered the glass from my eye, mouth agape. "Andrea," I said, voice scratchy. Then I cleared my throat and repeated it to the others. "Andrea and Filip . . . I saw them!"

"Andrea and Filip?" Jess asked. "Like our *great-grandmother* and *great-grandfather* Andrea and Filip?"

"Let me see that," Joseph cut in, taking the glass from my hand and holding it to his eye. It didn't take long before he spotted the two. His gaze was glassy for a moment as recognition seeped into his mind. "Andrea and Filip!" Joseph said with a chuckle. Then he examined the glass piece in his hands. "This must be Ghost Glass."

"Ghost Glass?" I asked curiously, and the twins echoed.

"Yes, a mystical piece of glass that allows you to observe ghosts. They cannot be seen with the naked eye, but they are easily seen with this magical piece of glass . . ." He brought the Ghost Glass to his eyes once again and examined the crowd. "Look at all these *ghosts*!" he cried.

We each took a turn to look through the Ghost Glass. Joseph was eagerly alternating glances between the Ghost Glass and his actual vision, depicting the differences.

"You know, they should really make something called Ghost Glasses—one lens would be like regular glasses while the other would be a Ghost Glass lens!"

We stared at him.

"Yeah . . . like that's going to happen." Janine patted him on the back. "Maybe you'll make that one day." Her voice was rich with sarcasm.

After Joseph's ghost-hunting excitement had finally dimmed, the five of us decided that touring Majestorium Square was no longer appealing. We headed against the crowd toward the exit, entering a long alley that led to the fields that surrounded Head Quarters. When we'd finally escaped the never-ending chatter of rambunctious sorcerers, I let out a sigh of relief. The alley was quiet except for a few sorcerers passing by: Some bowed at Adam's presence, and some were in awe at mine.

"Is that really her?" a boy asked a woman who looked to be his mother. The woman quickly whispered something in his ear and they hurried through the narrow alleyway.

After that deliberation I decided to keep my head low, face hidden from view of other sorcerers. I scanned my surroundings, noticing a strange woman pass by. She wore a thick brown cloak that was lined with dark fur. Her olive-toned skin seemed to gleam in the light, and her hair was thick and braided. There was a very strange but familiar tattoo located on her neck: the letter S surrounded by flames. It was the same tattoo I'd seen on Pedro's neck when we were in the Dungeons.

The woman turned her head and caught me staring at her tattoo. Her eyes met mine for a moment before she slapped her hand over her neck and scurried down the alley.

"Who's that?" I murmured to myself.

"Whom?" Adam asked, turning to face me.

"That lady . . ." I said, but trailed off when I noticed the alleyway was empty. The strange lady was nowhere in sight.

"I think you're just seeing things, Arica . . ." Janine concluded. "Perhaps it's just all this Sorcerers Underworld travel that's getting to you."

"Yeah," I said in agreement, pressing my hand against my head. "It was just her tattoo . . . I saw the same one on Pedro, in the Dungeons."

"Pedro . . . the Jail Guard?" Adam questioned.

"Yes," I confirmed. "I noticed a dark S surrounded by flames tattooed on his neck. And I saw the same one on that lady . . . but what does it mean?"

Adam turned suddenly, sweeping his eyes across the alleyway. "You mean you saw a lady . . . a *Shadower*?"

"What's a Shadower?" I asked, intrigued.

Adam heaved a sigh, contemplating the rose bush in front of him. I could almost see his weary reflection in the fresh morning dew.

"A Shadower is a sorcerer who has the ability to turn into a shadow, but this type of magic is banned. It's an illegal form of magic derived from a very sinister potion. The Shadowers was a menacing organization composed of six sorcerers. They were also known as the Cynical Six, going around and performing crimes in the form of shadows. They were deemed highly threatening to the magical society; however, their Shadowing powers soon began to drain and we were able to capture most of them, even their offspring. Pedro was one of them, but he turned himself in when his Shadowing powers disappeared. We decided to provide him with a form of punishment while also giving him something productive to do, so he is now forced to work at the Dungeons. His obeying powers work well as they help ensure that the inmates follow his commands and remain in their cells."

"So Pedro's . . . a criminal?" Joseph asked with a note of surprise in his voice.

"Well . . . he used to be, but he was one of the few who had actually turned themselves in, unlike the others. We've captured all five except for one, who's been snaking around the Sorcerers Underworld for decades. And now, she could be in Majestorium Square . . ." Adam trailed off, his gaze scanning the crowd of sorcerers.

"She couldn't have gone far," Jessica stated. "Maybe we'll find her hidden in the crowd! We just have to go look," she proposed.

Adam ran his hands through his golden hair, debating the idea. "I don't believe we'd find her that easily. Besides, she *is* a Shadower. I don't know how she maintained her power longer than the others . . ." He finished on a grave note. I turned my attention to a dirty glass window that belonged to the saddened face of an old novelty shop. Something was stirring near the corner of the window. It looked almost like a crow, its wings angrily fluttering up and down. The bird's feathers were black, but the tips of its wings were a bright, flaming orange, almost mimicking the sunset painted against a dark sky.

I turned, looking at the crow. It was now perched upon a small box, chirping at the wall. I turned my attention to the wall, examining the dark shadow that loomed against it. It seemed to flicker here and there, but the shadow did not belong to any figure.

I slowly crept down the alleyway toward the wall. The bird chirped louder, its wings fluttering frantically. Then it moved to the shadow, hovering there for a moment, and flew away, becoming a dark speck in the blue sky.

I returned my attention back to the shadow lingering on the wall. It seemed to take on the shape of a human—my shadow? I angled my head slightly and the shadow followed, but there was still something overtly odd about this shadow. I moved my hand toward the shadow and pressed it against the wall until I felt as though my hand were plunged in a giant bowl of Jell-O. I immediately removed my hand, clenching my fingers together until the jelly-like feeling subsided. Then, with a trembling hand, I urged my pointer finger forward until I felt my hand dip into the jelly-like surface. The shadow slowly flickered, showing the image of a woman with a dark braid and a tattoo on her neck—the same woman I'd seen in the alley. Then the image faded away, returning back to the dark, shadowy form.

"It's her," I said, almost as a whisper. Then I cried out, "It's her!"

"The Shadower?" Joseph questioned, leading the others toward me.

I replied with a trembling nod. Before the shadow-woman could move away from me, I plunged my hand back into the shadow and pulled forward. Her image flickered back to life and she fell forward, knees bent against the ground as her cloak hugged her form.

Adam's jaw hung at the sight of the woman. His expression darkened, matching the dark cobblestone ground beneath us. "Lyra?" he asked with disbelief.

The woman turned her head up, her deep, black eyes filled with pain. She nodded slowly, regaining her composure, and stood to face me and Adam. Then she touched the tattoo embedded on her neck and her face portrayed more pain. After a few brief seconds she looked at me as if she knew who I was. The friction between us was palpable. She was a criminal—a Shadower who'd been missing for decades, and now she stood before me with the eyes of an innocent child willing to be let go.

In one sudden movement she vanished, her shadow running across the walls and disappearing behind the aged trees.

"Run!" Janine cried, and everyone followed suit. We chased the shadow along the wall, passing through numerous obstacles along our path. Joseph was the closest person to reach out and catch her, but when his fingertips had barely skimmed her skin, he collided with a giant bin in front of him, his glasses crashing to the floor just before he did.

"Joseph!" the twins cried, rushing to him. We circled him and he began to regain consciousness. His eyelids fluttered up and down and a nest of dishevelled hair mopped his head.

"How many fingers am I holding up?" Jessica asked, holding her entire hand in front of his face.

Joseph groaned. "Five?"

"No, four, silly! You don't count the thumb!" she said with a giggle, and her sister joined in.

Joseph huffed. "Now's not the time to be joking around!" he said, scanning the walls. "She could be anywhere by now."

The twins suppressed a giggle. "Hey, Joseph, why is that every time you try to catch a girl she always runs away from you?" Then they burst into melodic laughter. Even I couldn't help but laugh along, too.

Joseph angrily fixed the glasses on his nose, stomping away down the alley. It was then that I noticed the sky before him as he walked away from the crowd of sorcerers. A dark shadow loomed over us, as though we were shrouded by a dark cloud. The sky seemed to disappear, replaced by a dark, wavering form. The figure seemed to swallow everything in its path.

Fear seeped into my veins and glued me to the ground. Then I felt a blast of wind hit me from the side, and the smell of the sea wafted toward me. The sea spray seemed to clear my senses, giving me an understanding of what this destructive force was: water.

A giant wall of water descended upon us, entering the alley of Majestorium Square.

"Fla . . . Fl—" Joseph stuttered.

"Flood!" I shouted, turning toward the rambling crowd. They averted their attention from the commotion and examined the sea of water that moved toward them. Almost immediately shouts and cries filled the air and the crowd began to swarm away from the descending water. I followed them, taking several glances back at the giant flood that knocked lampposts down and shook the roofs off houses.

"Adam, do something!" I cried to him as we ran.

Adam immediately pulled something from his pocket—a knife—and pressed the tip against his lip. He muttered a few whispers into the knife and suddenly the object released a glowing blue aura of light. He released the knife tip from his pale lips and pointed it toward the water. Layers of ice began to snake their way across the liquid landscape, causing the water to freeze. The rolling waves of water froze over, looming over my head. Tendrils of cool vapour escaped the ice as if a cold fire burned within it. I would have been swallowed by the giant mouth of water if not for Adam's power.

"Go," he said. "I won't be able to hold off much longer." He continued to point the knife at the barrier of ice. When I didn't move, he urged me on with the fearful look of his eyes. With one glance back, I headed toward the twins and began to gather the sorcerers to the other end of the Square.

"Hurry!" I urged, noticing the slowly cracking wall of ice. A loud crack emitted from the frozen scenery behind me and shards of ice began to fall like rain to the cobbled floor of Majestorium Square. More screams spiralled through the air as mothers and fathers covered their children's heads and took cover. The flood would break out any second now.

I was about to turn and run when I felt something cool drizzle down my back. I slowly touched the nape of my neck and felt freezing, icy water wash over my fingertips. Then I turned around and watched the icy mound break open and pour over the crowd, drowning them in the icy sea. I could barely see a look of horror set on Adam's face just before the sea swallowed him whole.

"Adam!" I cried. The crowd jostled against me, trying to head for an exit. I stayed put, trying to conjure a plan of some sort. I was *the* Prophetic Child—I had more power than I knew, and yet the only power that I knew I could access without question was levitation through my gemstone. I could try summoning Thoven's Bow, but what good would that do? The water was too destructive a force to battle against. There was no escaping it.

I held my breath and felt the cold, icy water splash my face and drown me into the sea.

* * *

A barely audible buzz sounded beside my ear, mixed with the sound of miniature waves crashing against my temples.

"Mm?" I groaned, opening my eyes to bare slits. A blue light washed over my eyes and I squinted to regain focus.

"Bookworm, come back here!" I recognized Joseph's voice. The blue light disappeared and soon the looming castles and stores that filled Majestorium Square came into view. "She's awake!" one of the twins called. I felt someone prop me forward and an immense feeling of dizziness washed over me. I noticed the twins, Adam and Joseph sitting in front of me, tiny waves of water lapping over their hands and feet.

"What happened?" I asked, standing up. Majestorium Square was in total wreckage: windows were broken, lampposts had fallen to the ground, and water spread thinly across the ground, shrouding our feet from view.

"I couldn't stop it," Adam explained. Janine and Jess stood on either side of him, their faces solemn. Joseph's leg shook anxiously. His Time Sprite (which I supposed was named Bookworm) was circling his head happily. Joseph warily eyed my neck, and then looked at Janine and Jess's necks, too. They were bare. Where were their gemstones?

I touched my neck instinctively and suddenly felt a large lump form in my throat. "M-my gemstone," I said, shuddering as a blast of cold wind broke through Majestorium Square. "It's gone."

Everyone was silent for a few long moments before Adam finally cleared his throat, cheeks red. "The flood was so powerful, filled with so much dark magic, that it must've carried your gemstones away along with it." His voice slightly gave out in the end, his eyes portraying a sudden onset of nervousness, but that was surely less than the boiling pot of rage I felt building up from my stomach. It took far too long for me to process this: I'd just fought in a deadly battle for these gemstones, undergone numerous obstacles, and now they were taken away by a *flood*?

I felt something creep up my throat, but I swallowed my revulsion with a dry tongue. Our gemstones. Gone. Just like that.

"It must've been Mira's doing," Joseph presumed. "Everyone thinks that she's the thief of the King's Jewel, so she must've become angry and created a giant flood without even realizing. It seems only logical, since she has extraordinary weather abilities."

Janine and Jessica nodded gravely. They touched their necks, wrapping their hands around the air that replaced the spot their gemstones should have been. I did, too. I felt so bare without my gemstone around my neck. My gemstone allowed me to access extraordinary powers, unlock a world beyond comprehension. It was the puzzle piece that connected the mundane mortal world to the mystical magic of the Sorcerers Underworld.

"I'm so sorry I couldn't hold the flood off any longer, Arica," Adam stated.

I nodded my head wordlessly, and then said, "You did what you could." I couldn't seem to say anything more. These past events were just too much to comprehend that neither the wolf attack, Golden Cave incident nor Ash's key sea monster attack combined could compare to the loss of the connection to my gemstone.

I could still remember the day my mother had given me my gemstone—my first day at Hill Valley. I remembered the feeling of warmth I'd had when she slid the gemstone around my neck. These three gemstones were passed down for generations, initially created by the Sorcerer Line as a way to create a superpower of some sort and take over the mortal world. No one knew what this superpower was, however, since my great-grandmother Andrea had taken the gemstones before the activating piece could be clicked into place. That was when Vina, who we thought to be the granddaughter of the Sorceress Wife seeking revenge, took the activating piece and time-travelled to my generation. She decided that by taking our gemstones—mine, in particular, since I'm the Prophetic Child—she could click the three gemstones into its pendant form, the shape of a heart, and activate the superpower by placing the activating piece in the middle. I had witnessed (without realizing) the activating piece, also known as the Prize of the Aradis, being taken from the small metal pyramid in the Golden Cave.

On Halloween night, during the battle for our gemstones, Vina explained that she was not the granddaughter of the Sorceress Wife, but the *actual* Sorceress Wife who had time-travelled into the future. Now, even after recovering our gemstones and entering the Sorcerers Underworld, we still faced another pressing issue. Our gemstones were gone, and I was more than determined to find them. After facing innumerable encounters at Hill Valley, I could face any obstacle—scorching deserts, ferocious snowstorms, anything to retrieve the gemstones.

"The gemstones could be anywhere by now," Jessica said, voice shaking. She and her sister exchanged weary glances, and then their fearsome eyes met mine. I rubbed my sweaty palms against my legs, but my pants were already wet from the vicious flood that had entered Majestorium Square.

I turned my attention to the sky, noticing small fluffy flakes falling from the navy-blue curtain that draped the world. I kept my eye on one of the icy snowflakes, taking note of the intricate maze of ice that formed this tiny flake. Then the snowflake touched my bare arm and I felt a warm sizzle against my skin. More snowflakes fell and bit my cheeks. My breath came out in gray-white tufts, so thick they were like cotton balls.

"More random weather patterns," Joseph stated. "We better head inside in case this turns into a storm."

We agreed wholeheartedly, and then left the beauty and magic of Majestorium Square to the mansion I'd awoken to just hours ago.

* * *

The queen's face was paler than a ghost as she pondered the missing gemstone situation. Adam had told his mother about everything that had happened in Majestorium Square (leaving out the maniacal faun, of course). The queen's face seemed to become a shade paler with each word he spoke, her face turning grave.

The five of us stood around the ring that bordered the electric blue Sphere as the queen gradually composed herself. She was pacing beside the podium, wearing a look of permanent contemplation.

"In order for this to be conducted properly, I'll have to take this matter to Council." The queen gave a resounding *snap* of her fingers and suddenly the room seemed to grow, expanding so that long, circular benches ringed the room. Ominous black smoke appeared along the benches, and sorcerers and sorceresses with long cloaks and pointed hats filled the empty seats.

"Wow," Janine and Jessica spoke. Even I was in awe of the Council, filled with hundreds of sorcerers extending so far they became inky blotches of blackness in the background.

"Ahem," the queen said, and the commotion rumbling through the Council came to an abrupt pause. "Thank you," she stated, leaning back on her gold-framed throne. "I have brought you here because an urgent issue has been brought to my attention: three gemstones, one belonging to the Prophetic Child, have gone missing. A magical flood swept them away, supposedly created by Mira due to the many accusations of her stealing the King's Jewel."

"Mira's doing?" some sorcerers cried, either fussing with their neighbours or nodding their heads in solemn agreement.

"An action on behalf of the Sorcerer Line, perhaps?" a man called, standing up. He was obviously an older man since his brown hair held subtle gray streaks. "Maybe the flood wasn't out of anger at all. Maybe she did it purposely, a way to show her loyalty to the Sorcerer Line since they believe she's the thief."

Murmurs of agreement followed, and the man almost seemed pleased with himself for suggesting something that seemed so pleasantly obvious. He sat back in his chair, disappearing into the jungle of cloaked sorcerers.

"You raise a strong point, Marus," Queen Magestaria agreed. "However, it still does not resolve our issue. Who is responsible may be apparent, but the location of the gemstones at this present moment is not."

"The Hall of Lost Gemstones," Joseph muttered beside me.

"What?" I asked with confusion. Joseph repeated what he said, only louder this time.

The crowd reacted with wary responses. "No one's been there in a hundred years," a woman called. She peered over her glasses with darting eyes, scanning the crowd. "Everyone knows that. And there is hardly a way of getting into that room, let alone the Sorcerer Palace itself. You'd have to travel far into the mortal world. Far . . . very far . . ." She ended with a trembling nod and the people around her helped her sit down in her seat as she began to ramble with a furious tone: "Far, far away . . . too far!"

The woman's words startled me, making the retrieval of the gemstones sound more and more impossible by the second.

"The mortal world?" Jessica asked. "That shouldn't really be a problem," she stated to the queen.

Queen Magestaria nodded her head, holding her hand up as though to silence the crowd. "I have a suggestion," she stated. "If you are heading on a journey for these magical gemstones, a search for the King's Jewel along the way seems standard."

Many people nodded their heads and spoke in vigorous agreement with the queen.

"I do not want to ask too much of you," the queen said after the rambling began to escalate. "You have just endured a turbulent relocation to the Sorcerers Underworld, so I believe a trip back home will be most welcoming."

A weight of pressure fell from my shoulders. *Home.* The thought of it made my insides warm and spread a feeling of happiness through my veins. I couldn't wait to see my mother, feel the fresh, earthy air across my skin, maybe even go back to school and see my friends. It felt like it'd been so long since I'd last seen Monika in the hospital, which I could barely believe was just a day ago in the mortal world.

"The five of you shall go on a journey to retrieve both the gemstones and the King's Jewel. But first, you will need a clue of some sort to help you along the way." The queen turned to her son. "Adam, please lead these young pupils to the Blessing River. I believe you know what to do."

Adam nodded his head. Then the queen said, "Thank you all for your time. Your input is graciously appreciated." Then she snapped her fingers once again and the benches dissolved, disappearing from sight. The crowd of rambling sorcerers vanished in dark smoke and the walls shrank until the room was back to its normal size.

"I believe you all should be heading off now. Time is ticking away."

"Yes, Mother. We'll see you soon." And then Adam led the way out the open doors and into the mansion, passing the columns and pillars that supported the tall structure.

As we silently crept past the Dungeons, I examined the cells. They were dark, evidently made of some rough stonework. Some cells were larger than others, extending into dark caverns beneath sparkling black rock. In a fairly small, cubed cell, I noticed a man's back faced toward me as he sat on the cold, hard ground. He was curled up, his backbone scarcely noticeable through his gray shirt. His black hair was ruffled and his hands held the cell bars in front of him. I continued to walk forward, but a dark wall covered the scenery. I turned the corner toward the mansion's exit and neared the man's cell, seeing his white knuckles furiously cupping the bars in front of him. I noticed a glowing orange-red light contained within his hands as he held the cell bars. When he removed his hands, an imprint of his fingers sank into the metal. He kept his head low, looking down at his palms.

A spiral of fire danced on the palms of his hands as though an invisible dragon were breathing into his palms.

The young man slowly lifted his eyes to mine; they glowed with a familiar spark, the fire lit in his hands reflecting in his depthless, charcoal pupils.

The eerie sway of the fire in his eyes was far too familiar. It reminded me of my first chemistry class, the boy I'd been working with in my lab with the Bunsen burner.

The boy from chemistry class: Geoff.

I felt ready to scream, but it never escaped my mouth. My throat seemed to swell, closing until my lungs screamed for air. I managed to suck in a deep breath, but my eyes rimmed with tears and my vision became blurry. When I'd finally blinked the tears back, the cell in front of me was empty. The cell bars were bent, as if someone had pulled two bars apart and escaped. A sizzle emitted from the searing cell bars in front of me.

Had I just seen Geoff escape? Or had I just been hallucinating the whole time?

I shook my head, looking back at the cell. It looked completely normal—no searing, open cell bars or young men with tendrils of fire curled on their palms.

But I couldn't dispel what I'd just seen. If it was true, and something in my gut told me it most certainly was, then Geoff had just escaped.

And maybe the other Sapphires had, too.

FOUR: THE BLESSING RIVER

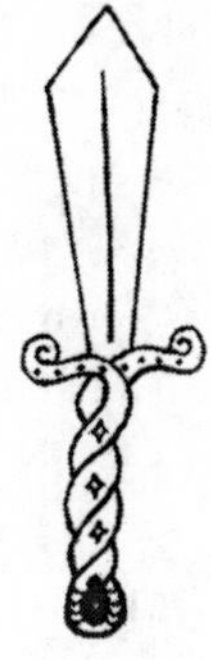

After several minutes of contemplating the situation as we walked through the vacant streets, we reached a sandy, deserted beach that led to the Blessing River. On our way there Adam told us about what the Blessing River was—a magical river where sorcerers and sorceresses could throw in their most precious trinkets or items, and receive them with a form of blessing, almost like a wish. Adam explained that we were heading to the Blessing River to obtain a clue that would help us pinpoint the exact location of the King's Jewel and possibly even the gemstones. We needed to find the gemstones and the King's Jewel before anyone else; if the Sapphires had truly escaped their prison cells, would they have done it to go after the gemstones? Now that they were gone, it seemed like a race to the finish line, and we had to get there—fast.

My toes sank into the sand as the water washed ashore, caressing my feet. A girl stood by the river, wearing a white linen dress and suede flip-flops. Her hair was entirely black except for one thick teal highlight that ran across the bangs that hid the right side of her face. She kept part of her hair tied in a loose bun, and her face remained solemn as she gazed at the sparkling blue water. When we drew near her, she turned around and started at the sight of Adam.

"Prince Adam," she said, taking a bow. "What brings you to the Blessing River?" When she lifted her head, several strands of hair had fallen out of her bun and loosely covered one of her emerald-green eyes.

"I'm actually here on assignment from my mother," he said, turning toward us. "Teal, this is Janine, Jessica, Joseph and Arica. Teal works here at the Blessing River," Adam told us.

"Oh, hello!" she said, and then shook each of our hands. She took my hand and shook it eagerly, but the rhythm of her shaking hand began to slow as a look of recognition crossed her face. "Arica . . . Arica Miller?"

"Uh, yeah," I said. I wondered how she knew my last name—did she recognize me? Had I met her before? Or perhaps word of my being the Child of the Prophecy had been spreading quicker than I'd thought.

"Wow," she said, giving each of us a particularly fond look. Then she shook her head, turning back to the river. "So, what can I do for you?"

"We're here to receive a sort of blessing for our journey," Adam said. "Our goal is to retrieve the gemstones and find my father's missing crown." He turned to me. "Arica, you must have some sort of sentimental trinket or keepsake to use in order to receive the clue, yes?"

"Um . . ." I trailed off. To be honest, I hadn't exactly expected to travel to another world on the night of the Halloween dance. The only thing I'd brought with me was my gemstone, and I didn't even have that here with me at the moment. In fact, I was still wearing my full on black shirt and pants that I'd sported for Halloween night.

"Arica, the metal necklace!" Janine explained. "The one we gave you in the cafeteria!"

"I don't have it," I said with sorrow.

"Since you're the Prophetic Child, you can conjure that necklace using your powers!" Jess told me.

I bit my lip. "I don't know, guys. I don't even know *how* to conjure Thoven's Bow. It just . . . comes to me."

Teal took a deep breath. "Maybe someone else could give a trinket?"

"Anything that belongs to Arica would be the strongest; it would give us the best clue. She is the Prophetic Child, after all," Adam said.

I sighed, moving toward the water of the river. I felt my knees sink toward the ground, back slouching forward. My hands left deep grooves in the soft sand. How was I supposed to conjure the necklace? I hadn't even gained full knowledge on my powers: The only power I fully understood was levitation.

But I couldn't give up; they needed a trinket, so I'd give them one.

I focused on the moving water in front of me, keeping the image of the metal necklace in my mind. After what felt like many strenuous minutes of concentration, I finally felt something cool appear in my palms. I turned my hand over and released my clenched fingers, revealing a solid heart locket in my palm.

"That's it!" Jessica cried. "You conjured the necklace!"

A feeling of pure joy came over me, and I began smiling in amazement. I felt light as air, exultant, even, as I held the necklace in my hand.

Teal bent down and placed the locket in her palm carefully. "This should be perfect."

Then we both stood and eyed the water, listening to the waves crashing against one another.

Teal closed her eyes and whispered something beneath her breath. Then she opened her eyes, surveyed the mystical water one last time, and threw the locket into the water. The locket swam along the water, and then sank beneath the waves.

The water turned a shocking blue, almost like lightning illuminating a dark sky. Then I noticed the metal locket making its way toward the shoreline. Teal extended her arm and the necklace slipped right into her fingers. The bright, blue water dimmed.

Teal held the necklace high as it glowed. Bright light seeped out of the metal locket as though the sun's rays were trapped within it.

I held out my hand tentatively and she placed the locket in my palm. The glowing aura around the locket disappeared.

"So . . . where's the clue?" I asked hesitantly.

"Well, it seems as though your locket has received some sort of blessing. When you open it, there should be a clue that will help you all on your journey." She ended with a sort of finality that seemed like a goodbye.

"Thanks for everything, Teal," Adam said. Teal smiled, but it looked pained, dark; although she worked for the Royals, she didn't seem very content about it. In fact, there seemed to be something darker hidden within her eyes, and she almost looked, for a lack of better words, *sad*.

"Bye, Teal," I said. The twins excitedly gave their farewells, too. Just as we were turning around, I caught sight of something on Teal's neck. The same symbol I'd seen on

Pedro's and Lyra's necks: the S surrounded by flames. It was a symbol of the Shadowers, a sinister group of people who had the ability to turn into shadows. Was Teal a Shadower? She was far too young to even look like one—she looked my age, maybe younger. I didn't want to say anything aloud, but rather kept it to myself until I would have some time to speak with Adam privately.

The five of us retreated from the sandy beach and headed toward an alley hidden in a crook behind a plethora of shops. The ground was still covered in water from the recent flooding incident. Adam seemed to know his way around—well, of course he would, since he was the *prince*—and soon we found ourselves nearing a large newsstand. On top, a sign read: get the latest edition of *Sorcerers Spark.* The lettering stood out, as though the letters were glued pieces bound to the lit sign behind it.

Adam lightly placed his hand on the *K* and wrapped his hand around the dark letter. The letter was covered in chipped black paint, as though it had been tampered with many times. Then he twisted his hand like he was twisting a doorknob and let it go. A creaking sound echoed across the alleyway. The newsstand began opening like a door, revealing an overwhelming sheet of darkness on the other side.

"Shall we go in?" Adam gestured toward the doorway. The four of us gawked at the darkness. Cobwebs dangled from the entrance and sickly green spiders crawled along the frame of the newsstand.

Joseph slowly backed away from the door with a sick expression, but Adam gave him a light shove, prompting him to enter the darkness. Joseph gulped loudly, and then slowly moved forward. Janine and Jess both gave him another hearty shove when a wave of anxiety crossed his face.

"Come on, Joseph! You're the one who keeps telling us you haven't been afraid of the dark since you were four-years-old!" Janine exclaimed, her British accent slightly thicker than I remembered.

"Uh . . . sure." He gulped again. It seemed like he hadn't been afraid of the dark since he was *fourteen*, not four, by the looks of things.

"I'll go in," I said confidently. Joseph met my gaze with a sigh of relief and gratitude. I began to walk into the creepy darkness, and suddenly shivered as a cold blast of wind swept from the side. I shook off the cold and headed forward. In the dimness I was able to make out a lit regular box farther ahead. Footsteps of the other four behind me grew louder as they followed in my tracks.

Adam approached the bright box and pushed the door open. Inside the rectangular structure was a lonely book sitting on a table. Then he moved inside and flipped the book open. It looked like one of those giant Yellow Pages books, but instead the front cover read: *Portal Station.*

Portal Station?

"I don't understand," Jess said. "How is this supposed to take us home? It's just a book."

"Not just any *book*," Joseph corrected, giving particular emphasis on the last word. "It's a Portal Station! It can take you to any location you can imagine! Australia, to the North Pole, you name it!"

"So the book is a sort of . . . portal? So we can *teleport*?" Janine asked. "Wow, that's *so* wicked!"

I couldn't help but gape in amazement, too. Adam was sifting through the papers, his eyes filled with intent and fingers careful.

"Where are we going?" I asked, wondering what he was searching for so keenly.

"The mortal world," he answered. "Hill Valley, to be precise." Then he turned to us, his pointer finger hovering just over the edge of the page beside the withered spine. "Who's ready to go back to that dance?"

* * *

Travelling to another world was even worse the second time around.

I clenched my stomach as soon as I fell to the cold, hard ground. A whirl of unease spread through my body as I breathed through gritted teeth. When I opened my eyes, I first noticed the large, circular fans placed high on the walls. There was a small window by the high ceiling and the room was painted a dark gray. We had entered the drama room.

It only took me a few seconds for the unfamiliarity of the room to sink in. Something seemed to have changed since I'd last been here. I propped myself onto my elbows to get a better look until I suddenly slid back onto the ground. With squinting eyes I noticed underneath me was a pool of water. In fact, the entire drama room looked like it'd been in a wild hurricane, the waves slowly crashing against my body and against the walls. I spat some water out of my mouth and regarded the room, noticing the twins and Joseph inching toward me. Adam was already standing by the doorway, his nose just barely touching the rectangular window that allowed him to view the hallway that linked to the school. The rhythmic beat of music still flowed through the air, and from what I could see through the small window, the moon still hung high in the sky.

How long had it been since my unexpected relocation to the Sorcerers Underworld? Twenty minutes? Thirty?

"Wonder what people will think when they notice the headmistress is gone," Adam said in a hoarse voice. Then he pulled out the knife he'd been holding when the flood broke out and whispered something unintelligible. His clothing was suddenly replaced by his usual janitorial outfit, and he held a mop in his free hand. He slid the knife into a secret pocket, but I could still make out the glinting emeralds on the hilt from his side. There was something very familiar about that knife—I'd seen it when we were fighting the King Scorzzard. It had a silver handle with the image of a long spider on the hilt. Yes, I could remember it clearly now: I'd been trying to conjure Thoven's Bow to defeat the King Scorzzard when the knife had caught my attention.

"You made that knife appear when we were fighting the King Scorzzard," I called.

Adam removed his eyes from the window and regarded me, his face grave. "Yes . . . I was trying to save you, but I was trapped in a watery portal. Vina trapped me there, how I'm not sure. The only thing I could do was send you this knife—my knife. The Wishing Knife." He gave his possession a glance, and I began to finally understand what this knife was. A Wishing Knife, probably one-of-a-kind, that could grant wishes. I didn't have time to delve deeper into the idea, because Adam was sighing heavily and looking thoroughly dissatisfied. He finished as though he didn't want to say anything more about the Sorcerer Line's evil deceit against him. I certainly didn't want to think of the battle that took place less than an hour ago, think of the possibility that our gemstones could have been lost forever.

The irony of the situation was as clear as glass. There was a possibility that we could have lost our gemstones to the Sorcerer Line, but even if we'd recovered them, they still would have been lost in the flood. Or maybe if they'd gotten the gemstones there wouldn't have been a flood after all. The flood had been created accidentally out of Mira's anger. The Sorcerer Line—mainly Vina—had accused her of stealing the King's Jewel and hiding it in a tornado somewhere in the mortal world. Maybe Vina wouldn't have accused Mira of this if she'd had the gemstones she planned to receive on Halloween night.

Adam gently clicked open the door, the four of us right behind him. As it opened, water gushed out of the drama room and into the hall. The water reached the feet of several students and they turned, peering at us with questioning eyes. Music echoed from the gym and filled the hall, wafting through the entrance to Hill Valley. A warm autumn breeze slid through the entrance as Mrs. Dovinsky squeezed her way through the doors, because her pumpkin costume was just a size too big to fit through.

"Ah," she said with relief when she managed to get through. Then, just as her shoes reached the slippery surface of water on the ground, she slid and fell backward. Her arms waggled through the air as she struggled to get up, her pumpkin costume restricting her from any movement other than a wiggle from her arms and legs.

We carefully neared Mrs. Dovinsky and helped her up. "Ah, thank you!" she said, then eyed the water that seeped out of the drama room. "Oh, dear! Zere is a flood!"

"Flood?" students whispered to one another. The news spread like wildfire, a sense of pandemonium slowly building as word crossed the school.

Soon enough the water that was once a few inches off the ground began wavering near our knees. Some students tried to flee from the flooded area, but the water was inescapable.

"Oh, no," Joseph said. "I think the portal didn't close properly. Maybe that's why all this water is coming through."

Adam nodded his head in agreement. "I'll close the portal. You four try and come up with some sort of explanation while I'm gone." And then he left for the drama room, dragging his legs through the rising water.

The crowd turned and gazed at us. I gulped, wondering what would be the most suitable response for the situation. I gazed down at my hand, and then caught sight of paper cups drifting along the water in my peripheral vision. "Vat are we going to do about this!" Mrs. Dovinsky asked, aghast. She was about to paste her hands to her cheeks but her costume restricted her from moving her arms that far.

"A pipe!" Jessica called suddenly. "There's a leaking pipe in the drama room. Nothing to worry about, the janitor's already left to go fix it." She gestured to Adam's figure which had soon disappeared into the dark room.

Many students streamed through the open entrance to Hill Valley. Their faces portrayed anger and rage, eyes examining the crowd.

"The entire African Jade campus is flooded!" a girl cried. Her hair was tied in a long braid and few strands stuck out, causing her to look even more infuriated than before. It then occurred to me that African Jade was the campus that was closely situated to the drama room and the main sector of the school. The other campuses were located farther back, meaning that the flood would unequivocally damage the African Jade campus, which remained closest to us.

"Where's the headmistress? We demand to speak to her!" she called.

A little too late for that, I thought. The headmistress, in light of recent events, was definitely not returning to Hill Valley anytime soon.

Or so I'd hoped.

"Uh—the headmistress won't be returning to school for a while," Joseph stated untruthfully. "She's out on a sort of . . . vacation." He gulped, scanning the crowd to see if they would believe his story.

"Vacation?" a boy asked. His freckled face was immediately recognizable—Jake's friend Ralph—and his ninja costume evidently assigned him as a member of Jake's posse. "At a time like this?!" he cried. I wondered why he would be so concerned with Lembrose's absence. Then I noticed his African Jade badge perched on his shoulder and realized he was a part of the flooding campus.

"My dormitory's flooded," another called angrily. "Where am I supposed to sleep tonight?"

Many others balled their fists and threw their hands in the air, yelling in agreement.

"Everyone, please, calm down!" Janine cried. "The gym isn't quite flooded yet. Students from African Jade will remain there for now." She turned their attention to the gym. They started nodding their heads, their protests coming to an end.

"There's a back entrance to the gym near the Australian Sapphire campus. You can sleep there unless otherwise notified," I finished.

After I spoke, the students began to file to the back entrance of the gym. Due to the sudden flood, the Halloween dance had come to a close. Adam had returned from the drama room, holding a wrench in hand. Then he turned toward us, wiping a bead of sweat from his brow. "It's all under control, the flood should be cleared by tomorrow," he said. We nodded and filled him in on the flooding of the African Jade campus.

"Isn't there something you can do about the flood? Use that knife you'd pulled out earlier?" Janine asked.

"Even if I did, the students would notice. It's best if we just leave this to the staff."

"But you're a *part* of the staff—" Joseph finished abruptly as his sisters both flicked him in the head. "Ow . . ."

"He's the prince, remember?" Jessica muttered to Joseph.

"Guys, maybe we should just focus on what we *should* be doing. We need to figure out a way to retrieve the gemstones *and* the King's Jewel, and I have a terrible feeling that someone else might be after them, too," I said.

"What do you mean, Arica?" Janine asked.

I gulped. The image of the searing cell bars formed in my mind. Was I supposed to tell them about Geoff's disappearance? But then again, I could've been hallucinating the entire time. The queen surely had the Sorcerer Line locked up, and I just had to believe that their imprisonment would remain that way throughout our journey.

"Nothing," I finally managed. "I just think that we should plan our retrieval for the gemstones before things get out of hand."

"You're exactly right," Jessica agreed. "I don't believe standing around here any longer will do us any good. How about we all go to our house and check out the clue we received from the Blessing River?"

"Good idea," Adam agreed.

We were all heading out the open doorway with the other angered African Jade members when I felt someone poke my shoulder. I turned around and saw Jake Macdonald, a freshman with messy, dark hair and olive-toned skin. I sifted through my memories and remembered the incident with him in the cafeteria this morning (yeah, *this* morning). The image of the two intertwined snakes on his shoulder still sent my insides spinning, but now I realized what had happened to both him and Monika. Ash had sent them both to the Sorcerers Underworld, which ultimately resulted in their receiving the image of the intertwined snakes somewhere on their bodies. Now that I thought about it, Ash had also taken me to the Sorcerers Underworld, but it had come across as a blurred nightmare. A few nights ago, as I lay in bed, Ash had used her powers to take me to the Sorcerers Underworld. When I woke I found her holding my wrist fiercely, as if she didn't want to let go.

"Hey, Arica!" he exclaimed. "I was looking for you in the gym before but I couldn't find you!"

I replied with a quick hello, noticing the shiny African Jade badge on his shoulder. Shouldn't he have been mad at me? I practically flooded the entire African Jade campus, and the rest of the students from African Jade had been giving me dirty looks ever since I stepped out of the drama room.

"Sorry, I was . . . busy." I swallowed hard.

"Oh, that's okay. Did you see that flood? It was so wicked!"

"Uh, yeah, I did," I said. *I was in it,* I thought, but I didn't speak my thoughts aloud.

"Anyway, I think sleeping in the gym tonight will be super awesome. Are you staying at Hill Valley over the weekend?"

"I'm sleeping over at my cousins' house tonight, but maybe I'll see you by the school tomorrow."

"All right," he said, but his eyes probed the crowd as though he had more on his mind. "Arica . . . I've been meaning to ask you something. Remember how we bumped into each other in the cafeteria this morning? Why did you run away when you saw that scar on my shoulder?"

"Um . . ." I ended abruptly, looking for some sort of explanation to cover up my actions.

Suddenly Jake's crowd of friends swarmed us and began blabbering incoherent sentences into Jake's ear.

"The snail, dude—" Ralph began.

"In the water!" another said.

"I think it grew!"

"You gotta see it, man." Ralph gave him an enthusiastic slap on the arm. "Hey, look, Jake's with his girlfriend again!"

"Ralph, how many times have I told you—"

"Yeah, yeah, I think he's just lying to us," Ralph murmured to another boy in the group.

Jake heaved a sigh. "I better get going. See you tomorrow?"

"Whoa, they've already planned a date . . ." Ralph muttered. Jake rolled his eyes.

"Yeah," I replied, and then left with the twins, Joseph and Adam. The trees' branches clawed the air in the cool, October night, and the bright, white moon illuminated the dark sky. We followed the sidewalk to the twins' house, which took less than a minute on foot.

Jessica had already rung the doorbell by the time I'd walked past their garden. A welcoming chime rang through the air, and then the door slowly opened.

FIVE: THE CLUE

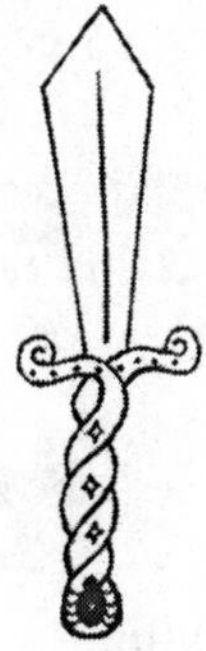

Aunt Elizabeth peered out the door curiously. She quickly closed it, opened a few more locks, and swung the door open. Her flour-spattered face covered the faint wrinkles near her bright, blue eyes. A floral apron covered her torso, also coated with patterns of baking substances. One hand was covered by an oven mitt, the other in a gardening glove that was painted in brown dirt.

She gave an awkward hug to her children, trying her best not to get the dirty glove/mitts on them. "Come in, I'm just making brownies!" she told us all (which I had a tough time believing because of her gardening glove), and then we strode toward the living room and took a seat on the sofas. Aunt Liz stripped her hands of the oven mitt and gardening glove and left for the kitchen. She returned with a bowl of brownies, steam escaping the elegant platter.

Aunt Liz hummed a happy tune as she plated the brownies. "They're egg-free, especially for you, Arica!" She took a seat on the chair behind her. "So, how was the dance?" I exchanged a glance with each of them. It seemed as though we'd made a silent but mutual agreement not to speak of what had just occurred over the past hour or so—three days if we were counting time in the Sorcerers Underworld.

"Fine," Joseph decided to reply, and we all nodded our heads.

"Ah, very well," Aunt Liz responded. "Oh!" she said suddenly. "I should call Claire! Surely she'd love to come over for a visit." She slightly rustled my hair before turning toward Adam.

"And who might you be?" she asked with both curiosity and wariness.

"I'm Adam. Adam Collins—"

Aunt Liz let out a long shriek, jumping backward with a start. The vase behind her nearly toppled to the floor, but it managed to remain on the wooden table.

"The—the *prince*?" She let out a small chuckle, hands against her chest. "Oh, my deepest apologies, Prince Adam. I didn't recognize you—"

"That's not a problem," Adam said, giving her hand a light shake.

Aunt Liz looked giddy, and then wiped her hand on her thigh probably due to the sweatiness. "Can I get anything for you?" she asked.

"No, I'm fine."

Aunt Liz left with a nod, dazed. When she'd disappeared from sight, the five of us decided we should head upstairs to observe the clue. We were just about to leave when Aunt Liz returned, phone in hand.

"No brownies?" she asked, her voice awash with disappointment.

"Um . . ." the twins mumbled. Janine lunged for the brownie bowl and stuffed a few in her mouth. "Mmm," she mumbled, crumbs falling out of her mouth. "Great." When she turned away she gagged.

"Arica's just going to stay over for the night. Adam, too," Jessica said as she made her way to the staircase.

We followed her, prancing up the stairs. Janine opened the bedroom door and we were suddenly enveloped by the warm autumn wind flowing through the open window. The rush of wind reminded me of outdoor camping with Kathy and Sam, roasting marshmallows by the fire and playing rounds of Truth or Dare. I'd last seen them on my birthday, which felt dauntingly long ago in comparison to my new life at Hill Valley, especially after receiving the gemstone from my mom.

The twins sat on opposite sides of the room: Janine's side was filled with red paint whereas Jess's gleamed green. I sat beside Jess and pulled the metal locket from my pocket.

Everyone leaned toward me, hands trembling as they stared at the necklace in my hands. Their faces remained anxious as my fingers grasped the locket and flicked it open.

Blue light poured out of the locket, bathing the room in its glorious colour. Bright, white words hovered over the necklace, which read:

A Triangle that forbids dark magic's ear is where
the Jewel of the King lies near.

We sat in silence as we contemplated the words that floated above us.

After a moment, Joseph piped up: "What do you suppose this *Triangle* is?"

"I've never heard of a sort of *Triangle* in the Sorcerers Underworld . . ." said Adam. "Is there one in the mortal world?"

"What about the Bermuda Triangle?" I asked.

"The Bermuda Triangle? You mean the mysterious place where boats, ships, and planes go missing?" Jessica asked with a shiver.

Adam chuckled, shaking his head. "There are many myths and tales about the Bermuda Triangle, but none of them are true. The real reason for the disappearing crafts is due to the magical current of the water. The Bermuda Triangle is actually the location of the Sorcerer Palace, where my family lives."

"So you're saying the strength of the magic surrounding the Sorcerer Palace is actually pulling all those things in?" Janine asked in amazement.

"Yes," Adam replied.

"That means the gemstones were washed away to the Atlantic Ocean—the Bermuda Triangle." Joseph tapped his chin.

"How are we supposed to get to the Bermuda Triangle?" I asked with confusion. "Teleport, maybe?"

"The Portal Station—we can just look for the location and it'll take us there, right, Adam?" Jess suggested.

Adam shook his head gravely. "The Portal Station can take you to many places, but the Bermuda Triangle—specifically the Sorcerer Palace—is not one of them, mainly for security purposes. We wouldn't want a bunch of sorcerers floating around the Palace and possibly being seen by other mortals." He shook his head again. "We'll have to find another way to get there. Perhaps we can find some information in a few books—"

Joseph's face lit like a light bulb. "Books?" he asked, though his excitement was not reciprocated.

"Oh, Joseph!" Jess cried. "Focus on the task!"

Adam chuckled wearily. "Well, yes, at the King's Library. I go there to research and read. It's truly a magnificent place."

"Wow." Joseph's mouth made a small O shape. "I've always wanted to go to the King's Library! It's at the top of my bucket list!"

We all laughed, but then I came to an abrupt stop when I heard sharp footsteps approach the twins' room.

"Quick, close the locket!" Jess cried. Just as the door opened to their room I'd slammed the locket closed, the blue light once again enclosed inside. I hid my hand behind my back and turned to see my mother.

Her hair was shorter than I'd remembered, dark brown just like mine, but her eyes were sparkly blue just like her sister's. I'd probably gotten my father's eyes—a deep, chocolate brown.

A sudden swarm of emotions came over me: relief, gratitude, guilt, and a thousand other emotions I couldn't pinpoint. I ran up to her and hugged her around the waist. "Mom, it's so good to see you."

"Um, honey," she said after furrowing her brows, "it's only been a few hours. I was just dropping by to see Aunt Liz and the twins and Joseph."

A murmur sounded from behind me. I turned and saw Adam clearing his throat, eyes tentative.

"Um, Mom, this is Prince Adam. Adam Collins . . ." I said, wondering if she would recognize him.

Adam stood abruptly and held out his hand. When Mom didn't return the gesture, he moved his hand back awkwardly. "I'm Adam."

"Yes, I'm aware of that," Mom said with cautious eyes.

"*Prince* Adam. Prince of the Sorcerers Underworld," I said, exaggerating the first word so she'd recognize his noble position.

"Ah," she said distastefully. "Yes, well, very nice to meet you." Her words were sharp, venomous. I wondered why she was acting so strangely, but then I supposed it was because of my mom's incomprehensible fear of magic and the magical world itself.

Mom slowly wiped away the creases on her shirt and turned to leave. "I'll just be downstairs, dear." Then she disappeared behind the doorway.

"What was that about?" Janine asked.

I shook my head, and then shrugged. "Hey, how about we get some rest?" I suggested, trying to rid of the unease from the tense conversation.

"Yes, we've had a long day," Adam said after a shred of silence. *"Days,"* he added with a chuckle.

We laughed along, and then prepared for bed. I stayed in the twins' room, whereas Adam stayed in Joseph's room (even though Joseph didn't particularly like that).

I laid a mattress on the floor and knelt into my comforter. The lights had all been shut off and everyone was silent in bed.

No. Not everyone.

The curtains by Janine and Jess's window fluttered in the wind as I lay awake in bed. The constant hum of cicadas and the chirp of crickets kept my eyes open, thoughts tense. I swallowed, took a look at the window, and silently crept out of my comforter. I was about to shut it closed when I noticed something lurking outside, like a dark shadow slithering past the window.

I spun around and checked the time. The digital clock read ten minutes before midnight, and yet it felt as if only a few minutes had passed by since we'd shut off the lights.

I leaned over Jess's bed, tugging at her silk night gown. She let out a soft groan and stretched her arms.

"Arica?" she asked a little too loudly.

"Shh!" I whispered. "I think something's outside."

"Huh?" This time Jess's mouth didn't move, but the same tone of voice resonated from the other end of the bedroom. It was Janine.

She lifted the thick blankets off her chest and scrambled out of her bed. "What's going on?" she asked.

Suddenly the twins' bedroom door clicked open.

First I saw a flash of stunningly beautiful blond hair, and then a mop of brownish-red hair that stuck out at certain angles.

Adam and Joseph slowly crept into the room. "We heard noises. Is something wrong?" Adam asked.

"I saw someone outside," I said.

"Outside?" Joseph's voice cracked.

Adam walked up to the window and peered outside. "We're going to have to get a better look," he said, and then moved toward the door.

"We can't go through the front door," Joseph denied.

"Yeah, we can't wake Mum!" Janine explained.

Adam tapped his chin and then pulled the knife from his pocket. He muttered something to the blade. Then his arm swung toward the window, directing the knife to the glass. The window seemed to grow bigger, the glass stretching like elastic. Adam retracted his hand and slid the knife in his pocket. Then he hoisted himself to the window pane and jumped.

"Oh!" Jessica gasped. "Is he all right?" We ran toward the window are peered down at the grassy expansion.

"I'm fine!" Adam cried, waving his hands in the air. "Just jump down!"

Janine scoffed. "And ruin this silk robe?"

"Come on," he pleaded.

"All right, I'll go," Joseph said, making his way toward the open window. The curtains beside him danced in the wind and seemed to irritate him whenever they stroked his face. He huffed, almost anxious as he looked over the window to see Adam's figure. He propped one leg on the frame, but the other stuck to the ground, as though the right side of his body wanted to move forward and the other didn't. It took much encouragement from the twins to finally get him to jump.

"Your turn!" Joseph called from the ground.

The twins made their way across, one after the other. Janine decided to go first after Jess kept crying, "But you're the older twin, now you go!" and Jess did not fail to follow. After they'd made their way down, I positioned myself on the window pane. My hands cradled the frame on either side. Then I closed my eyes, muttered a prayer, and jumped down to the ground. The wind whooshed up from the ground, but instead of falling downward I felt like the ground was moving toward me. What was once a bed of cold, green grass now felt like plush undergrowth.

I stood and faced the other four, their faces wild with excitement.

"We better search the surrounding area," Joseph suggested. "I'll search the front."

"We'll stay here!" the twins added.

"And Arica and I will check the back?" Adam asked, turning toward me for confirmation. I nodded my head.

After we'd all split up, Adam and I stood alone in the backyard. The trees looked like long, black poles with reddish leaves dangling from the branches. The evening remained frigidly quiet, so I decided to speak to Adam about the many questions that had entered my mind since my relocation to the Sorcerers Underworld. The latter of these questions was about Teal and the Shadower mark imprinted just below her ear.

"Yes, she is a Shadower," Adam responded, "but not one of the Cynical Six. She's one of their offspring: Pedro's daughter, who was captured a few years ago after an unexpected encounter with the Royals . . . or at least our assistants. One of whom was Vina . . ." He shook his head. "Vina was a trusted sorceress, a friend of my mother's. I should've known her intention at the school was only to take the gemstones." He buried his head in his two palms and then swept a palm over his soft, golden hair.

I slowly placed my hand on his shoulder. Many comforting words came to mind: *It's okay, it wasn't your fault, you tried your best,* but I couldn't voice any of them. Instead, I felt an odd tug from my waist. I peered down and noticed the metal necklace slowly reeling out of my pocket into pale, thin hands. Before I could even begin to understand what was happening, the person disappeared behind the trees, running with the necklace gripped firmly in their hand.

I immediately sprinted, running toward the vast expanse of trees. Adam was shouting something behind me, but his words were drowned under the rush of wind in my ears. I moved toward the person, sure this was the flickering shadow I'd seen outside the twins' window. Who would steal my metal necklace, and for what reason?

I continued to sprint, ignoring the subtle burn from my thighs as I ran faster. The strain in my legs brought the thought of Coach Anderson yelling (or as she called it, *motivating*) behind me to run faster back in PE. Not exactly the most charming thought.

The person was still in view; the chain hung from the same slender fingers. I could scarcely notice the inky black hair that tumbled to the figure's shoulders. It was hard to tell due to the darkness, but I figured this was a woman. The moonlight barely seeped through the open crooks of branches in the dim forest.

She was evidently heading toward a large, blue, electric portal ahead of her. Her emerald cloak rippled behind her, the tail of the cloak almost within reach. I kept my hand outstretched, continuing to chase the woman. The wind whipped my hair to and fro, but I managed to keep her in sight.

The portal was only a few feet away. With a grunt, I pulled on the cloak and the woman stumbled, falling to the mulch-covered ground. I, too, lost balance and tripped over her cloak toward a giant tree. My left shoulder slammed against the trunk and I fell to the ground, stunned.

I wavered in and out of consciousness, barely catching flashes of silvery light from beside me. I turned my head and saw my heart locket on the ground. The locket lay open, displaying hovering white words in the frigid air. I reached out and pulled the locket into my hands, but another hand clenched my wrist before I could move any farther. It belonged to the woman. Her other hand hovered over the locket in my palm, acting as a magnet when it lifted.

She released hold of me and loomed over my figure. A hood covered her head and made her expression even darker. Then she began walking toward the portal, the faint crunch of the ground beneath her feet resonating against the forest floor. The metal necklace barely clung to her fingers as she sauntered into the portal.

I managed to pull myself from the ground and run toward the woman. Then I dove toward the portal and pressed my hands along the edge of it. The portal was shrinking, slowly digging into my hands, but I ignored the strain against my palms and focused on the woman. She was walking toward someone, circling the chain of the metal locket around her fingers.

"We've got it," she said with a wicked smile, and then she turned toward me and gave a searing stare.

An invisible force pushed me back to the solid forest ground. The portal sealed off with one last burst of light, and then I was left alone with the eerily tall trees.

I lay on the forest floor for a moment, shuddering from the encounter with the woman. I pushed myself off the ground and crossed the dirty forest path to the twins' house, still jittering. It didn't take long for me to register the familiarity of the woman: her black hair, charcoal eyes, venomous tone.

The headmistress was back.

SIX: MONIKA, AGAIN

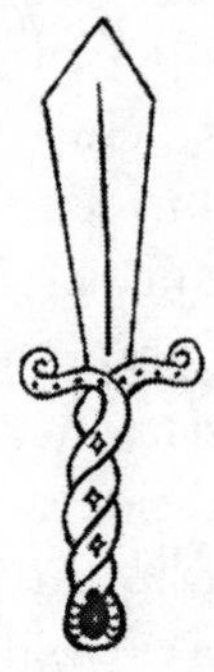

I studied my reflection in the hall mirror. Dark sleep-circles were planted beneath my eyes and my hair was messily untamed. None of us got much sleep last night, especially after I'd told them about my stolen locket and the headmistress. Their faces had remained thoroughly horrified during the retelling. Now, we planned to return to the school for a quick trip before leaving for the Sorcerers Underworld. Adam would lead us to the King's Library located at Head Quarters so we could do some research in order to find a suitable route toward the Bermuda Triangle.

"No time to fix up now," Janine said, tugging on my arm. The twins were already pulling me out the door.

"No breakfast?" Aunt Liz called from behind me, holding a plate filled with buttered toast.

Janine locked her eyes with the ceiling. "Not again!" Then she took a bite of toast and grabbed my arm, steering me toward their driveway. I stumbled toward the sidewalk, the twins behind me.

"And this is why I go to the breakfast buffets," she explained, holding bits of toast and saliva in her palm.

"Where are Joseph and Adam?" I questioned. A symphony of footsteps sounded behind me and I turned to see Joseph and Adam moving toward us. Joseph rubbed his arms as though his muscles ached from the jump last night.

"Oh, Joseph, your hair is a bird's nest!" Jessica stomped toward him and furiously finger-combed his hair.

"Ow, watch it! My scalp is sensitive—*ow*!" he cried.

Jessica gave up with a sigh. "All right, let's go before the buffet closes."

The sun beamed down on the first day of November. Wisps of clouds dotted the sky, but otherwise it remained cloudless. For many it'd be the perfect start to November, but for me it was just another reminder of the passing time—the time that determined who would retrieve the gemstones first.

The portal encounter last night had rocked me to my bones; it left me shivering even as I sank my teeth into a hot bagel in the open cafeteria. Lembrose—Vina—had certainly returned, and with a great amount of vengeance. She'd probably escaped her cell long before we'd even reached the Blessing River, so she must've known that my locket necklace would hold some sort of hint as to where she could find the gemstones.

The real question was, how did Vina escape? Had all of the Sorcerer Line escaped, too?

The hot chocolate burned my throat, and I didn't even realize that I'd been furiously chugging it down as I contemplated my thoughts. It left a sizzling feeling in the back of my throat after I'd swallowed.

"We should be heading to the King's Library soon," Adam advised, leaning toward us while sweeping the dirty cafeteria floor. He was once again dressed as a janitor, a name tag clipped to his pocket. The floor was still slick with water, meaning there hadn't been much clean up on the flood just yet. Angry African Jade members stabbed their food, irritably chomping on their breakfast as they contemplated the ground.

"I'm going to my dorm to collect some of my things," Jess stated. "I don't think we're going to be coming back to this school for a long while." Janine agreed with her, and then they left for American Ruby.

Joseph and I left the cafeteria, and soon we approached the drama room. A trickle of water seeped out the doorway, and I noticed many figures stirring about. All of a sudden the door burst open and many heavily-armed men in uniforms and badges that read POLICE began to place caution tape along the walls. A dark-haired man looking to be in his early thirties approached us, his rubber boots squeaking beneath him.

"Do y'all have any idea how this happened?" he asked with a heavy Southern accent.

Joseph's eyes spun toward me, then toward the officer. "There was a leaking pipe," he squeaked. I hurriedly agreed.

The officer eyed us for a moment before another uniformed police man barged up to the Southern officer, holding a receiver to his mouth. He let the receiver drop to his hips. "Officer Kit?" he asked.

"Yeah? Whatsamatta?"

"We've got a Code Ninety down at the station."

Officer Kit's eyes bulged. "A Ninety? But I thought we restocked on doughnuts yesterday!" The two officers eyed me for a second before continuing their conversation in hushed whispers. "Yes . . . yes . . . tell 'em I'll be there soon."

Officer Kit turned back to me with steel-gray eyes, his mouth pressed in a tight line. "You and your friend shouldn't a been walkin' round here. What're y'all doin' sneakin' 'round restricted areas? Y'all best get on movin' before they call ya to the station."

Joseph and I muttered an apology and turned to leave for Australian Sapphire, separating when we left for our dorms. As soon as I entered my dorm hallway a rush of nostalgia came over me. Memories of the time I'd spent with Monika and Ash surfaced, such as the hours we'd spent working on our chemistry skit.

A sudden sweep of hatred took over my emotions. Every moment I'd spent with Ash was just a way for her to ensure that I saw her as a friend, a person I could trust. Now the amount of trust I had for the Sapphires had dried to nothingness.

I entered the code into the digital lock on our dorm entrance and heard the welcoming *zing* as the door clicked open. Then I stepped onto the cold carpet and closed the door shut. Just as I lifted my eyes I heard a rustle coming from the bunk beds.

I turned my head and noticed someone lying on the lower bunk-bed. She was reading a book and sitting there as if it were any usual Saturday morning.

She was Monika.

"Oh!" I cried, fleeing to her, and then wrapped my arms around her and gave her a hug. She was wearing an extremely large cast and her hair was draped around her shoulders like a curtain. By the time I let go, her glasses were completely tipped on her nose and she had a cross-eyed look on her face as she examined them.

"Arica," she said, adjusting her glasses and blinking repeatedly. "Where were you last night?" Her voice turned interrogative.

"I-I," I stammered, feeling extremely overjoyed despite Monika's cold reaction. I felt as though I hadn't seen Monika in ages, yet my visit to the hospital had taken place just yesterday. Warm tears rushed to the brim of my eyes. How was I supposed to explain what had happened last night? What was I supposed to say about *Ash*?

She took a deep breath, eyeing her cast. "I'm feeling a lot better since you visited me in the hospital. Thanks so much for that," she said, placing her clammy hand on my elbow. She released it and quickly wiped it against her pants. "Listen, I wanted to ask you something." She sat a little straighter on her bed and eyed me cautiously. "About the cloaked man."

My chest tightened. The nightmare with the cloaked man still vividly played in my mind, and I was sure it had something to with Ash and the Sorcerers Underworld mark. She'd transported us during our sleep, making it look as though we'd had a nightmare.

"Yes?" I croaked.

"Well . . . I told everyone that I'd gotten into a baking incident in the kitchen, which made it seem like I'd burnt myself by accident, but really I have no idea where this came from. I just know that it came after that nightmare . . . after I saw the cloaked man. After I saw . . ." She took a shaky breath. "After I saw Ash."

"You don't need to worry about Ash," I said, but sounded more confident than I truly felt. "She's gone."

"Where?" Monika asked immediately, leaning forward.

"On . . . vacation." I gulped.

"You mean like the headmistress?" she asked, but she creased her eyebrows, as if questioning whether my statement was viable or not. "Don't you think that's a bit weird? How the headmistress suddenly left and now Ash is gone, too?" She absently tapped her chin, but then shook her head to release the thought. "So . . . she won't be here on Monday, when drama starts?"

Drama. Two months ago the course excited me, but now the word left me as empty as a gaping hole. I would have to leave school immediately in order to search for the gemstones, so there was no possibility in my showing up for the drama course expected to begin this Monday.

I nodded my head. "And I won't be here, either."

"You won't?" Monika asked with concern. "Why?"

Something deep within me wanted to let her know—to tell her all about the gemstones and magic and sorcery. I could never explain the situation with Ash and the intertwined snakes without her knowing; but for now, it seemed like telling her would be an unsafe bet.

"I just have something really important to do. But I'll be back—I promise." I swallowed. That was a lie—I surely wouldn't be returning to school any time soon. Not without the gemstones.

"Okay," she said, crestfallen. Then we stood and exchanged a hug.

In the midst of our embrace, I found myself thinking that one day I would fulfill that promise. One day, whether it would be in ten days or ten years, I promised myself I would tell her everything.

* * *

As soon as I left my dorm room I took the flight of stairs down to the cafeteria where I would meet with Joseph, Adam, Janine and Jessica. Many students peered over their heap of pancakes to see the twins and Joseph bickering loudly.

"You're telling Mum—" Joseph began.

"No, *you're* telling her—"

"But I just—"

"We flipped the coin and *you lost*," Jessica finished, folding her arms across her chest.

Joseph huffed. "Never been a fan of mortal money, anyway," he sneered.

I slowly took a seat beside Joseph, observing the crowd of students around us. One student had his jaw hung so wide that maple syrup was drooling out of his mouth.

"Could you keep it down?" I pressed. "Some students are going to start jumping to conclusions about what you mean—and specifically about the *mortal money*," I said, giving Joseph a light slap on the arm.

"All right, all right," he said, lifting his hands in the air. His gaze shifted and his eyes narrowed at the cafeteria door. He growled under his breath and muttered, "Oh, look, the prince lives." He angrily chomped on a carrot. Adam sauntered toward our table, wearing a thin white shirt with dark cuffs and denim jeans. His apparel looked almost out of place since he wasn't wearing his usual janitorial outfit, but I supposed he was just trying to fit in with the crowd. Some girls straightened in their seats and giddily waved as he passed. He gave a short wave back and the girls let out dreamy sighs.

"Hey, Adam," the twins called when he neared our table. "Where'd you get that outfit from?" Janine asked.

He lightly patted his pocket, an immediate gesture toward the Wishing Knife. "So, are you ready to head off to you-know-where?" he asked.

"Well, Janine has to—" Joseph cut off when Janine spoke.

"Ahem?" she responded with a guttural tone.

"I mean—*I* have to drop something off. A letter for Mum and Auntie Claire to explain where we are," he clarified.

"Oh, no problem," Adam said, waving his hand over the envelope that lay on the table. The letter vanished in a thin smoke. "I've just sent it off."

Joseph gawked at the spot the letter had once been, thin tendrils of smoke rising to his nose. He began coughing uncontrollably, his cheeks turning red. Adam waved his hand in a strange way, and then Joseph's bout of coughing came to an end.

"Um, thanks," Joseph responded, fixing his shirt.

"No thanks necessary," he stated. We quickly left the cafeteria and headed toward the entrance to Hill Valley, passing numerous celebratory Halloween streamers from the night before.

"The King's Library is located in the same mansion where the Dungeons and Sorcerer Council are located," Adam said, "except it's on a very high floor."

"Floor?" I pondered. "I don't remember seeing any stairs."

"That's because they're hidden. Only three people in all of the Sorcerers Underworld know where the library is located."

Joseph answered, "Your mother, your father—"

"—and me," Adam finished with a nod. He pulled the Wishing Knife out of his pocket and held it near his chest, the tip just barely reaching his lips. He unintelligibly muttered a few words into the knife. A thin, wiry trail extended from his lips to the tip of the knife, almost as though the words he spoke were passing through a small tunnel.

A blue portal emerged in front of us, bursts of blue light extending out. Adam was the first to walk through, followed by the twins.

"See you on the other side," Joseph said with a salute. Then he approached the mouth of the portal and disappeared.

I took a tentative step forward before I was surrounded by blue light. Colours danced around me, and then I found myself dazing at the ceiling of the mansion. Black dots swarmed my vision, and the last traces of the blue portal closed off the entry to the mortal world.

SEVEN: THE KING'S LIBRARY

"Isn't there an elevator?" Jessica groaned when we reached the staircase.

Just before we found the staircase, Adam had led us to a white column in the heart of the mansion. After knocking three times in very specific locations, the column seemed to cave in before revealing a very secretive door. Beyond that was a magical ringed staircase, gleaming gold with diamonds encrusting the railing. The stairs extended so high that they disappeared behind what looked like lingering rain clouds from above.

"Nope," Adam answered, eyeing the clouds.

"Then we better get walking," Joseph added with a huff. He pressed his right foot against the very bottom step, but as soon as he did, it seemed to disappear beneath his feet. He tried again, this time trying a different step, but he only stumbled when the step disappeared just like the last. They reappeared as soon as he moved out of proximity of the staircase.

"What?" Joseph asked, adjusting his glasses as if his eyes were playing tricks on him.

Adam advanced toward the staircase, placing his hand on the railing as he pressed both feet against the first step. He bounced, as if testing the step, and then moved forward. The stairs did not disappear beneath his feet as it had done to Joseph. "The staircase only recognizes the Royal family—no one else is allowed entry. But, if I move forward, you four can follow along; the stairs will not disappear as long as you follow my exact footsteps. Otherwise you'll be thrown over the railing and unconscious before you even reach the ground."

I gulped, lifting my eyes to where the top of the staircase was shrouded in gray mist. A fall from that high up would *not* be pretty.

Adam took a step forward, ensuring that his left foot stayed in place on the lower step. Joseph set his foot on the spot Adam's right foot had just been.

We all moved in single file, following the same process to ensure that our feet were placed exactly as Adam's feet had been. No one dared speak a word for fear of breaking our concentration. I followed behind Joseph, carefully analyzing his footsteps as we ascended.

A faint shudder ran through the staircase. I paused in place, holding the air in my lungs.

"What was that?" one of the twins whispered behind me. I would've shaken my head, but I was too afraid that it could cause me to stumble and, eventually, fall.

The rumble snaked up the stairs and eventually faded away. I slowly released the breath I'd been holding in my chest.

"All right, stay close," Adam reminded when he resumed the ascent.

I carefully followed Joseph's footsteps, keeping my trembling hands at my sides. When we were turning the final bend, I felt a sharp pang in my leg. I pressed my hand against the source of pain, wishing for it to subside; instead, the feeling only grew worse. I pressured both hands against my leg, straining to keep my footing. Before I could even comprehend the situation, I felt my body waver to the side and my right foot absently slipped toward the shining railing.

"No!" I cried, just barely catching my balance. The only sound I could hear was my heart hammering in my ears. My hands searched for the railing as I tried to set my feet back in place. I wrapped my hands around the railing and stayed in place.

After heaving many breaths and waiting for several long, tiring minutes, I finally convinced myself that it was safe to move forward. Adam, with much caution, slowly led the way to the top landing. The hardest part was passing through the thickening clouds. Sometimes a stray raindrop would fall from the clouds and hit me in the eye, making my vision even worse. I had to keep my hand pressed against Joseph's back to be sure that I remained right behind him and no farther back.

I gripped Joseph's cotton shirt in my hand; the worn tee was inexplicably calming, seeing that it was the only thing that helped me move along through the fog. Once in a while the fog would disappear, allowing us a few spare moments to shuffle forward.

A breath of relief sounded from ahead when Joseph tore his shirt away from my grip. He had reached the top landing, standing with Adam intently as they waited for me to move forward. Just as my shoe scraped the final stair, a loud shudder sounded from all around me. My foot hovered over the final stair as I looked at Adam.

"Don't move," he stated, keeping his feet firmly planted against the ground.

A loud *crack* sounded from behind me, gradually growing louder as it travelled up the staircase. I jerked to the right and banged against the railing, the diamonds etching deep grooves into my palm as I held on. Bits of matter rained from above, almost like white dust.

"What about now?" I yelled over the rumbling staircase.

"Move!" he cried, but before I could move forward I felt something beneath the step—a spring or coil—force me into the air. I flew over the railing and into the gray clouds. My vision became utterly useless until I fell out of the clouds and back toward the staircase. A scream escaped my throat and I kept my hands outstretched as I tried to reach for the twins' hands. My hands locked onto Jessica's, and I felt myself swing forward. I pushed my feet out from beneath me so that the impact would not harm my body, but the blow would still hurt nonetheless.

After my feet slammed against the staircase, my torso twisted to the left. My arm connected with the railing and I felt as though my bones had shattered. The world was nothing less than blurs of light that swished around me. Although the pain was almost unbearable, I forced myself to keep hold of Jess's hands. She pulled me up with unknowable strength so that my feet teetered on the edge of the steps. I pulled my weight forward, soon standing on the edge of the railing. The twins both helped me over to the platform: We leapt over the next few stairs onto the final landing, and the last disjointed step clicked back into place. The ringed staircase was immobile at last.

I stumbled on the platform and collapsed in Adam's arms, my left shoulder still crying in pain. "I-I think I broke something," I said, a crack leaking into my voice.

Adam examined my arm. "Nothing I can't fix," he said, but then his deep blue gaze became worrisome. "I should've been more careful with my steps," he said. "I should've—"

"It's not your fault," I stated, followed by a wince. "My arm—"

"Joseph, hold her up," Adam stated as he pulled the Wishing Knife from his pocket. The twins and Joseph propped me forward and Adam began to delicately trace the tip of the knife along my left arm. A warming sensation filled me, almost as though hot chocolate were seeping through my veins.

"I haven't practiced Healing in a while," Adam said once he'd finished, "but I think this should be enough to relieve the pain and fix your arm."

I nodded my head, rotating my arm from side to side. The pain had quickly subsided and my arm felt good as new. "Thanks," I muttered to everyone.

Adam pocketed the knife and we advanced along the high platform, turning past many dark corridors until we approached the grand, marvellous French doors: they were forest green with golden letters KL overlapping the infamous intertwining snakes.

"This is the King's Library," Adam stated. "A place where all of my father's research and data has been collected and put into various books. He even has an extremely rare collection of books that are restricted to public access."

Joseph wore an extremely large grin on his face, and his laugh was almost giddy. He took a step forward and extended his arm to turn the handle, but Adam held him back and restricted him from moving any farther.

"Do *not* step past this line," Adam stated. "We can never be sure if Simon's still here," he said.

"Simon?" the twins asked simultaneously.

"Simon the Chimera," Adam stated. "He guards the King's Library in case there are any unwanted visitors lurking nearby."

"What's a Chimera?" I asked.

Joseph eagerly opened his mouth to answer—go figure—when I noticed something ripple in front of the doors. It was a grand form, taking the shape of the front half of a lion with a mane that looked like strings of gold; the rear end was composed of a goat with two solid hooves for the back feet. It had a serpent's tail that was embedded with small green spikes, and great, scaly wings that spread so far they disappeared in the darkness of the next corridor. Its eyes were like coal, and its gaze was so direct I felt like it could see right through my eye sockets and into my mind.

Joseph took several steps backward, accidentally bumping into his sisters' shoulders along the way. The twins were far too shocked by the Chimera's appearance to even respond.

"*This* is Simon," Adam responded. The Chimera leaned toward him and he stroked his mane affectionately.

Simon turned his head toward us and a grunt escaped his throat. He opened his mouth to reveal sharp teeth, small bundles of smoke escaping his nostrils. Then he bellowed a column of fire toward us. We all plunged to the side, the heat barely scorching our skin.

"No!" Adam told the Chimera. "Bad Chimera!" He acted as though he were talking to a harmless dog rather than an extremely dangerous fire-breathing creature. "Sit!"

The Chimera reluctantly followed his command.

I wiped a few beads of sweat from my forehead and stood, noticing that a portion of my shirt had been badly blistered by the heat.

"We can change after," Janine noted. "For now, I think we ought to head into the Library before this Simon creature decides to attack us again."

Adam told the Chimera to move to the side in order to clear the path to the entrance. Once we'd crossed past the Chimera, we arrived at the doorway. Joseph was the first to reach the French doors. His trembling hand rested on the handle, but a slight smile seemed to form on his face. He took a deep breath before he opened the two grand doors, welcoming us to the wonder and magic of the King's Library.

The Library was unlike any library I'd ever seen. The walls were golden and the endless bookcases travelled along the floor, shifting toward walls or clicking in and out of one another. Books flew in circles around us, their words drifting off the page and spiralling through the air.

"My father's library," Adam said.

"Wow," Joseph said in amazement, turning in circles as he gazed at the moving bookcases.

Adam walked over to a grand bookcase that had just shifted against the wall. He pulled out an enormously large book that was leather bound with bright lettering that seemed to move across the cover. "This is a collection of my father's magical discoveries," Adam stated, passing the book to me. The paper inside was almost as rough as the tree bark from which it originated, thick but very delicate.

Joseph's face was so deeply buried in the book that he had to continually prop his glasses back from sliding down the bridge of his nose.

"Where are we going to find information on a route to the Bermuda Triangle?" Jessica asked, dulled by the book. Joseph seemed like the only person who could maintain a keen interest in books in the family.

"I could simply summon a book," Adam said. He sifted through his pocket and pulled the Wishing Knife out. "Or a lot of books, I suppose," he said, staring at the moving disarray of bookshelves. He muttered an incantation and waited for a book to move its way toward us. Even after Adam's display with the Wishing Knife, the books remained on the shelves.

Adam lowered his knife speechlessly. The books did not shift; all stood still. "My father must have put new enchantments on the Library," he stated. "Probably for security purposes after his crown was stolen. The Wishing Knife will not work." He slid the knife back into his pocket.

"Looks like we've got a long way to walk," Janine said after a sigh. Then she tugged on Joseph's arm. He lifted his head from the book reluctantly and then we set off into the maze of bookshelves.

* * *

We walked around the never-ending bookshelves for what felt like hours. Since they were constantly moving, it became even more frustrating to examine the books and select one that could help us on our journey.

"Didn't we pass that bookshelf a while ago?" Jess asked wearily.

"I don't know," her sister answered sleepily. "They all look the same."

Joseph looked fascinated by the world of bookcases surrounding him. His mouth hung in awe as he gaped at the bookshelves swerving around us.

As we turned past another bookshelf, I felt a cold blast of wind whip my hair and I shivered in place.

"Who turned up the air conditioning?" Joseph asked.

"It's like a freezer in here," Jessica commented, rubbing her arms.

"I'll check out the thermostat," Adam said. He strolled to an immobile bookcase and tipped the book forward with his pointer finger. Behind it was the thermostat: a big, white square with two faint pictures depicted on the surface. One was the sun and the other a snowflake. Adam checked the temperature with curious eyes and then spun the dial toward the sun, dramatically increasing the temperature.

"No!" a deep voice called out.

I immediately turned around, looking for the source of the voice. A shadowy figure sat by the wall, hidden between two bookshelves. The figure slowly stood with shaky movements and advanced forward. He seemed to move with a sort of limp, although I couldn't make out his facial features due to the darkness.

The bright, golden light of the Library first illuminated his shoes, then his torso, and finally his whole body. His appearance was both repulsive and intriguing—something I'd never witnessed before. His entire body glinted brown—his clothes, skin, everything. A long, brown glob formed on his thigh and dripped down his leg, supposedly causing the limp. His scent wafted toward me: milky, sweet, and highly familiar.

He was made entirely of chocolate.

"Hi," the chocolate man said. "I'm Arnold, Keeper of the King's Library." He looked down for a moment. "Don't let my scrumptious appearance deceive you," he added hastily. His Irish accent was easily detectable.

The colour drained from our faces. I tried to speak, but I felt my throat swell. His physical appearance was impossible—nobody could live in the form of *chocolate*. "As you can see, I'm just slightly melting, so I'd really appreciate it if you lowered the temperature," he said with a quick bow toward Adam. His right foot had almost completely muddled into a delicious fondue.

"Of course," Adam said, his gaze perplexed as he turned the dial back. Almost immediately the air seemed to become cooler, crisper.

"Ah, thank you." He took a seat at a study table and gestured us to join him. We reluctantly followed.

Adam was the first to speak up: "So, Arnold, Keeper of my father's Library—could you help us search for something? We're trying to find a book that could guide us to the Bermuda Triangle," he explained.

"The Bermuda Triangle, you say?" Arnold tapped his chin, leaving small smears of chocolate due to his melted fingertips. "I am used to receiving wishes as a prior genie, but of course I will follow the request of the prince," he stated.

"A genie?" I asked. "How'd you turn from a genie into . . ."

Arnold laughed. "I know my appearance may puzzle you, so perhaps I should clarify some things right now. My chocolate form was an accident. I was attempting to fulfill a wish for a young woman almost a hundred years ago in mortal time. I had no idea that in the future she'd become so sinister, so ominously evil . . ."

"She?" Joseph asked suddenly. He slammed his hands down on the table, causing it to shake. Tiny droplets of chocolate from Arnold's fingers rolled off his hands and dotted the wooden desk in an abstract pattern. The flowers set in the middle of the table shivered in the cool air.

He gulped, making a hollow, raspy sound. "It was a young woman," he said. "A young woman named Vina."

EIGHT: ARNOLD

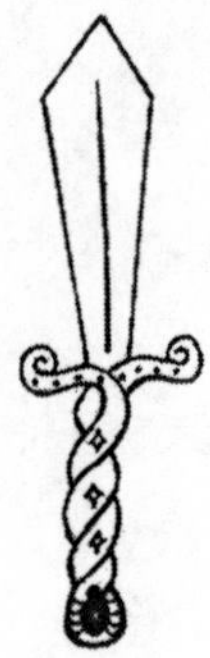

Arnold's blank brown eyes examined the five of us as he told his story. Every now and then a drop of chocolate would spatter our faces when his hands waggled through the air, but otherwise the atmosphere remained quite tense.

"And that's pretty much it, isn't it?" he finished. "I turned into chocolate, was pretty much socially unacceptable, and now I'm living the rest of my lonesome life in the King's Library. Luckily your father was gracious enough to allow me to stay here," he said, directing his attention to Adam. "Sometimes I like to take a stroll outside but Simon looks at me as though I'm a treat and I run back in," he added with a chuckle.

I replayed the story in my mind, feeling a mix of pity and rage coil in my stomach. Vina once had good intentions, trying to help her husband; but when he died, she'd become a different person. Her goal was to take over the mortal world, and do so with three beautiful gemstones.

"That's unfortunate," Adam said, then averted his gaze to the bookshelves.

Arnold sighed. "Yes, well, I've gotten used to it. Anyway, it seems you need some help finding a way to the Bermuda Triangle," he asked with a quick reverse on the subject. "I think I know just where to go."

Arnold led us through the bookcases, sometimes disappearing behind a bookcase but reappearing when he decided to march in another direction. We struggled to keep up; the twins' cherry-red hair flew in my face as we jogged along, and we dodged several bookcases that swerved nearby.

Here we are," Arnold stated, abruptly pausing in front of a grand shelf. Joseph just barely bumped into him as he came to a halt.

Arnold carefully peered at the spines of the books before he pulled out a thick wad of paper concealed behind a large novel. He began pulling the string that held the sheets together and carefully unfolded the papers. The sides were tattered and burnt, and the pages were embossed with messy scrawl.

Joseph examined the pages like a hawk, eyes darting as he moved from one line to the next. "This says a lot about the Shadowers. How do they have to do with the Bermuda Triangle?"

"They don't," Arnold replied in a thick voice, almost humoured. "It was what one of the Shadowers *did* that has to do with the Bermuda Triangle."

"One of the Shadowers?" Janine questioned curiously. "You mean like Pedro?"

"Correct," he affirmed. "But there were two different Shadowers involved in this. Two men named Quindle and

Benjamin, who'd gone on a journey to search for the golden dragon heart."

"The golden dragon heart?" I asked, intrigued. His story was becoming very interesting.

"Indeed. The golden dragon heart is legendary for maintaining specific powers over long periods of time; seeking this would ultimately guarantee that their Shadowing powers would last forever. You see, their power had begun to drain after a decade—give or take a few years—and so the two decided to go on a quest of sorts to search for the ingredient that could save them. But in the end they'd been captured in a place where no one could escape. Their only way out was to escape over water, and thus Benjamin decided to create a form of transportation. At first he'd decided to make a boat, but soon later he realized that a boat was far too small for the amount of passengers he wanted to rescue along with him. He created something else—a train. The Water Train."

"The Water Train!" Adam cried. "Of course!"

"I've heard of it," Joseph replied, tapping the rim of his glasses. "How will that help us?"

"Well, Benjamin died soon after and no one was able to conduct the Water Train, but since his power—you are aware of his power, correct?—was passed down to his son, the only person who could control it was him."

"Um, hello?" Janine asked, waving her hand in front of their faces. "There are some people here who have *no* idea what you're talking about." The twins crossed their arms and I nodded in agreement.

"Oh—right." If Arnold's cheeks could turn red, then they definitely would. "The Water Train—well, it's practically in its name—is a train made of . . ." He smirked. "Well, water."

"How is that possible?" I asked abruptly. I huddled beside Joseph and examined the papers he held. There was a diagram sketched in dark pencil: It looked like a train of some sort, except for the fact that it was, in fact, for sorcerers instead of mortals, and instead of riding on train tracks, it treaded on water.

"Benjamin, you see, had the power to create solid objects with water. Like I said before, he died in his escape attempt and the Royals found him. The Water Train was moved into the mortal world. It now travels within the Bermuda Triangle, almost like a cruise ship, where many sorcerers and sorceresses can climb aboard and enjoy a fun vacation or quick passageway to the Sorcerer Palace."

"That's it!" said Jessica, her voice overflowing with realization. "The Water Train travels in the Bermuda Triangle; it can take us to the Sorcerer Palace! And we *all* know what's in there."

I shook my head no. The twins almost seemed taken aback by my lack of knowledge. In my defence, I'd just learned about magic and the Sorcerers Underworld not too long ago, so I was still new to many of these magical places and concepts.

"As well as being the home to the Royal family"—Adam seemed content with this remark—"it also contains the Hall of Lost Gemstones."

The words rang familiarly in the back of my mind. Joseph had mentioned the Hall of Lost Gemstones at the Council before we'd travelled back into the mortal world. A lady had stood up from the members and said something about how dangerous the trip would be: *No one's been there in a hundred years,* she'd said.

"The Hall of Lost Gemstones," Joseph echoed. "All lost gemstones are sent there to be collected by their owners," he finished.

I decided to abandon the lady's frantic warning. If that was the one place gemstones go when they're lost, then we could surely collect them.

"If you're in need of your gemstones, that would be the perfect place to go. And remember—time is passing as we speak," Arnold added cautiously. "If you wish to travel to the Sorcerer Palace, then you must find a way to board the Water Train."

I set the papers against the bookshelf, my hand tracing the tattered sheets. "According to this calendar there's a stop at Miami."

"Great!" Adam called. "Surely we can teleport there. I'll just need to look through a few more books—"

"Adam, the stop is tomorrow," I informed coldly.

His face became grim. "I should still be able to—"

"No, you won't," Arnold interjected with a serious tone. "There's only one way to board that train, and that's with a ticket." He took his turn to examine the papers.

"Where do we buy tickets from?" Janine asked.

Arnold chuckled. "You don't *buy* tickets—you must find them. Tickets are said to be cradled inside seashells somewhere far within the Sorcerers Underworld."

"Where exactly?" Joseph pondered.

At first Arnold gave a hesitant response, but his voice was so low that I could barely hear him. Then he repeated what he'd said in a much stronger voice: "Topaz Sector," he informed.

"Topaz?!" Adam cried, a lightning-shaped vein popping out from the side of his head. "That trip would take a week."

"Well, unless you have a flying horse that can take you there, then I'm sorry. You're probably too late."

We remained silent with dismay. It was too late—there was no way we would make it to Topaz in time to receive the tickets to board the Water Train. Disappointment sank deep into my stomach, heavy as a brick.

"Wait," Jess said, her voice illuminating the dreary atmosphere. "We don't have a flying horse," she said.

"Thanks for stating the obvious," Joseph muttered.

Jessica gave him an uncomfortable stare. "But we do have something else: a royal dragon." She turned her eyes to Adam.

"That's right," Adam clarified. "We can travel to the Crigo Pit and fly the Crigoes there!"

"Where's the Crigo Pit?" I asked.

"You've been there once before," Joseph commented. "In the Drawer of Surprises."

"That's where all Crigoes live," Adam said.

My brows furrowed. "So the Drawer is actually a path into the Crigo Pit."

"Exactly!" Joseph looked overly delighted. "It's located right outside Head Quarters. We just need to go back down the staircase."

"Oh, not again!" Jess cried.

"If you're in need of a shortcut, I've got one here for you." Arnold half-smiled. Adam frowned. "There's only one way in and out, and that's the staircase . . ." Before Adam could finish Arnold had already stood up; he began trudging down the long blood-red carpet beneath his feet.

We exchanged glances and then quickly decided to follow. Arnold swerved around many bookshelves and we tagged along. My feet began to ache due to the tiresome walk.

"Ah, here it is." Arnold swiftly opened a light-blue curtain and we were left staring at a large metal circle planted against the wall. Arnold spun the handle clockwise three times before a loud *pop* sounded and the metal plate screeched open. On the other side was a vent or some sort of air shaft that tilted down like a slide.

I peered down the shaft. "And this will lead us to . . . ?"

"None other than the Crigo Pit!" Arnold exclaimed.

"Well, it looks much more promising than the staircase," Jess enthused, but her soft blue eyes widened with fear.

Arnold muttered an agreement, though his accent was so thick I couldn't understand a word he'd said. Then with a light shove he prompted us forward. We each took turns going down: Janine bravely slid down first, followed by her siblings. Joseph's whimper echoed down the shaft and I couldn't help but croak a very much needed laugh.

"Maybe I should go next," Adam said, his final words injected with laughter. Once his golden-blond head disappeared from sight, I shimmied my way into the shaft. I clutched the metal walls with both hands, and suddenly felt an odd sort of suffocation come over me. As soon as I took my first breath, I smelt a sharp, pungent fume that cut straight through my senses like a blade through air.

"Argh, it smells terrible," I said, plugging my nose.

"The smell wears off as you go down," Arnold assured, taking a step back. I took one last moment to survey the Library: its magical bookcases moved along the rugs as though they had a mind of their own.

I turned back, releasing my hands from the shaft, and lay back so I plunged into the darkness. The last thing I heard was Arnold's voice: "Oh, and don't forget, the seashells must be found in the maze!"

"A maze?!" I cried over the whoosh of my ears.

"Yup, good luck!" The rest of his words were drowned beneath the hum in my ears as I slid down the shaft, my heart thumping.

I closed my eyes and, after a seemingly infinite trip, I finally came to a stop. Two pale hands reached inside the shaft and took hold of my hands. Strands of untamed red hair dangled near the shaft and I realized it must've been one of the twins.

I managed to squeeze through the opening and emerge into a cloudy setting. The sky was overcast with angry clouds and fog ran along the ground in shadowy wisps.

"Memories," Jessica said as if she had come to a comforting, familiar place. "Remember when that Crigo tried to kill us? Ah, good times."

"Kill *us*?" I smirked. "More like me. I ended up unconscious in your room after that spiked tail sent me flying!" I exclaimed.

The twins giggled, though Joseph and Adam looked completely oblivious beside them.

"So we're supposed to *ride* these things?" Joseph asked hoarsely.

"Of course, I do it all the time," Adam encouraged.

As soon as Adam trudged forward, Joseph rolled his eyes. *"I do it all the time,"* he mimicked, though his mimic was not very authentic.

"Come on, Jocelyn." Janine and Jess both nudged his shoulders and they set off into the fog. We walked in silence for a few minutes; I sometimes tripped on a stray vine, but otherwise it was a smooth walk.

"Let's stop here," Adam said. We had approached a small stream that snaked along the ground to form the shape of a C.

I dipped my finger in the water, examining the leaves that had fallen into the stream. I cupped the water in my hands and then let it slip through the tiny cracks between my fingers. I was left with small pieces of dirt in my palm.

"This isn't drinkable," I complained. "We'll have to find another source." I turned toward Adam. He shook his head, which made me a little agitated. "But it's—" I began.

"Dirty, I know," Adam finished. He drew the Knife from his pocket and let the sharp edge glide across the water. The water began to glow bright green, illuminating the fog that curled over it. The water rippled in thin sheets.

I hesitated for a moment, but then dipped my other hand into the water and brought it out to see that it was clean. I glowered for a moment, but thought better of it: I surely didn't want to upset the prince. I swallowed the cool water down my throat and drank until my tongue was numb with the cold.

"Hungry, were you?" Adam asked. We'd pulled away from the group as they drank their water.

"Thirsty," I corrected, but my stomach growled and I cursed under my breath.

Adam found this amusing. "Maybe you'll learn how to do that one day."

"Do what?" I asked curiously.

"What I did at the stream just now, and what I did at the flood. My power—your power. I mean, you're the Prophetic Child! You just haven't learned everything you need to know."

"Like how to conjure Thoven's Bow," I said, arching my eyebrow.

He nodded. "It takes practice to conjure on the spot. You'd done well at the river, making your metal necklace appear. You know how to conjure objects, but with Thoven's

Bow . . ." He hesitated. "Sometimes the greatest weapons are the hardest to guide."

I half-smiled, impressed. "Where'd you hear that?"

"My father," he answered. "He taught me how to use the Wishing Knife when I was young. He was both a father and a teacher." His eyes suddenly widened, the corners of his lips twitching into a grin. "That's what you need—a teacher!"

"Who's going to teach me?"

Adam's mouth had just opened to respond when I heard a rustle in the trees. Behind the long, thin branches was a miraculously grand form.

"The Crigo!" I shouted, and the twins and Joseph shuffled toward us.

"Crigoes," Jessica corrected.

My eyes widened. Five Crigoes had stepped into the clearing, dipping their heads into the C-shaped stream. Each wore gleaming scales and bright wings that they kept cradled at their sides as they drank.

On their backs were four petals that surrounded each other like a flower. White petals signified a life to live, whereas black meant that the life was already gone.

One Crigo was especially familiar, its purple scales and defined sharp teeth immediately recognizable as the Crigo we'd seen Thursday evening in the Drawer.

Adam slid onto one of the Crigoes' backs. "This is Pepper," he stated, smoothing its scaly gray skin with his right hand. "Don't be afraid—they don't bite!"

I had a hard time believing this as I stared at its teeth. Maybe they didn't bite, but they sure did whip their tails mercilessly.

I carefully approached the purple Crigo, careful to steer clear of its razor-sharp teeth, and slid on with extreme caution. When the Crigo didn't react, I let out a breath of relief. The twins excitedly mounted their Crigoes, which were both fiery orange.

"Those are Crackle and Sniff," Adam said as the Crigo moved toward the twins. "And that's Lucy," he said, looking toward me.

"Lucy . . ." I mused. "Not exactly what comes to mind when I think of a huge scaly dragon."

He chuckled. "She was named after Lucinda, one of the first Crigoes to ever be found in the Sorcerers Underworld."

"Thanks for the history lesson," I joked, but my amused expressions slipped away when I heard Joseph's Crigo growl.

"Um—giddyup!" Joseph said fearfully. "Start your engines—open sesame?" Joseph ordered weakly. The Crigo continued to growl.

Adam took a few cautious steps toward Joseph. "Joseph, in order for a Crigo to fly you must pat one of its legs. Preferably the—"

"Left? Got it," Joseph said excitedly. He was probably overjoyed by the fact that he'd met a marvellous creature in the flesh rather than just reading about it in his endless array of books.

"No, Joseph, I don't think you understand—" Adam warned, but it was too late. Joseph had patted the Crigo's left leg and was plunged into the sky.

Joseph screamed as the Crigo flew vertically through the clouds. A few seconds after he'd disappeared behind the haze, he reappeared with the Crigo, swooping toward the ground. Joseph kept his head buried between his two arms as he clung to the Crigo's scales.

"Pat the right leg!" Adam called over the loud *swoosh* of the Crigo's wings flapping back and forth.

Joseph, without hesitation, peeled his right hand away from the Crigo and managed to pat the front leg on the right. The Crigo immediately lifted its head higher, and its two honey golden eyes turned down to the ground. It swooped down in loops and spirals until its feet gently hit the rocky floor. Beneath the slightly glowing haze above I now noticed the dark, royal blue of its scales, the tips of its wings ending in silvery feathers. The Crigo's tail slapped the water of the stream and caused a shower of water to rain on us.

I wiped my wet arms and slid off my Crigo. Then I ran toward Joseph, about to help him down.

"No, I'm fine," Joseph croaked, though his nails dug deep into the web that connected the dragon's scales to its iridescent wings.

Adam ordered Pepper to move forward. "Joseph, perhaps if you'd listened—"

"I patted the right leg, hadn't I?" he countered. His blue Crigo restlessly moved on the spot.

Adam let out a breathy sigh. "Skye is a bit of a dangerous one," he said. "But you must listen to what I say. I've had eighteen years of experience with the Crigo Pit, and you don't want to upset a Crigo." Adam rolled his right sleeve up to reveal a dark scar, snaking from his shoulder down to his inner elbow.

Joseph gulped. "Lesson learned," he said with a shaky nod. "I suppose we better head toward Topaz Sector."

"Now you're talking," Janine said, and then she patted the Crigo's right leg. It lifted its two front legs high in the sky as if it were a horse rearing before a race, and then flapped its wings. Crackle moved forward, sailing into the sky. Janine's whoops of excitement faded as she hovered farther away.

I followed suit, patting Lucy's right leg, and then the Crigo lurched into flight. My stomach lifted as we sped forward. The wind hit my face and caused my eyes to sting with warm tears, but I managed a smile. The twins' Crigoes both flew on either side of me. Adam and Joseph flew just behind.

I took hold of the gooey web that led into the Crigo's wings—the only thing that kept me from flying off—and steered forward. When I gently pressed on the right wing, it would lean to the right. I quickly learned the flight controls as Joseph pressed on about uninteresting facts.

I looked down at the Crigo's back and noticed a dark black petal imprinted on its skin. I'd made the Crigo unconscious after I'd hit it with a bow—which had turned into Thoven's Bow—and then the Crigo had awoken to its new life.

"Sorry," I whispered into her ear, which I supposed was the small slit on the side of her head.

The Crigo's lips seemed to curl up, almost as a smile. I smiled, too; it almost seemed like a silent forgiveness.

"Steer forward," Adam advised. "By nightfall we should reach American Ruby. We should be able to reach Topaz by the crack of dawn."

My mind reeled back to Arnold's words as soon as I'd plunged into the air shaft. He'd mentioned that the seashells must be found in a maze. I gulped. I'd had a bad experience in a Christmas ice maze once, and I promised myself that I'd never enter another maze again in my life. So much for that.

I decided to leave the maze information for later—we needn't worry about that now. After about an hour of smooth flight, I was beginning to slump toward the Crigo's back as if it were a bed. I tried to keep my eyes open, but the mundane gray clouds were so repetitive that I found myself falling asleep. I clung to the Crigo's back, feeling safe in the gentle flap of its wings, and dozed off to the rhythm of its beating heart beneath me.

In my dream I was light as a feather, my arms spread on either side like wings. The Crigo moved swiftly beneath me, sometimes rolling over so that I clutched back onto the web at the entrance of its wings. I clung to its scaly skin as Lucy flew forward through the warm wind, and I let out a laugh that made me feel lighter than air. Lucy continued to spiral through the sky gleefully.

Suddenly I felt a jerk underneath me and my hands flew upward. I took an infinitesimal moment to look around me and found that I was hanging upside down from my Crigo. My hands flew wildly in the ferocious wind and I felt a tingle of cold air linger around my fingertips.

All of a sudden I felt my legs slip, and my body jerked farther toward the ground. My feet were the only thing hanging on to the Crigo and I immediately felt them withdraw from their place.

I began to sprawl toward the ground, hands and feet flailing. My hair whipped around my head and the world looked like a messy painting.

Then all I heard was the long scream that escaped my mouth as I fell to the ground.

I jolted upright on the Crigo's back, strands of brown hair covering my vision. The sun beamed through the white clouds and I noticed two orange Crigoes flying just in front of me. Lucy snorted, tendrils of thick smoke dissipating in the air above.

I clutched Lucy's scales beneath my hands, immediately realizing that I'd just had a dream. I was still safely sitting on the Crigo as its wings shuddered from fatigue. The sky was much darker now—a shade of blue that perfectly balanced afternoon and evening. Beneath the wisps of clouds I could see city buildings and skyscrapers rising high in the sky; they were so close I felt like I could reach out and touch them.

"Finally awake, are you?" Jessica asked, her torso twisted toward me.

I smiled, but the bitter, cold wind caused my teeth to chatter and I frowned. I steered Lucy forward, my torso barely touching her back as I leaned toward her. Lucy sped in front of the twins and I looked back with arched brows.

The twins were laughing, readying their Crigoes to move forward when their faces displayed pure horror. I followed their gaze and found myself caught in the middle of some sort of air battle. Magical flying creatures soared my way; I steered Lucy down and we swooped beneath the endless flying crowd.

"Looks like we've hit downtown," Adam said with a grimace.

The whinny of flying horses and the snorts of other creatures I'd never seen before sounded from above. They galloped and flew along the invisible path of the air, sometimes stopping to allow pedestrians (like Time Sprites or pixies) to cross.

"Downtown?" I murmured. "In the *sky*?"

"Things can get pretty hectic around here," Adam explained.

"We need to find another path out of here," Joseph said, steering toward me. "We can't stay down here forever.

The buildings are going to get in the way." He pointed to the vast city that spilled before us.

Lucy snorted in agreement. Her eyelids fluttered with tiredness.

"Let's make a pit-stop," I suggested. "We can let the Crigoes rest and"—my stomach growled right on cue—"get something to eat," I finished.

"Right," Jess agreed. "The rush will die down once we've finished, and I'm starving." She and her sister both nodded their heads synchronously.

"What's that?" Joseph murmured, his thin lips barely moving. His trembling finger pointed to a yellow-orange palace hovering in the sky, so bright and gleaming that I could barely look at it. Small windows dotted the palace all around.

"It looks like gold!" Joseph said incredulously. He pushed farther, and I could almost feel the shakiness in Lucy's bones as she struggled to move ahead.

As soon as we neared the palace, a horrible smell invaded my nose. It smelt like old lingering cheese.

"Joseph . . . I don't think that's gold," Janine said with a shaky voice.

As I inspected the palace I found that Janine was correct: the palace was made entirely of cheese, with small holes sinking deep inside.

"Swiss cheese," Jess murmured. "This looks like a cheese palace."

Another growl sounded from my stomach. "Maybe we can find some food here."

"Hey, look! There's a drive-thru!" Janine enthused.

"It's a fly-thru, Janine," Joseph corrected. Many winged creatures lined the cheese palace, waiting to make their order. The words THE CHEESY PALACE were imprinted on a dark façade that loomed over the palace entrance.

"Then let's go!" I steered forward, and the others trailed behind me as we flew to The Cheesy Palace.

NINE: CAMPFIRE

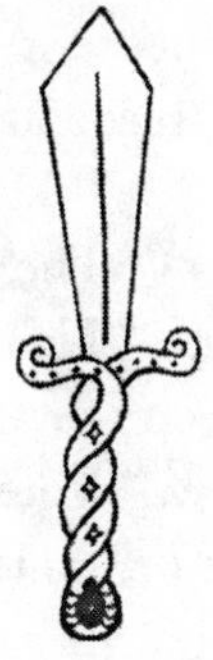

"Would you like to hear our specials for today?" the man asked for the millionth time in a monotonous voice. He was standing before an open window at The Cheesy Palace's fly-thru.

"No, thank you," I repeated. "We want five cheesy cheeseburgers, please."

The man wore a purple shirt covered in cheese stains. His name tag was flipped upside down and his features were worn by weariness. "Would you—"

"No!" I said, but I didn't mean to shout. Agitation poured over me before I could stop myself. "I mean—no thanks. We just want five. But one has to be veggie."

The man arched his brow as if this was an utterly confusing demand, and then moved his fingers at a snail's pace toward the register. "Twenty-five cents is your change." He struggled to find a quarter in the avalanche of coins spilling across the register. "Uhhh . . ."

"Keep the change," I said quickly.

He knitted his brows together. "Okay?" he murmured confusingly. Just when he'd found a quarter he grunted. "Would you like a receipt . . . ?"

"No," Joseph blurted behind me. His Crigo grunted irritably.

The man let out an unnecessary sigh. Our food appeared on the fly-thru pick-up table, small wisps of vapour rising from its spot.

"Thanks for choosing The Cheesy Palace, where everything is fit for a prince." He looked up lazily and then jumped back as if he'd been shocked. "Oh, Prince Adam," he said, giving a slight bow. "Would you like to hear—"

"No, thanks . . ." Adam trailed off as he struggled to read the man's name from his name-tag. ". . . Bert?"

"It's pronounced Be—" The man belched midsentence. He warmly smiled to himself and patted his stomach.

"We'll just be going . . ." I said with revulsion as I picked up the bags. Lucy moved forward and stopped by the outer edge of the parking lot—well, more like a *flying* lot, since we were still hovering in the sky. We ate our burgers in silence. The food was chewy and bland, and not at all very cheesy, but it was enough to end my hunger until our next stop at nightfall.

"Where do you think our next stop will be?" Jess asked once she'd devoured her burger.

"American Ruby," Adam answered. "We can set up a campfire and rest there till morning."

The sound of a warm, earthy campfire was very uplifting. The sky was already dimming alarmingly fast, a moving canvas that highlighted the brightness of the moon. The crescent was barely visible at the moment, but it was sure to become visible beside the stars at dusk. The extra food that was fed to the Crigoes helped motivate them to fly faster. We had flown over dense, green forests and sparkling lakes and rivers that extended toward the horizon. The moon was scarcely visible on one side of the sky; the glowing, orange sun beamed as it set on the other. Buildings and homes looked black against the moving sun, streaks of fiery orange subtle against the yellow sphere.

Adam had found a place to rest after few minutes of searching, and our Crigoes settled in the dusty clearing within the forest. We dismounted our Crigoes and let them roam.

"We'll have to start a fire," I decided when I planted my feet firmly on the ground.

"I'll get some wood," Jess said, her words strung together sleepily.

"No, I'll go look," Adam declared. "I think we need some rest for the day."

Jess did not disagree. She tilted her head to the side and settled beside a log, instantly falling asleep.

Adam came a while later holding a bundle of logs in his arms. Joseph helped settle them on the ground before Adam produced a fire with his Wishing Knife. The fire was small at first, a harmless glow, but soon it grew into long, lingering flames that whipped as the wind blew. A warm crackle sounded and small glowing pieces that emerged from the fire floated through the air like tiny orbs.

I slumped toward the ground and leaned against a long log. Adam accompanied me on the other side, lowering his knife back into his pocket.

"Long day, huh?" he asked once everyone was asleep.

I kept my eyes closed, the warmth of the hearth dusting my eyelids. "Very," I added.

"You know, I never got to finish what I was telling you by the stream in the Crigo Pit."

"And that was . . . ?" I questioned, opening my eyes to bare slits to view his unreadable face.

"I want to be your teacher. To teach you all about magic and sorcery," he added. "How to conjure objects, recite chants, and use weapons like *Thoven's Bow*."

I smiled at that, meeting his gaze. "Okay, Teacher. What's the first thing I need to know?" I asked, crossing my arms.

"Well, if you want to know how to conjure objects well, we'll have to start with something small. Like a whistle."

I lifted my eyebrows. Adam cupped his hands together, and then in a matter of moments he was holding a silver whistle in his hands. The whistle lifted into the air, small golden wings fluttering on either side.

I was genuinely surprised, but he was the prince, after all. "That's amazing. But I can't do that without my gemstone," I denied.

"Sure you can. Your power runs through your blood, not your gemstone. You've conjured things before—like the metal necklace. All you need to do is envision the object in your mind. Believe that it is so undeniably real that it will appear right in front of your eyes."

I huffed, unsure of myself. Adam urged me on, so I closed my eyes and focused on the image of a whistle: the round, solid shape, the sharp edges, and eventually I felt something hard formulate in my palm. I opened my clenched hand and saw a whistle, exactly as I'd seen it in my mind.

The whistle fluttered in the air for a moment before it fell back into my palms.

"It's a good start," Adam encouraged.

My eyebrows made a *V*. "A good start? That was great! Let me try again—"

Just as I was raising my hands, Adam caught them in midair and stared at me with intense eyes. "Arica, don't get giddy on yourself. You need time. And this takes a lot of practice. You have undeniable power, but it's very hard to learn and control within a few days' time." I opened my mouth to speak, but then closed it quickly. I felt like a fish underwater. "Let me try again," I pressed. "I'll try harder this time—"

"Listen, Arica, I think you have potential." He sighed, lowering his eyes and muttering something to himself. His intense gaze flickered back toward me. "But maybe you're not quite there yet. Maybe you need more time . . . ."

"What?!" I practically yelled. "Weren't you just saying that I'm able to conjure objects like Thoven's Bow, and learn how to recite chants, and—"

"Arica!" he whispered harshly, ending my rant. "Keep your voice down, I don't want to wake them." He jutted his thumb at my sleeping cousins.

I pursed my lips, ready for a comeback. My head felt like a boiling pot of water ready to explode at any second. "You've been the one telling me that I'm able to conjure objects and do things beyond mortality! I'm the Prophetic Child, yet now you say I'm not *ready*?" I wrenched my hands from his and gave him a concentrated stare.

Adam shook his head. "I didn't mean it like that," he said, taking my hands in a caring gesture.

"Save it." I pulled my hands away from his grip and stomped toward the grassy fields ahead of me. After several minutes of strenuous walking, I finally took a rest on a grassy hill and stared at the dome of the sky above me.

I took deep breaths until my anger had finally dissolved. Now I felt guilt; I shouldn't have lashed out at Adam, but I couldn't restrain my irritation. He was right, and I knew it—I just didn't want to accept it. A part of me wanted to go back to the campfire and confide my apologies to Adam, but the more dominant part told me to stay here.

I lay in the grassy meadow, the grass swerving beneath me. The moon kissed the tops of cliffs in the distance and birds, or it could've been some other winged creature—you never know in the Sorcerers Underworld—flew across the landscape.

Suddenly something flashed orange in front of me—a fire. I looked down and saw that the grassy plain dipped low like a valley. The entire valley glowed orange, and I noticed dark figures moving about. I walked forward carefully, nearing the figures when I suddenly felt an invisible force pull me forward. I fell to my knees and looked up. I was within the vicinity of the fire, and as I looked back I noticed the thin shield of a force field creating a bubble around the valley. I'd entered some sort of force field.

Whispers sounded around me, but nobody was there. The words were daunting and unfamiliar: "Welcome to the Death Field." The voice was creepy and breathy, and I suddenly had a mental image of an old man raggedly breathing those words into my ear.

A shiver ran down my spine and I prohibited myself from visualizing the thought again. I had no idea what the "Death Field" was, but I supposed it was a place for dead sorcerers. If the other five sectors of the Sorcerers Underworld allowed the living (and occasionally ghosts) to inhabit them, then this was the place the dead came to after they'd . . . well, *died.*

A thought sprang to my mind. Something that I could never shut out of my brain because it'd been lingering there since I'd first heard of the Sorcerers Underworld.

I could see my father.

It seemed impossible at first—the thought that I could see my *dead* father—but now everything fell into place. I could see him as long as I had Ghost Glass, the powerful lens I'd found at Faun & Sons.

With the idea firmly planted in my mind, I sprinted back to the clearing where the Crigoes rested. The leaves tickled my arms as I moved, both anticipation and excitement shuddering through me.

When I approached the clearing I observed the sleeping figures of my cousins and Adam. Light snores sounded from Joseph, and the twins both seemed to be sleep-talking to each other, which was undoubtedly strange. Adam's back faced toward me, and he lay in the same position I'd left him in. I took a step toward him and then paused, biting my lip. I couldn't speak to him now—our fight would have to be resolved tomorrow morning.

I hesitantly pushed toward Joseph, careful to make the crunch beneath my feet barely audible. I leaned toward him and moved my hand toward his robe pocket. I could almost see the black-framed figure jutting out of his pocket. I carefully slipped my finger and thumb into the pocket, and then firmly placed them around the frame of the lens. As I carefully pulled the Ghost Glass from his pocket, Joseph began to stir; I remained frozen until he returned to his sleepy groans.

In one quick motion, I slid the lens out of his pocket and into mine. Carefully looking around the clearing, I turned around and found myself face-to-face with Joseph's Crigo. Skye grunted with dismay.

"Shh," I whispered, pressing my pointer finger vertically against my lips. Skye grunted again, but shifted quietly out of the way. I quietly treaded along the sandy dune of the ground beneath me and escaped the clearing. Once

I'd returned to the warm and dense forest I felt a sense of relief. I traced the ghost of my footsteps back toward the grassy meadow, where I met the fire valley. The force field swallowed me again and I found myself back in the valley with the scorching flames.

I excitedly plucked the Ghost Glass from my pocket and held it to my eye, peering across the landscape. Several figures whose skin ranged from pale white to scarcely transparent swarmed the ground. A young girl obliviously walked right through me, holding a ragged stuffed bunny under her right arm. Older men crossed the fiery ground, none bearing any remote resemblance to my father. I lowered the Ghost Glass from my eye shakily. I decided to investigate deeper into the landscape when a man flashed in front of my eyes. He was no less than thirty with long, greasy hair and silvery eyes. His pupils were so depthless that I could almost see right through them and into his mind. Small gears clicked and swerved in his brain, and his face was slowly becoming paler. He ruffled the papers in his hands and eyed me warily.

"Another one? Ugh," he said, rolling his silver-gray eyes. "Listen, you can't just *walk* into the Death Field. I have to assign you a Sector first."

I stared at him with a blank face, my hands rigidly tucked in my pockets. We continued to stand in the same uncomfortable positions before he loosened himself from his stance and pulled a stray paper from his pile.

"You realize you need to sign some forms first, right?" he told me.

"Huh?" I asked.

He rolled his eyes again. "Are you even dead?"

"Are you even living?" I retaliated.

The man let out a strange laugh, almost robotic. "No one is *living* around here."

Well, obviously, I thought. *It's called the* Death Field *for a reason.*

"I may not be alive, but at least I'm not a ghost. Sometimes living people stumble in here and I'm the only person they can see." He grunted. "Anyway," he spoke, "you need to fill out some forms. What's your name?"

"Arica—"

"Your last name," he sneered.

"Miller," I said, my voice shaky as he examined my face.

The man shook his head, strands of greasy hair plastered to his face, and then returned to his papers. "Sign these pages and you should be good to go," he huffed.

I took the pages from his hand and ruffled through them disconcertingly. "I would like to be placed with my father," I said. "His name is Aaron Miller."

The man heaved a sigh. "Don't they all," he muttered.

I lifted my eyebrows, turning my lips down in a frown to portray a sense of sadness.

"Ugh, fine. But just because you're young." His eyes traced the endless names on the yellowed pages. "I don't see his name here. He mustn't be registered properly," he added. "Newbies. I shouldn't have given him a raise—he's still a trainee. Darwin! Get out here, your break ended five minutes ago!"

A short, blond man trudged out of a small office just behind the greasy-haired man, his shoulders slumped. "What is it, Hansel?" he whined. "I was playing my new—"

"Cool it," Hansel said. "Darwin, have you assigned anyone by the name Aaron lately?"

"Lately?" I asked. "He died fourteen years ago."

The two men stared at me, baffled. "Fourteen years is pretty recent when you've been living for all eternity. I know I don't look it"—he gave a toothy smile—"but I've been using some ole Wrinkle-Be-Gone. That stuff works wonders for your skin!" He lightly patted his face, and then returned his attention to me. "Oh—right. Aaron. Register him lately?" he questioned, turning to Darwin.

"Nope, can't remember," Darwin answered. "Listen, can I go back to my game—"

"You have all of eternity to play your stupid video games," Hansel answered cynically. "Help this young dead girl to Sector Five, will you?"

Darwin eyed me for a moment, and then nodded his head, never leaving my eyes. "Sure." Darwin turned and I quickly followed; he walked the circumference of the force field before turning near a muddy, rotten shack. The Roman numeral for the number five, V, was painted on the doorway.

"Here ya are. Have a fun afterlife." Darwin sprinted away from me quickly, muttering something about the next level of his game under his breath.

Once Darwin had jogged out of sight, I pulled the Ghost Glass back up to my eyes and headed toward the door. The door was already open, light bouncing off the reflective handle, and I headed inside. With each step I took, the floorboards creaked beneath me. It was so dark I couldn't even see any figures with my Ghost Glass.

"Hiya there!" a girl's voice sounded. A large, brown eye curtained by thick eyebrows peered back through the lens. I stumbled backward and then her whole body came into view. "Hi," I croaked. "Listen, I'm looking for my father—"

"Father? Well, you'll be lucky if you find him. No one usually comes down to Five. I'm all alone here." She pouted unconvincingly.

I sighed. "Right." I placed the lens back in my pocket and decided to leave—this girl would be no help to me. I was just walking out when I heard her cheerful voice chanting in my ear:

"Go up by the cliffs! That's where most of the newcomers go! Otherwise your dad's probably roaming the Sorcerers Underworld like a free ghost—lucky him." She faintly whimpered behind me. "Has your translucent skin come in yet? You sure don't look like a ghost. And why were you holding that thing to your eye?" A rush of wind surrounded me as she circled my form, her ghostly laugh sending a chill down my spine.

I closed my eyes, trying to shake her words out of my mind. Was this entire trip for nothing? Could my father really be out there, roaming the streets and villas of the Sorcerers Underworld?

"Uh—no. And it . . . helps me see." I cleared my throat. "Anyway, thanks for the tip, but no thanks. I'm not going to spend all my time jogging up cliffs to see if my father is there." This girl was evidently lying. The Death Field didn't even extend beyond the cliffs. She was just looking for a new cabin-mate to live with for all eternity.

I jogged out and traced my path back, the girl's haunting laugh echoing behind me.

I was startled when Hansel's figure popped in front of me. "Hansel—um—"

"I thought Darwin sent you to Sector Five!" Hansel said cruelly, and then he pressed his lips in a thin line. "Newbies . . ."

"I'm just checking out some of the amenities. You know, I hear there's a ghost spa." I swallowed hard.

Hansel's forehead made wrinkles deeper than an ocean. "I've worked here all my life and I haven't even heard of this *ghost spa*? Darwin," he said, saying the trainee's name as if it were a swear word. "Where is this spa?"

I pointed in the opposite direction I was heading.

"Ah, indeed." Then he left, excitedly pulling at the edges of his cloak as if he were a little boy and jogging past the immense fire.

I exited the Death Field's invisible force field curtain and trudged back to the forest. I moved sulkily; I was disappointed by the fact that I hadn't seen my father, and with the vast geography of the Sorcerers Underworld, I had no idea where he could be.

I moved through the forest, searching for the clearing where everyone was sleeping, but I couldn't find them. Had they relocated? I couldn't see any figures nearby—had they noticed I was gone? Left and searched for me? I quickened my pace and swerved around the endless trees, gripped with fear.

I kept forward until I spotted a figure moving through the woods. The reddish hair was distinctly familiar—one of the twins was moving toward me.

"Jess—or Janine! Where's the campfire?" I asked, but the figure disappeared. A dark shadowy figure reappeared right in front of my eyes, and I realized it wasn't one of the twins. In fact, what I'd seen were the reddish-orange streaks of Ash's hair.

"Hello, Arica," Ash said.

I stumbled backward, hitting a tree trunk. I dug my nails deep into the ridges of the tough bark and let out a terrified shriek. What was Ash doing here?

"It's been a while, Arica." She sauntered toward me. "Did you see us escape?" Ash cocked her head to the side, eyes blazing. "We made it out of the cells. But you couldn't tell your poor little family, could you?" She gave an evil grin.

My head spun in circles. Ash's face repeated four times in front of me. "W-what are you talking about?"

Ash suddenly gripped my shoulder and our noses were almost touching. "We're retrieving the *gemstones.*" She gave an ominous laugh.

I spat in her face and she stumbled back, wiping her nose. Then she gulped loudly. "You better run fast, Arica, before we find the seashells."

My brows furrowed. "Why are you going after the seashells?" I said, voice tremulous.

"Why do you *think*?" Her eyes narrowed at me. "We want to go to the Water Train, too. And there are only nine more seashells left in the maze, *Miller.*"

My heart lodged in my throat and I felt bile rise to the edge of my mouth. How did she know about the maze?

"Five for us, four for you. Do the math."

No, I thought. *She's lying.* But a part of me knew when Ash was lying and when she was telling the truth—and at this present moment, she was telling the truth. There were five Sapphires, and five of us. We needed ten shells altogether—one of us would be left behind.

"We'll see who gets to the maze first." Ash's lips curled in a sinister half-smile. "But then again, there's no way you'll make it in time. Maybe you should just go back to the world you belong to. The *mortal* world."

A searing pain shocked my wrist and I looked down to see the intertwining snakes mark etching deep into my skin.

Before I could even comprehend what was going on, Ash pounced toward me, her nails like the claws of a lion.

I ducked and then rolled beneath her, moving to where she'd once been. A sickly *snap* sounded when Ash hit the tree. But when I turned toward her, she was standing up, her pupils lighting like balls of fire.

"I can take you back," she said. One side of her hair was frizzy and untamed due to the fall. She looked almost crazy—she *was* crazy. "I can take you to the mortal world." She flashed toward me and gripped my wrist. I kicked and flailed, trying to release my wrist from her grip. "There's nothing you can do. Not even your Prophetic Child powers can save you n—"

A loud *bang* sounded and Ash sprawled toward the ground, her neck crooked. Looming where she had once been was Adam, breathing heavily as he held an enormous piece of driftwood in his hands. He dropped the wood to the ground and helped me up.

It took a while before I finally regained composure. Adam wrapped his arm around my shoulders, steadying me.

"How'd you find me?" I finally asked.

Adam gave a short laugh. His golden hair ended in a small curl that touched his brown eyebrows. "I couldn't sleep. Not after that fight. I saw you come back to Joseph—you took the Ghost Glass. I silently followed you through the forest and waited near the force field. You took hours, but I guess time passes much more quickly in the Death Field. Then I realized what you were doing . . . ."

"You know about my dad?" I asked.

"I know more than you think," he answered. "Did you see him?"

"No," I replied, my voice low. "I couldn't find him. But anyway, that's not important right now. Ash just came—"

"I saw," Adam interjected. "I haven't any idea how she could've escaped the cells—Pedro guarded them so carefully—and now she's after the gemstones . . ."

"I'm sorry I didn't tell you," I said, my thoughts stirring. "The Sapphires had escaped, and I should've known they would follow our path."

Adam shook his head. "Listen . . . about before. Your powers . . . they're extraordinary. I was just so amazed by how quickly you were able to conjure a whistle after barely two minutes of training." He looked sorrowfully into my eyes. "I was jealous—"

"You were *right*," I told him. "I'm still adapting to my powers. It takes time. And I was only able to do that because I have such a great teacher." I smiled widely.

"So what about Ash?" He looked over my shoulder fearfully.

I shook my head. "We just have to make sure the Sapphires don't make it to the maze before us—"

"The maze?" Adam asked curiously.

I realized I hadn't informed Adam—and my cousins for that matter—about the maze where the seashells were kept. I sighed. "I guess I have a lot of explaining to do."

A sudden rustle sounded from the forest behind us. Ash was waking up.

"Save it for the flight," Adam said hurriedly, and then we sped through the forest to the blazing campfire.

* * *

Joseph was the hardest to wake up.

The twins had tried shouting, flicking, and even lightly kicking, but nothing could wake him from his deep sleep.

Even the overtly fragrant smells of roses from the bushes would not cause a single stir.

"Wait—I've got it!" Janine lowered herself near Joseph's ear and yelled, "Joseph, I've got your calculator!" she taunted.

"W-what? Mum?" he said groggily, pushing himself up from the ground. "Where is it? Where's my—"

"Well, that woke him up," I said with a playful smile. Joseph looked heartbroken when he realized we didn't actually *have* his calculator.

"Hurry, let's get on the Crigoes," Jess added, looking at the tinge of the bright blue sky that was breaking out of its dark twilight shell.

I mounted my Crigo, still breathless from my encounter with Ash, and then patted her rear right leg. We soared into the cool, frigid morning air, and I felt my lips curl into a smile.

Adam took the lead this time, directing us to Bahia Topaz. The trip was eventless besides the twins' and Joseph's reactions when I told them about the maze. Adam also filled them in on the Ash encounter, explaining our need to find the maze quickly.

"Where are we going to find a maze in this mess?" Jessica said pessimistically. She looked down at the tops of trees sprawled beneath us.

"How about we check out a map," Adam suggested. He pulled a small wad of paper from his shirt pocket and began to unfold it. The wind picked up and it carried the paper into the air. "No!" I cried, pushing forward, but Adam halted my Crigo.

"What are you doing?" I asked him. "The map is flying away—"

"Just wait," he responded dismissively, staring at the drifting sheet of paper. I regarded him with a confused look and shifted my gaze to the paper. It was flying back toward us, faintly rustling as the wind guided it, and then the next part happened in a blur. The paper seemed to freeze in midair as though it had hit a glass window in front of Adam's face.

"Map," Adam stated. "Bahia Topaz."

Thin, black lines began to scrawl themselves on the paper, an abstract drawing. Soon enough an image of the Topaz Sector had formed on the page, encrypted with vigorous detail.

"Wow," I murmured, absentmindedly steering closer toward the map. The map was dotted with forests and lined with streams that seemed to move on the paper. Small stick figures walked along the cobbled roads and down alleys. Buildings shot up high in the sky and something resembling Big Ben was placed in the exact centre. Just behind it was a square scribbled with squiggling lines—the maze.

"There it is," Jess stated in wonderment. "I can see it."

I twisted my torso and viewed the scenery before me. The first thing I noticed was the clock—two hands (and I mean *actual* hands) depicted the time. It had an intricate Victorian frame that shone golden-brown and the structure was magnificently tall. The tip of the structure was shrouded by moving clouds. On either side I could just barely see the edges of the maze's structure.

"Let's go!" Joseph shouted excitedly, gearing Skye forward. We'd steered around the Big Ben look-alike and found ourselves overlooking the maze. The top seemed to be shrouded by some unknown shadow or lingering storm clouds, but a stone structure was still visible underneath.

"Let's head to the side and look for an entrance," I suggested. We agreed and then Lucy plunged face down toward the maze, the smells of honey and faint mist lingering as we drew near.

The Crigoes settled on the ground noisily and we slipped off their backs. Sniff and Crackle sniffed the air with their snouts and snorted gray-black clouds of smoke into the sky.

"We've arrived at the maze," Adam declared. Ahead lay a plethora of stone walls that interweaved intricately only to meet several dead ends. I walked toward the front of the maze and pressed my hand against the cold stone wall. It felt more like a rough quilt rather than smooth as I expected.

Immediately a gray face made of stone protruded from the wall. I yelped and yanked my hand back. It began uttering words in a raspy tone: "Enter at your own risk. I had entered once and never returned, now entrapped in these walls. Beware."

The face dissolved back into the wall as if it had never appeared in the first place. Its words still rang faintly in my ears. My heart was thumping loudly as I thought back to the Christmas ice maze I'd ventured in with my mother years ago. A dreaded sensation of fear washed over me.

Adam moved forward, disregarding the face's apprehensive words of caution.

"How exactly do we get inside of this maze? I mean, there's no doorway—no carved entrance."

"How about we look overtop?" Joseph asked. "I'll take Skye up and look around." Joseph mounted his Crigo and flew up. He was about to push forth over the maze, but an invisible wall stopped him from moving any farther. Joseph looked disgruntled as he struggled to move through the barrier, but had no such luck.

"Do not cheat the maze," a haunting voice echoed around us. "You cannot overlook the maze nor fly over it to your destination. Find passage through the stone wall and move along as all the others have."

"Others?" I breathed shakily, my thoughts immediately shifting to the Sapphires.

Janine gulped loudly. "Wonder what happened to them."

"They don't exist, that's what happened." Joseph advanced to the stone wall where the eerie face had once been. "Do you think that's what'll happen to us?" he asked. "We'll just turn to stone?" His face turned grave. He then assembled his hands so that his index fingers and thumbs created a triangle, and then a blinding white-yellow light hit the stone, blazing like sun flares. Nothing happened.

I lowered my head and then sighed. Janine was leaning against the wall, her ear pressed against the cold stone. "I feel like I can hear something on the other side, but there's no way to get in!" She banged her fists against the wall and then tipped her forehead against the stone. I yelped when she plunged forward—half of her body had sunk into the maze, but her legs were still visible on the other side.

Joseph immediately yanked on her legs, trying to pull her out, but I stopped him. "Don't you see?" I asked. "This is it—this is how we get into the maze!"

If I could see Janine's head, it was probably nodding. Her legs flailed back and forth and she slowly sank deeper until her entire body disappeared.

"Let me try!" Jess cried excitedly. She placed her hands and face in the exact same way Janine had, but she immediately yelped when her sister's head loomed out of the stone.

Janine muttered an apology to her sister and turned to us. "Come on in, everyone!" she said, her cherry-red hair tumbling over her shoulders when her torso came into view. "I found the maze!"

TEN: A-MAZE-D

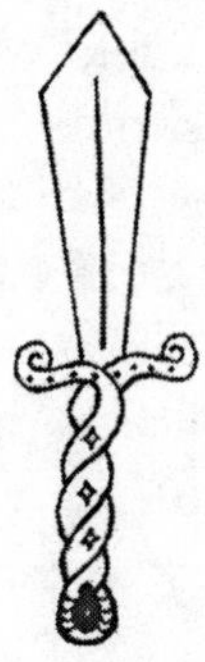

The first thing I saw was the dark haze that spilled in front of us. The intoxicating smell of honey and blossoming flowers filled my nose. I kept one hand on the cool stone wall, and the other firmly pressed at my side. A faint *whoosh* sounded every time someone stepped through the maze wall from the outside.

"Wow!" Jessica's voice echoed through the maze and I felt her shoulder bump into mine. "Sorry!" she managed. "It's just so dark in here!"

"I know," I responded, shifting forward. The fuzzy gray haze seemed to disappear as I moved farther into the maze. "Just stay close."

We shuffled through the darkness slowly, but I wasn't able to make out many shapes or forms in the darkness. Finally, after only hearing the sound of our feet squeaking along the floor, Adam spoke up:

"Joseph?" he asked. He was squinting through the haze and moving his arm from side to side. "Joseph, where'd you go?"

"Joseph?" I asked. I was sure he was right behind us, but sure enough, Adam was right. I could only see Janine, Jess, and Adam. No Joseph in sight.

My lungs seemed to shrink. More calls for Joseph, all with no answer. I clung to the wall and took a step forward. *Where is Joseph?* I thought. He was the last to step inside. I wanted to believe that he was just fooling around—that he'd show up around the bend, his face red and choking from laughter, but he didn't.

"Oh no," Jess said, her face perturbed. Her voice shook with worry.

Adam muttered absent thoughts, wondering how Joseph could've gotten lost just steps into the maze. At that moment, I felt like the maze was mocking us, saying, *"Hey, I can take you any moment I want. You'll never make it through alive."*

We debated Joseph's absence for a few minutes, anguished by his disappearance. In the end we (mainly Adam) decided that looking for him would make us lost ourselves. Instead we trudged forward, moving quickly in order to secure our five shells before the Sapphires could get to them first.

Adam stayed in the lead, wielding his Wishing Knife whenever we turned a corner. After several minutes of reaching dead ends, I let out a doubtful sigh.

"Let's move to the right," I suggested, and Adam nodded. Adam used his Wishing Knife to trace X's on the paths we'd already gone. It helped narrow down the routes we could take to find the seashells.

We were passing through a dark corridor when a loud shriek emitted behind me.

I turned and saw Janine flailing as she was sucked down a dark shadowy pathway. A large concrete slab came down and blocked us from moving forward. Janine was out of sight.

"Janine!" I yelled, banging against the concrete slab. I pressed my head against the slab and continued banging my fist until it turned pinkish-red, my agony only elevating with each bang. Tears dripped from my eyes when Janine's hollow screams drifted away. Both Joseph and Janine were gone, and we hadn't even approached the seashells yet.

Although I didn't have time to pay much attention, I noticed that Jess, too, was in anguish. Her twin had just disappeared, and so had her brother. Tears streaked her face. It took a few minutes of Adam's convincing, but finally, she nodded her head. We had to move quickly if we even wanted a chance of survival, let alone find the seashells.

Adam moved cautiously, always looking back to see if we were still present. We moved through the eerily dark maze, soon finding a small clearing. I moved forward and saw a ceiling overhead. The dark hood seemed to watch down on us, faintly ruffling like a billowing blanket. No. The hood wasn't rustling—something above it was.

I stepped forward and held my breath as I listened to the rustling sound overhead. The sound vibrated along the hood, down the stone walls and beneath my feet. A miniature earthquake swept the ground and I struggled to stand on the floor upright.

Before I could move, something caught my attention: a small feather that was gleaming gold and spotted with brown dots fell from the hood and landed on the edge of my shoe. Then I looked up and gulped.

A giant, shadowy figure flew to the ground, its inquisitively dark eyes burning into mine. It had the head of an eagle and the body of a lion, its talons sharp and menacing. Its golden wings spread sharply at either side, and in the light its dark pupils faintly shone red.

The three of us had already broken into a run, streaming through the maze.

"It's a griffin!" Adam yelled beside us. "Vicious creatures, but they're highly attracted to golden objects!" he shouted. We continued sprinting through the maze, the griffin flying just behind us.

"Split!" Jess called. The three of us separated without question, and I took a sharp right turn into a nearby corridor. It was quite dark and gloomy and all around very quiet.

I remained frozen still, ragged pants escaping my throat. The only thing I could hear was my breathing. My body shivered as I touched the concrete wall to my right, and I peered around the corner to check if the griffin had disappeared.

The path was quiet and deserted. I took a hesitant step forward, whispering Adam's and Jessica's names. No response.

I was just turning back when I felt the griffin's talons grip my arm. Its cold claws dug into my skin and it lifted me high in the air. It flew above the maze, but I paid no attention to the sprawling stone walls below me. Instead I kicked and flailed in its icy grasp, shrieking for help.

I bounced and sprawled when I collided with the ground. The griffin had let me go, leaving me cornered at a dead end. Small beads of blood appeared where its talons had dug deep into my skin.

The griffin rustled its wings and peered down at me. I had nowhere to escape. My mind shifted to Adam's words—he'd said that griffins are attracted to golden objects. There was only one golden object I could think of: Thoven's Bow.

The griffin was closing in on me. I struggled to keep the image of Thoven's Bow in my mind with the sound of the griffin padding toward me. My cranium felt like it was about to implode; but, to my relief, I felt the cool bow and arrow form in my hands.

A loud squawk sounded from the griffin when it saw the Bow in my hands. I held it up high, aimed just over its head. With a sudden shift of my fingers the arrow sailed over the griffin's body. It turned, mystified by the golden object. Another arrow magically placed itself in the Bow and I aimed it again, only this time I aimed for the Sorcerers Underworld mark on its ankle.

"Don't do that."

I jumped back and searched for the source of the voice. "Adam?" I asked hesitantly.

"Go for its wing—that way it can't fly back. Then you can easily shoot its ankle."

"I'm perfectly fine shooting it now, Adam," I said confidently, but inside my stomach coiled at the sound of his voice. It was low and familiar, a little different from Adam's tone.

"I'm not Adam," he said sternly.

My arms went limp at his statement. If this wasn't Adam, then whom could it be? "It's going to turn around in a few seconds. It'll attack if you don't move soon."

"How do you know—" I stopped speaking when I noticed the griffin shifting toward me. Its talons clawed the moist floor.

"Hurry," the mysterious voice said. "Before it's too late."

Too late? My mind scattered, trying to reason out what I should do next, but the griffin itself was so overpowering physically that I felt helpless.

The griffin sauntered forward and then pulled Thoven's Bow out of my hand with its beak. It sank its teeth into the gold matter as if it were a chew toy.

I gasped, but immediately afterward I felt someone, presumably the boy, grab my arm and pull me to the side. We moved to the side wall and I noticed a crack just big enough for our bodies to fit through. I crawled through, the man just behind me, and dusted my hands off when I managed to stand. I twisted the angle of my feet sharply, ready to attack the guy if anything were to happen, but I stopped in my tracks. I found myself face-to-face with Rowen. His face was pale and he had small, red scratch marks on his left cheek. His eyes were hazel-orange and his hair looked almost brownish-blond.

"What are you doing here?" I asked.

"I'm saving you," he said.

"Maybe I didn't want to be saved." Completely untruthful.

"Well, it kind of looked like it." Rowen huffed. "Arica, the Sapphires are here. And I know you think I'm one of them—but I'm not. I was put under Sleeplock because I'm not like the others. I never wanted to be evil, but they forced me to be."

"How do I know you're not just saying this under that potion?" I asked, my voice wild with panic. I crossed my arms to look more interrogative.

"It's five," he said darkly.

"What do you mean, *It's five*?" I carefully inspected his dirt-smeared face.

"Five o'clock was the time the Sapphires fed me Sleeplock. I found these orange contacts at a thrift store yesterday"—he pointed to his eyes—"and I've been wearing them to fake the symptoms. I even pretended to sleep-walk last night to make the Sapphires sure of my obedience. They've allowed me to take my doses on my own, so I've been secretively slipping them down the sewers."

I regarded Rowen carefully. "Prove it," I said. "Take them off."

Rowen gulped, and then nodded his head. He lightly pressed his pointer finger against the lens and the hazel-orange of his eyes transformed blue. He held the contact on his finger so that one eye was sunset-orange and the other a deep, sea-blue.

"Do you believe me now?" he asked, taking off the other contact.

I closed the narrow space between us, looking deeply into his irises, and caught a whiff of a sweet vanilla scent. His eyes were a shade of blue that seemed almost too perfect, like two orbs filled with the icy, cold ocean.

I wasn't sure if I should've believed Rowen or not. He was under Sleeplock, after all, so I remained suspicious, despite the fact that Rowen was not truly a part of the Sapphires' evil plan.

Our noses were just barely touching when I heard a distant noise. I drew my face from his and turned around.

Adam's footsteps resonated as he walked toward me, Wishing Knife in hand.

"Arica," he breathed, "have you seen the—"

Adam's voice suddenly caught in his throat. His face was swelling purple, and he looked like a noose was squeezing his throat and restricting his air flow. Suddenly, he looked as if he was drifting backward without even moving his feet.

"Adam!" I called, running toward him. Adam's eyes were fathomless. I reached out to touch his hand but his figure disappeared into the darkness behind him. I ran into the dark alley, peering around the stone walls, but I could not find Adam anywhere. I repeated his name over and over until my throat was sore from yelling. Then I turned back to Rowen with frantic eyes.

Rowen approached me calmly; when he was close enough that I could smell the whiff of vanilla lingering around his body, I could see that his eyes were frantic, too.

"It's Cale," Rowe answered. "He's taking everyone away—hiding them behind giant concrete slabs. The concrete is full of pieces of metal so that he can levitate them wherever he wants."

"Cale's been doing this?" I asked, stunned. It was only a matter of time before a giant concrete slab would come down in front of Jessica, and eventually me.

He nodded his head gravely. "We should move quickly, before one of the other Sapphires finds us."

I quickly agreed. We'd gone so far into the maze that we would *have* to reach the seashells soon.

"Rowen," I asked as we jogged through the labyrinth, "there are only nine shells, meaning nine tickets. There are ten of us altogether. And if you're separated from the crowd . . ." I hesitated, and then continued, "then they might not spare one for you."

"I figured," he answered. "But they could just take all the shells from you if they get there first. That way you guys won't even make it on the Water Train."

I gritted my teeth, sprinting faster. "And do you know where they are?"

Rowen shook his head. "But I know where they're going. They took the west entrance to the maze, which means they'll be coming out of this exit." Rowen pointed to a dark alleyway.

We moved in silence, keeping to ourselves. I was concentrated on the faint lingering smell of honey from afar. I felt drawn to it like a moth to a flame.

Rowen sniffed the air. The stone maze walls were turning damp, green moss blossoming over them.

"Do you smell that?" he asked, sniffing the air again and touching the mossy wall beside him.

"I think it's honey—but where's it coming from?" I said, walking deeper into the maze. As soon as I said those words we reached an opening in the maze. In the clearing I saw bright, green leaves tangled with one another and the air became much more humid. It felt like we'd entered some sort of greenhouse.

Rowen scavenged through the leaves and walked deeper into the greenhouse. I followed just behind him. Pink flowers lazily blew from side to side, and the green lawn that lay ahead of us was perfectly manicured. The scene was picture perfect: Bees swarmed around the colourful bed of flowers and the honeycombs set nearby oozed of a lusciously viscous golden colour. The invigorating smell of honey filled my nose once again.

A large butterfly with a swirling purple pattern on its wings sat on my fingertip. "What is this place?" I asked. The butterfly flew away when I spoke.

"I have no idea," he answered, entranced. He moved toward the honeycombs and observed the dripping honey. He placed his finger under a comb and let the honey fall to his index finger. Then he carefully licked the viscous liquid.

"Mmmm," he said. "I haven't tasted something so good in days."

I leaned in, intrigued to taste it, but the few remaining seashells kept me alert. "I don't think this is a good idea," I said. I peered around—the scenery was almost too charming, too welcoming. Behind this cheery guise I noticed peeling flakes of who-knows-what stripping off the walls, glaring cobwebs that stretched over the grass, and a hot, flaming hand that was barely visible behind the stone wall.

That last bit of information took a while to digest, but when I finally understood what it was, I yelled, "Duck!"

A ball of fire flew where our heads had once been and Geoff stepped into the greenhouse. His hands were fiery red, almost the same shade as his red ears.

He threw another ball of fire toward me, but I sprawled toward the grass. The flame flew against the stone wall and caused the wall to melt. Giant globs of stone trailed down like teardrops.

I was just standing up when an idea formed in my mind. I decided to peel the honeycomb off the wall—the bees were busy near the flowers—and throw it toward Geoff. I ran to the honeycomb and struggled to pull it from its sticky hinge against the wall. The humidity of the greenhouse was not helping, and Geoff's flames were growing steadily. I had scary flashbacks of chemistry class disrupting my focus, but I shook them away. I finally managed to break off the honeycomb, and before Geoff could hurl another ball of fire toward us, I threw the honeycomb at him. The honey sprinkled him at first, but then the substance coated his skin and he became awfully sticky. He struggled to release hold of the sticky bond between his fingers, but was distracted by the swarm of bees rushing toward him.

"This way!" I yelled, pulling Rowen along with me. We escaped the humid greenhouse and sprinted around the stone walls. The paths were much darker than they had been before, and we seemed to be hitting a lot more dead ends. After two minutes of wordless sprinting, it seemed as though we'd tried every imaginable path.

Rowen twisted his body from side to side, his face injected with worry. An eerie candlelight flickered from above, illuminating the endless walls around us.

"There!" Rowen pointed. He moved toward a cold, stone wall. "Look at this."

"What do you mean? We already went there and we didn't see—" That was when I saw it: a small, circular tunnel embedded at the bottom of the wall. The gloomy light cast from above made it barely visible.

Rowen wiped his hand around the outer edge to wipe the dust off, and then stuck his head into the gaping hole in the wall. Then he wiggled his body through and slowly disappeared. I stood there for a moment, and then felt my skin prickle. I didn't hear Rowen moving at all.

I stuck my head into the hole in the wall and searched for Rowen. "Rowen?" I asked. Nothing. I moved out of the hole and contemplated it. "Rowen," I said, this time sounding more worried than I'd hoped, "it might not be sa—" My voice turned into a scream when Rowen stuck his head out of the darkness.

"Boo!" he shouted, and then doubled over in laughter.

I fell back onto my elbows and gasped in pain. My heart beat wildly fast and a scowl permanently drew itself on my face.

Rowen's laughter echoed down the tunnel. When I stood up I gave his shoulder a shove, and he pretended to feel hurt. "Ouch," he muttered playfully.

I was about to reply, but my mouth clamped shut when I surveyed the darkness of the tunnel at knee-level. The tunnel was barely large enough for me to crawl through, and the griminess made me recoil.

"Ladies first," Rowen said, gesturing to the tunnel.

I gave him an uncomfortable stare which he found oddly amusing, and then I crawled through. The gloomy light that seeped into the tunnel seemed to reflect off the stones that were deeply embedded in the walls. They looked black, though they were smooth. They almost reminded me of my gemstone. I swallowed back the lingering memory of the cool stone against my neck; the feeling of dread and horror when I found out it was gone. It only made me more determined to progress farther into the tunnel.

I pushed my thoughts back and focused on my steady breaths as I crawled along the floor. Eventually the mouth opened into a wider cavern, forking into two paths.

"I hear water trickling," Rowen murmured beside me.

"Me too," I replied. "And I've had a bad experience with waterfalls in the past." My thoughts shifted back to the Golden Cave. Surely that was something I never wanted to experience again.

"I see," Rowen speculated. "Well, seeing as you're so afraid of waterfalls and mazes—"

"You know I'm afraid of mazes?" I asked with an incredulous tone.

Rowen glued his eyes to the ground. I soon realized that I'd forgotten all about Rowen's power—mind reading.

I shook my head playfully. Rowe looked up with a hopeful glint in his eyes.

"Can you stop that? Mind reading, I mean," I asked, partially annoyed and surprised.

"Fine. Sorry. I've been doing that a lot with the Sapphires, trying to figure out what they're up to. But it's like they've put this giant wall in front of them and I'm blocked from looking into their minds. Maybe because they think of me as an outsider in their group. Well, at least that's how I feel."

"At least you're not a part of them," I said. "Just the thought of Ash and the others makes me cringe."

He gave a short, staccato laugh. "Imagine *living* with them. I have to wear these silly contacts and follow through on every one of their plans."

My memories flooded forward. I'd never really thought of Rowen's position with Sleeplock—how he'd acted when he was forced to drink it, the time we'd spent at the river when I saw the memory of that woman feeding it to him . . . .

"Rowe . . . do you remember the river? After the wolf attack? I'd seen this memory of you when you were young. This lady was giving you a bottle filled with Sleeplock . . . and she said she was related to you. Does that mean . . . that woman was . . ."

"Vina Lembrose," he answered. "My great-grandmother. Correct." It was a fact, but he said it almost lazily, as if he'd come to terms with it.

A shiver ran down my spine. The thought of Lembrose—the Sorceress Wife—being Rowen's great-grandmother was just too bizarre to comprehend. Every Sapphire was a descendant of the Sorcerer Line, a group whose goal was to use our gemstones to overrun the mortal world. Rowen was the only one without evil intentions. After his parents died—and I had no idea how they had at the moment—Lembrose cared for him. But she'd changed him—forced him under a periodic sleep (for twenty four hours, to be precise) with a potion that would make him think as she did.

"Let's take the other path," I reasoned, mainly because I wanted to stay away from the sound of trickling water. I forced myself to push my thoughts back for two reasons: to confirm I would not dwell on depressing facts, and to make sure Rowen wouldn't creep into my mind and hear my thoughts.

"Okay," he agreed. We took the path to the right and walked silently along the crunchy path. The air was moist and the tunnel walls felt wet beneath my palms. I trudged alongside Rowen for a few minutes before we hit a dead end.

"Great," Rowen said, his voice strangled down to a whisper. "Should we take the other path?"

My heart sank in my chest. "I guess so."

Just as I was about to turn around I caught sight of a tiny hole in the middle of a plethora of sparkling rocks. My finger could just barely squeeze right through.

"Look at this," I said, pointing to the hole in the wall.

"What about it?" he asked warily.

"What about it?" I questioned. "This could lead us out of here—toward the seashells." I lowered my left eye to the small opening and peered inside. Through the hole I saw many sparkling objects sprawled along the floor. Some were flat against the ground, whereas others took on the shape of a cone. They looked smooth as glass, ranging in hues from pale blue to ivory with pinkish spots dusting the surface.

My spirits lifted—the seashells were only a few feet away from us, almost within our grasp. But the solid tunnel wall blocked the way. How were we supposed to reach them?

"Rowen," I said hastily, "they're here."

"Who's here? The Sapphires?" he questioned worriedly.

"No—I'm talking about the shells," I corrected.

He lifted his eyebrows and then ran toward the hole. He pressed his eye against the opening, his hands resting against the cool tunnel wall on either side of him, and immediately gasped. "There must be hundreds of them."

"I know, but I thought Ash said there were only nine?" My thoughts swirled.

"With tickets," he added. "There are hundreds of shells, but only nine with tickets. We have to find the specific shells that can transport us to the Water Train."

"And how do we know which ones will take us there?"

Rowe rubbed the side of his neck. "You know how you can hear the sound of the ocean through a seashell? We need to search for the ones with the sound of a train whistle," he responded, a little too matter-of-factly. "That's what the Sapphires said, at least."

I met his gaze uneasily. "Then we need to find a way to get past this barrier."

Rowe leaned against the wall, a smirk playing across his face. "Hey—I'm just a mind reader. But you . . . you're the Prophetic Child! Or at least that's what's going around the Sorcerers Underworld. All the Sapphires envy you. Only you can find a way out of this." His white knuckles knocked on the barrier.

I swallowed an immense feeling of expectance; everyone believed that my powers were infinite, yet I hardly had the time to practice them and realize my full potential. At least I'd been able to conjure Thoven's Bow when I'd seen the griffin. Conjuring objects was something familiar to me now. But breaking through walls? Not so familiar.

I looked back through the hole. *If only I had some sort of extreme super-strength abilities,* I thought, *I could easily break through this wall.*

The thought didn't seem very likely. Instead I concentrated on the hole, forming an image of a cracking wall in my mind. Before I knew it several fissures were slithering in a million different directions. I gave the wall a shove and it broke into crumbling pieces of stones and rocks.

Rowen muttered something like, "That was amazing," but his voice muted when he saw the shells. An endless ocean of seashells lay on the floor below us, sometimes piling so high they formed a mountain in the valley of rocks.

"I guess we have some digging to do," I said quietly. I plunged into the layer of shells and held them to my ear. I heard the whispering waves crashing against one another, the sound of the ocean spiralling so deep within the shells. The sound always mystified me, but it also brought a feeling of disappointment. Every shell I picked was the same as the last.

"This is impossible," I stated worriedly. Rowen looked just as discontented. He was placing a pinkish-blue shell to his ear when he yelped in surprise.

"Arica—I hear the whistle!" He swarmed through the shells, kicking them aside as he held the shell aloft. He placed it next to my ear and I was extremely astonished to hear the sound of a train whistle. The faint *chug* of the train was also audible. I could just imagine smoke billowing overtop.

"One down, four to go," I murmured. Rowen placed the shell carefully in his pocket and scavenged the grounds. I hurriedly held the shells to my ear, discarding those that held the tranquil sound of the ocean.

Rowen and I were overly excited each time we managed to find a shell. We had collected four shells when we heard a pair of feet shuffle along the ground. I turned to Rowen, but he was motionless in his spot. We remained so silent that even the swirling ocean sounds emitting from the shells were audible from a distance.

A giant shockwave slithered under the ground. The cornucopia of shells exploded like a volcano. My breath was knocked out of me as I plunged back through the air. I landed on the hard ground, gasping for air. I planted my hand against my stomach and winced. Something had definitely bruised.

Rowen lay on the ground near me, his arms and legs sprawled in separate directions. A livid purplish bruise was blossoming on the side of his face. A thick substance oozed out of the cut on his lip.

"What was that?" Rowen struggled to lean against the concrete wall beside him.

I sat up, wincing in pain. The shells I'd collected were still safely tucked in my pockets. "I don't—" I was just about to finish my response when I saw Cale sauntering forward. His gloomy gray eyes were dark with malice, and his brown hair was long and messy.

"Rowen, Rowen, Rowen," he said, his voice deep and taunting. "Looks like you haven't gotten your dose for the day." He shook his head, staring into Rowe's deep blue eyes. Rowen stood shakily, but his build was still strong even in comparison to Cale.

"I don't need a dose to tell between right and wrong," Rowe responded.

Cale pursed his lips and then turned his eyes to me. I still sat on the ground, shaken.

"I'm sure you'd like to see your cousins, wouldn't you? And that prince, too." He lifted his hand to a concrete slab toward the right and it lifted. Cale must've known these walls were packed with metal—it was undoubtedly a great advantage for the Sapphires. This was hardly a maze if they could throw aside each wall with such ease.

Joseph came out first, his glasses crooked and eyes wary. Cale lifted a slab to his left and out came the twins. Jess must've been caught earlier on. Finally Adam sauntered through, his face red from exhaustion.

"You have only four seashells," Cale stated. "Wouldn't you, the Prophetic Child, be so noble to let your family take them? Wouldn't you stay behind and fight until your last breath?"

A voice inside me kept saying yes, but I remained silent. Cale was lifting a piece of metal—it looked like a part from an air vent—and threw it toward me. Instinctively I threw the piece aside. I felt stronger than I ever had before, because now I was accessing my levitation power without my gemstone.

"We'll find the last shell," I promised. "And we'll be the first to get to the train."

"What makes you so sure?" he responded. "The others could be on the train this very minute. My seashell could be right beside my feet for all you know." He leaned down and picked up a shell, holding it to his ear.

A sinister smile spread on his face. "Looks like I've got a ticket to Miami." He set the shell in front of him, and almost immediately a swirling torrent of water sprayed outward. Cale was sucked into the water and disappeared in the rocking, vacant shell. The seashell disappeared in a shower of golden dust.

Adam was the first to react, sprinting toward me. Everyone crowded around in a circle. We explained that we'd gotten four shells, but we still needed one more. Rowen was missing a ticket, too—if the other four Sapphires had left without him, then they had probably already decided on leaving him here alone.

"There's still one shell left," I explained. "If we find it soon we can get to the train before the Sapphires can board."

We all broke into separate directions, overwhelmed by desperation. My worries were mounting faster than I could count. Maybe we'd never make it to the train in time. Maybe they'd leave without us, and the Sapphires would be the first to reach the Hall of Lost Gemstones and retrieve the gemstones for the Sorcerer Line. And then what? Vina would place the three gems together in a pendant and put the activating piece in the middle, initiating the superpower. Their plans to rule the mortal world would take place sooner than I could comprehend.

"Um, guys?" Rowen called worriedly. We turned toward him. I followed his gaze and saw the foreboding griffin flying in circles overhead. Its wings rhythmically shuddered up and down, causing dirt to swarm around us like a sandstorm. When it landed it gave a resounding squawk, rustling its feathers. It seemed to be protecting something behind it—a giant nest of eggs, each the size of a large boulder.

I suppressed a scream.

Adam unsheathed the Wishing Knife and the blade shone like a ribbon of shining steel.

The griffin moved back warily. I could barely see a glinting seashell in the middle of the pile of eggs. It was the only shell we hadn't checked, so it had to have a ticket to the Water Train.

"I see the shell," I whispered to Joseph. If you can create a blinding light to distract the griffin, maybe I can go in and get it."

Joseph nodded. He summoned a bright white light to his fingertips and I immediately felt my eyes strain to look ahead.

"Quickly now," he said, squinting at the bright light emitting from his fingertips.

I took a deep, steady breath, and then ran forward. My eyes were just slits as I dove for the remaining seashell.

The griffin made a horrible sound—a mixture of a tremendous roar and a deafening squawk—and flailed its wings toward me. I landed clumsily in the middle of the nest of eggs. The giant white shells were specked with brown dots that were so tiny they were barely visible. As I stared at an egg in front of me, a crack began to slither its way through the shell and it split open.

Two beady eyes poked out of the shell, bright as incandescent bulbs. Then its entire head poked out. A gooey green slime formed an intricate web around the creature. Then its wings spread out on either side of it. When it crawled out, I noticed that its body was in the form of a lion. Its talons drilled into the floor as it sauntered toward its mother.

More cracks followed. Small eagle heads were poking out of the eggs; some yawned or croaked at the sight of their new world. Other shells tumbled along the floor in attempt to break free.

I grabbed the seashell and made a mad dash for the others, sprinting through the muddle of eggs. Joseph was practically drowning in his own sweat when I'd reached them. He let the bright light fade away and Rowen and I spread the seashells along the floor.

"Okay, the seashells will transport us to the Water Train in a few seconds," Adam informed. "If we move quickly we can get there first, and the Sapphires will be—"

A loud whimper sounded from behind me. I turned around to see the griffin holding Rowen by a single talon through the back of his shirt. He dangled in the air above us, his mouth agape with fear.

"Hurry, Joseph, cast that light back toward the griffin's eyes!"

Joseph was reluctant and weary at first, but I urged him to try and he did. The light blinded the griffin for a moment and caused its talon to slowly slip out of Rowen's shirt. I dove toward Rowen—with what plan I was not sure—but he fell to the ground before I made it there. He lay on the floor, unconscious, his chest barely moving an inch. I regarded his face; it was calm, and much less apprehensive than before. Probably because he was no longer being held by a giant eagle-lion hybrid, but that wasn't the point.

"Arica, we have to get going!" Janine called, tugging on my shoulder. I turned around and noticed the spiralling tornadoes of water as they protruded from the mouths of the seashells.

I laid my hand on Rowen's arm, then on his hand. His fingers were cold as icicles. Then I stood, realizing that we had no choice but to let him stay here.

"I'm coming," I told them, and Janine nodded solemnly. The twins plunged into the water simultaneously before their shells disappeared from sight. I turned back to Rowen, my seashell burning in my hand. A plan was formulating in my mind—I wasn't sure if it would work, but I had to try.

I smashed the tip of the shell against the ground. A jagged shard cascaded from the bright seashell and into Rowen's upturned palm. I took the shard and held it to the side of my head; a faint train whistle buzzed in my ear.

"Arica, what are you doing?" Adam asked.

I disregarded his troublesome question and placed the shard back in Rowen's palm. Hopefully the shard I had broken off would be enough for Rowen to make the train, but there was no time to debate that now. I set the seashell in front of my shoes. Joseph and Adam followed.

"Are you ready?" I asked. A torrent of water was spiralling out of my shell, along with Joseph's and Adam's.

"Ready," Joseph responded, taking a wary glance back at Rowen.

I was just about to pounce into the water when the smell of eggs invaded my nose.

"Are . . . are those scrambled eggs?" I asked, taking a look back at the few remaining eggshells. The yolks had turned into piles of overly cooked eggs.

"Yes . . . that's my fault," Joseph confessed. "The light I produced may have been a little too strong. You see, the incandescence of the light can also produce extreme heat levels, in which—"

"This isn't exactly an appropriate time, Joseph," Adam warned, his head tipped toward the restless griffin.

"Uh, right," he said, his cheeks flushed with embarrassment, and then three of us plunged into our seashells. Mist coated my eyes and the lingering smell of burnt eggs trailed behind me.

The world became an ocean of blackness. The right side of my face smacked against a warm, grinded substance, and then I opened my eyes to see an endless desert of sand.

ELEVEN: THE WATER TRAIN

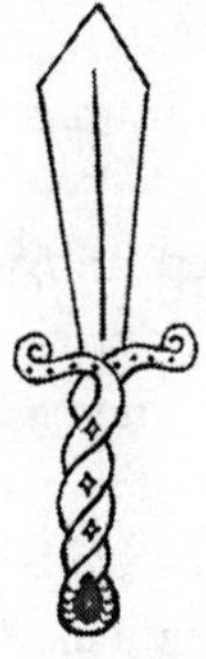

The sand beneath me held the texture of breadcrumbs, sometimes thickened by the lapping water nearby. I soon realized that we'd landed near the Atlantic Ocean, and occasionally the spray of salty water would linger in the air. Palm trees swayed in the warm wind, and the sky was a tropical blue. Not a cloud hovered in sight.

"Welcome to Miami," Adam called. He was sitting in the sand, gazing at the sparkling ocean in front of us. I stood beside him, brushing grains of sand off my clothes. I turned my head and examined the twins giggling at the sight of their brother. Joseph was extremely frightened when he'd awoken to his body completely buried in a tomb of sand.

"Okay, c'mon," Joseph growled. "Get me out of this!" His neck turned so red his anger was palpable.

Adam gave his Wishing Knife a twirl and the sand disappeared from Joseph's body. Joseph clamped his hand to his chest and breathed a sigh of relief.

"Oh, Joseph, you're burning up!" Janine called. I tried to hinder my laughter, but I couldn't help myself. "Joseph gets the most *horrible* sun burns. Once back in England he'd forgotten his sun screen and the next day his back was covered in thick drying peels!"

"Hey," Joseph defended, standing up, "that was a really hot day. And I didn't put it on because *someone* used it all up!"

"Okay, okay," I settled, moving between the three of them. "Let's find some shade. The train should be coming by soon." As soon as I finished speaking I felt the nape of my neck tingle with beads of sweat. The sun beamed down, so hot I felt like I was being baked in a giant oven.

I led us to a row of giant palm trees that lined the beach. Joseph was the first to collapse under the tree's expanse of shade. I leaned against the trunk and sat next to the twins. The heat was so unbearable I could barely form a thought in my head. It wasn't until a long, cool wind travelled past us that I remembered what I was wearing. My black cardigan was beginning to feel like it was made of heavy steel. My jeans coiled around my legs tightly, and suddenly I wished I had a change of clothes.

Adam unsheathed his Knife and began muttering an incantation. I felt my heavy clothes disappear, replaced by a tank top and shorts. I looked as though I was about to spend a lovely day out at the beach, but as tempting as that seemed, that was not the intention of our trip.

Janine and Jess were stunned by their matching clothes, and Joseph became irritable at the sight of his. He wore an orange Hawaiian shirt covered in floral white orchids, and his board shorts were just a size too small. In the sunlight his hair was a dark coppery brown, just barely drooping over his sapphire eyes.

"Ugh!" Joseph whined. "This is far too uncivilized—"

"Just relax, Joseph," I told him. "We're boarding a mystical train to the Bermuda Triangle—we have to look the part," I said.

"Fine," Joseph replied, his arms crossed in disgust as he regarded Adam. The twins almost swooned at the sight of his muscles; he wore a dark tee with matching board shorts, but his were a perfect fit.

"Okay—now that we look as though we belong, we have to act like it, too." Adam drifted through the sand, Janine and Jess trailing behind him. I took hold of Joseph's arm and towed him toward the ocean's edge. The water carved and shaped the sand as it lapped over our toes.

I was just nearing a long line of people—sorcerers waiting for the train, I guessed—when I heard a boy in front of me say, "Here it comes." The boy wore a tight orange surf shirt and black board shorts, and was pointing to the expanse of the ocean. His surfboard was tucked between his torso and his arm, and he had wavy brown hair that was cut just near his ears. His skin was deeply tanned, and small freckles dotted the bridge of his nose.

Just after he spoke, the boy seemed to have changed. He looked a bit different—lighter, in fact, which didn't make much sense since he should've been tanning with all the heat. For a moment I thought I could see right through him, but then I realized the blazing sun was distorting my vision. He looked completely normal after a few seconds.

A tall wave approached the long line of sorcerers. At first I was frozen by the sight of the wave—it looked like it could swallow us whole—but then I realized it must've been the Water Train. The wave transformed into the shape of a long train, and the water seemed to glint as the sun beamed down. The train was immense, looking as though it had many floors. What was most odd about it was the fact that it was completely made of water, yet in just seconds it turned solid and was a deep shade of green. Long golden drapes curtained the windows along the sides. Tufts of smoke that looked a little more like ice trailed alongside the train as it chugged toward us.

It moved along the invisible train tracks of the water as it skirted the water's edge. My hair whipped against my face as it streaked past. I felt as though I were at a railroad crossing and a train with endless cargo was flying by.

"Wow," I muttered under my breath. I took a quick glance at the twins, who looked especially excited, and then at Joseph, who looked quite horrified. Perhaps it was because his shorts were a little too tight for his liking.

"Let's get in line," Adam said, gesturing me first. The line quickly shortened and I found myself near the front, just behind the boy in the orange surf outfit.

"Ticket, please," a man called. The surf boy handed him a small blue piece of paper and disappeared from his spot.

I stepped forward. In front of me was a man looking around the age of eighteen, wearing a badge that read ANDRAE, CONDUCTOR. He had short, choppy brown hair and glinting brown eyes. He seemed very young to be the conductor of the Water Train. I wondered if he still went to school—if they even had that in the Sorcerers Underworld.

"I'm Andrae, Conductor of the Water Train," he said, and we exchanged greetings. He seemed quite cheerful for the most part, though I noticed his eyes were a permanent dark brown that seemed almost saddened and secretive. As if he had a past he didn't wish to share. But I wouldn't guess that from his bright smile.

Andrae paused. "Can I have your ticket, please?"

I suddenly felt something heavy land in my pocket. I fished out a small, square ticket with a depiction of a seashell on the front.

I passed the ticket to Andrae. He observed it for a moment before a machine quickly swallowed it. "Have a good trip," he stated. He lowered his hand to a large green button on the control panel, but my gaze was no longer on his hand. I had noticed a strange marking hidden near the nape of his neck. It was half covered by his hair, but I could still make out the Shadower imprint.

A thought surfaced in my mind: Arnold was telling us about the Water Train and how the creator of it had died. His son had become the conductor of the train, who I supposed was Andrae. That meant Andrae was a Shadower—or one of their offspring, at least, just like Teal.

Andrae's finger hit the button and shadowy gray wisps began to surround me. I disappeared in a plume of gray smoke and reappeared on a large wooden deck. I supposed this was the back end of the train, and also the highest floor (since I could see the sky above me). A large juice bar was set up in the corner, and tables littered the floor. Sorcerers of all kinds were strolling along the deck, enjoying their vacation.

I started at the sight of Adam appearing in front of me. The twins and Joseph were not far behind.

"Wow, this train is incredible!" said Jess, tugging her sister along as she ran to the juice bar. I swerved around the tables and came to a halt as I approached the juice bar. The twins were both holding strawberry banana shakes, and I ordered the same.

A blond woman, whose frizzy hair was tied in a thick braid, handed me my drink with a stiff smile. I tried to thank her, but she whipped away from me and began taking other orders. I took a sip of the drink and turned around. My eyes rested on a teenage girl who was crouched on one knee, nursing what looked like a broken bird's wing. The bird shuffled restlessly on its feet, and the girl slowly brushed her pointer finger along the crooked wing. Immediately it began to straighten back to its normal shape. Testing both wings, the bird fluttered anxiously on the wooden floor, and then flew off into the warm air.

The girl smiled contentedly before turning to me. The wind blew her short, choppy black hair across her face, but I could still make out her startling gray eyes. At first I thought she was walking toward me, but then I realized that she was taking a seat at the juice bar. She seated herself to my right and ordered a papaya drink. The frizzy blond-haired girl came with her order in hand a few seconds later.

The girl took one last sip from her thick papaya drink before setting it down slowly. It wasn't until this moment that I noticed the many defined maroon-purple highlights in her midnight black hair. Her eyes were just as I'd seen them before: a stormy shade of gray that made her look wise and content. An emerald-green gemstone hung from a velvet thread was placed around her neck, and she wore a ratty rock-and-roll T-shirt and jeans.

"Hi," she said openly. "I'm Raven Lilac. I'm guessing you just got on this stop?"

"Yeah," I replied delightedly. "With my cousins and Adam—"

"Adam?" Raven questioned. She scanned the deck and then her eyes fell on Adam, who was strolling toward us with Joseph. "Oh," she said absently, and then directed her words to Adam. "You look . . . familiar. Like Prince Adam."

"Yes, I am," Adam responded smugly.

Joseph grunted behind Adam and then picked up his drink from the juice bar. He took a swig and then spat it out almost instantaneously. "Ew—who ordered mango?"

The twins giggled beside him, and then introduced themselves to Raven. "I'm Janine, and this is my sister Jessica." She extended her hand and their palms met for a few long seconds.

Raven set her cup down on the bar counter. "Did you all just arrive on the Water Train?"

"Yeah—it's our first time here. We're trying to get to the Sorcerer Palace," Jess explained.

"Do you guys want a tour of the top deck?" Raven asked. "I've gotten pretty used to this place, since it's my destination for work."

"Work?" I questioned. It seemed as though I could only speak one syllable at a time lately.

"Yeah. I work for The Kite Postal and Gift Services. I'm a Kite Collector—I go around collecting kites. People can strap their messages, gifts or other trinkets to magical kites and send them wherever they want to go. Mortal postal service is pretty average in comparison." She gave a half-smile, but it gradually slipped away. She placed two fingers on her emerald gemstone necklace. "Not like Mom or Dad really approved of my job, anyway," she said, murmuring the last part.

"Why not?" I asked. She looked up, surprised, as if she thought I hadn't heard.

"Oh—well . . ." she said, smoothing down her shirt. "This is my dream job—I would love to tour the world someday. But my power—the power from my mom's side of the family—is the ability to heal animals and, occasionally, people. I'm a Healer."

"So that's what you were doing before?" I asked. "You were fixing that bird's wing."

She nodded swiftly, a smile lighting up her face. "Exactly. I've been practicing my powers since I was young. There's a lot of pressure put on Healers. With this kind of power comes high expectations. Especially from parents." She sighed heavily. "It's okay, though. The Water Train is amazing. I'm sure you're all going to have an awesome time here."

"Aaaah!" Jess shrieked suddenly. I gasped and turned my attention to her. Jess was drawing away from the crowd. "What *is* that thing?"

I looked down and noticed a small hairless creature. It looked like a muskrat, but when it spread its pinkish-golden wings, I thought otherwise.

"This is Musky," Raven said, picking up the strange creature from the ground. "He's my pet, a Muskig."

I turned and saw Adam suppressing a gasp. "I thought Muskigs were extinct!"

"Not all of them. Especially this species. He's part muskrat, part pig. And he has wings, so . . . part bird, too." She widely smiled.

Joseph stared in awe. "My mum always wanted a pet dog, but I always asked her for a Muskig. Fascinating creatures, they are!"

Raven laughed melodically, and I laughed along. Musky flew off Raven's upturned palm toward her straw. "And he loves papaya," she added.

"So, were you assigned to work on the Train?" Janine asked. We were streaking down the long deck toward the shuffleboard station.

"Yeah. I sort of volunteered. A lot of kites come down here this time of year. And I'm trying to earn a merit—it'll help me get promoted to a higher ranking. Then I can travel across the entire mortal world and collect kites. Maybe then my parents will understand my love for travelling." Her eyes glazed her surroundings. "Anyway, I suppose you guys ought to head to your cabins. Did Andrae assign you each your room number?"

I exchanged a glance with Jess, whose brows were furrowed in confusion.

"No," Joseph said. "We just . . . *appeared* here, if that makes any sense."

Raven laughed again, but this time no one joined her. She ended abruptly and cleared her throat. "I should've known. I was just recently told that I would get a new roommate." She looked down at a shrivelled piece of paper in her hands. "Arica will be joining me in room 432, and I suppose the boys will be rooming with Drake."

"Drake?" Joseph and Adam asked uneasily. Joseph almost let out a groan but stopped himself when I shot him a warning stare.

"Yes. And the twins will be with Summer."

At this the twins groaned, "But it's autumn?!" in a weary and confused way.

"Looks like you guys need some rest in your cabins." Raven frowned at a drop of water that had fallen on her paper. We all looked up and noticed large rain clouds swirling overhead. Subtle streaks of lightning flashed down toward the horizon of the ocean. A storm was approaching.

Raven shook her head, and then pulled something extremely strange out of her pocket. This wasn't your regular inanimate object; she was pulling out a dark gray chameleon, its beady eyes like two marbles jutting out from the side of its head.

"This is Newt," Raven stated. In my mind I wondered if she was some sort of crazy pet lady—I mean, she had a flying muskrat-pig already—but she explained that Newt was actually something she used for her work: "He's a weather lizard. They can tell you the weather pretty much anywhere based on the colour of their skin. I could simply say a place anywhere in the world and Newt's skin colour would inform me of the weather. I always check the weather in advance to see if it's nice enough to collect kites." Her finger trailed along Newt's scales. "Newt here is an Egyptian Snocker. Since his scales are gray, it means there's a thunderstorm heading our way."

"Thunderstorm?" echoed Joseph uneasily.

"Yes—and a bad one, too." She examined Newt's scales as they turned a shade darker.

"Well, we'd better get indoors," Adam said, taking a newspaper from a news rack and holding it over his head.

Raven nodded her head. "I'll lead the way."

* * *

After a long tour through the Water Train (which was quite gorgeous), we finally reached our cabins on the fourth floor. Raven unlocked the door with a key-card and we walked into the frigid, cool air. The cabin was extremely spacious. A bunk bed was placed at the side of the room, and a retro green couch sat lonely in the corner. A silver TV sat atop a wooden dresser, and across the room a few suitcases littered the ground.

"Prince Adam must have had your luggage magically transported here," Raven concluded. "If you want, you can take a bunk. I share this room with another girl. Her name's

Violet. She's probably out somewhere, so take what you can before she comes back. She can be a little feisty."

"And she can be a little sneaky, too," sneered a voice from the front entrance. I swiftly turned and regarded a girl smirking as she leaned against the door. Her hair was soaked with pinkish highlights (did everyone have highlights around here?) and she wore long black boots that reached her knees.

"I'm Violet," she said, extending her hand, but apparently I was too slow in returning the favour, so she let it drop back to her side. "You must be Arica. I got a Notification while I was out swimming," she said, harshly hinting toward Raven. "I told you not to send me those while I'm out."

"Well, how else am I supposed to talk to you?" Raven replied. "Arica, you can grab the upper bunk, I guess. Looks like Violet's got the floor mattress tonight."

"Me?" Violet asked aggressively. Then she shook her head. "Fine."

I kept my lips pressed firmly shut long after their deliberation had ended. Violet was immersed in a sci-fi TV show, and so Raven suggested that I meet Summer in the next cabin over with the twins.

"Summer speaks French," Raven notified, "so I hope you paid attention in school."

I groaned. The only thing I really knew was some German from my mother's side, but otherwise I was an Anglophone.

Raven and I exited our cabin and continued forward. The door opened just as I lifted my hand to knock.

"Arica!" Janine and Jess cried, both embracing me in a hug. "Finally, someone I can speak some *English* to."

"Ooh!" a voice sang from inside their cabin. The room practically mirrored ours, except the curtains were much more frilly and the cabin was neatly painted in hues of pink. "Eez zat a visitor?"

"Oh, no," Jess wailed. Suddenly a girl wearing baking mitts and a yellow sundress burst through the door. Raven began to introduce me, and I was surprised by her knowledge of the language. Summer turned to me with an extremely pleased expression on her face.

"Arique Miller?" she asked, her hand (well, oven mitt) clamped against her mouth so her words sounded muffled. She pronounced my last name like *me-eh.*

"Uh, yeah." My voice was strained.

"In ze flesh! Such an honour, it eez!" She furiously shook my hand with her hot mitten, her blond ponytail bobbing restlessly. "My name eez Summer LeBlanc."

Raven leapt across the cabin and landed on a green sofa that exactly matched the one in our cabin. "Summer here is Drake's girlfriend. Drake's sharing a cabin with Prince Adam and Joseph across the hall." She pointed down the dimly lit hallway.

"Oui, oui." Summer's eyes went into a dreamy state. "Il est mon chaton!"

The twins eyed me as if to ask what that meant, but I shook my head. Her words were nothing more than gibberish in my mind.

Raven cleared her throat and stood, and then translated the words Summer had said: "She said 'He is my kitten.'"

The twins gagged with revulsion and stumbled out of their cabin. I trailed behind them as they approached Joseph's room.

"My word, I honestly don't know how I'll handle living with that girl for who-knows how many days." She abruptly paused before Joseph's cabin door and curled her lips in a smile. "Jocelyn? Are you there?" Janine pressed. The door was slightly ajar, so Janine pushed it open. What I saw was definitely not what I expected.

Clothes were strewn all over the beds and floor as if a volcano of laundry had just erupted. Books were also scattered recklessly on the shelves (probably Joseph's doing), and the curtains looked lopsided. The whole place had an air of complete disarray.

"Hey!" a boy called. He had jumped out from the washroom and looked as if he'd just woken up from a good nap. A mop of brown-black hair sat atop his head, and his skin was the same colour as the walls—an olive-brown. When he approached us, I realized his eyes were chocolate brown despite the startling silver flecks visible in the light above us. He quickly grabbed a leather jacket from the ground, threw it on, and then regarded the three of us. A grin spread across his lips, and his eyes held the wildness and excitement of a hungry wolf.

"There's no Jocelyn in this cabin, but there is a Joseph!" He gave a slight smirk. "Name's Drake. Not the rapper, if you were wondering," he added, "but I get that a lot."

"So you're Summer's boyfriend?" I clarified. I hadn't exactly pictured him as the rocker type.

"The one and only. I'm guessing you're Arica and the twins. Prince Adam told me about you. Have you all settled in?"

The twins swapped weary glances. "Well . . . we'll unpack later. Summer's a little busy in the kitchen and we didn't want to . . . um, well . . . *disturb* her."

Drake looked amused, which was a little unsettling. "I'm guessing you two don't speak French. Neither do I," he confessed, "but she really starts to grow on you."

“Is that so,” Jess breathed, but it sounded more sarcastic than a question.

“Well, we’re not staying on the train too long,” I said, trying to uplift the twins’ stoic mood.

“Really? Because the Water Train is a beautiful place to live; especially this time of year. Summer and I have been living on this train for a while now. Maybe we could all meet up tonight and get to know each other? There’s a really big buffet on the upper deck every night—the food magically replenishes itself whenever anything runs out,” he explained.

“That’s a great idea!” Raven called behind me. Her Muskig, Musky, was gently hovering over her shoulder. “That’ll be a great way for these newcomers to get to know everybody.” She gave a reassuring smile.

“Great,” Drake confirmed. “We’ll meet on the upper deck this evening. Sounds good?”

“Sounds great,” I corrected, and then Raven led me back to our cabin.

* * *

After a few hours, I decided to sort out a few of my things (in which Violet was giving me a few disdainful glances) in the dressers. My clothes magically unloaded themselves from my suitcase and neatly stocked themselves in the drawers. Brooms swept the floors whenever a mess appeared, and as Violet claimed, the room changed colour depending on the mood.

“Wonderful,” Violet grunted when the walls turned a cheerful yellow. Then they slowly began to pale into a marble gray. The picture frames that hung on the opposite wall rearranged themselves to form a saddened face.

My body sank into the upper bunk as I finally took a chance to rest. Our cabin felt like a replication of my dorm at Hill Valley, but this was much more magical.

"Can you keep that thing *away* from me?" Violet asked, swiping away Newt the Egyptian Snocker when he crawled up her leg.

"Sheesh," groaned Raven as she pulled Newt into her arms.

I surveyed the room on my upper bunk and noticed an empty bowl sitting on a wooden desk. "What's that?" I investigated.

"Room service," Violet answered with a mysterious grin.

"Room service?" I asked, but my thoughts derailed as I watched a mountain of candy pile into the bowl. My jaw hung in wonderment.

Violet chortled, popped a candy in her mouth, and then stood abruptly. She strutted toward the door and then leaned against the frame. Her eyebrows lifted. "Coming?"

"Where?" I asked, puzzled.

"To the *buffet.* People do eat in the mortal world, right?" she sneered.

I curtained my face with my hair to hide my red cheeks. "Right," I responded. Just as I was about to jump off the bunk, it lowered toward the ground and then tipped forward. I slid off and nearly stumbled.

Violet gave a half-smile, and then clicked her heels together before escaping the cabin. I joined Raven and Violet as they submerged into the dim elevator light, and then we ascended to the upper deck.

A rush of warm wind slithered into the elevator as the doors drew away from each other. The evening glow of the moon bathed the train in a ghostly light, but the flashing neon glow of the lights strung above us compensated for that. The air was alive with excitement; kids, teens and parents were daintily enjoying their food as the sound of classical-turned-rock music filled the air.

"The Water Train glows different colours each night. Tonight it looks to be blue," Raven explained as she walked toward the side railing. I looked down and noticed the glinting reflection of the moon against the train, but the blue aura still remained strong. The water remained inky black, rippling here and there when a sea creature would surface.

The twins arrived in the elevator and streaked toward us. We secured a table near the juice bar and then set off to grab our food from the buffet. Violet remained immersed in something she must have found highly intriguing on her cell phone, and a spoon magically transferred food onto her plate.

We settled at our table and devoured our food. My stomach had been crying for a mere morsel of food for the past few hours; the last bit of food I'd had was a tasteless veggie burger from The Cheesy Palace. Even my Crigo, Lucy, had found that food revolting.

"Oh, this is much better than Mum's cooking!" Jess exclaimed. I had to admit that the food was extravagant (I went with the salad), but it could've just been the magical preparation that was making it seem so appetizing.

"I've had better," Violet voiced monotonously. She stabbed her fork into her cheesy baked potato and then gave each of us a glance. "I know Raven's here for her work and all . . . but why have you three decided to board the Train?" She intertwined her fingers and let her chin rest on her knuckles.

"We're . . ." I turned to the twins.

"Going to the Hall of Lost Gemstones?" Violet pulled the words straight from my mouth.

"Where'd you hear that?" I asked. My voice was a hint harsh.

"Word travels fast," she answered with a mysterious tone. She abruptly stood, and then drifted toward the elevator.

"Wait!" I called. I didn't know what had come over me, but I had the sudden urge to ask her this: "Where's your gemstone?" I immediately sealed my mouth shut. She slowly spun her torso, her eyes burning like a flickering candle. I squeezed the napkin on my lap, not daring to leave her eyes.

She looked at my neck. "Where's yours?" she answered. After releasing a short laugh, she turned back and left the deck.

I remained stunned. A million thoughts trickled in at once: *Did she lose her gemstone, too? Or is she just hiding it like my mother used to do?*

I silently completed the rest of my food. When the dessert buffet opened, Joseph, Adam, and Drake had finally exited the elevator and approached our table.

"Boys," I huffed under my breath. "I thought you guys were going to meet us before the buffet *started*."

"Sorry," Drake said, his voice barely apologetic. "Summer's a clingy one," he added with a chuckle. "Anyway, we just wanted to check out the desserts. I think I saw pie . . . I really love pie." He displayed a toothy grin. "Where's Violet?" he asked.

"She just left," I explained. An uncomfortable silence wafted through the table.

"Oh," Drake responded. "No problem. Summer should be coming down soon, anyway. At least I hope," he added, muttering the last part.

"Where is she?" Janine asked. "I haven't seen Summer since she was baking. Then she just . . . sort of . . . disappeared."

"It was really odd," Jess agreed. "She wouldn't even demonstrate her power when we asked her what it was! And the weirdest part is . . . she doesn't even have a *gemstone*."

I cleared my throat, tipping my head toward Drake.

"That's all right," Drake said. "Summer doesn't wear her gemstone . . . not after France. It was quite a traumatizing event. She doesn't like to talk about it. But even if she did, I still wouldn't understand because she'd be speaking French." He managed a laugh.

I nodded my head. "And what about your power?" I asked. "You have nothing to hide, do you?" I joked.

Drake's face paled to the colour of white milk. "O-oh," he stuttered. "Well, you see . . . I can't show it to you."

"What do you mean?" Joseph asked. "Is it like my sisters' powers—something you can't really display?"

"No . . ." Drake trailed off. "I can definitely show it . . . but only from time to time. I'm still . . . well, learning it, you could say."

"I see," I responded, even though everyone at the table was clearly confused by his vaguely described power.

A voice surfaced from the excited chatter. "Ah, zer he eez!" Summer, now wearing a white floral dress, was skipping her way toward Drake. She planted a light kiss on his cheek. "How eez everyone?" she asked as she settled at the table. The atmosphere remained icy with silence.

"I will take that as good," she joked. She dug into a slice of cherry pie. Adam began talking about the refreshing room service bowl, but I averted my attention to the faint tug of the tablecloth beneath me. Something cool tapped my leg and I flinched.

Jess noticed my reaction. "Arica, are you okay?" she asked.

I smoothed the napkin on my lap. "Sure," I responded. "I just dropped something." I ducked under the table and hid behind the cloth to see a blood-red clutch set on the deck floor.

My hand slithered toward the clutch slowly. I was merely inches away when a white flash erupted in front of my eyes and blinded me for a few seconds.

"Wha—"

"Arica!" a voice called. "Shh!" A hand clamped my mouth.

I squirmed away from the person's hand and regarded the man's body as it slowly squeezed out of the clutch. His entire body from the waist upward was visible.

"Rowen?" The name came out as a whisper.

He breathed slowly. "Arica. Sorry about clamping your mouth."

An airy laugh escaped my throat. "What are you doing here? I mean . . . how'd you get in that *pouch*?"

He chuckled. His eyes were an ocean blue, meaning he'd escaped another dreadful dose of Sleeplock. "It's Ash's. She uses it to transport around the Water Train. But that's not why I'm here. I have to give you something." His hand unclenched to reveal three green wrappers. Inside each was a green candy.

"Candy?" I asked. "Listen, I'm already having dinner—"

"This isn't *candy*, Arica. Take one of these tonight—and make sure no one sees you. Come out of your cabin and go to the deck if you must. Then meet me near the cauldron."

"*What?*" I whispered. "What is this all about?"

"It's a way for me to meet you. Take them." He outstretched his arm and I carefully plucked the wrappers from his palm.

"Did you manage to get onto the Water Train? I mean . . . outside of this pouch . . . you're not still in the maze, are you?"

"No, we got out of the maze. What you did back there, with the shell . . . I couldn't believe it. You didn't have to break it—it may not have worked."

"It was nothing," I said modestly. "Where are you guys now?" Saying *guys* instead of *Sapphires* now felt too casual, but Rowe wasn't really a part of them, so I decided not to use the name.

"I think I'm in a basement of some sort, at the bottom of the Train. I really don't know, but that's where we're staying. They've been keeping a clever eye on me. It's hard to escape Sleeplock when they force it down my throat. Luckily the effects have been wearing off earlier than they think." A rush of murmurs sounded beneath him. "I need to go. Promise you'll meet me tonight?" His eyebrows lifted and caused deep etches of wrinkles to cross his forehead.

"I promise," I said in a hushed tone.

He hesitated for a moment, examining my face, and then disappeared back into the clutch. It disappeared as soon as he had.

"Arica, is something going on down there?"

I quickly shot back into my seat and regarded the faces of everyone at the table. "No . . . just kind of dropped my fork." I waved my fork in the air to make it seem more believable.

"I thought I heard voices," Joseph commented.

"Voices? No, you must be imagining things," I said, and then I stuffed my mouth with a spoonful of pie as an excusable way to stop answering questions.

Drake shrugged. "If you say so," he murmured, and then he continued his conversation with Summer.

Adam was giving me an uncomfortable stare, as if asking me, *What really happened down there?*

I shook my head and then avoided his eyes—and everyone's eyes for that matter—for the rest of the dinner.

TWELVE: DUNGEON DROPS

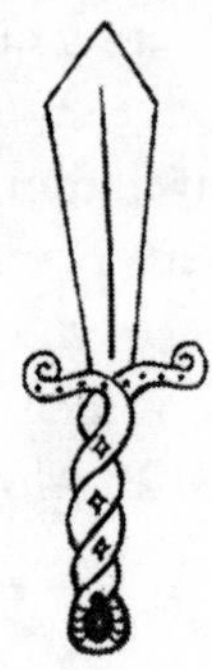

The clock struck on the midnight hour. As tired as I was, I couldn't seem to fall asleep. Not after that conversation with Rowen. Violet's loud snores had been ringing through my ears for the past few hours, and Raven had been sleep-talking some very strange things.

"Down," I whispered. The bed slowly lowered, meeting Raven's face for a moment. I gently slid off the bed and crept toward the door.

The picture frames on the wall rearranged to create a question mark, as if wondering what I was doing, but I disregarded that. I quickly opened the door and escaped into the hallway. The door groaned with a screech. I kept my hand firmly gripped on the handle, my heart still thumping when I viewed their sleeping faces.

Raven rustled in her bed, muttering, "Can you close the door please? Can you close the door please?" Her voice sounded lulled and sleepy. Then she collapsed into another chorus of snores.

I carefully exhaled a breath, sure that she was sleep-talking, and then closed the door. I escaped into the cabin hall. The door closed silently, and the dim lights above me illuminated nothing more than shadows on the walls. I fished for the candy in my pyjama pocket and pulled out a glinting green wrapper. I hadn't noticed this before, but the words Dungeon Drop were engraved on the wrapper. I extracted the circular candy from the wrapper and held it up to my face.

Take one of these tonight—and make sure no one sees you. Come out of your cabin and go to the deck if you must. Then meet me near the cauldron. Rowen's instructions were still clear in my mind.

I sprinted up the stairs, not bothering to take the elevator—taking the lift alone in the dead of night didn't seem very appealing—and made my way to the upper deck. My hand was carefully clenched shut to conceal the Dungeon Drop. I spied around the deck to ensure that everything was clear, and then lifted the green sphere of candy to my mouth.

"What are you doing up here?"

I jumped backward and dropped the candy from my hand, sending it sprawling down a vent. I turned to face a handsome boy wearing a familiar orange surf shirt.

I struggled to speak. "I was just . . . getting some fresh air."

He eyed me oddly. That was when I recognized him—he'd stood in front of me before we entered the Water Train.

"Ah," he breathed. "Sorry to startle you. It's just . . . curfew and all. Can't set up a bad example for the youngsters."

"Right—sorry. I'll just go back."

"No!" He sealed his mouth shut as if he wished to take back his outburst. "Wait. I'm Logan Burke," he said, extending a hand.

"Arica Miller," I said.

He let his hands drop to his sides and gave me a smile, as if he knew my name before I'd even introduced myself. His smile then faltered and he gripped the side wall, looking like he was about to hurl. His face turned ghostly pale.

"Are you okay?" I asked as he closed his eyes in frustration. Logan took a sharp breath and then turned back to me, an apologetic look in his eyes.

"Sorry, I get seasick sometimes," he explained nervously, rubbing his elbows.

I stuffed my hand back into my pocket to double check that I still had the other two Dungeon Drops. They were still there, as I presumed.

"Of course!" he exclaimed suddenly, as if a mild revelation had come over him. "I saw you before the Train came. There's been a lot of talk about you searching for the King's Jewel around the Sorcerers Underworld. Is it true?" His interest sparked a hopeful glint in his eye.

"Uh—yes. I'm trying to get to the Sorcerer Palace . . ."

"Me too!" he exclaimed, but his features remained calm. Then he pressed his lips together so they were as thin as paper. "I suppose you should get back to your cabin."

"As should you," I countered playfully.

"Right. What level are you on?"

"Four," I pronounced, my hand still dug deep into my pocket. I cradled a Dungeon Drop in my palm.

"I'll lead the way," he stated, gesturing for me to move forward. He trailed behind me as we descended the steps. We discussed some things about the Water Train for a while, and then I made it back into my cabin hallway.

"This is my stop," I said, careful not to wake my roommates.

Logan nodded, his dark brown eyes never leaving my face. "I'm staying just down the hall, in case you need anything. I'm sure I'll see you tomorrow, then?"

"Tomorrow," I breathed.

With a tip of his head, Logan disappeared around the hall bend. I stood bound to my spot as I quickly pulled another Dungeon Drop from my pocket. Before anyone else could interrupt me, I threw the candy in my mouth and felt as though I'd turned into a puddle of gently sinking mud. A revolting sensation spread in my mouth.

The next thing I knew, I was lying on the floor of a dark cement basement. Balls of dust hovered in the air like clouds, and the barest hint of life came from a fire on the opposite end of the hall. A substance was bubbling in a cauldron above it, sometimes spilling over the giant bowl's edges.

I suspiciously walked toward the cauldron. It hissed and spat bubbles of a murky liquid over the top. My face was barely visible in the rippling reflection.

"Finally," a voice whispered. I turned and saw Rowen gently sifting his fingers through the sandy cement beneath him. He stood and viewed his face in the cauldron. The substance in the cauldron was turning a bright green, illuminating the basement with an eerie light.

"Hi," I muttered, but my voice was slightly muffled by the candy in my mouth. I'd almost completely forgotten about the Dungeon Drop until the familiar revolting taste took over my mouth. I spat it into my palm and turned to Rowen with a bitter expression.

"I know, it tastes bad," Rowen commented. "Dungeon Drops are made to simulate the taste of dragon spit, you know."

"You're not helping," I remarked.

"Sorry, but you wouldn't have eaten it if I gave you a warning."

I turned back to the cauldron. "Is this . . . Sleeplock?" I observed his eye colour: a light aquamarine.

"No," he denied. "Apparently it's much worse. But the Sapphires won't tell me what it is. That's why I called you here. The Sapphires . . . they're not only involved with the gemstones." He swallowed. "They're involved with the Jewel's thief."

I gasped. "Did . . . did *they* steal the King's Jewel?"

"Of course not," he said. "They wouldn't be able to do that while in the Dungeons. Not until they escaped, that is. I just know that the thief is their accomplice; the thief is using them to help him or her with their plans."

"What are the Sapphires doing to help the thief?" I asked.

He sighed, almost exasperated. "They've been collecting things for this cauldron. I don't know why the thief needs this, but it's obviously for an important reason. They keep talking about how they're going to retrieve the gemstones for the Sorcerer Line, and they also keep talking about this one other thing they need. They say the thief needs one of Prince Adam's possessions."

"Adam's?" I questioned. "Why would they need something of Adam's?"

"I don't know. But I thought I'd warn you. There must be hundreds of sorcerers on the Water Train; any one of them could be the thief. And if the thief is trying to get one of Adam's possessions, then it's possible that his roommate could be the thief."

"That's not possible. Joseph is my cousin—he didn't steal the crown. And his only other roommate is . . ."

Rowen lifted an eyebrow.

"Drake," I blurted. "At the buffet tonight, Drake was talking about how he couldn't demonstrate his power . . . but why?"

"That could be it. Maybe he's involved with the Sapphires . . . or perhaps he's gaining power from the King's Jewel. This could be worse than I thought."

"I don't think *Drake* would be the thief. I just met him, and he certainly doesn't look like a guy who would steal the *crown.* I mean . . . he's just . . ."

"Arica, that's what they *want* you to think. If you keep an eye on him, then we'll be able to tell if he's the thief for sure."

I swallowed, a seed of uncertainty growing in my gut. "Is there anything else you wanted to tell me?"

He opened his mouth to speak, but hesitated. "No. That's all. Just return tomorrow for an update. You have two more Dungeon Drops, right?"

"Actually, I only have one."

Rowe frowned, but I interrupted him before he could speak: "Long story. Some guy was talking to me—"

"Guy?" His restrained his voice from anger. I wouldn't understand why he'd be angered by this, but for some reason I felt content.

"Don't worry about it. I'll just focus on Drake."

"Good," Rowen responded, not so angry. "Listen, the Sapphires are probably looking for me; they're readying another dose of Sleeplock. I won't be able to talk to you until midnight tomorrow."

Rowe's face became blurry, almost like someone was stretching his face from a hundred different angles. I reached out to touch him, but my hand swiped through him as though he were a hologram. The taste of dragon spit filled my mouth, and then I landed back on the upper bunk in my cabin dorm.

Violet rolled off the mattress, rubbing her eyes. "Arica? Where'd you go?"

I jolted up only to bang my head against a portrait on the side wall. Those things were really starting to annoy me.

"Nowhere," I answered, injecting a hint of sleepiness in my voice to sound more convincing.

She grunted. "I thought I saw you leave—"

"You must've been dreaming," I denied, gently resting in my bed again. When she didn't respond, I decided to end the conversation. "Goodnight."

She sleepily pulled the covers over her head. "Whatever you say," she muttered, and then she returned to her peaceful snores.

*   *   *

I rubbed my sleep-crusted eyes the next morning, just faintly conscious as I walked to the bathroom. I washed my face as though I were a zombie, almost falling forward into the sink. My muscles ached with tiredness from the night before, and I used my toothbrush to try and scrub the taste of dragon spit off my tongue. It was while I was brushing that the smell of something burning invaded my nose.

I wiped my mouth and walked back into the cabin, eyeing both Raven and Violet. They both seemed to have smelt it, too.

An unsettling *bang* came from the hallway. I swung open the door to find Summer, her face covered in black powder and ashes.

"Oh, my!" Summer said, staring at the smoke billowing from her cabin. "Zis is all my fault," she said, frowning.

A flock of firemen arrived just after she spoke. Janine and Jess stood close by, weeping while they explained the story to Adam, Drake, and Joseph.

Supposedly, Summer decided to wake early that morning to create a nice breakfast to share with Drake for their two-month anniversary, but she was startled when a knock came at their door. A man looking in his teen years with dishevelled black hair entered their dorm without consent. Then all Summer remembered seeing were columns of fire, and the man had disappeared.

"I recognized him," Jess murmured. "I didn't want"—she hiccupped a breath—"to believe it."

"Who did you see?" I asked, my voice trembling.

She wiped away a few tears and then said, "A Sapphire member. Geoff. Oh my days, I don't know how this happened . . ."

The firemen began filing out of the hallway in a single file line, muttering in their very specific lingo. By the time they'd rounded the corner, Violet popped out of the doorway discreetly.

"Are they gone?" she asked. Raven slithered through the door behind her.

"Yes," Summer muttered, her voice muffled. She was weeping into Drake's shoulder.

Something hardened in my throat. If Drake truly was the thief, then maybe this entire thing had been a set-up; maybe Jess hadn't seen Geoff. Perhaps it had been Drake, trying to distract everyone so he could steal what he needed from Adam.

I moved toward Drake, a negligible hint of sympathy in my eyes. "Where have you been?" I snarled.

Drake gulped. "I . . . I had to . . ."

"He was beezy!" Summer cried, and then she fell back into Drake's arms. I supposed the proper translation for "beezy" was "busy," but you could never be sure with her thick accent.

"Come on," Drake encouraged, leading Summer down the hall.

Summer's cabin was dark with dismay. Her frilly curtains had shrivelled; the miniature kitchen was burnt to oblivion; and their drawers were crouching deep into the corner, almost as though they'd moved away from the fire.

"Where are we supposed to stay?" Janine whimpered.

"Andrae—the conductor—should be able to relocate you to a new cabin," Adam informed. "What I think is more important is why Geoff did this."

I nodded, about to disclose my opinions about Drake, but thought better of it. Now wasn't the time to be pointing fingers. "We should be notified of your new cabin soon. I think we all just need to settle down and get some breakfast," I suggested.

The twins nodded in agreement, and we headed toward the elevator with meagre conversation. The breakfast buffet was already open on the upper deck, and we were all delighted to take our first relaxing moment since the fire. Rays of sunlight crept along the deck and illuminated the morning sky. The waves made subtle crashes against the train as we advanced farther into the Bermuda Triangle.

"What do you think people see when they notice the Water Train?" Jess pondered.

"A giant wave?" I guessed. Mortals were unable to see practically anything magical; if I'd levitated a bowling ball people would probably think they'd seen a plump bird hovering in the sky.

"Interesting," Janine mused, but she still looked sad.

"Hey, everything's okay," I said, trying to lighten the mood.

"I know, but I'm still a little shaken. Why would someone do this to us?" She gazed at the wooden floor, a transparent tear rolling down her right cheek.

A clatter sounded from the other end of the table. Violet had just arrived, looking sleepy with dark rings under her eyes. They seemed to blend with the poorly-drawn eyeliner she'd probably rushed to put on this morning.

She dug into her breakfast. The twins were discussing some of the amenities on the Water Train, and Violet remained uninterested.

"Any interesting events going on today?" Joseph poked at the raspberry muffin that lay on his plate, trying to stimulate some sort of conversation.

"Not that I know of," Violet answered monotonously.

"I'm collecting some kites this morning," Raven informed. "I was wondering if any of you guys wanted to help me out." She raised a fork to her mouth, and then hesitated, awaiting our answer.

"Again?" Violet sighed.

Raven shot her an icy stare. "It is my *job*, you know. And it might give Janine and Jessica something to do while their cabin's being . . . fixed."

Jess and Janine both liked the sound of the idea. I agreed to help, too. Joseph and Adam left to find Drake and check out the wave pool—technically it was more of a bathtub in comparison to the Water Train, but it was still a good way of passing time until we would reach the Sorcerer Palace—and the twins, Violet, and I followed Raven downstairs.

"It's my job to collect any kites and make sure I send them back to our main quarters. I've collected all sorts of kites in my days, but I'm always surprised when a golden kite shows up."

"A golden kite?" I asked. "What's so special about that?"

"Golden kites can only be used by Royals," Violet explained. "And they're charmed with very old magic; no one could intercept the kite's path."

"Could we see one?" Jess asked excitedly.

"Chances of seeing a golden kite are slim. Last time I saw a golden kite was during my first week of training. Golden kites are a rarity, but since we're nearing the Sorcerer Palace, we might be able to catch sight of one." Raven then guided us toward a room at the corner of hall. A giant circular handle was set against the doorway, almost like a steering wheel. Raven spun the wheel sideways and the door groaned as it slid open.

The room was strewn with kites. There must've been at least a hundred in all. Some kites were blue, some yellow with green spots, or black with sparkles . . . .

"Look! There!" Janine pointed toward a golden kite that hovered at the corner of the room. She immediately ran toward the kite, but then stopped as though she'd reached a glass door when she was a few feet away from it.

"Like Violet said, the kite cannot be intercepted," Raven explained.

"But there's a note attached," Jess observed. "How could there be a note? Unless this kite is meant for someone on the boat . . ."

"Maybe it's meant for Adam," I surmised. "I mean, it's the most logical explanation."

"We wouldn't know for sure unless we saw who it was addressed to. And no one but the receiver can view that."

"Then let's get Adam," Jess said, her sleek red hair shining as sunlight spilled through the open window.

"Slow down," Raven said. "We don't know if Prince Adam is the receiver. It could be meant for anyone."

Janine huffed. "Well, maybe Arica can get a better look." Janine probed me with two gentle fingers and I was lightly pushed forward. I began to make my way to the golden kite, feeling slightly vigilant. Once I was only a few inches away from the kite, I felt my breath choke in my throat. The air felt thick, as though I were walking through a wall.

"Do you see anything?" Raven said, but her words sounded muffled.

"What?" I asked, turning on my heels. When I turned around I noticed their figures looked fuzzy; I couldn't tell the twins apart, and Raven's face was distorted.

Glancing back at the kite, I felt a cold blast of wind cut straight through me. The kite hovered toward my face, glowing as though it were literally made of gold. The ruffled note began sliding out of the kite and smacked me right in the face. The breeze died down as I read the rushed font:

Dear Arica,

You may be aware that I, the thief of the King's Jewel, am aboard the Water Train. I am here to tell you that this is true; but I seek another possession of the Royal family. Prince Adam is the keeper of a dagger that is very dear to me. Hand me this object and I will give you the King's Jewel in return. Do this once you've entered to the Sorcerer Palace, and do not inform anyone else of this note. Remember: I am darkest when the sky is bright.

"Arica, what do you see?" one of the twins asked. I turned to view their faces, the air curling around me suddenly misting up like fog. I walked forward and their faces turned back to normal. I held the paper in my hands with apprehension before handing it to Raven.

She didn't respond for a long moment. Then she lifted her cloudy-gray eyes up to mine and said, "There's nothing on it."

"What?" I asked, taking the paper from her. The crumpling sheet remained blank.

"Is this some kind of joke?" Violet asked, averting her attention from her nails. "Seriously, Arica, we know you're the Prophetic Child and all, but you could at least show us one little letter."

My jaw dropped to the floor. "I didn't do anything—I mean, the note just became blank when I gave it to you."

She snorted. "Right. Come on, Arica. Just because you get messages from the Royal family doesn't make you any more special." Then she twisted her body around and strutted down the corridor.

I turned back to the twins and Raven. "You guys believe me, right?"

The twins swapped looks. Raven said, "I don't know, Arica. A blank message wouldn't have come from the Royal family . . . but if it was addressed to you . . ." She shook her head. "I don't know," she answered numbly. "It just doesn't look good."

"Janine? Jess?" The hurt was evident in my voice.

Jess grasped my shoulder. "Raven's right. This doesn't look good. But that doesn't mean I don't believe you!"

"Exactly. What did the note say in the first place?" Janine asked.

I swallowed loudly. "It wasn't from the king or queen—it was from the thief. The one who stole the King's Jewel."

"That's impossible," Raven denied, but her voice shook. "This kite can only be commanded by royalty."

"Maybe it has been commanded by royalty. Since the thief has the Jewel, maybe the Jewel believes it's being commanded by a new owner . . . the new king."

Everyone's facial expressions stirred. "Then the thief has more control than we'd ever imagined." Raven cleared her throat. "We really need to read what it says. Let's take it to Adam and see if he can figure out how to read it."

"But this note must be bewitched by dark magic," I explained. "Deciphering this would take forever. It's impossible."

"Then we'll just have to make it *possible*," Jess said.

I huffed, and then nodded my head. "Fine. Let's go," I said, and then Raven led the way to the fourth floor.

* * *

"It's not working," Adam said, frustrated. We were all standing in his room, trying to make the blank paper reveal the words it had shown earlier. He blew a breath of air into the top of the Wishing Knife and touched the tip to the scroll once again. It remained blank.

"Maybe we should talk to your mother," Joseph said. "Is there a way to call her?"

"No. The Water Train has specific rules for connections with the outside world. I'm afraid it's not possible." Adam's face was grim.

"Can't Arica just tell us what it said? I mean, she's right here." Drake crossed his arms firmly.

I thought about what Drake had said. If he didn't know what was on the paper, could that mean he wasn't the thief? Or was he just lying, trying to stay below the radar?

I placed a finger to each of my temples. "I don't exactly remember—"

A snort came from the open doorway. "She doesn't want you to know. She's hiding it from all of us. Don't you see?" Violet's voice was recognizable.

"I'm not hiding anything," I said fiercely, rooted to my spot. Violet's eyes looked ablaze.

"Oh, yeah? I know you think Drake is the thief. I heard you say it last night. In your sleep." She snorted again.

"What?" Drake's mouth slid open. "Why would you think that, Arica?"

"Is that true?" Adam asked, shooting me a stare.

"Well—no. I mean, yeah, but—"

"I can't believe this," Drake muttered furiously. "And of all people, I was going to trust you with my—"

Thudding footsteps sounded from the hallway. Andrae, the Train Conductor, appeared before the doorway beside Violet. He was panting, as if he'd just run here.

"Andrae?" Raven asked quizzically.

"Sorry to intrude," he said. "I've just been getting some strange signal from this room." He was staring at a golden tablet in his hands and furiously reading something. His hands flew over the screen, typing in several commands, until a weird beeping sound commenced.

"You see? It's detecting something strange. Some other creature on the train," he said, seeming exasperated.

"Creature?" I asked. "But . . . I thought the train was open for all magical people."

"It is," Andrae answered. "All magical *sorcerers* and *sorceresses.* It wasn't designed for vampires, or goblins, or who knows what else." The beeping grew louder.

"Let me see that." Violet tore the device from his hands and furrowed her brows. "Look at the battery. It's low."

"So?" Joseph asked. "That's a pretty trivial detail if you ask me."

Violet became angry. "If the battery is *low*, there could be something messed up with it. It could be broken. Corrupted, for all we know."

Joseph was about to retaliate, but I interjected before he could speak. "How can you be sure?"

Violet gave the device one last glance before handing it back to Andrae. He took it gingerly, examining the plating on the outside. "Well . . . I just am." She didn't answer as confidently as she probably wanted to, but at that moment I wasn't questioning her tone. I was wondering why she would know such a thing; why she would be turning down the possibility that someone on the Train could've been non-magical, or that Andrae's device was simply *broken.* Did she possibly have something to do with this?

Drake cleared his throat. "Um, guys, maybe we should listen to Violet." I shot him a stare, but then realized that maybe he was right. Maybe I was being too overly judgmental. Violet hadn't said anything wrong, had she? She was just bringing up a possibility. A suggestion at most.

Andrae sighed. "Sorry, again," he said, gripping the device with both hands. Andrae was giving Drake a strange glance now, but he quickly turned away and left. I turned to Drake, too, and examined his face. He looked disturbed.

"I'm hungry," Drake said suddenly. I realized that the change in his emotions had passed extremely quickly; he'd been mad at me only minutes before because I'd accused him of being the thief of the King's Jewel. Either he wanted to avoid further conversation, or I was just overanalyzing the situation. The latter seemed more likely.

Joseph, too, rubbed his stomach. Then Drake supplied, "How about we grab something to eat quickly?"

"Sure. The note doesn't seem to be revealing anything, anyway," Raven observed. She patted me on the arm. "Let's head upstairs?"

I was so preoccupied in my thoughts that I hadn't even realized she'd asked me the question. I finally agreed, and then turned to Adam. He muttered something about figuring out what the note said later, and then handed me the blank paper. He left ahead of me, just behind Raven and the others, so that I was the last one remaining in the room. Giving the paper one last glance, I stuffed it deep into my pocket and left.

The blank note burned a million questions into my mind the entire way up to the deck.

THIRTEEN: VIOLET'S PHONE

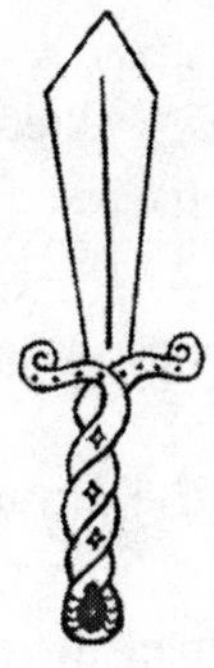

"Vere eez Drake?" Summer groaned as the evening commenced.

"The cabin just got fixed, Summer," Janine explained with a twinge of annoyance in her voice. "Can you calm down for just one minute?"

Summer scoffed, but relaxed in her chair. We were lounging on the deck chairs, trying to relax, but obviously that wasn't working for Summer. The blank paper still wasn't revealing any information whatsoever, which kept Adam and some of the others irritated, too.

The thief's trade was still clear in my mind: give him or her a dagger (probably the Wishing Knife), and in return they would give the Jewel. I wanted to tell Adam to keep his Wishing Knife safe—to guard it from harm—but my words faltered.

Jess was feeling paranoid now, too. "We haven't the faintest idea where the Jewel is, or why the thief is sending

Arica strange blank messages . . . It's just plain *weird*, isn't it?"

"We need something to take our minds off of this," Raven suggested. "It's a beautiful evening! Why don't we go—"

"I am going downstairzz," Summer announced. She stood from her chair and walked to the elevator. Drake arrived at the lounge chairs just after Summer had left, a quizzical look set on his face.

"Did something happen?" he asked, taking a seat on the chair beside me.

Adam whispered to the Knife and an image glowed from the tip. In the image, Summer was angrily stomping into her cabin. She slammed the door shut and the image dissolved into fog.

"Why is she angry? I mean, I understand the whole cabin thing, but—" Raven began.

"It's nothing," Drake finished, and his tone had a finality that left everyone silent for a few long minutes. My gaze was transfixed on the stars above us. They looked almost as though they were moving, rearranging to form different shapes and faces.

"Drake . . ." I spoke hesitantly, but remained quite enough for only him to hear. "I'm sorry about thinking you were the thief. I shouldn't have jumped to conclusions."

He didn't speak for a long moment; but when he turned, his face had a youthfulness and innocence that I hadn't expected. "No harm done," he said.

I warmly smiled, but my smile melted when I thought back to our conversation. "You also mentioned something before. You said you would trust me with . . ." I trailed off.

Drake was suddenly very interested in his shirt. "I . . . I just felt like I could trust you. Since the moment I saw you I felt like I knew you. It was like I'd known you all my life, and right there and then, I wanted to spill my darkest secret." His face hardened.

"And what's that?" I whispered.

He kept his voice low. "I wish I was a regular kid. Not who I really am. I feel like part of me really is normal. Mom always told me I have a—"

"Hey, Jocelyn!" Janine yelled, a little too loudly. A few passengers lying nearby gave her dirty, annoyed glances. "Look at those fireflies!"

Hovering lazily against the dark sky were four distinct fireflies, producing a soft green glow.

"Ah!" Joseph called. He didn't even retort to Janine's nickname for him, probably because he'd gotten so used to it by now. "Chemiluminescence at its finest!"

The twins groaned. Raven chuckled.

The fireflies swam through the air in random patterns. Their glowing bodies seemed almost hypnotizing, captivating. They looked more like green orbs painting the sky.

Then they moved toward Joseph and began swirling around his head, moving so quickly they created a band of green light.

"Whoa—wow!" Joseph exclaimed.

The fireflies escaped suddenly, shrouded by the bright lights that hung above us in strings. Joseph looked around glumly in search of the fireflies that had disappeared.

"That was interesting," Adam murmured to himself, relaxing in his seat once more, transfixed in the unmoving stars. I wondered why he gave such a sarcastic remark, though it was probably just the tension that had been building between Adam and Joseph since they'd met.

"What were you saying? Your mom always said you had a . . . ?" I prompted.

"I . . . I . . ." Drake's smile melted to grimness. "Never mind. Too much to explain, I guess. It's no big thing." He shifted a bit more, seeming suddenly uncomfortable with the conversation.

"Oh . . ." My hopes felt deflated. What he was about to say surely didn't feel like "no big thing," but I didn't exactly feel like probing through his feelings any further. It only seemed to inflict pain on his normally cheerful visage.

"Fireflies, mazes, and chocolate men! What next?" Jess exclaimed.

"Chocolate men?" Drake questioned. "Uhh . . ."

I let out a chuckle. A chocolate man really did seem pretty crazy at first thought.

"It's nothing," I answered. Drake gave one last quizzical look, and then left the topic.

"Ugh. Fireflies," a voice commented from behind us.

I turned to see Violet, who was wearing pyjama pants and a shirt displaying a flower that looked way too cheery for her normal day-to-day outfits. Her hair was set in a braid down the side.

"Can I take that chair?" she asked, but then she moved toward the seat between Raven and me before anyone could respond. The silence remained for longer than I'd hoped.

"What's wrong with fireflies?" Joseph asked after a moment.

Violet wrinkled her nose. "Hmm. I dunno. Just kind of . . . bright," she responded.

"I think fireflies are great," Raven objected.

"Whatever," Violet said, shrugging.

Joseph looked taken aback, as though someone had insulted him and he was unsure of how to respond. "Well . . . I'm tired. I think I'll head back to the cabin."

"I second that," Drake added. They both hurriedly made their way off to the elevator.

"What was that about?" Jess asked. "I mean, I know Joseph's weird and all, but really—even he doesn't sleep this early."

"It's been a long day, hasn't it?" Violet reasoned. "I mean, with Summer's cabin and everything . . . I guess they've called it a day." She plucked out her phone from her pocket and began scrolling through texts. The white light from the screen cast an eerie glow against her skin and made her look somewhat ghost-like.

Raven grunted suddenly. "Violet, how many times have I told you? No phones on the Train."

"Yeesh, it's not like I'm *talking* to anybody." Violet continually flicked her finger upward, causing a stream of texts to fly across the screen.

"C'mon, Vi," Raven said, acting sympathetic. "It's been proven to weaken the strength of a person's magic. Plus, Newt gets scared when that thing buzzes."

As if on cue, Newt scrambled up from Raven's side and hid in her sleeve. His marble-sized eyes were dark, causing small lumps to form on her cuff.

Violet let out a throaty sigh. She placed the phone beside her reluctantly and succumbed to staring at the stars, just as Adam had. In fact, Adam seemed to be trying not to take part in any conversation at all—I'm not sure why—whereas the twins were chatting to each other excitedly.

Violet, after unsuccessfully trying to stare at the sky, stood from her seat. "Anybody want anything from the juice bar? It's on me."

"Wow. That's . . . polite," Raven pronounced with difficulty. "But no thanks."

"Thanks, but no," I declined.

"Hey—it's your loss, not mine." Violet's tone returned to its normal carelessness. Then she trotted off to the juice bar, the sound of her footsteps fading quickly.

Violet's phone, sitting on the lounge chair, buzzed almost immediately. The screen flickered to life; a dark black box with the words new message appeared, along with several other notifications.

A reoccurring *buzz* sounded every time she received another text. Everyone else was too preoccupied to notice the buzzing of Violet's phone. I decided the only polite thing to do was stop the buzzing by tapping the screen.

I clearly thought wrong. A flood of messages appeared on the screen. I didn't want to feel invasive, but the sight of the name "Geoffrey" caused me to freeze. I inconspicuously moved closer to her phone and peered at the screen. With my unfortunately not-too-great eyesight, the font was just too small and blurry.

But I did manage to catch sight of the word "jewel."

Before I could truly understand the conversation, I heard the sound of Violet's boots clicking against the floor. Reluctantly, I shifted my gaze and waited for Violet to take her seat. Once she had, I couldn't help but stare at her.

Violet took a long sip and then noticed my unmoving gaze. "What? I asked you if you wanted something. If you want a drink now, go get it yourself," she snarled.

"Uh . . . uh, sorry." I swallowed roughly, and then redirected my attention to the ocean view. Why was there someone named Geoffrey texting Violet? Just seeing his name on the screen caused my insides to twist. Geoffrey . . . Geoff. As in *chemistry* Geoff? *Sapphire* Geoff?

It must've been a pure coincidence. There was no way that Geoff and Violet could be linked.

But then again . . .

I shook my head. I would not allow paranoia to devour my thoughts—not like they had with Ash back in Hill Valley.

"You know, this mango juice is actually *really* good," Violet commented. If Joseph were here, he would definitely be scowling; but I had other thoughts on my mind. Perhaps Violet texting a person named Geoff was a coincidence, but the word "jewel" appearing in their conversation did not seem like wholesome luck.

Violet took one last sip while checking her texts. The tip of her nose nearly touched the screen. Her eyes widened as she read the texts, which only caused me to become even more apprehensive.

"I'll be right back," she said quickly. The expression on her face seemed almost worrisome, but she then she lifted her chin as if to mask it. She abandoned her juice and pocketed her cell phone before heading to the washroom located at the corner of the deck.

"I . . . I've gotta go, too. But I'll be back." The string of words came out rushed, and Raven furrowed her brows as if to question my words. Before I could regret what I was about to do, I left my seat and followed Violet to the washroom.

Violet moved with a quick, intent pace toward the washroom. Once the door had shut closed behind her, I counted to five and then carefully opened the washroom door. By the front was a mirror, so I could easily check if Violet was standing nearby or had entered one of the stalls. The scene looked vacant enough, so I entered.

A few ladies were adjusting lipstick by the mirrors, and gave me strange glances when they caught me looking at them. I quickly looked away and then hid in a stall, trying to contemplate the situation. I felt stupid at the moment—I had no plan, no idea of what was to happen.

But, luckily, in that short moment of panic in which I was standing in the stall, I caught sight of Violet's boots in the next stall over. The short *clicks* that emitted from the stall must've been the sound of the keyboard on her phone—she was texting someone.

In that instant, I pushed myself out of the stall and stared at the mirror. I knew what I was about to do. If I took a look into Violet's stall, I might be able to see inside, and even better, figure out who she was texting.

After pretending to fix my hair, I took a few steps to my right. I slowly turned my head to peek through the gap in the stall. I could see Violet's black-and-pink hair, but she was looking down and ferociously texting.

I took a step closer to the stall, and saw a bright red light emit from the phone. Someone had texted her, but the name was unclear to me.

And then it all happened in a blur. I was leaning forward, trying to get a better look at her phone, when the stall door had opened. Violet was standing there, staring at me with blazing eyes, as I fell forward. My hands began flailing, grabbing for something to hold on to, and then . . .

Splat. My nose hit the door. A stinging feeling swam down the bridge of my nose. I held it for a long moment, eyes shut and burning. After a few heavy breaths, I looked up to find Violet still staring at me. She was slipping the phone in her pocket when she said:

"Arica! What are you doing here?"

"Uhh," I groaned, still holding my nose. I blinked my watering eyes a few times. "Oh, uh—sorry," I began. "I was looking for you . . . to make sure you were okay."

"Well, you found me," she said, moving toward the sink. "And why wouldn't I be okay? I was just going to the washroom."

I tried to think up a lie quickly. Unfortunately, I wasn't the best liar.

"I just wanted to make sure, I guess. You left kind of quickly."

"And you followed me pretty quickly, too," she said, eyeing me carefully.

I shrugged, as if to pass it off, but my nose was stinging like crazy. I grabbed it with my right hand and forced myself to control my breathing.

"I'm sorry, Violet," I said, still holding my nose. My voice sounded kind of nasally. After another few steady breaths, I removed my hand and looked up.

The washroom was completely void of people except for a few ladies adjusting their lipstick. Violet had vanished—gone, disappeared. I found myself saying, "Where did she go?" but the women were just looking at me as if I was insane. One woman gave me a glance and shrugged. She seemed to know as little as I did.

How could Violet have left so quickly? She hadn't sprinted out of the washroom, had she?

I walked out of the washroom and back to the lounge chairs, feeling dazed. Violet wasn't there, either, but I sat on my lounge chair anyway.

After a few minutes of staring at the stars, I blurted out a question unknowingly. "Where's Violet?" I asked. Janine and Jess were giving me a stare, their left eyebrows both raised.

"What do you mean?" Raven asked. "I thought you followed her. You left in such a hurry, anyway." She looked around at everyone else as they nodded. They must have noticed my apprehension. To be honest, I was probably just bottling all this stuff up because I didn't want to come out with the wrong suspicions about Violet.

"I think you should go to bed, too, Arica," Adam said. "I was just about to head down myself. I'll take you there."

Before I could even respond, Adam stood and offered his hand. I took it and stood, and then waved goodbye to Raven and my cousins.

Adam was silent on the way down, and I couldn't have been more thankful. I definitely did *not* want to talk about Violet's mysterious disappearance any longer, and Adam seemed to want to keep to himself, too.

I wondered why he was being so quiet. Could he have known the thief wanted his Wishing Knife? That was the only possible dagger on the Train, anyway. He might've been mad at me because I didn't tell him. But then why would he have offered to take me back to my cabin if he was mad at me? That didn't make any sense.

"Here's where we part ways," he said. "You'll be all right?"

"Of course," I said, and he nodded. "But—"

"But what?" he asked. "Is there something concerning you?"

I found it strange how Adam still sometimes talked in a noble manner, just like he had back at Hill Valley. Of course, after I'd found out he was the prince, I knew he didn't talk like that all the time. But it seemed like every time something concerned him, or made him upset, he used that tone of voice.

"Just—just have a good night." I pasted a fake smile on my face.

"Okay," he breathed, and I could tell by the sleep circles under his eyes that he really needed to rest.

I sluggishly opened the door and fell onto my bed. I noticed Violet wasn't in the room, which for some reason didn't bother me because I didn't feel like talking to anyone. I only wanted to fall asleep, alone, in the darkness . . .

I felt as if I were plunging into a dark, black hole. Into a darker world . . .

And I knew I was about to have a nightmare.

The first thing I saw was a strange blue light and a cloaked man. I was cupping the cell bars, crying—screaming—to be let out. To be freed.

But the man only kept his hand suspended in the air as he emitted the light. Creatures of all sorts—goblins, werewolves, beasts of all kinds—were banging against the walls. But one by one they began to follow the man's orders as the blue light passed them. A look of relief washed their faces, and they looked as if they'd been lifted from a curse that kept them perpetually doomed.

The man had finally made it to my cell, but the blue light weakened. I had done everything in my power to make it go out. My mind was concentrated on the light and I felt beads of sweat break out on my face.

The man lowered his hand with cautious red eyes, and then moved the other to his hood. He gripped the hood with one hand, and slowly brought it down . . . .

I felt as if someone had gripped my heart in their fist. Violet's pink hair fell around her shoulders, and her strange devilish red eyes glowed sinisterly.

"Violet?" I blurted. Her bright hair illuminated the dark essence of the jail cell. How could I have not noticed it was Violet before?

"It was always me," she said, her voice hissing in a scathing chorus. *"Always."*

"No!" I shouted. "He—it—it can't be you!"

"Why not?" she asked. "You saw me talking to Geoff about the Jewel."

"Are—are you the *thief*?"

She smirked. "Not exactly." She pulled the hood back over her head, and suddenly all that was left of her face was an empty, unknowing darkness. The cell bars were starting to melt in my hands; in fact, the whole scene felt like it was falling apart. Cracks and fissures formed on the floor. My body slipped into the gaping rivers of blackness on the floor, and then I sank into a world of darkness.

My eyes opened wide with alert. I pressed my hand to my chest to feel the sweatiness of my palm against my running heart. Fragments of the vision ran through my mind. Violet had revealed herself as the supposed "cloaked man"—but was this vision real? Or had I just been so stressed and paranoid by the washroom incident that I'd had a false nightmare about her?

Just in the midst of my thoughts, the door to our cabin opened. A harsh yellow light bloomed from the hallway and caused me to squint. Violet entered the cabin, her cell phone pressed to her ear.

"Yes . . . I know . . . I'll find my ring, I probably just misplaced it . . . Oh!" Violet had flicked on the light and realized that I was in the room. Her jaw remained hung for a moment before she regained her normal poise. "Uhh . . . I'll call you back." She lowered the phone from her ear and ended the conversation with a click of her finger.

"Uh—hi." I wanted to say more, but my throat felt dry with suspicion. That nightmare had not done well to release my doubts.

"S-sorry," Violet stuttered. "I just came here to look for something. My ring." She swallowed, and then directed herself toward her bed. She began ruffling through the blankets as though looking for something. "It was a really precious ring. A jewel," she said.

At that moment, I felt a lump rise in my throat. Had Violet been using a metaphor? Or was this "jewel" I had read in her text conversation really just her missing ring?

If that were true, then I'd taken everything all wrong. My worries had all been over a ring that Violet had lost. And Geoff? Sure, it seemed like there was a link . . . but otherwise, I couldn't simply assume. Look what that had gotten me—another nightmare and unnecessary paranoia.

"Ugh. Can't find it." She lay on the mattress, arms outstretched, and sighed heavily.

"I'm sure you'll find it soon," I said, trying to steer my eyes away from the harsh light. "Could you turn off the light, please?" I asked.

Violet sighed again. "Sure. Guess I should sleep, anyway. Raven will be back soon . . . and you know how goodie she can be." I wasn't quite sure at all what she meant by this at the time; Raven did seem like the rocker-ish type, but then again she *worked* on the Water Train, so she would evidently have to set a good example for others. By that, I supposed curfew fell as a topic under that list of enforcements. So did cell phone usage.

Violet turned off the light and settled on her mattress. I stared at the ceiling for a long moment, contemplating a certain question in my mind. I knew I couldn't sleep if I didn't bother asking Violet.

"Violet?" I asked.

She groaned. "What?" she asked. "Suddenly wanna stay awake now? Make up your mind."

"No . . ." I sighed. "I have a question."

I could picture Violet pursing her lips. "Go on."

"Well . . ." I struggled to put the words correctly. "Have you ever been to . . . to a jail?"

Violet sniggered, and then stopped. She probably thought I hadn't been serious. "Do you really think I'm the type of person who would go to *jail*?" She kept silent for a moment. "Wait—don't answer that."

I laughed. "I didn't mean it that way. I meant . . . have you ever been to the Sorcerers Underworld Dungeons before? I mean, like, *seen* it?"

Violet turned in her bed. "Hmm . . . yeah. Yeah, I've been there."

I swallowed. "And . . . and you've seen a cloaked man there?"

"Cloaked man?" she scoffed, and then went serious. "No. Not a cloaked man," she replied vaguely.

"Okay . . ." I responded, my voice dry. I was trying to see if she would spill any more details, but she didn't bother saying anything else. Suspicion continued to fill me.

Raven entered the cabin suddenly. "Ouch! Who turned off the light?" she asked. She stumbled over to her bed and then rested. "C'mon, Newty," she said calmly, "it's bedtime." I could hear Newt scampering up the bunk beds.

"Yeah," Violet responded casually, and I had a lingering feeling that she was directing her next sentence to me. "No more talking. It's bedtime."

FOURTEEN: FOOTPRINTS

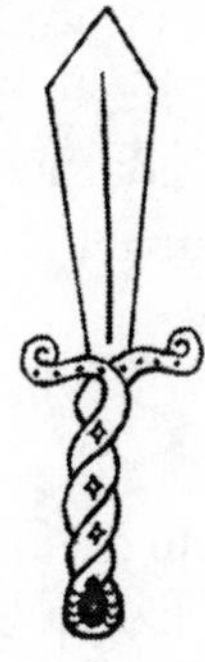

I woke up the next morning to clouds and rain. It rained for a while, and I just stared at the ceiling for a good half an hour before deciding to get up once the rain stopped. I groaned, lifted the covers, and headed for the washroom. On my way there, I noticed a small sticky note attached to the empty mattress on the floor. In that instance I realized that Raven and Violet weren't in the room. The note read:

> Headed out to eat breakfast with everyone. Thought you would like to sleep in. Meet us on the deck.—Raven and Violet

I pocketed the note and headed toward the washroom. It was nice that Raven and Violet had let me sleep in—especially after a very weird night—but I later contemplated the fact that Violet may have not wanted to wake me up *because* of last night.

A sudden knock came at the door while I was brushing my hair. Could it have been Violet coming back to check on me?

But why would she, after last night's weird encounter? She seemed pretty irritable with me, too, and had wanted to get some sleep. Her ring was missing, after all. I felt pretty silly to think that the "jewel" she was referring to was the actual King's Jewel. But she wasn't talking about the Jewel; she was talking about her prized-possession: her ring. Something she would never let out of her sight.

The knock came again, but this time with a man's voice. "Arica, you in there?"

I froze mid-brush, staring at my reflection in the mirror. The voice was slightly familiar, and I knew it couldn't belong to Adam or Joseph. Even Rowe's voice didn't match.

I gave myself one last look in the mirror, and took a deep breath. When I opened the door, I recognized the man's tight-fitting surf shirt and matching board shorts. Logan's deep-brown hair was slicked back, and almost looked glossy in the dim halo of light emitting from the ceiling.

"Hey," he said. "What's up?"

"Uh, nothing," I replied. What was Logan doing at my room at this time of morning?

"Adam told me you were in here," he said, his mouth in a half-smile.

"You two know each other?" I asked incredulously.

"Yeah, we're kind of like old buds." He let out a nervous laugh.

"Oh," I said, and then he pulled out a bright blue surfboard from behind his back.

"Wanna join me?" he asked.

"Oh," I said, taken aback. "It's kind of early, don't you think? And I don't surf."

"I didn't mean you had to surf. I was going to go later, anyways. I kind of just wanted to show you something." There was a hopeful glint in his eyes, as if he'd known me for so long. But I'd only met him two nights ago. Why was he suddenly so interested in me?

"I need to eat breakfast," I said, grabbing a sweatshirt. "I should go."

Logan furrowed his brows, looking disappointed. "Arica, wait, I didn't even get to talk to you yesterday!"

I stopped myself halfway to the door. "I'll talk to you later, Logan," I said, remembering the exchange we'd had just before I'd eaten the Dungeon Drop. He'd promised to speak to me the next day. But now, when I thought about it, why had he been alone on the deck in the first place?

Giving him one last glance, I trotted down the hallway toward the upper deck, leaving him alone to his thoughts.

* * *

"Last night was a real buzzkill," Violet murmured, stabbing her egg yolk with a fork. "Who goes to bed at nine?"

I rolled my eyes. "I was tired," I muttered, but no one seemed to hear me over Summer's excited rants about her new shipment of pink curtains.

"Now I have *rose* curtains again! Yay!" she said, clapping.

"And just in time for your birthday, too, eh, Summer?" Drake said, putting an arm around her shoulder.

"It's today?" Janine asked, her mouth full of half-chewed scrambled eggs.

"Non, Janine. Demain," Summer replied. When nobody understood what she'd just said, Raven translated the word by telling us it meant *tomorrow.*

"Oh," Jess said with a bright smile on her face. "Are you having a party?"

"Nah, we wanna keep it simple, right, Summer?" Drake said, eyeing her cautiously.

"Oui, oui!" she agreed.

"Oh, okay," Jess said, looking a little down. "That's cool."

Drake let out what sounded like a fake yawn and stretched his arms. "Oooookay then. Guess I'm gonna head *downstairs.*" On the last word, he gave a weird signal to Adam and he nodded. Joseph stood, too, and followed them along the wooden deck. Adam took one swift glance back at me with an open smile and waved me over.

I wondered what was going on. The girls at the table didn't seem to notice, though. Violet was once again immersed in her cell phone; Raven was conversing with Janine and Jess about rock bands; and Summer was daintily cutting into her breakfast omelette.

Leaving my napkin on the table, I turned around and followed Adam to the elevator area. I found the three of them talking rapidly to one another, but with hushed voices, as though discussing some private matter.

"Summer's going to love this," Drake said, grinning widely. His teeth were so white I could barely look at them. He must've had a good orthodontist.

"I know," Adam replied. "I've always loved surprise parties."

"I don't know, guys," Joseph countered. "It seems kind of . . . big. I would just prefer a night of the History Channel and some reading."

The other two just stared at him as if he were an alien.

"Uh, guys?" I said, shifting toward them. "What's going on?"

"Arica, you came!" Adam said, placing a hand on my back and pushing me into the group.

"Okay, we need a girl's opinion. Surprise party or no surprise party?" Drake asked.

"Uh, I guess it depends on the girl," I said shakily. "Does Summer even like surprises?"

"For sure," Drake said cheerfully. "I brought her to the Water Train as a surprise trip. And it's been the best months of my life."

"Where are your parents?" I asked suddenly.

Just after I spoke, I realized I shouldn't have asked that question. My thoughts swam back to last night. Drake had said he was keeping a big secret from me. From all of us. What if it was about his parents?

"They're . . . busy. I kind of needed a new life, so I came out to the Water Train. It was the best decision I've ever made."

Joseph cleared his throat after a while, and said, "So, surprise party or no, Arica?"

"I think yes," I said, in a bit of a daze. I was still thinking about Drake and his family. I remembered his words faintly: He'd said his Mom always told him he had a . . .

"Okay, tomorrow we need to decorate the upper deck," Drake said, interrupting my thoughts. "We're going to need as much help as we can, but we need to keep this a secret from Summer. And Arica, tell the twins and Raven and Violet."

"All right," I said, feeling a bit overwhelmed.

"Cool," Drake replied. "I guess we should go back to the table. Don't wanna make Summer mad!"

Adam and Joseph laughed along with Drake as we made our way back to the table. But throughout the rest of the breakfast, I didn't really feel like talking to anyone.

I was silent, filled with my own thoughts about Drake and Summer . . . .

And then there was Logan. He wanted to show me something this morning, but I left him quickly to meet everyone for breakfast. But now that I thought about him, his offer didn't seem so bad. I didn't know what he wanted to show me, but it must've involved water if he wanted to surf. And right now, that sounded pretty good.

As if on cue, I saw Logan's bright blue surfboard out of the corner of my eye. I turned around in one swift motion and saw him heading toward our table. "Hey, guys!" Logan said. Then he directed his gaze toward me. "You done eating breakfast, Arica?" he asked.

I bit the inside of my cheek. "Uh, no. I heard you need to wait fifteen minutes before swimming if you've just eaten," I said, trying to look down at my food so I could avoid his eyes.

"We're going swimming?" Janine and Jess said excitedly. "Awesome! Let's go get our bathing suits!"

"No, no—" I was cut off.

"Awesome, Logan!" Adam said, giving Logan a short handshake. "I'll meet you there in a bit."

"Guys, we're not going swimming!" I finally said. Everyone looked toward me like I was a lunatic.

"No—I invited Arica to come somewhere with me," Logan corrected.

"Oh," Joseph said, suddenly sitting straighter. "Well, I don't think that's a good—"

"Sounds good to me," Violet said, as if she wanted to get rid of me. "I guess we'll meet you later, then, Arica."

"I don't think I want to—"

"Go on, then!" Jess said with her perky accent. "Logan's waiting!"

I gave a grim smile, and then stood. I felt slightly better knowing I could walk around.

Logan took me to the elevator and back down to the fourth floor. I looked at him weirdly, wondering where he was going to take me, but for some reason I didn't say anything. I followed him out of the elevator once we'd reached the fourth floor, but then he didn't move another step. Instead he stared at the wall, as though contemplating the choice of wallpaper. Then he turned his head and studied my face intensely.

"What?" I asked. "Is there something on my face?"

He shook his head. "You're the Prophetic Child," he identified slowly.

"Well, yes . . ."

"Why didn't you tell me?" he asked.

"Well, that wasn't exactly the first thought that came to my mind," I said, "but—"

"Never mind," Logan interposed. "Listen, there's something I want to show you. It's sort of weird . . . and I felt like—you being the Prophetic Child and all—I should tell you about it."

"About what?"

He sucked in a breath, and then turned back to the wall. "About this."

"The *wallpaper*?" I questioned. "Um, it's nice, I guess," I said.

He chuckled. "No, I meant"—he pointed to the small brown swirls that adorned the walls—"this design. I've been staring at these swirls all day. They look so familiar."

"I suppose . . ." I contemplated, though I wasn't quite catching on to what he was saying.

"And isn't it strange how this wallpaper is only decorated on this floor but no other?" When he saw the expression on my face, he laughed. "You start to notice these things after a while," he explained.

"Uh huh," I replied.

"But the strangest part is where the swirls stop—look closely." He leaned forward, and I followed. The brown swirls did indeed stop right smack dab in the centre, but it seemed to form a small dot right at the tip. After a few seconds of scrutiny, I realized that the tip of the swirl formed the shape of a snake head.

"A snake?" I asked.

"Yeah, that's what I thought." He moved his hand along the wall to the following swirl. "Look at this one—the snake faces the opposite way as the last. And the pattern continues along the whole wall."

"So? Maybe the interior designer wanted to decorate it this way. It's no big deal."

"That was what I thought," he said, his voice tightening, "until now. Does it make sense for the snakes to face opposite ways? It almost reminded me of a symbol . . . the symbol of the Sorcerers Underworld."

"So . . . you mean to say the wallpaper has something to do with the symbol? But what?"

"I think it's meant to cleverly represent some sort of exit. There has to be something behind this wall."

"How are you so sure?" I asked.

"Because . . . because . . . I saw this girl yesterday, when I was leaving my cabin, and she was just sort of standing in the middle of the hall. I turned around for one second, and then the next second, she was gone," he explained. "And it's not like she just vanished or anything like that. If she had, there would have been some trace of it—a white smoke in her place or something. So she must've gone in . . . in through the wall."

"What girl?" I asked suddenly. "I mean, what did she look like?"

Logan scratched his chin absently. "I don't remember. She just had lots of highlights. Like *a lot.*"

I involuntarily shivered. There were only two possibilities at the moment: Raven or Violet. The latter was the only one that seemed even remotely likely.

"So she went *through* the wall?" I asked.

"If that even makes sense," Logan agreed, "but yeah. And I thought if she did . . . then maybe you could, too."

I regarded the wall carefully, and then brushed the swirls with my hands. Then I pressed my ear against the wall and listened intently: a slow, rhythmic ticking sound came from the other side, almost like a metronome.

"What is that . . . ?" I asked. The ticking steadily grew faster, becoming hypnotizing. I closed my eyes and focused on the rhythm, suddenly immersed by the sound. *Tick, tick, tick . . .*

The sound was the only thing that seemed to exist in the world—not even my thumping heart could be heard over the penetrating *ticks* that emerged from the room.

Without warning, I felt my feet lift from the ground. In one millisecond, there was no surface beneath my feet, and in the next, I was resting on the solid ground once more. I forced my eyes opened and found myself staring at a dark canvas of a wall.

Where had I gone? I shifted my position and spied through the darkness—I couldn't tell if I was in some dark room, or rather at the mouth of a dark forest. The air felt chilly, but it was probably just my sudden nerves that caused my teeth to chatter and arms to tremble. I pressed my hands against the wall, still trembling, and pushed. It was hard as concrete, and stable, too. My breath quickened.

"Logan?" I said, sounding more frantic than I'd wanted. "Hello?"

No response came. Then, suddenly, the ticking sound reoccurred. It was no longer a sharp, ticking noise, but rather a much deeper thumping. Like a clock whose heart was draining of life; a mere, unstable ticking that could end at any possible moment.

"Arica?" came a voice. It was Logan, from the other side of the wall from which I stood. "Whoa—where'd you go?"

"Logan, I'm on the other side!" I cried toward the wall. "It was the ticking—focus on the ticking, and you'll come through!"

"Ticking?" he asked. "I don't hear any—oh."

"Yes—*oh.* Now focus on the sound," I ordered.

"Sure," he murmured, and then there was silence. After much patience, a shadow flung itself into the darkness on the other side of the wall. There sat Logan's body, hunched over, as though he had run a long marathon.

"Logan?" I grabbed his hand and helped him. He wheezed uncomfortably.

"Come on, it wasn't that hard, was it?" I joked.

"Ha," he laughed, "maybe not for *you*, Miss Prophetic Child." His smile softened, and I could almost imagine his ears twitching at the sound of the steady clock's heartbeat coming back to life. "So, about that ticking noise?"

"Yeah, about that . . ." I turned to survey the darkness. There was scarcely anything lit, which just made the place feel even creepier. "I guess we follow the sound."

Logan moved forward, and I kept a careful hand on his shoulder as I followed. The ticking progressively grew louder as we approached the unknown source. When it felt like the ticking noise was unbearably close, we stopped. I bent down and tried to make out what I could in the darkness. My hands moved forward and gripped a cold, metal object.

A memory enveloped my mind. I was back in the Golden Cave, holding the Aradis in my hands. Then I was running into the crevice while Lembrose surveyed the area, and her eyes fell upon me . . . .

I came back to my senses, darkness swarming my vision. The cold metal was still present in my hands, and I knew in that instant I was holding the Aradis.

"Oh my gosh," I murmured. "It's the Aradis."

"What's that?" Logan asked suddenly.

I stood slowly, feeling the grooves in the metal. It had been damaged, most certainly—but how did it appear here?

"Cale," I whispered.

"The vegetable?" Logan asked. "What does that have to do with this?"

I ignored his inquiry. "Cale was here. And if Raven or Violet were here too . . ." I swallowed loudly. The ticking, I realized, had stopped once I had held the Aradis in my hands.

"Whoa—don't shine that thing in my eyes," Logan said, shielding his face. I realized that the metal shimmered slightly in what scarce light was present.

"Wait—this is perfect! It could act like a flashlight!" I moved the Aradis and began to shine it on the ground. My shoes came into view, followed by our footsteps along the dusty ground.

"Aaah!" I screamed suddenly. A small, gray snake appeared in the light, its eyes venomously red.

"That thing looks ancient," Logan commented, "like my old uncle Ian."

The snake hissed once, but then darted out of view. I struggled to bring my heart rate back down, breathing heavily. Logan laughed.

"It's not funny," I said, moving forward. I was tracing our footsteps back to the wall.

"Clearly not." Logan seemed amused. "Wait—look at that!"

"I'm not falling for any tricks," I said, still focused on the ground.

"No—I mean these aren't our footsteps. Unless you're wearing size seven boots with diamond patterns on the bottom."

After little examination, I realized Logan was right. These definitely weren't my tracks, and they looked pretty fresh in the dust.

"Someone was here," I theorized.

"Probably the girl I saw yesterday," Logan said.

I bent down and examined the footprint further. If I could find someone with this pattern on their shoes, then I could possibly figure out which girl Logan had seen—and if she had any connection to bringing the Aradis here.

"We should go," Logan said, placing a hand on my shoulder. I agreed quietly, and then we both headed toward the wall. The Aradis felt like slippery, limp piece of metal in my palms.

"I'll go through first," Logan said. "Er, if I know how."

I laughed. For some reason, the wall looked like it was a rippling pool of water. I stepped forward and felt absorbed by the wallpaper, and then emerged on the other side.

Logan stumbled through the wall and almost ran into the elevator. He gave a short laugh, and then examined the Aradis in my hands.

"I think I'll hold on to this," I said before he could suggest the same. "You know—for safe keeping."

"Oh . . . yeah sure," he said, looking thwarted by my suggestion. "So . . . want to swim?"

I regarded the Aradis: just another reminder of Hill Valley and the Sapphires' involvement in my life.

"Sure," I said. "That sounds great now."

After I hid the Aradis in our cabin, Logan and I left for the pool. He'd grabbed us some cool pineapple drinks, because the sun was beaming mercilessly now. I tried to act cool and calm around Logan, as if nothing was bothering me, but I knew I had to survey people's shoes to see if I could find the matching diamond pattern.

Although I was clearly zoned out, Logan was telling me a story: "And then she was like, 'But I ordered a *medium* salad, not a large!' Oh, man, it was hilarious!" he said, clearly amused by his story. He sighed. "She got the large, anyway. Uh, Arica—are you listening to me?"

"Oh—yes, I am. Very funny story. Could you excuse me for a minute?"

Logan looked a little discomforted by my suggestion. "Oh, okay. No prob."

I gave a tight smile. "Thanks."

I spied a pair of shoes with a diamond-shaped pattern on the bottom. Revealing a hint of a smile, I put my drink down and walked toward the lady wearing them. She was sporting a large, white floppy hat and a matching white eyelet-lace dress down to her ankles. She caressed the necklace on her chest as she stared at the open water.

I also noticed a long lock of thick, navy-blue hair protruding from the hat. She must've had highlights, like Logan said about the girl who'd entered the room.

"I found them," I muttered to myself. The lady, who was once staring at the ocean, now looked over at me with questioning eyes.

"I'm sorry? What was that?" she asked. She sounded Australian. Her eyes were piercingly blue, and her face was scarcely pale.

"Oh, nothing," I said. "Just . . . uh . . . admiring your shoes."

"Yes, well, this is my first time wearing them," she said, surveying her ankles, and then sighed. "They're not too comfy. I think I should just return them."

I couldn't think of anything to say, so I just nodded. If this was the first time the woman was wearing her shoes, then she couldn't have been the one in the room Logan and I had found. I sighed in sorrow. "They're very . . . nice."

She smiled, her teeth now framed by dark red lips. "Thank you. Sorry to leave, but my husband is calling me," she said. "Nice meeting you." And then, turning so pale she was see-through, she lifted her feet off the ground, and then looked as if she was *floating*. She hovered in the air for a second, and then flew off.

I stood in the same spot, stunned, as Logan walked toward me. "Who was that?" he asked, pointing at the floating ghost lady. She now sat at the juice bar with a man looking to be in his thirties.

"Uh, I don't know," I said in shock. Had I just seen a ghost? A dead woman?

"Looks like a ghost to me," Logan said. "They're allowed on the Train, you know."

"Seriously? So this whole Train could be haunted by ghosts?" I said sarcastically.

"Ghosts don't haunt people!" Logan said protectively, slamming his pineapple drink on a nearby table. "They're just regular sorcerers who didn't get their chance in life like everyone else."

I stared at him, confused by his abrupt and angry speech. "I-I'm not that thirsty anymore," I admitted. "I think maybe I should just go back upstairs—"

"The diamonds look *amazing*," I heard a girl say from a few feet away. I looked at her using my peripheral vision, and then straightened my stance when I noticed her shoes. My stomach filled with butterflies when I noticed the bottom of her shoes had diamond-shaped patterns, too. She was crossing her legs, one over the other, as she showed them to a boy beside her.

I gasped a little too loudly and the girl seemed to have heard me. She looked up.

"Excuse me?" she asked, turning around.

I stood, mouth open in an *O*. "Uh, I, uh—"

"Hey, I'm Logan," Logan said, shaking hands with the girl politely. She had bright red hair, with light streaks of pink, and a slightly pointed nose. Her tanned skin shone brilliantly in the sunlight.

"Amelia," she replied while shaking hands with Logan. "And this"—she pointed to the boy beside her—"is my brother Jace." She turned to me. "What's your name?"

"I'm Arica Miller," I said. "Nice to meet you, Amelia." I eyed her shoes once more. "Where'd you get those?"

"In one of the gift shops," she said in a careless tone. "Why? Do you like them?"

"They were really expensive," Jace added. "Mom had to pay hundreds of dollars!"

"Well, it's not like that mattered, Jace," she said, shoving his side.

"What do you mean?" Logan asked, suddenly intrigued by their conversation.

"Our parents are filthy—" Jace was cut off by Amelia's high-pitched voice.

"Rich!" Amelia finished. "They're rich. They paid for this place to be redecorated."

"Oh," I said. "But didn't this Train once belong to a man . . ."

"He died," Amelia said in a *duh* voice. "So, like, my mom paid. No big deal."

Jace nodded. "So, basically, the shoes cost a lot," he said after a while. "Like *a lot*—"

"What size are you?" I cut in, not even feeling guilty for having interrupted Jace, who was now invested in his iPhone.

"I'm size nine," she replied, and my heart sank. She couldn't have been the unknown shoe-owner.

"Oh, there's Violet!" Amelia said suddenly, mixed expressions written on her face as she pointed across the deck.

I could feel my jaw drop. "V-Violet?" I said, not even glancing back. "The one with pink highlights?"

"The one and only, unfortunately. We used to be roommates," she said.

"What do you mean by *used to be roommates*?" I asked.

"She . . . got a little . . . strange," she said sourly. "I didn't like her."

"W-what—"

"She told me her secret. I thought she was crazy for a few days, sitting there in our room. But soon I learned who she really is. And I can't handle it anymore. I was thinking about telling Andrae."

Jace only nodded solemnly, still focused on his phone.

"What's the secret?" I asked, leaning in.

"She was telling me . . . it's hard to explain so quickly," she whispered, and then gave her ring-adorned fingers a wave. "Just remember, it's her *cell phone*."

I shook my head, clearly confused. I turned to look at Logan for help, but he had disappeared.

Amelia stood up abruptly. "Here she comes!" she said. "I have to go. Come on, Jace," she told her brother, and they left with a startlingly quick pace.

"Hey, Arica," Violet said. "What's up?" She casually took a sip from her grape juice.

"Nothing much," I said, trying to stay calm after Logan and Amelia's abrupt departures.

"Wanna head back to the cabin?" she asked. "Raven says there's a *How It's Made* marathon on the Discovery Channel."

"Oh, cool, I love that show," I said, although the words in my mouth tasted bitter with lies; I'd only watched a few episodes of the show in my entire life.

"Awesome. Let's go," she said, and we headed down the elevator and returned to the fourth floor with minimal conversation. We made it to the cabin and I plopped onto my bed, noticing Raven had taken the mattress for the night. She was lying on the mattress while reading and giving the TV occasional glances.

"Hey, Raven," Violet said, throwing her phone to the lower bunk.

"Hey, guys!" Raven replied cheerfully, but she was still deeply rooted in her book. The cover read *The Life of a Muskig*.

"How about that marathon?" I said.

Violet pressed her maroon lips together and then searched the bunk for the remote. She finally appeared out of the blanket avalanche with a remote in hand, and began flipping through the channels so fast I could barely see what was on the screen. She stopped (after at least a hundred clicks) on the Discovery Channel, and let out a relieved breath.

After a few minutes, Raven cleared her throat in a weird way, as if to announce something. But she only turned her attention to Violet and said, "Do you have my shoes?"

I nearly choked mid-bite on my M&M. My mouth remained frozen as I regarded Violet squirming on the lower bunk. What shoes was Raven talking about?

"Uh, I think they're—oh, here! Found them." I saw her arm poke out beside her as she held shiny silver sandals. I noticed a diamond pattern on the bottom and the number *7*.

"Good. I thought I'd lost them," Raven said, and the two of them chuckled. I sat there, eyes still warily trained on the shoes, jaw dropped. Raven couldn't have been the shoe owner . . . she couldn't have had something to do with the Aradis. She couldn't have—

"Thanks, Raven," Violet said lazily, interrupting my thoughts, "for letting me borrow your shoes yesterday."

FIFTEEN: CONFRONTATION

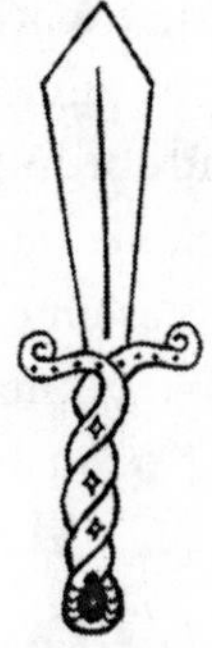

The night passed quickly. I spent the next morning with Janine, Jess and Violet. Violet had somehow managed to seem awfully normal, even after last night when she'd given Raven her shoes back. That meant *Violet* had been the person sneaking around in that weird room. They were *her* footprints—or at least that was the only conclusion I could draw.

Violet extended her arm, handing me a Morning Sunshine smoothie. I took it reluctantly, and then stared at the clouds drifting slowly in the pale sky. Beside me, the twins were noisily playing some weird twin telepathy games.

"Guess what colour I'm thinking of," Jess said.

"B-blue . . . No, wait, yellow . . ." Janine replied, struggling to find the right answer.

"You're not looking into my eyes hard enough!" Jess said, slamming her juice on the table. Some orange juice spilt out of the glass, but she didn't care. "Look harder!"

Janine looked at Jess, then down at the drink, and back at Jess again. "Orange! It's orange!" she cried.

"Yes, finally," Jess breathed, sitting back in her chair.

"Guys," I interrupted, "when should we start setting up for Summer's party?"

The twins pondered this silently. "Maybe we should ask Drake," Jess said after a minute. She leaned to her right, and noticed that Violet had abruptly left. The *click* from her shoes faded on the wooden deck as she retreated.

"All right," I said, still eyeing Violet warily. Obviously she didn't care about hanging out with the twins and me. She seemed to change her personality a lot while we were on the Train. Sometimes she seemed all right, and other times just downright weird. Today was one of those weird days.

"Let's go to Jocelyn's cabin, then," Janine said, picking up her smoothie. We left and arrived at their cabin minutes later, and by then it was probably noon. Adam and Joseph had just opened the door to leave the cabin when we arrived at their door. Why were they leaving their cabin?

"Hey, JJ," Janine said, trying to give Joseph a high five. "What? New nicknames are always healthy for good relationships, right? I think I read that in a magazine somewhere."

"We were going to go to Arica's cabin, actually," Joseph said, lifting his glasses to his eyes, but they just sloped back down his nose. "We were going to talk to her about the party."

"We were going to see *you* about Summer's party, too!" Janine exclaimed.

"I think we need to decide on a time for the party set-up," Adam said, joining the conversation. "How about six? That'll leave us plenty of time to do whatever we want until then."

We all agreed and split off. I headed back to my cabin, but the twins stayed behind to bug their brother.

Violet grunted as soon as I walked into the cabin. "Back already . . ." she murmured monotonously.

"Yeah," I responded, my voice a tad bitter. I plopped down on my bunk and felt something stir beneath my legs. When I looked down I saw Musky flying toward Raven's dresser, where he seated himself comfortably on the wood.

"Wonder when Raven will be back," I speculated.

"Hopefully not soon," Violet snarled. I couldn't help but observe her change in attitude.

"Do you know about Summer's party tonight?" I said, trying to change the topic without ruining the mood.

"Now I do," she chortled. She paused, staring at the ceiling. "I'll go talk to Drake about the set-up and leave you alone with your thoughts." Her boots made short thuds along the cabin floor before she entered the hallway. I would've told her we'd just spoken to Joseph and Adam about it, but I didn't feel like talking.

Violet left abruptly, but she turned down the hall toward the right. That wasn't the way to Drake's cabin; obviously her talking to Drake was just some kind of excuse to leave.

I sank deep into the cushion beneath me, pondering several things that mainly had to do with the King's Jewel. Was it possible that the crown was hidden somewhere on the Train? Since the thief was aboard the Water Train, the idea seemed likely. I wondered where it could've been hidden; perhaps behind one of the grand statues at the dining hall? Or possibly in the giant safe on the first floor. Maybe even in the basement . . . .

Something cool was tapping my leg. I realized it was the tips of Musky's wings brushing my legs as he flew over my bed. He seemed to be carrying something strapped to his back. It looked like a leather-bound book.

"Let me see that," I murmured, unravelling the thick rope that tied around his belly. Musky snorted gratefully as I managed to pull him free of the twine. Then I lifted the book to my face. A piece of parchment peeked out from the side. I slid the paper out and stared at Adam's familiar scrawl: *Found this on the deck; most likely sent through a portal from my father. I thought you'd like a look.*—Adam

After lowering the note, I studied the book's leather cover. The surface was grimy and somehow much more faded. The symbol of the Sorcerers Underworld was still present, but it was barely recognizable from the last time I'd seen it at Hill Valley.

I flipped through the book until I fell on one page in particular: page forty-nine.

The page was riddled with pock marks and scratches. It looked as though someone had tried to completely obscure any information that the book had provided on the Prophetic Child. Somehow one part of the paper remained unharmed. I hadn't seen this part before, but it almost looked as if it had been scribbled in using a fine pen:

> *The Prophetic Child maintains power that is superior to any other sorcerer's. It is rumoured that it can be harnessed in some way; there is, in fact, an incantation that allows one to take a part of the Child's aura of power. This power cannot simply be bottled up, but rather transferred through a powerful chant:*

The powers of the one that holds the Bow,
No lack in time will ever show.

The price that passes the magic as such
Shall destroy the depth of the Child's touch.

I locked my eyes on the final sentence. What did the "depth" of the Child's touch mean? The Prophetic Child's powers? I shuddered. I hadn't actually speculated the thought that someone could try to *destroy* or *steal* my powers. I hadn't even known there was an incantation that could allow a sorcerer to do such a thing.

I lightly pressed my finger against the deep etches the pen had left in the paper. Someone had clearly written this in, and the last person I'd seen with this book was Ash. I'd first thought it belonged to Ash, but clearly (after reading the note Adam had attached) it probably once belonged to the king, and now the prince.

A sudden knock came from the door.

"Arica?" a deep voice called.

I looked up, startled, when I heard the man's voice. I tucked the book under my comforter with lightning speed and jumped off the bed.

Someone opened the door just as my hand brushed the doorknob. There stood a man with aquamarine board shorts and a tight-fitting orange surf shirt.

"Logan!" I said, trying to remain calm, but my voice came out a little squeaky. I suppose I was still shaken after reading the strange chant that was written in the book.

"Hey, Arica!" Logan replied. "I'm sorry about leaving yesterday. Something happened—"

"It's fine," I said, and he smiled with relief.

"Wanna swim, then? We never got to go yesterday, with the footprint thing and all."

"Oh," I said, my mind still focused on the book sitting on my bed. "I don't know—"

"Come on," he said, urging me forward. "It'll be tons of fun. I've invited everyone to come. And it should be a great stress-reliever before the party."

"How do you know about the party?" I asked. If word had gotten out to the other members of the Water Train, then did Summer know, too?

"Adam told me," he said, and I innately breathed a sigh of relief. "Now come on!"

I frowned, but his suggestion was beginning to sound enjoyable. "All right," I said, and we entered the elevator.

Adam and Joseph were already in the pool. Joseph shivered in the frigid water; Adam seemed contented by this.

"Logan!" Adam called, waving us over.

"Hey!" Logan waved. "Be right over!" He turned to me. "You're not wearing that in the pool, are you?" he asked, pointing at my jeans. When I didn't respond, he said "Hello? Earth to Arica?"

"Oh, sorry," I said. "I was just thinking about you and Adam. How do you guys even know each other? You said you were—"

"Old buds," he finished. "I used to work at the Sorcerer Palace. That's kind of why I'm going back. The king finds my power useful for the Crigoes."

"What's your power?" I probed.

"I can basically talk to animals. I work better with sea animals, but I've gotten pretty used to Crigoes. There's a whole dungeon full of Crigoes in the basement."

"Basement?" My voice trembled, but remained curious. "Where?"

"In the Sorcerer Palace. Where else?" he replied casually, gently stirring his right hand in the water. "That alligator over there says your aura is disturbing him."

"Alligator? Aura?" I pondered frantically, searching around.

Logan laughed. "I was just kidding about the alligator. But seriously. Ever since you've boarded the train, all the animals find you so . . ."

"So . . . ?"

He huffed. "I don't know."

"What did they say about me?" I investigated.

"Seriously, I don't know. But they act weird around you. Your aura is really strong."

"What *aura*?"

"Your powers!" he said, as if the answer were obvious.

My eyebrows made a *V*. "What about them?"

"You're the Prophetic Child! You said so yesterday. Your powers are so strong they create an aura . . . . You'll have to do something about that."

"What are you talking about? I don't have to get rid of my powers, do I?" I questioned, horrified.

"No! Of course not!" he said, waving his hands in front of him. "I'm saying you need to keep cautious. And you leave a scent, by the way."

I quickly smelled the back of my hand. "What scent?"

"Only animals can smell it. A strong scent comes off of you if you use your powers too much. The dolphin told me."

"Dolphin?"

"Kidding! I'm kidding. Gosh, you really don't get sarcasm."

I rolled my eyes. "So how do I get rid of it?"

He pursed his lips, and then his eyes shot toward me. A theoretical light bulb hung over his head. "I know a spell," he revealed.

"What is it?"

"Well, it's not supposed to be used in public." He wrapped his arms around his knees after taking a seat by the pool's edge. He observed the sparkling pool in front of us.

"Why?" I asked.

His face twisted in a weird way, as if he smelt something horrible. He didn't answer.

"Logan!" Adam called from the pool. "Come on in! The water's warm!"

"I'm coming!" Logan called. He turned his head toward me. "Are you ready to go in?"

"Uh, no, but thanks," I managed. I didn't feel like swimming anymore.

He wrinkled his brows, and his happiness deflated. He kept staring at me warily, as if I would change my answer, but when I didn't, he jumped into the pool.

I observed the pool as giant waves swallowed the crowd whole. Some kids cried with excitement and accidentally caused their powers to erupt uncontrollably. One kid began flying upward. Joseph managed to help by sending a beam of light toward him. The kid, flailing, sailed straight back into the water. A group of lifeguards rushed over to the scene. I moved out of the way and headed toward a few lounge chairs. When I looked over the immense, glittering pool, I noticed two bodies in the distance. They looked like Janine and Jess. I veered around the pool and approached them, but from behind they no longer looked like the twins. The two looked very similar and recognizable at the same time . . . .

They began descending a spiral staircase with anxious speed. I kept far behind, but managed to stay in view of the two.

"Shh," the first girl said. "Okay. Is the plan set for tonight?"

"No. There's a party tonight," the other replied.

"Party?" she yelled, and the word bounced along the walls. I ducked behind the bend on the staircase, both intrigued and terrified.

"Yes, and I have to go. We'll have to do it before the final stop."

"You're delaying plans far too much—"

"The time will come!" the girl whispered, her voice injected with a dose of harshness.

"Fine. But you know where we're . . ." Her voice lowered.

I kept my ear pressed against the side of the railing, trying to drown the sound of my thumping heartbeat out so I could hear the next girl speak: "I know. We can't do anything tonight. The other boy . . . when the moon appears . . ."

"She'll have enough to deal with. Tomorrow," a voice finalized.

The staircase trembled beneath me. Someone was climbing the staircase.

I spied the deck in front of me, and then dove into a corner behind a large plant. A boy passing by gave me a strange look, but I disregarded his confusion. Instead I kept my eyes glued to the opening of the staircase.

"Arica! What are you doing down there?"

I turned my head to see Logan near the edge of the pool. His arms were folded on the slippery deck.

I looked back into his brown eyes, scrambling for an answer. In my peripheral vision, I saw a figure entering the elevator. The girl that had been coming up the stairs disappeared behind the cool elevator doors. I hadn't managed to get a good enough glimpse of her before the elevator took off.

"What are you doing down there?" he repeated.

"Uh, I dropped something. But I found it." I stayed glued to my spot. My legs burned from staying in my crouched position for too long.

He removed his folded arms from the deck. "Are you coming in?"

I removed my eyes from his and stood. "I don't think so. You should stay. Have a fun time."

"No, wait!" He climbed out of the pool and then wiped himself down with a towel.

"Listen, I've gotta go—"

"Do you want to hear the spell or not?" He took a step toward me.

"What?"

"I can tell you a spell. It'll slow down the aura—make you . . . *smell* nicer, for the animals' sakes."

"Gee, thanks."

He rolled his eyes. "Seriously. I wrote it down." He patted his pockets, looking confused. "I think I left it in my cabin. Wanna come?"

"I'm supposed to be setting up for the party." My cheeks reddened. This was an obvious lie. Set-up wasn't supposed to begin until six o'clock sharp.

"I'm sure you've got some extra time," he said, strolling toward me. He clicked the elevator button and stood beside me in silence, keeping his head high.

I sighed, knowing I couldn't escape. He walked into the elevator squarely, and I reluctantly followed by his side.

The quaint elevator music played a lovely tune until a short *ding* sounded when we reached the fourth floor. The doors opened to the narrow hall, and Logan strolled toward the left. Just as he reached his cabin, he sighed.

"What's wrong?"

He patted his pocket. "Forgot my key-card. Wait here—this will only take a sec." He disappeared back into the elevator with a short wave.

"Arica!" two mimicking voices chimed. I turned to see the twins.

"Hey!" I called, mildly surprised by their appearance. "How are things with Summer?"

"Not good," Janine replied. "She's starting to figure out that we're up to something. We're going to have to get the party ready sooner than we'd expected."

"What do you mean?" I asked.

"I *mean* we have to go—now!" She tugged on my arm and jabbed her thumb at the elevator button.

"It's too slow," Jess muttered. "Let's take the staircase."

"Whoa, whoa, whoa," I said hurriedly, regarding them. "I'm supposed to wait for Logan."

"Well, he'll just have to wait for you, won't he?" Janine stated, and then the twins led me back up the stairs.

"Honestly, can't this wait?" I whined. "I was just figuring out how to smell better—"

"*Smell* better?" Jess retorted. "How about you try something called *perfume*."

"I meant with my powers," I clarified.

The twins stared at me with glassy, innocent eyes.

"There's a strong smell that can apparently exude from me when I overuse my powers," I explained.

"Since when are you *exuding* too much power? You don't even have your gemstone!" Janine denied. "And I certainly don't smell anything. Even without my necklace, I still have a pretty good sense of judgement."

"Janine! Jess! Arica!" Drake called, his head peeking over the top of the staircase. "I've just made Summer stand in line at the hot dog stand downstairs. That'll literally take hours."

"Good idea!" Jess agreed. "How can we help?"

Drake's body became more visible as we reached the upper deck. He wore a T-shirt that displayed a rock band I'd never heard of, and his eyes were wild with stress and excitement. He looked as if he hadn't gotten much sleep.

"So, let's start setting up, then?" Janine suggested.

"Yeah," I agreed. I moved forward, but then realized that Drake and the twins weren't following me. They were staring at me intently, but I had no idea why.

"What?" I asked.

"Do you really think we're gonna set this up *manually*?" Drake asked. "You're the Prophetic Child! Summon some stuff up!"

I supposed I hadn't realized how easily I could access my powers, even without my gemstone. I lifted my hands and envisioned the deck adorned with banners hanging from the string of lights above, and soon enough, the tables rearranged themselves to form a giant S. Flowers began to bloom magically from vases on each table, and a warm, dim glow emerged from the lights, making the deck feel as warm as melted butter.

"Summer is going to love this. I can't thank you guys enough!" He reached out for a hug, but soon looked as if he was about to vomit. He bolted down the stairs and retched.

"Oh my days!" Janine exclaimed. "I'll call Raven. She'll know what's wrong."

"No!" Drake yelled harshly from below. He cleared his throat. "I'm fine. Probably something I ate. I'm just going back to my cabin." I heard a chorus of footsteps and no more. Drake had left.

"What's wrong with Drake?" I asked.

"I don't know, but I don't want him to miss Summer's party! We really should call Raven—"

"Who needs to call me?" Raven asked. She had just appeared from the elevator, and was now strolling toward us. "Do you guys need something?"

"It was Drake," I explained. "He was fine just a minute ago, and then he ran off and threw up."

"Ooh," Raven said, and then she inhaled sharply. "Probably those nasty hot dogs. I better make sure Summer doesn't get those."

"Yeah, wouldn't want the birthday girl throwing up now, too," Jess said. Her twin chuckled.

I agreed, but still didn't feel like a hot dog was the reason for Drake's sudden disappearance.

"Newt, weather report for tonight, please," Raven said, placing the Weather Lizard on her hand. Newt gleefully turned a beautiful shade of navy blue.

"Looks good," Raven said. "Tonight should be cloudless. Perfect for the party." Newt scampered up to her shoulder and hid in the folds of her hair.

"Newty, I'm ticklish!" Raven laughed. I noticed Newt lying comfortably beside her neck, but he didn't look so navy blue anymore. In fact, he looked a deep, charcoal black.

"What happens when Newt turns black?" I asked Raven almost absentmindedly. I was regarding Newt carefully, wondering if my eyes were betraying me.

"It means something bad, or evil, is stirring. Or perhaps just some really horrible weather. Why?" Newt emerged from her hair, orange now, just as he had looked when I'd first seen him.

"Nothing," I replied quickly. "Let's go to Summer."

But in the back of my mind, I knew something was wrong. If Newt had turned black, then that meant something bad would happen. I was hoping Newt had just misinterpreted something, that he was mistaken. Unfortunately, that didn't seem likely. I tried to remain calm as we descended the staircase, but I still couldn't shake the fact that, just possibly, there was something bound to go wrong tonight.

SIXTEEN: CELEBRATION

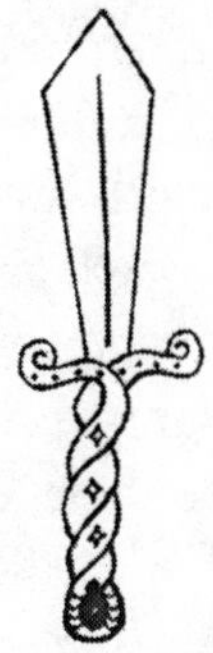

By 7 pm the deck was full of commotion. Raven, Violet, and the twins were standing with me near the elevators. Raven had supplied us all with dresses and other necessities for tonight's party (discreetly, of course, to make sure Summer wouldn't notice), and she'd also sent messages through The Kite Postal and Gift Services to several cabins to invite them to the party. Staring at the cluster of people, it seemed as if every single sorcerer and sorceress had been invited. Even Newt and Musky tagged along, with Raven's discretion.

I was currently staring at a cherry pie with a feverish look in my eyes. Steam wafted from the holes lightly pressed into the surface, and plump red cherries spilled from the sides when I cut into the oozing filling.

"Drake said to wait," Joseph sang annoyingly. "Not until Summer comes—"

"Joseph, Joseph, Joseph!" Jess cried. "Could you *possibly*, just *once*, stop acting like Mum? It's like the Hill Valley feast all over again!"

Joseph clenched his hands. "I. Am. Not. Acting. Like. Mum!" Joseph fumed. His face flushed tomato red.

"Ugh!" Janine cried. "Don't eat this, don't do that—"

"Janine! Jess!" I moaned. I looked back at the pie sulkily. "Joseph's right. We have to wait for Summer. She'll be coming up soon." I examined the sky's face as it darkened.

The twins reluctantly stopped talking. I pushed the plate of pie aside, stomach growling.

Violet glanced at her watch and let out an exasperated sigh. "Seriously, is she coming or not?"

A boy, whom I recognized as Logan, frantically ran across the deck. "Everyone, hide, quick! Summer's coming upstairs with Drake!"

Murmurs swept through the crowd, and a hushed sense of fear spiralled in the air. The twins and I sat tucked under the table. I held my breath as footsteps thudded up the staircase.

When Summer's feet were visible near the entrance, we all sprang out from behind the tablecloths.

"Surprise!" we yelled. Summer, dressed in a strange outfit I suppose she'd bought from France, looked horrified, and then delighted. She yelped and covered her face with her hands.

"Zis is pour *moi*?" she asked, looking at the streaming banner above her. The words HAPPY BIRTHDAY, SUMMER! were neatly pasted on the banner.

"I cannot believe zis!" she exclaimed, and then she leaned forward to give Drake a tremendous hug. Drake looked a little startled, but still pleased by her reaction. He wore a tie, which I found completely unexpected for his tastes. The way he was dressed tonight reminded me of something—of someone . . .

"Well? Pie time?" Adam prompted, holding the cherry pie in his hands.

"Definitely," Drake replied.

The crowd rushed over to the buffet, and the juice bar was suddenly shrouded by figures. I collected my food hurriedly in the rush, and grabbed a seat at a table close enough to overlook the ocean view. Moonlight shimmered along the ocean surface; the moon looked distorted and rippled on the moving water.

"There's only one more night on the Water Train, you know," Adam informed. "Andrae told me."

"Ah, pour vous," Summer inquired. "But I want to stay on zis train forever." She turned to Drake affectionately. He tore a grin, but his eyes portrayed sadness.

"Like the pie?" he asked finally. He took a bite and chewed slowly, as if savouring the taste. Then he stood abruptly, a weary look crossing his face. "I'm not very hungry anymore."

"Non?" Summer asked worriedly. "Why not, mon cherie?"

He bit his lip and turned away, moving toward the railing. I dropped my napkin on the table and followed him.

"What's wrong?" I asked, observing his face. He looked younger, but his face was weathered with stress. Small laugh lines were visible near his lips.

He looked at the moon. I followed his gaze to the bright, circular face that peered over the world. "It's so far away," he stated.

I didn't quite understand what he was trying to say, so I only lifted my eyebrow. "Yes . . . but there's nothing we can do about that."

"Yeah." He looked down at the ocean. "It's so far away . . . but it has a strong connection to me. Like me and my brother."

"Brother?" I questioned.

"Yeah. We were separated at birth—my mom told me about it. He lived with my dad, but I haven't heard from them in a while. My dad was a conductor. He loved mortal music. He used to study it so much that he decided to move to the mortal world. Heck, my dad was *named* after Mozart." He laughed.

I wondered why he was revealing so much to me rather than Summer, who was daintily eating a salad.

"And then he died unexpectedly. I don't even know where my brother went. As for my mom . . . she left, too. And just before I boarded the Train, I met Summer." His eyes lit up. "That just got me thinking about how much I care about Summer; how much time I spend with her, and how much time I wished I'd spent with my family."

"My dad died when I was younger, too. The thought would always cross my mind, but one day you learn that they never leave you."

"Who?" he asked, his eyes still glued to the ocean.

I hesitated, and then said, "The ones you love."

At this, his face turned green. He slapped his hand over his mouth.

"Drake?" I asked, hands placed on his shoulders. "What's going on?"

He stared at me with wild eyes, but then his eyes seemed to change. They became hungrier, darker, and somehow more oval-shaped. He fled the deck and ran back down the stairs, just as he'd done earlier in the day.

"Drake!" I called, running after him, but halted when a large shadow spread across the deck. A cool wind whipped from the side, and the lights above us flickered and died out. The deck had become eerily dark. Yelps and whispers filled the cool air.

"What haz happened?" Summer cried, looking over the Water Train's railing. She turned toward me, her brows deeply furrowed.

After she spoke, I noticed dark figures moving through the water. At first they looked like thick squiggles, but as they approached they became clearer. The ocean they moved through looked like black ink.

"The Black Trench," Violet whispered with a shudder. "The darkest part of the Bermuda Triangle is the Black Trench. It's filled with horrible, ravenous sea monsters . . ." Her voice became a whisper and she clamped her hand over her mouth. Everyone's mouths hung agape with fear.

The dark shadow disappeared in the water. For a moment, it seemed as if the monsters had disappeared; as if all was well.

As quick as a light I felt a stabbing pain in the small of my back. My vision turned black, but I could still hear and feel the wind around me. The palpable fear that was once surrounding me had disappeared. The air suddenly felt moist, and beads of sweat formed on my forehead. The blackness of my vision slowly dissipated until my normal vision returned. The first thing I saw was bright, red curtains that drew around the room in a circle. Then my vision illuminated a man who wore a blindingly white suit, and stood before a table covered in blue tablecloth that looked like moving water. A clear glass ball filled with foggy cloud wisps lay on the cloth. The man's face showed the barest hint of emotion—amusement.

Everything seemed so silent in here. But where was *here*, exactly?

"Hello there!" the man said, a crooked grin spreading over his face. "Would you like me to predict . . . your *future*?" He shuffled a deck of cards in his hands.

I wondered if I'd heard him correctly. "Sorry," I said absently, rubbing my forehead. "What did you say?"

"Your future, dear," the man continued, delicately moving the cards in his hands. He seemed very tranquil. "I can foretell it, if you wish."

"Future?" I asked, a part of me intrigued, but then remembered the situation I was in. Perhaps I was just hallucinating, having a strange delusion after seeing a shadow in the Black Trench. But then why did all this feel so real?

"Um . . . no. No thanks." My throat was suddenly very dry. When would this strange hallucination end?

"The cards are calling you. You cannot walk away." The cards in his hands had spread out into a fan. "Pick one," he said softly, lowering the cards toward me.

I was about to shake my head, but then I heard something very strange. *"Come . . ."* the cards said, over and over. *"Come . . ."*

The words continued until I felt like they were grabbing my arm and forcing me to pick a card. My fingers tingled and shivered as they inched toward the deck. I gently plucked one card from the pile and stared at the moving image.

"Well? What is it?" he asked anxiously.

I looked up speechlessly. "K-king . . . king of hearts," I managed.

His brows rose, and wrinkles formed on his forehead. "The king you say? How intriguing. How very intriguing . . ."

I stood in place awkwardly before setting the card down on the table. "Sorry, I really have to go—"

"Arica Miller," the man said, and I wondered how he knew my name. His tranquil expression wavered. "I see the Train is in some trouble now." He wrung his fingers together uneasily. "We have entered the Black Trench . . . a very dark, dark, foreboding place," he added hauntingly. His fingers moved up to his brownish-gray beard and began stroking it. "Your card?" he asked after a moment.

"I already told you, it's the king of—"

"*Show* it to me," he clarified.

After a moment's hesitation, I handed him the card from the table. He regarded it carefully.

"The crown . . ." he muttered after a moment. "Where is the crown?"

I took the card from his hand and looked at the image of the king. He kept moving back and forth, as if he were pacing around his room. The crown that had once been on his head was now missing.

I shuddered involuntarily, and the thought of the missing Jewel sprang to mind. I thought back to the thief and the note he or she had given me. The thief was definitely on the Water Train, but *where* exactly was the thief keeping the Jewel?

The man took the card from my hand and began shuffling it into the deck. He fanned the cards out again and told me to select one. I pulled out a joker. Instead of wearing his usual hat, the joker was wearing a crown: the Jewel.

All colour drained from the man's face. "It seems as though you will confront the joker—the thief—in a mere *ten minutes*!" the man cried.

"T-ten minutes?" I gasped. The man nodded, pondering, and looked deep down into the crystal ball. The wisps that were once white and cloud-like looked like dark thunderclouds.

A feeling of eeriness curled around me. I felt the urge to leave, immediately, because the man was slowly gazing up with a look of horror spread across his face.

"You share something with the thief . . . something you would never think possible."

"W-what?" I clenched my fists to stop them from shaking.

He moistened his lips slowly, his breath coming out ragged with phlegm. He spoke one word, one syllable, and at first I didn't register what it was. I didn't want to believe what it was.

I stumbled backward, disbelief building inside me, and then without truly discerning what this meant, I ran from the man's table. Tears formed in my eyes, making the curtains look like a giant blob. I ran farther, and then stopped as I felt the same strange stabbing pain in my back. The world dissolved into blackness, and I felt as if I could hear the forceful ocean waves roaring in my ears.

I had reappeared on the deck. During all this, my brain was moving a hundred miles per hour. The single word he had said had disappeared from my mind, blocked out now, because I didn't want to remember it.

I turned to see Adam. He was standing by the railing, looking calm, as if I had never left. But *had* I left? I couldn't exactly figure out what had just happened.

Adam's face looked long and pale in the moonlight. He pulled out the Wishing Knife from a niche in his pocket and held it to his lips. As he whispered words into the tip of the knife, his breath came out in cool puffs of smoke. I wondered how his breath could possibly show on such a warm evening, but then I, too, saw my breath come out in puffs. The hairs on my arms rose—it didn't feel like it was cold, but rather the eeriness seemed to make everything, mainly the atmosphere, feel icier.

Adam finally let the Wishing Knife go, and a glowing blue aura surrounded the blade. Everything around us seemed to grow darker; I could barely make out anyone's faces on the deck now, apart from the whites of the twins' wide, fearful eyes beside me.

"How long do you think it'll last?" a man asked nearby. I turned and noticed Logan, wearing the same orange surf shirt and matching shorts. "How long?" he asked again, intrigued.

"I—I don't know," I muttered, staring into his wide eyes. "I've never been in the Black Trench before."

"Maybe we should go down below to the safer floors," he said, his gaze shifting to the bright moon, which now shed the only light on the deck.

I noticed that Adam was still standing near the railing, and Janine and Jess remained by my side. "It's not working," Adam said with aggravation. He held his knife out to illuminate the ocean, but it seemed as if the blue light would dim whenever it moved near the water. "The water here is charmed. We can't see anything."

Raven headed toward us (I could only recognize her in the dimness due to her highlights), and then nodded toward Logan. "The guy's right. We need to move to lower floors. We don't know how the safe the Black Trench is—or what sort of *monsters* are lurking below us." She gave Violet a particularly harsh stare. "C'mon—Newt is getting scared."

"Please," Violet replied harshly, "How would you know if *Newt* is scared?"

"Now's not the time to fight, *Violet*," Raven said, maybe a little too angrily. "Let's get a move on."

Violet crossed her arms, but the fear was still evident on her face. "Yeah. Fine."

Several of the sorcerers on deck had already decided to leave. The elevators were crammed full, and the stairs were also flooded. I was about to follow the crowd when Janine shot into view, her face sickly pale, as if she'd just thrown up. She grabbed both of my shoulders and gazed at me intensely with her bright blue eyes.

"Arica . . . Arica, I saw something."

"Saw what? A monster?" I asked frantically.

"No—I mean I *saw* something. A . . . a *vision*." The last word came out as a shaky whisper. "Of something flying over the Train."

"Flying . . . as in a bird?"

"No . . . something bigger," she said, her body trembling now. Janine opened her mouth to go on, but then her attention was redirected to the sky. I removed my gaze from the pandemonium of sorcerers flooding the deck and focused on the sky. It looked like a sheet of endless darkness and nothing more.

"I saw it taking me, Arica," Janine said worriedly. "And then I saw Jess—oh, Jess, looking so very worried about me. Oh my—" Janine choked on her words. She pressed her hand to her mouth as if she couldn't go on.

"You saw *it* taking you? What do you mean, *it*?"

"I—I don't know. But whatever it is, Arica, it's coming. I was on the deck when it happened. And it's going to happen—soon. *Very* soon."

"C'mon, Janine!" Joseph called. He pulled her by the arm and dragged her using his scrawny arms. "Let's go!"

"No!" Janine said, pulling away and running toward the middle of the deck. She pointed her face toward the sky, and the wind began blowing harder. I heard something like a splash of water, and then ran to the railing and bent my body as low as I dared. Something was stirring in the water below, causing calm ripples to walk along the surface.

I bent closer, the fog of my breath clouding my vision, and waited. The wind grew calm for a moment. I stared at the water, watching the pattern of ripples slowly grow larger and larger, until a figure emerged from the blackness. It looked like a green splotch, but then it flew into the sky and I could barely catch sight of it. I spun on my heels and watched as the green figure flew over the train in a grand arc. By the time it hit the ocean on the other side, I noticed what was wrong with the picture. The green splotch looked all too familiar in its movement; I'd seen the fireflies place themselves in a similar formation earlier on the Train.

And then, as I stared forward, my stomach twisted into seventeen knots.

Janine was gone.

"Janine?!" I called, turning in circles. I buried my face in my hands, my mind spinning with realization. Janine had gone, perhaps been kidnapped, just as she'd envisioned only a minute before. She'd watched her own fate echo in her mind.

"Where on Earth—?!" Joseph cried. He was scanning the deck frantically. "Where's my sister?"

"It was her vision," I explained numbly. "She saw herself getting captured—I get it. The fireflies—that green splotch—they were a distraction. For it to take Janine . . . ."

"It?" Joseph replied, infuriated.

"I—I don't know." I felt like an ice cube had slid down my throat, and as much as I tried to hide it, I could feel tears beginning to burn in my eyes.

It seemed as though Raven, Violet, Adam, and Jessica had noticed the situation, too. Jess stepped forward, clearly distressed and shocked, and looked as if she was about to run forward and off the Train itself. I ran to her and steadied her before she could do anything irrational.

Jess looked just as bewildered as her brother. "What took Janine? Where is she?" Jess looked like she was going to sob, but then something stopped her. She turned up her nose and pressed her lips together. "I smell it. The evil . . ."

I wondered how she could possibly access her powers, but now wasn't the time to ponder. We were in a difficult situation, and if Jess was sensing some evil powers in control of Janine's capture, then we were definitely in trouble. "I've never sensed anything quite like this," Jess said with surprise and numbness. "It's not something *human* that captured Janine. It was something in the water—in the Black Trench."

"You don't mean . . ." Raven swallowed gravely. "I mean, I've heard of creatures in the Black Trench, but I haven't travelled on the Train enough to really know," she excused. "If they want Janine . . . they want someone who has visions—who can see the future."

"*They*? I thought it was an *it.*"

"Not if we're talking about the Water Guardians," Violet explained, and then lifted her eyebrows when my face remained blank. My ignorance caused her to groan. "I don't think I could fully explain them properly. But if we're near the home of the Water Guardians, then it can only mean one thing." She paused, and then, in a haunting voice, she said, "Mermaids."

Joseph looked up, aghast. "Mermaids . . . you mean those fireflies were a distraction for *mermaids* to take her?"

"That's not possible," Raven rationalized. "Mermaids can't just walk onto the deck and take a human. No—there must've been some other magical force involved."

"Are you saying she just . . . *vaporized*?" Adam suggested. "Even *I* can't make a person disappear. Only my father would know how."

"Father?" I questioned, my voice hoarse. I swallowed loudly, the lump in my throat still aching.

"He has the ability to summon a person at his will . . . . Well, he could still do that if he had his crown. But he doesn't," he denied. He ran his hand through his golden hair.

Joseph looked down, his face a mask of sorrow, and then suddenly jerked his head up. "Wait—that's right! He doesn't have his crown, but the thief does! Which means the thief is in charge of this—of taking Janine."

"But I thought there were mermaids involved?" I questioned. I rubbed my forehead. It was all too confusing, and if I was going to sort out these answers, I would have to figure it out myself.

Jess quivered in her spot. She seemed extremely fazed by the situation, the moonlight just barely illuminating the tears streaming down her face. She finally spoke up: "I've got to go down there," Jess said, and by "down there" I supposed she meant the water; it was clearly where everyone thought Janine had gone, since Violet had proposed the involvement of mermaids. "I *have* to get my sister!" she continued with a shrill voice.

"Jess, you can't go down there. I won't let you get taken, too," Joseph decided. "But Arica . . . Arica could go down there without getting hurt. Her powers would save her."

I nearly hesitated, but I knew wasting even a second could mean precious time lost to find Janine. Like Joseph said, I could protect myself with my powers—but then again, what was I actually protecting myself *from*?

"I'll go, too," Adam said. His breath came out heavily, and I could tell something was on his mind besides Janine's capture. Sweat beads glistened from his forehead.

"No—if there's something in the water that's potentially harmful, you have to protect the others." I pointed to his Wishing Knife. His eyes followed my hand, and then he nodded. Of course he would nod; it was his duty to protect others. Even back at Hill Valley he'd been protecting me to ensure that Lembrose was doing her job. As a noble, it was manufactured in his genes. Protecting others was second nature for him.

"Joseph, Jessica, Raven, Summer and Violet should all stay here with me," Adam said. "We don't know if anything's going to attack the Train anytime soon. We are in the *Black Trench* after all," he explained, though his expression looked pained. "Joseph, be ready to blast light if anything shows up. Raven—send out a kite to see if we can get a distress signal out. Perhaps someone at the Sorcerer Palace could contact us. Jessica can sense if any more evil will show up. And Summer and Violet . . ."

At this moment, I realized that Adam hadn't even had a proper introduction to Violet. Well, at least one I hadn't seen. But there wasn't time for introductions right now. Adam was surely trying to figure out what Summer and Violet's powers were, but the strange thing was, even *I* didn't know what their powers were. They never wore their gemstones, and they didn't even bother bringing up their magical abilities.

"I'll just keep a lookout," Violet rushed, and Summer nodded silently by her side, looking down. "Arica, you should go. Janine needs saving—*now.*"

I swallowed. "But how do I get down there?" I really wanted to say: *"How do I get down there, in the water, with a bunch of vicious sea creatures and mermaids that I have to fight off all by myself? Not to mention I need to save my cousin!"* though I knew my inner ramblings weren't exactly appropriate for the situation.

"That won't be a problem," Adam said. The Wishing Knife appeared in his right hand. He held it to his lips, murmured an inaudible sentence, and then extended his arm toward me. The blade was placed horizontally to my body.

"Here," he said. "Take it, and you should appear wherever Janine is safely."

I lingered there for a moment, and then grabbed the glowing blade carefully. As soon as my fingers met the blade, I felt as if I had gripped a hot stone. The last thing I saw was Adam's face slowly dissolving into a mass of blackness.

The only sensation left in my body was the hot, searing pain I felt in my fingertips from touching the blade. Slowly, the sound of my beating heart began to throb in my ears. The blade still burned my fingertips, and then, in a split second, the pain vanished. I felt as if a cool wave of water had enveloped my hand and extinguished the invisible fire that was lit to it.

My eyelids flew open. At first, everything looked like a distorted mush of blue and green, but then my vision cleared. By the looks of it, I was planted right in the middle of a giant ocean. The water around me looked sea green, and small creatures which I recognized as fish travelled to the reefs in front of me.

I took a breath, expecting my throat to swell and choke up, but instead I felt like I was taking a breath of fresh air. For a moment I felt as light as a feather, but then I snapped back to reality. I was in the Black Trench, though all my mind could formulate was: *Why does the water look so green if it's called the Black Trench?*

At that instant, I turned my head and noticed that something was approaching me—something that looked an awful lot like a shark. A scream issued from my throat, but it sounded more like a giant gurgle. Tiny bubbles escaped my mouth as I wriggled my arms back and forth, struggling to reach the surface. When I broke through the water, the first thing I heard was Raven's voice:

"Where's Janine?! Did you save her?"

I sputtered, heaved in a load of air, and rubbed my eyes. Strangely, the water looked like a giant expanse of blackness from above.

"I—" I managed half of a gasp before my voice was cut short. Two icy hands wrapped around my ankles. I was forced back into the water. My eyes were wide with alert as I struggled to look back at the figure that was pulling me down.

The icy hands felt like handcuffs on my feet. I kicked and flailed, but its hands were like metal. Finally, the hands released hold of me. Before I could move an inch, I felt long green strips of something that looked like seaweed being wrapped around my body. They tightened around my arms, legs, neck, everything but my face. I felt like a giant piece of sushi.

The figure moved in front of me. It was a girl, but she was not wholly human. She had no legs, but rather a long tail of green scales that ended near her waist. Diamonds and pearls glittered from her necklace. A starfish charm hung on the bottom of the necklace, and she held a trident in her hand. Even before I could comprehend anything else, I knew that she was a mermaid.

She poised the trident against my neck. "You know not of the waters you enter," she said. Her voice made me cringe, like hearing nails on a chalkboard. Her fire-orange hair spread around her in long strands, and her skin was white as snow. The mermaid's cheeks, though, were so sallow they looked gray. Her eyes gleamed silver; she gave a penetrating stare that drilled straight through me.

A growl escaped her throat. "Your friend is very valuable. Not as valuable as *you* . . . but still important." She clucked her tongue. "Ah, it would be a shame to rid of someone so valuable from this world." The trident's tips dug deeper into my skin. I flinched.

The mermaid laughed in a low, guttural tone. Then her eyes narrowed. "She sees if it will be taken. You must make her see!" She pushed me to the side. My view spun toward Janine, who was positioned against a rock, her body entangled in a web of seaweed. A cage of mermaids surrounded her. The scene reminded me of the snakes coiling Jess during the battle on Halloween night.

The mermaid spun me back around by the shoulders. "Make her see, and you shall be freed." Her mouth curled into an ominous smile. Short, gray fangs protruded from her upper jaw.

I felt the seaweed tighten around me until I nodded. The mermaid looked pleased for a moment, and then returned to her grimace. She prodded me forward with her trident, because I was struggling to move through the water with the seaweed stuck to me like glue. Finally the wrapping loosened, and I was free to move toward Janine.

The mermaids surrounding her dispersed at my arrival, and then I found myself staring at an unconscious Janine.

"Janine," I called, my voice somehow audible underwater. "Janine? Can you hear me?" I gently tugged at the seaweed that encircled her body. Her eyes were closed, cheeks flustered, but then she looked as if a bolt of electricity had awoken her and her eyes shot open.

"Arica!" she cried. "What are you doing here? The mermaids will see—"

"They already know," I explained, wondering how she was able to speak underwater as well. "They want me to tell you something. They need you to see . . . they need you to look into the future."

"Why?" Her voice quivered.

"Hurry . . ." the mermaids taunted. Their bright tails illuminated the darkness beneath me.

"Because . . . I don't know. But they'll let us free after. Just make a vision come to you."

Janine looked up. The Water Train was a moving silhouette above the water. "I've never done it before . . . I don't think—"

"You did it just before, on the Train," I encouraged.

"But that was different," she explained. "I wasn't trying . . ."

"You can do it again. Trust me."

Janine nodded her head grimly. Then she closed her eyes and pressed her lips together firmly. After a few tedious seconds, her entire body began to shake.

"Janine?" I asked, my chest tight with concern. "What's going on?" I took hold of her shoulders. Her entire body shuddered as if an earthquake were passing beneath us. I called out her name again, but she didn't respond. For a moment I was afraid that she wouldn't ever stop; that she would never see the vision and we'd be trapped here forever.

Suddenly her eyelids lifted to show her eyes: a startling sea-blue that made her look frantic and horrified. She stopped moving. "I saw it," she warbled, half-whispering. "You were holding it."

"Holding what?" My hands trembled at my sides.

"The Jewel—the crown! You had it!" she exclaimed. "But it gets worse. The mermaids . . . I think they're working for the thief. They want to know if you're going to take the crown from him or her."

"Well?" the mermaid prompted. She'd appeared from nowhere. Her voice was cold and venomous.

I spun around quickly. The mermaids were surrounding us, moving closer as the seconds ticked by.

"What does she *see*?" a blond mermaid asked. Her eyes were a startling shade of blue and her lips were as green as the seaweed that entangled her hair. "Our master is waiting! We must tell him! What does she *see*?" the fiery orange-haired one asked.

Janine's cries became audible. "Don't tell them, Arica! They're working for the thief!"

"Silence!" The orange-haired mermaid stuck her trident at Janine's neck.

"She sees nothing," I said firmly.

"Liar!" a mermaid yelled from the crowd.

"She can't control her powers yet! We don't have our gemstones!" I reasoned.

The orange-haired mermaid gritted her teeth, a growl escaping her throat. She released the trident from Janine's neck. Janine slumped down, heaving.

"No matter. I—and only I—can see through the falsity of your claims." She pressed her hand against her necklace. The starfish charm began to glow, and a golden light radiated from her body. A faint, distorted noise, like a chorus of voices, sounded from her necklace.

The mermaid smiled widely. The sounds grew louder, and I soon recognized it as music. A somewhat cheery tune, complete with violins and fiddles, but a haunting voice later drowned out the cheeriness of the song. A woman's voice elevated an octave with each note, until it was so high I was sure I heard glass breaking. The voice ended abruptly. A shred of silence hung like thick smog in the air, and then the mermaid looked up. A smile curled on her lips.

"Lies," she finalized. "I demand the truth; our master will not do with anything otherwise."

I shook my head, examining the crowd. "Tell us who the thief is, and then we'll reveal the truth." There was a strange confidence in my voice that I surely wasn't feeling inside.

The mermaid cackled. "You still haven't figured it out? Why, surely I thought it would be right under your nose . . . ."

"Tell us who it is!" I demanded. The mermaids looked taken aback.

The orange-haired mermaid came closer. She began circling me, eyes wide.

"You're very . . . young. And so . . . *eager*." The mermaid moved so close to me that our faces were mere inches apart. "I will propose something to you," she began. "I'll show you the thief. But then you must obey. You must tell me what she saw."

I didn't hesitate. "Deal."

The mermaid half-smiled. She lowered her trident and turned, moving toward a curtain of giant seaweed. I followed behind her, passing the crowd of mermaids as they rumbled with laughter.

I moved through the layer of seaweed with some difficulty and found myself at an odd cave entrance. The mermaid moved to the side of the cave, pressing her ear against the rock. I, too, lightly brushed my ear against the rocky enclosure. A hollow *ping* reverberated off the dank walls, as if someone was mining inside.

"Master is at work," the mermaid whispered gently. She turned her eyes on me. They began turning a faint red colour. "Which means you must tell me the vision, or I will not pass such information in return."

"No. Show me the thief and . . ." I gritted my teeth. "And *then* I'll tell you what she saw."

Crinkles formed between the mermaid's brows. "As you wish." She drifted toward the entrance of the cavern. Two torches were lit on either side, emitting a strangely inviting heat. I didn't know how torches could possibly be lit underwater, but I had a theory. One name crossed through my mind over and over: Geoff.

The mermaid led me into the cavern, and I felt as if I'd walked into a giant bubble. The cavern must've been enchanted because it was not filled with water. It almost reminded me of stepping into the Golden Cave, except this setting was obviously much darker. The hollow *ping*s became louder with each step I took inside. The mermaid seemed to float on invisible water (which made it look like she was hovering) as she headed toward a bubbling cauldron. I recognized the cauldron as the one I'd seen in the basement the night I'd met Rowen with the Dungeon Drop.

"Massster," she hissed, "is busy. He cannot show his full form."

"Full form?" I questioned. "How am I supposed to know who this is if I can't see the thief's full *for—*"

"Quiet!" she snapped, but in a harsh whisper. "Ah, here he comes."

I saw a pair of feet, beneath a ruffling cloak, shuffle toward the cauldron. The figure added tiny green leaves to the frothing substance, and then hurried off.

"I have shown you the thief. Now you must inform me of the vision," the mermaid stated, turning toward me. She clenched her teeth menacingly.

"What do you mean? I didn't even *see* who it—"

"See?" She scoffed. "I did indeed say I would *show* you thief . . . which I have done. That was our agreement. I would never reveal his name."

I could feel the heat in my cheeks. "*Tell* me who it is, or the deal's off."

"We only refer to him as Master! You do not deserve to know his name." Her eyes began glowing yellow. "What does the Visioner see?" she implored.

Rage boiled inside me. "This wasn't our deal. *None* of this was our deal. If you want Janine's vision, you won't have it." I'd never felt more determined and stubborn in my life.

The mermaid turned the corners of her lips down to form a small grimace. "Deal . . . what a mundane mortal word to use. Mortals always expect the truth to surface from a world of lies; one day they must realize that a lie is only a secondary version of the truth."

My cheeks burned. I clenched my fists with rage. "Let us go," I demanded.

She cackled. "Let *you* go? A deal we have made, yes, but you have not yet fulfilled your requirements."

I looked through the murky water. Everything seemed so peaceful from down here.

"Where is the Knife?" she interrogated.

"Where is it?" another seethed.

My mind throbbed wildly. I had the Wishing Knife with me when I appeared in the water, but since then it had completely slipped my mind. Where had it gone? Maybe it was charmed to magically return to its owner—Adam?

"I don't have it," I said weakly, thoughts running through my mind.

The mermaid made a very strange growl, one that reminded me of the wolves in Bailey Park a week before Halloween night.

"If such a situation seems of no matter to you, then I must tempt you to see otherwise." She pointed to a giant castle on my left side. A blue aura enveloped the castle, causing undefined shadows to bounce along the ground. I hadn't noticed this before, but two unkindly mermen guards held tridents poised to protect the entrance. "The home of the Water Guardians," she captioned. "Such a horrible place—a prison for the aquatic, if you will. It holds the most sickly, unearthly creatures, to portray the"—she smirked—"*disloyalty* of the Royal family."

"Disloyalty?" I pondered.

For a moment, it looked like steam was coming out of the mermaid's ears. "Yes, *disloyalty*," she said, giving each syllable an equally irritated stab of cynicism. "Do you believe we follow the Jewel's thief for no apparent reason? He is our Master, for the Royals abandoned us in the Black Trench. They have not let us roam freely among the mortal world; a watery curtain restricts us from moving past the Bermuda Triangle."

"Have you ever thought that maybe they don't want mortals to *see* mermaids?" I probed, but I immediately wished I hadn't spoken.

This time I was sure I could see smoke escaping her ears, and possibly even nostrils. "No. But they still believe in those futile fairy tales, do they not?" Her voice escalated with anger. "You see, child, we wish to serve our master as best we can. We are both on the same side—against the Royals. They regard themselves so highly. But why is it that they do not see our troubles? That it is always the most innocent who are found in places for one who is guilty?"

I swallowed roughly. For once, the mermaids' case was actually making sense. I still didn't believe the Royals were as bad as the mermaids set them out to be, but the leader's innocence was really starting to beat down on me. Or maybe it was just her own charmed powers causing me to feel sympathy for her?

"Please, you have to let us go," I said. "I feel terrible—really, I do. But if I speak to Prince Adam, I'm sure he'll listen to me. I'm sure he'll find a way to make you feel like you're not . . . trapped anymore. Not contained in the Bermuda Triangle."

The leader's grimace lifted ever so slightly. "Do you speak of the truth?" she asked. I was sure she could check by using her power, which she had performed earlier with her starfish charm necklace, but she seemed to have genuine interest in hearing my answer.

I cleared my throat. "Of course. But, please, you have to release us. Let us get back to the Train so we can confer with the prince and set things right."

Some mermaids had permanent scowls set on their faces, but the leader looked hopeful. "Yes. Of course—anything that will aid my sisters would be most appreciated." I noticed that her tone was unequivocally different from what it had been when she had first spoken to me.

"Well . . . I think we'd really like a spell or something to help us get back to the Train." I nodded toward Janine, and the seaweed was beginning to loosen around her body. She breathed a long sigh of relief.

"Yes, yes, of course," the mermaid agreed eagerly. "Anything to help us get away from such a torturous place." She raised her trident and closed her eyes. It almost seemed like some strange mermaid ritual ceremony was going on, with the mermaids bowing their heads and looking somber. I bowed my head, too, just in case.

In that instant, I heard a *buzz* from beside me. I lifted my head to see if the mermaids noticed, but the leader was still concentrating hard on the spell with her eyes closed. I turned to Janine, but her head was bowed too.

Buzzzz. The sound felt too close for it to be beside me . . . but the only closer place it could be was *inside* me.

Arica? Can you hear me?

I jumped, but it was sort of difficult to do in the water. I recognized Joseph's voice in my mind immediately. "Joseph?" I said mildly.

A black-haired mermaid looked up from the crowd. "Joseph? What is Joseph?"

I stopped mid-breath, realizing I had spoken aloud. Some of the other mermaids were looking up now, wondering what was disrupting the 'ceremony' that was happening.

"Oh . . . Joseph." I swallowed. Janine turned to me, eyes wide. I felt paralyzed in place.

"Joseph," Janine began, tearing her gaze from me, "is a place. Uh—where we're heading, actually. To Joseph." She gulped. I nearly laughed.

"Ah," the mermaid said with cognition. "Indeed. To Joseph, then!" she said, raising a trident.

The others seemed confused, as if they weren't sure if they were supposed to be angry at us. Instead, they recited the words of the black-haired mermaid: "To Joseph!" they called. The main mermaid, whose sallow cheeks were now somehow less gray, opened her eyes. "To . . . Joseph?" she questioned. "If the Prophetic Child says so . . . then it shall be done." The leader looked much more defiant. "Yes—to Joseph, they are heading!"

I turned to Janine, who was sporting a grin. We turned back to the mermaids, and I began to see a sort of water tornado spiralling around us. The mermaids were giving giddy waves, some still scowling, but mostly the scene had becomes the antithesis of what I had arrived to.

My vision began to darken. The mermaids' voices were audible as they cried, "Onward to Joseph!" and "Send a postcard!"

Joseph's voice buzzed in my head again. *Arica, you won't believe what's happened.*

How are you communicating with me? I thought, though I could feel the edges of my mind becoming blurry. Joseph's voice was beginning to fade, along with my vision.

Adam lent me the Wishing Knife. Oh gosh, Arica—have you got Janine? Are you safe?

Yes, I managed, but I couldn't put in any more thought. My brain was slowly turning into a puddle.

You won't believe who's up here—what's happened to him—oh, I can't explain much now. Just . . .

Joseph's words slipped away. I spiralled into darkness, and then woke with a start. The first thing I saw was the deck floor, and then, in front of me, a man wearing strange dress shoes and trousers.

"Arica!" Joseph cried. He bent down, but all I could make out was his glasses on his face. The blurriness finally subsided. Janine was standing on the deck beside me, completely suffocating in Jess's strong grip. Jessica warbled on about something that was too British for me to define, but finally she managed to stop her tears. The twins embraced one another, and in that moment, I was sure they hadn't been this close since the womb.

"You're safe!" Raven cried. She ran over and gave us both hugs. Violet, too, attempted at making a hug, but instead she stuck with a handshake. I was happy she was even attempting to make some sort of polite gesture.

"Where's Summer?" I asked, scanning the deck. It looked almost vacant for the most part, besides the juice bar. "And Drake?"

"You see . . . that's what I meant to tell you . . ." Joseph began, but he seemed too stressed to continue. He instead turned toward the opposite end of the deck, and I followed. Sitting there were Drake and Summer, holding hands with grave faces.

I advanced toward them slowly. "Hey," I said when I was within hearing distance. Drake's ear seemed to twitch at the sound of my voice.

He looked at me absently, then back at Summer. "I'm sorry, Arica. I was going to tell you earlier," he muttered. "I was going to tell you . . ." He quickly hid his arms behind his back as if he didn't want to show me something.

"Tell me what?" I asked. Imaginary gears began clicking in my head.

Drake looked down wordlessly. I noticed that something was very different about his face. His hair seemed thicker than I remembered, and he seemed to have acquired a light case of morning stubble in a matter of minutes. His eyes seemed wider, too, and his arms hairier.

"I need to go," he said suddenly, moving toward the staircase beside the elevator.

"Wait, Drake!" I called, but Adam pulled me back.

"He's going through a tough time," Adam explained.

"What tough time?" I said, struggling to understand his words.

Janine and Jess only looked down, shaking their heads. "Drake must miss him so much," they said.

"Who would he miss?" I asked, most likely looking crazy in front of everyone. "Tell me!"

"Mon chaton," Summer squeaked from behind me. "He . . . Oh, mon chaton!" She began sobbing into her hands.

Her exclaiming *mon chaton* over and over wasn't helping at all. In fact, it only made me more infuriated.

She kept her head buried in her hands. "Go find my Drake! You must talk to *heem*." She extended the last word.

I took a few steps back. "I don't know—"

"Please!" Summer lifted her face from her hands, her face streaked with mascara and tears. "You would know more about his life than anyone else."

"Me?" I said, aghast. "Why would I know?"

"Go! Find heem! He will explain everything."

I knew I couldn't fight any longer. Without taking a glance back at my cousins, I turned and ran down the stairs to Drake's room.

SEVENTEEN: RELATIONS

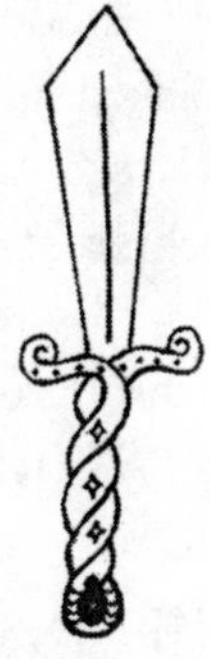

I fled down the stairs quickly, and then paused as soon as I made it to the fourth floor. The air felt much more humid down here, and I could feel perspiration slicking up my palms. As soon as I made it to the hallway, I heard a door slam shut. The sound had undoubtedly come from Drake's cabin.

The noise caused me to jump back, but I knew that I had to move forward. For some reason, the air was so thick that I felt like I was breathing through a pillow—the exact opposite of the atmosphere on the deck. My heart raced unhealthily as I moved closer to his cabin.

My shaking fingers finally tugged on the handle. The door slid open smoothly, revealing a dark setting. I could barely make out the bunks. Portraits lined the wall, now displaying pictures of wolves and coyotes strutting up mountains cast with shadows.

"Drake?" I whispered. There was a slight shuffle from the corner of the room. I noticed a back facing me; a boy crouched on the floor before a tall mirror.

Slowly, I advanced to the mirror. Drake didn't bother looking up, so I crouched down to try and catch a glimpse of him. The hairs on his arms stood upright, and the hair on his head looked like an attacked bird's nest. His shirt looked like it had been ripped from several angles—probably some new unsuccessful fashion statement he was trying to create.

Summer's words ran through my head. Why did she want me to talk to Drake? What was his big secret? I sat behind him warily, my throat dry. The air seemed even hotter in his room. "It's pretty humid down here, don't you think?" I finally managed after a long silence. I moistened my lips.

Drake shifted an inch to his right. "I can't handle cool temperatures. That's why I couldn't stay up on the deck. It leads to greater chances of . . ."

At first, I had no idea what he meant to say. Then my mind reeled—the pieces were beginning to come together. The hairy arms, ripped shirt, his strange hungry, oval eyes.

Could Drake be . . . a wolf?

"Arica, I really did want to tell you before," Drake managed. He turned to me, and his eyes gleamed hazel, like pools of liquid gold. In that instant, I saw the eyes of a wolf staring back at me—not human eyes. Definitely not Drake's eyes.

"That's your secret," I concluded. "You're a . . . a were—"

"Werewolf?" he asked, and then gave a cold laugh. "At first thought, yeah, I guess. My mom was a werewolf. Dad . . . Dad was an animal shape-shifter. And since I'm a dude, I'm an animal shape-shifter just like my dad, too." He spoke quickly, as if he'd been waiting to get that off his chest.

The news left me in a state of shock. If Drake's father was a shape-shifter, he would inherit that power. How could I not realize this before? Drake had never really shown any signs of being a werewolf—or shape-shifter for that matter. But one particular line seemed to be pounding in my head over and over; it was from the conversation I'd heard this morning, between two girls on the staircase near the pool. *The other boy . . . when the moon appears . . .*

When the moon appears—as in a werewolf's change at full moon? Drake did seem to have a lot of connection to the moon, as he'd said earlier before the entire mermaid incident.

"Why shape-shift into a wolf first, then? I mean . . . have you ever changed into anything besides a wolf?"

"A wolf seems like the most instinctual thing, with my mom being one and all. But I did change into a dog once . . . not sure of the type though." He ended off with a heavy sigh.

"You must go through a lot of shirts," I joked, even though on the inside my stomach was crawling.

His expression looked tortured. "Yeah," he responded, his tone huskier than what I remembered. He cradled his legs with his arms, and I just barely caught sight of his black claws expanding into dirty nails. "Yeah, I do," he continued. "What's it matter. I'm off the Train now. My secret's leaked. I'm not a full sorcerer." He stared out the small window perched at the corner of the cabin. I followed his gaze. The full moon glared down on us.

"You didn't have a choice," I suspected, turning back to him.

"No," he agreed, and then we lapsed back into silence. He didn't speak for a while, so I shifted into a more comfortable position against the wall.

"Summer knows," he finally admitted. "Summer was the only one who knew."

"How long has this been going on for? The . . ." I struggled to put my words correctly. "The . . . *changes.*"

"It's only happened a few times. It's happened quite a bit since I turned fourteen. My birthday was a few weeks ago. This is the first time I've been exposed under a full moon—I think that's what triggered the whole wolf thing." He grew silent, his head buried. He seemed so young, innocent. I would guess that he'd be just a normal freshman back at Hill Valley if he wasn't a werewolf; he seemed to have been stripped of his childhood.

"I think I know how to control them," he voiced. "The changes," he elucidated. "It helps when I listen to music."

"Music? Like . . . *calming* music?"

"Yeah," he answered. "Classical. I'm into classical."

I smirked, which made him look a bit dissatisfied with his comment. I quickly cleared my throat. "You just seem like the rocker type," I explained.

He shrugged absently. "Mom likes—liked—rock music," he corrected. "Dad loved classical. His name was Wolfgang . . ." He trailed off, a hint of a smile growing on his lips. "I know. Ironic. Dad's side of the family descended from shape-shifters, but mainly wolves. *Lots* of them. And he conducted a lot, Mom said. My first middle name is Sebastian, for Sebastian Bach. Honestly, these composers had such weird names," he added after a brief moment. "My brother's first middle name is Amadeus, from Mozart."

"You mentioned your brother before," I clarified. "So . . . is *he* a shape-shifter too?"

"Dunno. I mean, he would have to get his powers sometime . . ." he concluded.

We sat in silence once again, and then a light bulb lit up in my mind. "You said your brother lived in the mortal world. Where?"

Drake pondered this. "England? I'm not sure. I think it had British in the name, but that's all I can remember."

A lump the size of a small rock formed in my throat. "British . . . British Columbia? Was that it?"

He pursed his lips, drawing his eyebrows together in contemplation. "Yeah, I guess. Can't be sure. But he went to some posh boarding school after Dad died. Lives with our aunt now."

"H-Hill Valley?" I stuttered, my palms beginning to sweat.

Drake pursed his lips. "Sounds about right."

"Drake . . ." I said after a moment. My mind reeled. "What's your name?" At this, he raised his eyebrow. "Your full name," I added.

Drake gave an audible swallow, and at that moment, I couldn't think of anybody else except that one African Jade freshman I'd met a few months back. I could see how familiar the two looked: the same messy black-brown hair, dark eyes, innocent smiles . . . .

"Drake," he said. "Drake Sebastian Romulus Macdonald."

EIGHTEEN:
AN UNPLEASANT FAREWELL

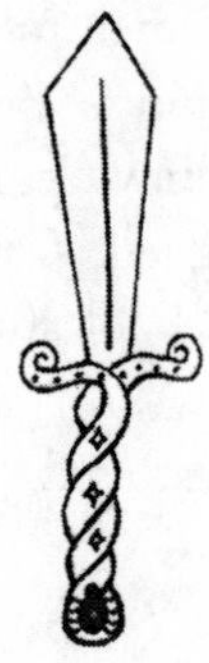

His words were like blows to the stomach. Drake sat, unmoving, impassive. He didn't look the least bit fazed, which I found odd. Then again, he didn't know that I had once met his brother, whom I'd assumed was a regular mortal attending school.

"Jake," I whispered. Warm tears rushed to my eyes. "Oh, Jake Macdonald . . ."

Drake shifted uncomfortably. "Yeah. That's my brother. How'd you know his name?" he asked curiously.

"I attended school with him—Jake. He was a freshman . . . just a regular boy. But he'd been traumatized a lot. With Ash . . . her friends . . . the mark of the Sorcerers Underworld appearing on his skin . . ." I trailed off.

"Whoa, whoa," he said, shaking his head. He pressed his hands to his temples. "What d'you mean, the Sorcerers Underworld mark appearing on his skin? And who's Ash?"

I took a deep breath, and then replayed everything that had happened to Jake over the past few months. Drake looked a bit startled by this.

"And all this time . . . my brother hasn't even known . . ." He trailed into speechlessness.

I held his shoulder, but then let go when I realized how much I was sweating.

"Sorry. I turned the AC down to make the room warmer. Cooler temperatures lead to greater chances of . . . you know. The change," he explained.

I nodded slowly, but still didn't feel quite comfortable with the stuffy air. Drake heaved a loud of carbon dioxide out of his system, and then shook his head.

"And to think this all started when I turned fourteen," he said, his voice tender.

I raised a brow. "When's your birthday?" I questioned.

He didn't hesitate to answer. "October thirteenth."

"And you're fourteen?" I knew he'd already stated the fact, but I had to reassure myself.

"Yeah . . . ?"

"But . . . but Jake's thirteen. I think. You couldn't possibly be born so close."

Drake smiled, his lip quivering slightly. "Jake's fourteen. Must be. Mom said I'm ten minutes older."

My heart nearly stopped. *Ten minutes?* "Then . . . then you must be . . ."

He carefully regarded himself in the mirror. "Yeah. Like Janine and Jessica. Twins."

The mere syllable made my shoulders tense with unease, with shock. "Twins," I spoke stoically. "But surely not . . ." I stared at his reflection.

"No, not identical." He chuckled wearily. "I haven't seen him in a long while, but people say we look only a little alike. When you put us side by side, I guess." He tilted his head against his fist and pressed his thumb into his cheek. "I just wish I could've seen him. I mean, I did when we were little, but after that . . ." He heaved a sigh. "We're like magnets. Can never be kept apart. We're both halves of the other; and my whole life I've been missing the other half. The other piece of me."

I could only imagine what it was like to be kept away from a sibling—a twin, especially. Being an only child my whole life, it made me wonder how different things could've been if I had a sister or brother.

He kept his jaw taut, and then turned to me. I could see the similarities more now, the replicated features on his face. And somehow, Drake seemed to take on another persona: a rocker, a much more confident version of his twin's self. But at the present moment, I could've probably mixed up Drake with Jake based on his innocence and vulnerability. If Drake's hair was the least bit longer, his face a bit less square, I could've identified them as twins on the spot. I felt a bit stupid, being unaware of my own schoolmate's relation with sorcery, and his having a twin. Drake and Jake—their names rhymed, for goodness' sake!

Drake heaved a sigh. "Thanks, Arica. For coming down here. I mean, when I change . . ." He swallowed what I guessed was a seed of revulsion. "I'm different. Horrifying. A monster."

"You're no monster," I said, giving my voice a certain edge of confidence. "I mean, everyone on this train is—well, according to mortals—abnormal. I'm a sorceress. You're an animal shape-shifter. Is that such a big deal?"

"For Andrae, it must be," he managed. "He's probably having a fit right now. And Summer . . ." He looked as if his heart had been cracked in half. "Oh, Summer. She might be kicked off the Train with me for knowing about my true form."

"Why would Andrae be angry?" I asked.

"Because . . . because I snuck on the train. There's no way for a guy like me—a descendent of werewolves—to get on the Water Train, only meant for pure sorcerers and sorceresses."

"But then how'd you get on the Train? You couldn't have just snuck by with the magical borders . . . ?" I ended it as more of a question.

Drake turned his head, scanning my face, his eyes now a deep chocolate with flecks of silver. He looked uncomfortable. "It wasn't easy, I'll tell you that much," he said with a rough laugh. Then he gulped, and his brown eyes lifted to mine. "I'd better get packing. The whole Train must know I'm a shape-shifter now." He sighed with exasperation, but then finally nodded. "I'm just another menacing creature in their eyes." He paused. "I've gotta go. Prince Adam and Joseph should be coming back soon. I don't think I can face that right now." He lugged a giant suitcase toward his bed and began stuffing his clothes and extras inside.

"No," I said as he began stuffing his suitcase. "I won't let you leave. Just because you're not a pure sorcerer doesn't mean you deserve to be punished like this. Maybe you could ask for a stay at the Water Train. I'm sure I can convince Andrae."

Drake's face was unreadable—he looked rather sleepy. "Thanks, Arica. But maybe we should just let it go. There's a fireworks celebration tomorrow. Do you want to join Summer and me? And everyone else will be there, too. It will be a great farewell . . ."

"Or not a farewell at all," I said, relating back to what I'd said before.

"Right. But you're leaving, too. Tomorrow night is the stop for the Sorcerer Palace. You are going there, right?"

Suddenly a knock came at the door. Drake and I exchanged a few questioning glances.

"Go," he told me, his voice just above a whisper. "Hide!"

My muscles tensed for a moment, but then I lunged into the miniature closet, nearly knocking down a broom along the way. I tried my best to remain still, but I still shuffled quietly to the right to try and peek out the thin slit of the open closet doorway.

A man entered the room, looking a few inches taller than Drake. He had a bit of a lanky physique, as if he'd been overly tired, and ruffled brown hair. It had to be Andrae. His eyes were stern, but it was hard to make out his facial expressions in the darkness. His Shadower marking was visible from my side; it looked as if a hot stone had seared the emblem onto his skin.

"What are you doing?" Andrae asked. I expected his tone to be harsh, but instead it seemed a bit polite.

"Packing," Drake answered monotonously. "You and I both know I can't stay on the Train."

Andrae swallowed. "It's against the rules," he confirmed, but it didn't seem like much of a statement. "The Train-goers won't be pleased."

"I know," Drake answered coolly, heaving his suitcase toward the door.

"I never said I would kick you off," Andrae finally managed after a tense silence. He shifted his eyes around the bedroom, and then his eyes landed on the closet door. I stiffened, unsure if he could see me through the thin slit.

Making a sudden movement would give me away. I had to remain still as best I could.

"Are we alone here?" he asked, his feet making short thudding sounds as he approached the closet door. He laid his hand on the handle, about to pull it open, but Drake abruptly pushed it closed. My heart beat louder than a drum.

"C'mon, Andrae," Drake said, his voice slightly muffled. "We're alone here. Anyway, I have to go off at the next stop. Tomorrow's the fireworks—"

"Drake . . ." Andrae began, his tone much softer. "I know what it's like to be different. Outcast. When I was younger, I had no place to stay. I lived at orphanages with my best friend . . ." I imagined him shaking his head. "My friend . . . she was like Summer to me. We never really had a chance to . . ." His voice faded, and then reappeared. "Not since the Royals took us. I don't want you to experience what I had when I was outcast. The Water Train is like a safe haven."

"Not for me," Drake retorted. "Well, anymore. Only for sorcerers. Werewolves, goblins, other mythical creatures—what about them? Aren't we just as competent? Just as deserving to have a spot on this Train?" Hurt grew in his voice.

Someone sighed—Andrae, I guessed. "I agree. But when my father created this Train, it was only under the intention that he could rescue people from an inescapable city. It was only made for pure sorcerers. And when they caught him in his plan, everything crumbled. I was found, punished to run the Train. It's not so much of a punishment anymore. The only thing I miss is . . . her."

A sudden rumble caused the floor to quake. I nearly staggered to the side, but I kept a firm grip on the broom that was neatly connected to the wall.

"Our next stop is the Sorcerer Palace," Andrae continued, noticing the ship's rocky movement out of the Black Trench. "And you don't have to leave the Train. I'm allowing you to stay."

"But, I—"

"Take my word: you both deserve to stay." He paused. "Are you sure no one else is in here?"

"I'm sure!" Drake said, but his voice cracked at the end, making the statement less convincing.

Andrae sighed. "It's okay, you can come out now."

I straightened my back reflexively, eyes bulging. The stillness in this closet was haunting.

All of a sudden I felt an odd presence beside me. It was almost like a person was standing there, but from what I could see in the darkness, there was no one here.

"Drake?" I whispered, struggling to push open the door. "Are you still there?"

Drake's quivering voice did not sound until a while after I'd spoken. "Ye-yes," he managed to say. "Arica, I . . . I think he's in there."

"What?" I said in a wrenched whisper.

"Shh," I heard from beside me.

In that instant, I screamed, jumping from my spot. I flung open the closet door and hit the ground hard. Drake was looming over me, wide-eyed, his jaw hung low.

Through the darkness, Drake's face was still quite fuzzy. Then, unsure if it was my imagination, I saw strange white-gray particles floating beside him. I thought maybe they were particles of dust, but they were coming together in a weird form—the figure of a human. A shadow formed from the particles, and then, from the legs up, Andrae's body reappeared.

"Whoa—what the heck did you just do?!" Drake said, sounding exuberant and horrified and surprised all in one sentence.

Andrae gave a stiff smile. "I'm a Shadower, remember? Can turn into a shadow at any moment I like. I used to think my power was weird, but I've gotten used to it now."

The world felt hazy. Then Andrae's words began to seep in—everything made sense. Andrae had used his powers to turn into a shadow, which would explain the Shadowers symbol on his neck. Pedro had had the same one, and so had Teal. "I thought when they found you . . . I mean, wouldn't your Shadowing powers stop working? Aren't they illegal?"

"They haven't disappeared *fully,* but they will soon. Might as well take advantage of it while I still can. But the Royals still keep an eye on me so I can't escape." He sighed heavily. "I don't think I need to tell you that Summer's party is cancelled."

"Checked off my list," I said, still in shock. My muscles felt like jelly.

"Then I guess you heard everything we were talking about," Andrae surmised. "About . . . the Royals."

I nodded, propping myself up from the floor. "But you're not harmful at all. Why are the Royals treating the Shadowers like this?"

Andrae shrugged. "Technically, I was never even supposed to be born. That's why the Royals hunted me. And my friend. I never had a home to live in because I was always on the run. But that was years ago."

"Why don't you talk to Adam?" Drake suggested. "He's a great guy—I'm sure he'd understand."

Andrae only shrugged. "I don't know. It was his family—or his servers—who took me away from T—" He stopped himself before he could produce another sound. "I mean . . . my friend. They made me take up this job on the Water Train. I haven't seen her since." He stared at the floor.

"What's her name?" I asked.

Andrae looked puzzled for a second. "You wouldn't know her."

"Maybe I would."

Andrae looked a little frustrated. "I'm not supposed to be talking about this. It's getting late and I've gotta go back to the cockpit. They're waiting for me."

"I'll walk with you on the way there." I took a step toward him.

He sighed, his lips scrunched in a grimace. He looked defeated. "All right. Let's go. Goodnight, Drake," he said.

Drake, sitting on his floor, looking slightly appalled and confused, gave a quick wave to Andrae. "Will I see you at the fireworks display tomorrow?" he questioned.

"Of course," Andrae said with authority.

"Good," Drake said, looking like a giant weight had been lifted from his shoulders. "Thanks for your help, Arica. And thanks for letting me stay, Andrae."

Andrae gave him a warm smile. "My pleasure."

* * *

"So your father was a Shadower?" I asked Andrae, though the information was familiar. We had exited Drake's cabin and headed to the elevator.

"Yes. He was a member of the Cynical Six. I'm sure you know about them, right?" He continued after I nodded. "Well, my father's name was Benjamin. He created the Water Train after a treacherous journey to find a golden dragon heart. He went on the journey with his friend, Quindle, another member of the Cynical Six. Quindle went missing before he could join Benjamin on the Water Train. My father died shortly after. I never saw my father—ever. But it doesn't matter, because I never knew either of my parents, anyway. I guess my mother sort of . . . left me."

I laid my hand on his shoulder. "Don't say that."

"It's the only explanation. It's been nineteen years, Arica. But I guess you can relate—with your father and all."

I took a step back. "How do you know about my father?"

Andrae looked amused. "Isn't it obvious? The story of his capture was all over *Sorcerers Spark* thirteen years ago. Maybe even longer than that."

"Capture? My father died in military battle—that's what my mom told me," I said quickly, but the words started to feel less truthful. Mom wouldn't lie, right? Andrae was just getting confused—mixing up my father with someone else.

Andrae lifted his eyebrows. "*Military* battle?" he said, looking aghast. "No . . . I remember it all very clearly. I was young, maybe five, in my first orphanage, when I saw the newspaper. When my friend *showed* me the newspaper," he corrected. "Your father was captured, Arica. He was captured . . . and . . . and killed." The last word was barely audible. "Killed by an unknown villain."

My ears felt numb. There must've been something wrong with my hearing. "What do you mean by *unknown villain*?"

With a fragile voice, Andrae said, "I mean they don't know who killed him. But whatever you thought before, Arica, was wrong. He wasn't in any military battle. He was in an actual battle—a battle of magic. In the Sorcerers Underworld."

I wanted to hide it, but it was too hard to fight back the fresh ocean of tears swimming in my eyes. A thousand questions ran through my mind at the speed of light. *No,* I thought. *No, no, NO.*

Andrae looked unsettled by this. "Hey—Arica, I didn't mean to upset you." He placed a hand on my shoulder delicately. "I just thought you knew what happened to your father."

I was overwhelmed. Andrae looked blurry in front of me due to the tears, and my mind was just as cloudy. I couldn't process this information—*my father was murdered.* And probably by a sorcerer in the place of all magic. My intestines crawled, and I felt like throwing up.

"Sorry, Andrae," I said, and wiped my eyes. I turned, muttering a barely audible goodbye. With the little strength I had, I steered myself toward my cabin. I plunged into the room and closed the door loudly. My watery eyes still made everything look blurry, but to my luck, the room was dim. The TV was flipped to the Discovery Channel, and Raven and Violet were both sitting on their beds. I guessed tonight's sleep was on the mattress.

As soon as the door shut loudly behind me, Raven and Violet simultaneously turned their heads.

"What happened?" Raven asked, noticing my tear-streaked face. A loud *boom* came from the television.

Raven plopped her popcorn bowl on the ground, not caring that Musky was now nibbling the kernels that had fallen to the floor, and ran to my side. She gathered me in a tight hug. "Hey, it's all right" was all she said, but I immediately felt better by her touch—probably because she was a Healer. Did Healers have the power to fix emotions, too?

"What happened?" she asked once she let go. Violet was staring at both of us with wide eyes. She seemed a little discontented by my face, but still kept eating her popcorn; she was also stealing quick glances at the screen to watch the mating of a peculiar bird species.

"I just had a little talk with Andrae, and things didn't turn out so well, that's all." I wiped my face quickly to hide the tears that swam out of my eyes like rivers.

"It doesn't seem like that's all. Maybe you're getting out your emotions from everything that's happened today. I know you put a lot of hard work into getting Summer's party ready."

"No, no. It's not about that," I said with a weak voice. "I just need some sleep."

"Then take the bed tonight. I'll take the mattress," Raven suggested.

Before Raven had even finished speaking, I had already lain on the mattress and wrapped myself in the warm, fuzzy blanket. I forced my mind to become blank. The day's events were too much to consider at the moment.

Raven patted my back. "Get some rest. You're going to need it."

* * *

I woke feeling relaxed.

Today was the last day on the Water Train, and I didn't want to waste it by thinking of the dreadful things that had happened the day before. After all of my encounters on the Water Train, I was looking forward to a day of peace. But considering what had occurred each day previous, I knew that wasn't possible. The Sapphires were on the loose, our gemstones were missing, and the Hall of Lost Gemstones was merely hours away. If the Sapphires made it there before us . . . Well, there would be trouble, to say the least.

After a hot shower, I reappeared in the room to find Raven and Violet making the beds. Or at least Raven was making her bed. Violet was "supervising," more so glancing at her cell phone whenever it gave a dismal buzz.

Bands of light shone across the room through the porthole at the back. Violet squinted, almost shrinking away as if the light were lava. "Gosh. Someone call Mr. Sun. It hasn't been this hot since Keller went out of control last summer."

"Keller?" I asked, running a towel through my hair.

"Fire girl. Lost control of her fire power and had to go to a medical institute for a while," Violet explained.

"Oh—I didn't know," I said. My thoughts involuntarily steered to Geoff.

"Obviously," Violet retorted. She returned to texting on her cell phone.

"I'm sending out a few kites today," Raven began to break the tension, "so I won't be around for too long. But I know it's your last day here, Arica, and I don't want to leave you alone." She placed a frown on her face.

"Don't worry about it. I'll be with the twins if you finish early," I said with a thin smile.

"Thanks so much, Arica. I'll be finished by tonight for sure. We can watch the fireworks display together."

"What are those fireworks for, anyway?" I asked.

"Well . . . they're not like *real* fireworks, the human-made ones. We use fireflies! They make coordinate patterns and . . . voila! Fireworks, essentially. They only come out a few times a year in the Bermuda Triangle," she explained. "Like that other night on the Train! Anyways, tonight's the last night before your stop at the Sorcerer Palace. We need to celebrate!"

I lifted my eyebrows, feeling more knowledgeable than I had twenty seconds ago. It sort of felt like I was getting a math lesson from Joseph, except I actually understood what she was saying.

"Right. Thanks. I'll see you there too, Violet."

Violet abruptly looked up from her cell phone. Her face was contorted; half-pained, half-wistful. "Right. It's tonight . . ."

"And I'm leaving tonight," I added, unsure if she'd caught that fact.

"Yes. I know." She stared at me with a glassy look in her eyes. "See you then."

"Um, okay? Later," I said as I walked out the door. There was something odd about how Violet had said "See you then," as if something weird was going to happen.

"Arica!" two synchronous voices called down the carpeted hall. "What do you plan to do on this fine day?" Jess asked.

"Something relaxing," I said with a smile.

"How about we hang at the arcade downstairs?" Jess suggested. "I hear it's much better than mundane mortal arcades. This one's got holographic screens and a huge spin-the-wheel game where sorcerers actually fit inside!" She giggled. "But I haven't actually been there. Joseph told me about it. Apparently he went mad crazy last night after Summer's—well, almost—party with this maths video game and went bollocks!"

"Why is Joseph so obsessed with math?" I questioned.

"He's odd like that. So, are we going to the arcade?" Jess asked.

"Definitely!" I said enthusiastically, immediately feeling better once I ringed by arms around the twins' shoulders.

But a nagging sound kept ringing through my ears the entire time we were playing at the arcade. It was almost as if something was haunting me, trying to tell me something. I couldn't figure out what it was.

A buzz came softly by my ear. I spun around to find Violet leaning against a brick wall. Her bright pink hair was slightly puffy and frizzy; she looked maniacal.

"What are you doing here?" I asked.

"Raven and I have been searching for you. The fireworks display is about to start."

My mind spun. "It can't be night already . . ."

"Well, it is," Violet said, walking forward.

"How—"

"No time to explain," she said, grabbing my arm. "Seriously, we have to move. Like, now." She caught my arm and dragged me toward the stairs.

"Violet, stop!" I said, pulling her hand off my arm. "What about the twins?"

"They're already on the deck." She had a strange look in her eyes: one looked larger than the other, and her hair seemed even frizzier now.

"Are you okay?" I asked, staring at her. "You look kind of . . ."

"It's all this heat," she admitted. "My hair gets frizzy when it's hot." She looked down, embarrassed.

"Oh," I said, immediately regretting my comment. "Sorry."

"Whatever," she said, shrugging it off. "Let's go to the deck."

A load of sorcerers was standing in a large, open area; they were all intently talking to one another, ignoring Violet and me. But that didn't seem to matter to Violet. We were stuck in a small corner of the deck. The sound of glistening water was like music to my ears.

"Isn't it beautiful?" I said as I held the railing, facing the ocean. The sky was becoming dark alarmingly fast.

"Not really," Violet snorted. Her phone vibrated. She slipped the phone out of her pocket and quickly texted something I couldn't see from my distance. Sometimes, while texting, she would give me a few wary glances. I couldn't bring myself to look away.

"Who are you talking to?" I took a cautious step forward.

Violet kept staring down at the screen, but an ominous smile crossed her lips. "A friend."

"Cell phones aren't allowed on the Water Train. How are you texting?"

Violet looked up, and I was sure I'd never seen this kind of hatred on her face before. "I'm not," she replied, her voice somewhat deeper, icy with resignation.

This would evidently be her typical answer, so I lunged for the phone and took it from her hands. I knew the move was a bit rash, but I wasn't thinking about that at the moment. All I wanted to see was who Violet was texting—and why it was so important.

I took the phone from her, staring at the dark midnight screen, and saw nothing but a red bar and the words: battery low.

Violet smirked. Feeling defeated, I handed back the phone. Normally I would never act in this way, but Violet's texting was beginning to get on my nerves. Then, just as she took the phone from my hands, she used her other hand to grab my wrist. Her grasp felt like a ring of lava encircling my skin. I gasped, knees buckling, feeling no sensation besides the exploding pain along my wrist; a feeling I'd recognized from the moment Ash had sent me to the Sorcerers Underworld . . . .

"Arica, Arica, Arica." Violet bent down beside me, but the fresh tears coating my eyes caused her to swim in and out of my vision. "I thought you'd catch on quicker."

"What are you talking about?" I said, trying to articulate each word powerfully. My lips suddenly felt dry. Tears still stung my eyes.

Violet smirked. "I guess to qualify as the Prophetic Child you have to be oblivious, too." At this moment I noticed a key necklace that looked exactly like Ash's slip out from beneath her shirt. She snickered, and then said suspiciously, "I have my sources."

It took all my willpower to inject as much cynicism into my words as possible: "What *sources*?" I spat.

"A friend—or sister, for that matter. I thought you would see the resemblance between us."

"You have a sister?" I asked, though I didn't sound very surprised with the pain still manifesting along my wrist.

"Yes. She's a year younger—red hair, key necklace? I'm sure you've got it figured out." She stood from her position and pulled me with her. "I'm one of *them*. I'm like the Sapphires. A descendant of the Sorcerer Line!"

"But h-how?" I stuttered. "Why?" My stomach roiled with rage.

"There are not only five great grand-children of the Sorcerer Line; I am another. But Ash had already taken her place—and I was just another Underworlder. A member of the Graves family." Her crooked smile was thin and mocking. "But those were the old days. I don't want to be recognized as a Sapphire, as you call them. I want to be known as Violet Graves; never living in the shadow of my sister, never coming second, always getting the attention I never had . . ." Her voice became a melancholy whisper. "So the Sapphires pretended to be your friends—and I watched by the sidelines." Her voice was gravelly—a bit revengeful.

"I know you saw that room behind the wall. The one with the Aradis. But you never figured out what it was for, did you, Arica? The Aradis didn't just hold the activating piece. It's a communication device, where I could speak to the thief. Yes, we're aligned," she said, her grin exuding a sort of non-existent power. "But I'm not here for the thief. Heck, I'm not here for Ash. Not even Vina." She said the final name with distaste. "I'm here for myself.

"But now it's time to end your reign, Miller. And I know exactly how to do it." Violet sauntered toward me, the cell phone in her hand expanding and changing into a massive bronze machete.

I couldn't believe my eyes. "W-what—"

"I can't believe Ash isn't here to see this. I bet she would love to see you *die*!" At the last word she swung her machete and missed her target (my head, surely) by mere inches. She tried again but only fell forward. When her machete smacked against the deck floor, a ball of icy blue electricity surrounded the weapon. She lifted it, satisfied, and checked her reflection in the bronze edge. I could've sworn I'd seen Violet's reflection cruelly smiling back, but for some reason it looked more like Ash. As if she were actually trapped inside the weapon, waiting to come out.

She was now just in front of me—and I had nowhere to go but into the water.

This was it. This was the moment she'd been waiting for. Her big win. Her victorious finale. The fireworks began to spark, and I saw fireflies dancing from the corner of my vision.

"It's time!" she cried, and ran toward me, her pink-streaked hair flying behind her ears. Without time to think, I side-stepped at the last second and rolled off to the side. Violet had leapt toward me, her machete aimed at my throat, but she failed to realize her mistake. I had jumped out of the way just as she soared into the air, arms cradled around her, eyes bulging. Violet, creating a grand arc in midair, flailed with her machete in hand. And then, soon realizing she'd gone too far, flung her body over the railing.

The last thing I heard was a deafening *bang* from the fireworks, and Violet's scream as she plunged into the water.

NINETEEN: DEPARTURE

"Quick, someone, go get the Life Raft!" a woman yelled.

Many minutes had passed since Violet's mistakable falling, and everyone had averted their attention from the fireworks to the corner of the deck where I stood, shocked in place. After many retellings of the story, firemen (the literal extinguisher guys) and police officers came running to the scene. Adam and Joseph and the twins were all standing next to me with grave faces. Raven had just made it too; to my surprise, she wasn't very taken aback by what had just taken place. She said Violet had always been mysterious and weird. But I didn't think she was *this* crazy.

A man looking at around twenty-years-old leapt toward the water, extended his arms in a perfect upward parabola, and turned into a giant, red raft. I'll admit it was shocking at first, but most people seemed to find his transformation completely normal.

"So Violet is a descendant of Luminista?" Joseph asked for the fourth time.

"She's crazy! And I knew it, too. I was just too scared to admit it," Raven added.

"Her machete . . ." I began. "I think it was some sort of communication device. Of course, a normal cell phone would never work on the Water Train. But it wasn't. It turned into a bronze machete before my eyes. And Ash was in it! She must've been speaking to her somehow. If that's even possible," I added, my thoughts scrambling.

Drake, who'd been given several stares since he arrived on the deck, took his turn to speak. "First the mermaids, and now this crazy-awkward-mad-revengeful sister. Even to this extent, this is definitely considered *weird* in the magical world."

"I agree," Raven supplied, becoming a bit angered. Newt, glowing green, looked a bit shy and tucked himself neatly under the cuff of her shirt.

"Andrae hasn't even heard," Janine added. "He'll be furious—"

Right on cue, Andrae came stomping along the deck floor. His eyes were hooded, and his eyes looked red from tiredness. He looked like he hadn't caught much sleep.

Andrae cursed, overlooking the waters. The Life Raft man had come back empty handed.

"Sorry, dude," he said, lowering his parabola-shaped arms back to a linear fashion. "No girl out there. You sure you saw her dive in?"

"She didn't *dive,*" I explained, exasperated. "She . . . *fell.* It was an accident. She was trying to . . ." The words could not formulate in my mouth. How could someone ever declare, almost lazily, "Yeah, she was trying to kill me with her cell-phone-machete thing. No big deal."

"Obviously the thief and his comrades are on the boat. Violet could've been working with them," Andrae added, slapping his hand against his neck and rubbing with forlorn anxiety.

Joseph wrung his hands together uneasily, and then looked at me. "This is all just very strange, Arica. I mean . . . *Ash's sister* on the Train? Who knew! Who knew the descendant of Luminista—" Joseph was just about to dive into another grand chorus of *who-knews* when Jessica cut in.

"Joseph, honestly, *stop* with the descendent of Luminista thing! Now that we know she's a descendent of the Sorcerer Line, why do you think she's been on the Train? And what exactly was she trying to hinder *you* from doing?" She indicated me with a shaky finger. "Taking the Jewel?"

The Life Raft man looked around and noisily blew out a long stem of air. "Yeah . . . I dunno what you dudes are talking about, so I'm just gonna go over there . . ." He trailed off, jutting his thumb to the dessert table, and left.

Andrae had not realized the departure of this man, but rather kept his eyes glued to the ground in concentration. "Horrible," he spat suddenly, his rage becoming evident. "All these horrible things happening, all in quick succession, all because of . . ." He struggled to put the words correctly. "Because of the thief."

"But we can still retrieve the Jewel," Adam said with noble stature.

"It'll be hard," Andrae admitted. "Whoever took this Jewel has caused many problems to such poor and innocent people. Question is, why did the thief take the Jewel in the first place?" Andrae asked.

"We may not know the thief's motives," I said. "But the queen asked us to get the crown back for her husband, and that's exactly what we'll do." *However we do it,* I added in my head. I still wasn't sure where we would find or meet the thief; the only plan we all really had in mind at the moment was reclaiming the gemstones at the Sorcerer Palace.

Andrae affirmed my hope with a nod. "I wish all the best for you guys, really. Last time I went on an adventure like this . . . things didn't really work out." He gave a grim chuckle. "Anyways, the Train will be docking at the Sorcerer Palace soon. Maybe we can get a few more fireworks in. That is, if the fireflies aren't too scared after Violet's . . . um . . . *incident.*"

Incident seemed to be a pretty popular word nowadays, or maybe I was just getting myself into more "incidents" than I could count.

"Strange," someone said, coming from behind me. I turned to see Logan, his fingers stroking his chin absently. His dark eyes met mine. "Remember when we saw Violet's footprints in that room? Maybe it could've had something to do with the Jewel—the thief."

"Room?" Jess inquired.

"I'll have to explain it to you guys later," I told them, and then redirected my focus to Logan. "I don't think Violet's the thief. She probably is connected to the thief, since she knows the Sapphires, but she mostly just seemed like a revengeful sister in my eyes. Maybe she was going to that room for some other reason? Just a way to communicate with the Sapphires?"

Logan pondered this, and then wandered to the railing. He observed the ocean. "Looks like we'll never know the answer to that question. She's gone."

"But not dead, surely?" Joseph said, his voice shrill.

"No—probably not," Adam presumed. "She could have transported herself to the Sorcerers Underworld straight after plunging in the water. That is her power, isn't it? I mean, it was Ash's power."

I was surprised by Adam's knowledge, but he was the prince, after all.

"Exactly . . . which was why she wouldn't say what her power was yesterday. She's an Underworlder." The revelations came together quickly.

Logan looked pointedly at the elevator. "I think we should head back to our cabins and pack our stuff. We'll have to be docking soon, right, Andrae?"

"Very soon, by the looks of it. We should near the Sorcerer Palace in less than an hour, actually," Andrae said, almost solemnly, as if he were wishing this moment wouldn't come.

"Why do you have to pack your bags, Logan? Aren't you staying on the Train?" Adam asked.

"I'm getting off at the same stop as you," he stated. "I've been called for some work with the Crigoes—you know, with my animal telepathy powers and all."

"Oh," Adam answered. "The more the merrier, I guess," he said, laughing, but hearing laughter felt strange at the moment. Especially with sorcerers still running about looking for where Violet could've gone. The pandemonium never seemed to end on this doomed deck.

"Maybe one day we can all board the Train again—but this time only for fun!" Jess said, chuckling at the end. The thought was actually quite uplifting, but I wasn't so sure when we would ever get a chance like that. I was continually encountering new enemies—whom I'd *assumed* to be friends at first, like Violet and Ash—and if this kept up, we were surely doomed.

The dark, misty night curled around us. The sky seemed much cloudier now, and in the distance a sort of glowing orb was visible. At first I thought it might have just been another set of fireflies, but then as the Train inched closer, the outline of the palace was beginning to take shape.

"Is that the Sorcerer Palace?" Janine said incredulously. She squinted into the distance.

I had never seen the Palace before in my life, but in that instant, I thought I had never seen a more beautiful architectural structure in my life. It was definitely a palace you would envision for a king or queen, looking radiant and strong, with a slight medieval feel to it. The stones lacing the corridor looked like bricks of gold, and the whole palace appeared as if it was floating on the mystical water.

"We're closer than I thought," Andrae estimated. "We should be docking by the time you've finished packing your bags." He turned to us and examined our motionlessness. "Uh—and by that I meant *go*."

"Oh," Adam said, seeming slightly fazed by the appearance of the castle. "Right. Yes." He shook Andrae's hands and then headed to the elevator. The twins, Joseph, Raven, and I followed eagerly.

After a quick five minutes, the twins had their bulky matching suitcases parked by their sides in the middle of the landing floor. This was the lowest floor on the Train, mirroring that of a lobby in a grand hotel. A chandelier was hanging above us, exhibiting strands of golden light, and in front was what I guessed to be Andrae's private conducting room, where he steered the Train.

"We're on course," Andrae informed once we'd settled our bags on the floor. "Just a few more minutes, I would say, before we reach the entrance."

"Thanks for everything, Andrae," Joseph added, seemingly appearing from the elevator. Adam followed close behind. He held out his hand for a handshake, but his actions seemed a little awkward and limp. Typical Joseph.

Jess turned to me privately and looked slightly fearful, red strands of hair curtaining her face. "Arica . . ." She paused. "I know things have been weird. Here on the Train. But we have to go get our gemstones back. Even if we don't meet the thief, or retrieve the Jewel, we'll do what we intentionally set out to do: take back our gemstones." Her blue eyes were steely with both fear and hope.

Her twin nodded. "As much of a train wreck this has been," she said, and shortly laughed at the pun, "we can get our gemstones back. Get our powers back, even if we are learning to use them without our gemstones. I mean, can you really believe it?" she asked incredulously. "We're literally minutes away from our gemstones . . . The ones great-gran Andrea had taken so long ago . . ."

I took in a deep breath, trying to prohibit any thoughts of the Sapphires or the thief from my mind. Instead, we rejoined the group and I took some time to say my goodbyes to Musky and Newt. Raven also handed us cards with an address on them.

"If you ever need to contact me, just send me a kite," she said, indicating the card. "We can chat any time." She pasted a lively smile. I gave her a hug, and immediately felt like I was losing another friend. No—not losing. Just moving farther away from another. It ached to think of when I would next see her and Andrae. Plus, it felt weird having to leave the Train altogether; it was now almost like a second home, a place to find comfort in when all was lost. That was what Drake had done, of course: found refuge in this place and stayed with Summer.

While I was giving Musky a pretty gracious scratch behind the ear, Drake and Summer arrived, arms linked, from the elevator. They headed toward us, looking slightly solemn, though I noted that Summer seemed to drag Drake forward. Drake was probably still not that comfortable with appearing publicly after his *transformation* on the deck the previous evening.

They approached us slowly, and then Drake spoke up: "Summer and I have been talking," he said, giving Summer a quick glance, "and we think that as much as we love the Train, it feels wrong to stay on board any longer. We're docking off at the next land stop."

"What? Why?" Janine asked, pained. "Summer—you love the Train! Trust me, I know. I heard you sleep-talking about it at night. And sometimes in French, too," she added, a bit horrified and disgusted. As much as the twins would've loved to help out at the party, they still weren't very close friends with Summer.

"She thinks it's about time I see my brother," he said. "I think so, too. Jake is out there. And we have to tell him who he really is. And maybe I'll be the first sense of family he's had in a while." He gave Summer's hand a squeeze.

"That'll be a long journey," Jess said. "I mean, travelling all the way to British Columbia—it's not a very easy task without a plane ticket."

Drake nodded, but her worries didn't deflate his confidence. "Don't worry. I'm sure we'll find a way."

"Tell Jake I say hi," I said, remembering the innocence of the freshman boy, his great group of friends who were always chanting Jake's name. I gave Drake a final hug.

"I'll see you back in British Columbia," I stated with finality.

"Yes." He nodded with a grim smile. "I can't wait."

* * *

Janine and Jess were the first to hurry off to the docking station, located at the west edge of the landing deck, just beside Andrae's control room. Andrae had gone back to steering, muttering some strange lingo into a speaker phone, and currently my nose was pressed against the warm glass window. The ocean beneath us was magnificently large, sparkling like a diamond. The Palace lay on the water as if an invisible island was beneath it, and the highest tip seemed to disappear in the clouds.

I nearly jerked to the side when I felt someone tap on my shoulder. I turned to see Logan, and then breathed a sigh of relief.

"Didn't mean to scare you," he said with a faint laugh. His brown hair became even lighter in the streaming moonlight.

"It's okay," I said, still a bit shaken. "How are you?"

"Fine, I guess. Excited to get back to work."

I found his commentary to be the exact opposite of his facial features. His cheeks seemed blanched, almost as if he was a ghost, and his eyes glazed.

"Are you sure?" I asked, unconvinced.

He looked as if he'd just been found guilty of a crime. Then he stared down at his leg and pulled up his pants to reveal his ankle. A small but very dark bruise was visible just above his anklebone, and slightly reminded me of the bruise Jake had had on his shoulder back at Hill Valley.

"Oh my gosh. What happened? Are you all right?" My thoughts gushed out.

"Yeah, fine. Nobody's noticed my limping so far." He snickered to himself. "It's okay, though. I just got it last night, when we entered the Black Trench . . . . It just got so dark. I tripped and landed on my ankle in a really bad way." He gave it one last glance and then let his pants slide back down. A thin smile played on his lips. I still wasn't sure why his bruise didn't convince me of the pallor of his face, because even after, he kept clearing his throat and looking very pale. I wasn't sure if he was just feeling sea sick or nervous, but that was the only appropriate reason that made sense at the moment.

An extremely loud fog horn sounded from above, causing the floor to shiver below us. I gripped the window pane as the Train trembled.

"Could that be any quieter?" Logan joked.

"I suppose a bruised ankle did nothing to your sarcasm," I added amusingly.

"Nope, didn't change a thing." He threw a cargo bag over his shoulder. "You coming? Andrae's gonna ship us off the docking station."

"All right. I'll be right there," I said, warily staring at the corner of the deck. The memories from a mere *hour* ago—perhaps less, as it felt—flooded forward. That was where Violet had tried to push me off the Train. But her plan had backfired. Instead of sending *me* in the water, she had accidently flown off the landing and landed in the water with an ear-splitting *splash*.

"Okay," Logan said a little shakily, disrupting me from my thoughts. "I'll meet you . . . er . . . outside."

As he limped away, I grabbed my suitcase. But before I could pull myself forward, my eyes wandered to the Sorcerers Underworld mark etched on my arm. It had mostly faded away when I had first entered the Water Train, but now it seemed to have come back with an unknown vengeance. I remembered Violet grabbing my wrist, and how much it reminded me of going to the Sorcerers Underworld; clearly Violet was no different than Ash when it came to powers.

But in reality, Violet seemed to be like more of the *crazy* sister, and Ash the less impatient of the two.

"All leaving the Train, please go to your docking stations for your arrival at the Sorcerer Palace. I repeat, please go to your docking stations. Thank you," I heard Andrae say on the loudspeaker.

"I guess that's us," I heard from beside me. Adam was standing a few feet away, giving a stern and disconcerted glance at the window. "We should go."

I nodded, took a deep heaving breath, and felt like butterflies had filled my stomach. Adam had turned away, so I followed quickly, and then we were holding our suitcases on the grand docking station.

The docking station looked like a deck that could fit in a backyard; not too large, but big enough to hold the numerous sorcerers that were on it now. Each sorcerer moved forward in a linear fashion, gripping their bags tightly, until they reached the end of the dock. They each disappeared in a plume of smoke, reappearing on the platform to the entrance of the Palace.

Joseph prodded me forward in the midst of my thoughts. "Go on, now. Don't be afraid." He spoke with a tremble in his voice, as if he was convincing himself.

I realized that the line had already disappeared quickly. Adam was gone, too, meaning he was probably standing at the platform. I had only a few more feet to go until the edge of the dock, where the only safety beyond lay in the glittering dark ocean. I moved forward carefully, the dock making creaks beneath my feet, and then, suddenly, I felt like I'd been trapped in a box. All oxygen seemed to leave me, my vision turned dark, and every sensation within me felt lost. Although it only lasted a millisecond, I was sure I would never forget the experience.

I reappeared on the deck, my vision suddenly sparking to life, and sucked in a breath. Oxygen coursed through my veins. Adam's figure appeared before me, followed by Joseph and the twins, all looking just as stunned as I probably had.

"The effects wear off," Adam explained, brushing off his clothes. His eyes gleamed in the moonlight. "How about we head inside?"

Joseph looked apprehensive, and then spoke suddenly. "Remember a while back, when the queen ordered that council? There was an old woman saying bad things about the Sorcerer Palace—how it hasn't been occupied in a while? How *nobody* has been here in centuries?"

"It's a bunch of birds' poop in my opinion," Jess supplied confidently. "I mean, if no one's been here in centuries, why would this be a stop on the Train? And how else are people supposed to retrieve or get their gemstones in situations like ours?"

Jess had made a good point, but Joseph did not look shot down. "I'm only summarizing what the woman said, Jess."

"He's right, though," Adam said. I wasn't sure if I'd heard him correctly. Had Adam actually acknowledged that Joseph was . . . *right*? Joseph always seemed to have disliked Adam for some reason—probably because he was the prince and a supposed know-it-all about the Sorcerers Underworld, too.

"I—I am?" Joseph's lip trembled. I had to pat his back to calm him down, and then laughed at the shocked expression that crossed his face.

"We'll just have to go inside and see," I said, giving everyone firm glances, and then we faced the doors of the Sorcerer Palace.

TWENTY: THE SORCERER PALACE

The solid doors shut closed behind us, and I turned to view the scenery. The air was sweet like honey, and the walls were gold. In an odd way it brought me back to the King's Library—Simon, the Chimera, and Arnold . . . .

"Whoa," Joseph shakily whispered.

Shimmery white curtains flanked us on either side, and ivory doves circled the air. One flew overhead and released something from its claws: a red-velvet bag, sort of like a coin pouch, with golden string around the top. The bag fell clumsily into my hands.

"What's that?" Jess asked, staring at the bag in my hands.

"I don't know," I said. I unravelled the golden string and opened the bag. A sort of vacant darkness was all that seemed to lie inside, but when I placed my hand inside the velvet, I realized that there was something leathery in the bag. I pulled out the object, which happened to be four times the size of the tiny bag, and felt my heart leap into my throat. Ash's, or really Adam's, book had been inside the bag. The Sorcerers Underworld sign seemed to glow, as if it were a radiant bulb of light, from the leather cover.

"Where'd this come from?" I asked, completely aghast.

Adam seemed particularly shocked. "It's my father's book!" He examined the velvet bag, and then came up with a small tag in his fingers. "Look at this. This bag is from the Water Train, most likely a gift shop."

Joseph took a glance at the bag. "There's a sort of diamond shape at the front, like a kite," he observed. "Do you think Raven sent this? As a sort of good-bye present?"

"Dunno," Jess replied. "But it's really strange. I mean, wasn't that the weird book we saw back in your dorm at Hill Valley, Arica? The one discussing the Sorcerer Line?"

My thoughts melted to a giant pile of mush, but I forced myself to stay collected. "Yeah. I thought it was Ash's . . . but clearly I was wrong. It came to me on the Train. On Musky's back. Adam gave it to me." Adam acknowledged this fact. "Why would Raven send this?"

"It used to belong to my father, but then I wrote my initials in the back," Adam added.

"Guys . . . I know that book may be important and all . . ." Logan took the book into his hands and stared at a certain page. "But look." He turned his head up and stared straight ahead. We followed his gaze robotically, fear glazing our eyes.

Logan and the rest of us examined a large statue by the foot of endless circling stairs. It seemed to resemble some important figure in the Sorcerers Underworld, and held the same features as Adam. Most likely King Thoven, whom I'd never seen before in my life, and yet his noble stature and kind, wise eyes felt almost comforting. He wore a long sash that curved back up around his waist, and held a dagger in his right hand. I noticed a depiction of a snake drawn on the hilt along with several gems.

"King Thoven," I said, but it accidently slipped out as a sort of question. Logan, thankfully, nodded.

"And there's the King's Jewel!" Janine said.

Even before she'd finished talking, I saw the crown glittering across the corridor. It was hovering in midair, but it seemed to be moving away from us, as if being taken. A mysterious dark blob behind it swivelled carefully around the bend. I almost thought I saw pale fingertips coming out of what looked like a cloak.

"Where did it go?" Joseph wondered, squinting through his black, thick-framed glasses.

"I don't know," I muttered. Whose hands were those clutching the Jewel? Was it the thief?

I turned toward Logan and noticed him transfer something from the book to his pocket. Had he ripped a page out, or were my eyes betraying me?

"Isn't that the Hall of Lost Gemstones?" Logan asked, walking toward the bend.

"Stay back," Adam warned. "I think I saw the thief."

"Me too." Jess's voice quivered. "Maybe you should call your mother, Adam."

Joseph lifted his sleeves. "No need. I can beat the thief."

Janine tried to hide a laugh. "Okay, hold on, Mr. Know-It-All. How exactly do you plan on doing that?"

"My power," he said, as if stating the obvious. "The light exuding from my fingertips will be plenty enough to knock out the thief."

"What if it isn't the thief? What if it's King Thoven?" I inquired. "You can never be too sure. The thief was on the

Train. How could he have gotten off at the same stop as us?"

"Arica's right," Joseph realized, running a finger over his lips. "We need to be careful."

"I think we should go. You're right, Logan. That is the Hall of Lost Gemstones. That's where we'll retrieve the gemstones," Adam informed.

Janine and Jess led the way, swerving through the halls with ease. Adam followed behind swiftly, whereas Joseph isolated himself from the pack, muttering things to himself. Finally, we reached a dead end. I stared ahead hopelessly, and then turned around.

"Where's the Hall?" I asked.

"Dunno," Jess replied. "But this is really strange. Look." She pointed to a portrait hanging on the wall. "Who do you think that is?"

"My grandfather," Adam answered. He pulled out his Wishing Knife and gave it a longing glance. Then he held it forward, right next to the poster, and indicated the Wishing Knife in the photo. "My grandfather was the one who found the Wishing Knife," Adam informed. "He said he'd found it at the bottom of a magical ocean in the American Ruby Sector. It had been fashioned of purely magical elements; it's able to cut through almost any fabric, metal—you name it." He put the Knife away.

"It looks different, though," Joseph commented. "See the lines etched on the side? It sort of looks like an eagle."

"It is," Adam agreed. "The Knife can transform into whatever animal is etched on the blade. The image changes every time it's handed down. Mine has a spider. Which reminds me . . ."

"Wait! Look at that!" I interjected. "See that door in the photo? The one that's open in the back?"

"Yeah?" Janine asked, though she didn't sound very interested. She acted as though it were a small, superfluous detail.

"If you look at the room as a whole . . . then we're in it. That door should be right over there . . ." I spun my eyes to the right, and as if by some miracle, the exact same doors stood there, shining radiantly. The door handles were long, lengthy swirls of brass. The Sorcerers Underworld symbol was stained proudly on the two doors.

"Do you think that's it? The Hall of Lost Gemstones?" Janine asked.

"We'll have to go and see," Joseph said. He moved ahead of us with strange confidence, placed both hands on the handle, and slowly pushed the doors forward.

* * *

It seemed like a whole separate world on the other side of the door. I felt as though I were entering the Golden Cave again: The whole hall glittered, the walls studded with gems, so much so that I thought they were literally *made* of gemstones. Ahead of us lay a giant podium that glowed radiantly. A thousand separate smells invaded my nose—salty sea spray, the smell of a new book, the whiff of a bouquet of roses . . . .

We all stared at the walls in concentration. They were covered with glittering gemstones of all different hues and varieties.

A whisper sounded from the walls around me. At first I thought someone else was speaking, but when I noticed no one else's mouths were moving, I knew that was false. It was difficult to detect what I was hearing at first, but the voice gradually grew louder. *Come* . . . it said calmly. *Come* . . .

"Do you hear that?" I asked abruptly. "The word *come* . . . over and over . . ." I pondered.

"You hear it too?" Jess asked. She softly touched a ruby red pentagonal gemstone in the corner of the wall. "Mine's coming from here . . ."

"Over here!" Janine called. She leaned against the back wall, near another gemstone identical to Jess's. "I hear it . . ."

"And Mum calls *me* the crazy one, sitting up all night reading," Joseph muttered.

"It's the gemstones," Adam theorized. "They're calling you, aren't they? My dad used to tell me stories about the Hall of Lost Gemstones."

"Calling? Are you bloody mad—" Joseph was cut off.

"Shh, I hear it again!" Janine cried. "Get me something to pluck my gem out with!" she said to Joseph, hair crowding over her forehead.

"What?" he said, raising his hands. "Don't look at me, Janine! I don't have tweezers."

"You can't *pluck* it out," Adam explained. "My father told me that the gemstone is just supposed to . . . well, *come* to you, if that doesn't sound crazy."

"Unfortunately, it kind of does," I joked. Before I could really theorize how we would get Jess and Janine's gemstones off the wall, I heard a sort of faint whisper emanate from the walls.

"Come . . ." I heard. The faint tone slightly reminded me of the mermaids' whispery (but evidently harsh) voices. The word repeated over and over, as if stuck on replay.

I followed the source of the noise, and then found myself right in the centre of the Hall. A diamond that looked much like my own was planted between a hexagonal topaz and a thin, gleaming amethyst.

Caught in the radiance of my gemstone, I trailed my finger lightly over the small nick in the corner. A thought of my moving back in the summer enveloped my mind, and I remembered the small shard of the diamond that had somehow broken off. The shard had punctured my palm and caused two very distinct memories (one of my mom, and one of her and Aunt Liz) to surface. With the shard missing, was my gemstone truly any different than how my mom's had been? I realized that the shard had broken off when my mom had thrown the gemstone in a small box . . . But why had she thrown the diamond? Out of frustration? Mom had never really been a fan of magic. Though the missing shard seemed trivial, I could only wonder if my gemstone had been affected in any way. I certainly hadn't felt anything strange when practicing levitation at Hill Valley, but I still felt unsure.

The walls began to shake in the midst of my thoughts. My gemstone squirmed from its place on the wall, and before I truly understood what was happening, I realized that the gemstone was . . . well, *moving*. The cut diamond was beginning to tip forward; I pressed my hand against the wall and felt the corners of the diamond dig into my skin. It had been a long time since I'd held my gemstone, and it felt like one of the most relieving and joyous things in the world.

I turned to see Janine and Jess both holding their identical gemstones. The velvet ribbon looked to have fashioned itself on the rubies again magically. When I looked down at my gemstone, the ribbon was there, too. Even the minuscule interlocking piece, which allowed the three gemstones to click together, was placed proudly at the top of the diamond.

A sea of colours swarmed in front of me. I realized that the walls were beginning to change; the gems were beginning to rearrange, looking like a giant game of *Bejeweled,* as if to make up for the missing spaces where our gems had been.

"We all set?" Logan asked, looking around nervously. I wondered why he looked so jumpy all of a sudden. Didn't he have a job to go do with the Crigoes? He really had no need to stand here with us as we were retrieving our gemstones.

"Yes," Adam said firmly. "That's one thing off our list. Now we just need to find the Jewel."

"Easy peasy," Joseph said sarcastically.

"How exactly are we going to get back when all this is done?" Janine queried. "Get home, that is."

"It shouldn't be hard, since my father keeps one of those portal phonebooks in his chamber upstairs," Adam inquired.

"The phonebook we used to get back to Hill Valley? But I thought we couldn't just *flash* into the Bermuda Triangle. I mean, that is why we took the Train, right? Surely we can't just flash *out.*"

"With my father's power, I know there's a way to teleport out of here. The Train was, of course, our only option of getting here."

I turned to view Logan's face and found it to be a canvas of boredom. He stuffed his hands in his pockets, and then turned to me casually. "Arica, can I—er—talk to you for a sec?"

I looked back at my cousins and Adam to find them deep in conversation. They didn't look as if they would notice my absence, so I agreed.

Logan led the way out of the Hall of Lost Gemstones, and as soon as everyone was out of earshot, he said:

"Remember when we were talking the other day? About how I could hear animals' thoughts?"

"Yes?"

"I wanted to talk to you about the spell. The one that would get rid of that smell—you know, when you use your powers too much. We were walking to my cabin, and then you just sort of disappeared."

"Oh, right. The twins—"

"It's okay; you don't have to explain," he said. He fished out a piece of parchment paper from his pocket and began to open it.

"What is that?" I asked. "Wait—is that the sheet you ripped out from the book? Ash's—Adam's—book?" My face flushed red-hot.

He didn't look up, but rather smiled to himself. Then he stared at the parchment and began reading something aloud: "The powers of the one that holds the Bow, no lack in time will ever show. The price that passes the magic as such . . ."

As he spoke, I began to feel extremely tired. Even with my gemstone hanging around my neck, I felt as if every drop of power inside of me was draining.

And then I knew what was happening. "This isn't a . . . a *smell* spell," I said, my voice nearly cracking. "I know this spell—it's the one to steal some of the Prophetic Child's aura. My magic." My face flushed even redder.

Logan's eyebrows creased deeply. He'd never seemed so angry before—in fact, for most of the time I'd spent with him, I'd only seen one emotion playing on his face: carefree joy.

"What . . ." My voice faded. I wanted to trip over backwards, but my muscles felt like solid ice. Logan's face seemed to change. No, the features weren't changing—his face was changing, becoming paler, and he almost looked like a ghost.

"I am who I am, Arica," he said, examining his hands. They became clearer as well, becoming pale gray. The colour in his clothes and skin slowly seeped away, as if being sucked by a vacuum. Were my eyes deceiving me?

"It's the spell." He sighed, the corners of his lips turning down. My heartbeat became short, painful stabs. I didn't dare breathe.

He sighed heavily. "I was never gonna show you a spell that would take away the smell that's produced when you use magic. Heck, there is no smell. I mean . . ." He struggled to convey his thoughts. "I'm not here to work. I don't work at the Sorcerer Palace. You could say I'm sort of . . . *normal* now."

"Normal? *Normal*? You call this . . . *this*"—I pointed at his slowly decolouring skin—"*normal*?"

He sighed again, but this time it sounded almost inhuman. "I've needed you. And your powers."

"My *powers*?" My stomach twirled. "You must be out of your mind."

"Yeah. Well, maybe I am. But at least I feel alive now. Before I followed you out of the Death Field . . . life was different."

"You followed me out of the Death Field?" Another invisible blow to the stomach. Bile rose up my throat, but I forced it down and focused. My eyes were slowly becoming blurrier, and I began feeling light-headed. "When? Where? *How*?"

"When you guys took those Crigoes—that stop you made in the woods. As soon as you showed up in my cabin, I knew I had to follow you out. You were alive—I could feel it. My sister was being a bit of a snob if you ask me.

Yes, that girl was my sister," he said after my jaw hit the floor. "And I've wanted out of the Death Field for longer than you know. My sister says she lives alone, but that's not true—I visit that cabin all the time. She just likes to say she's lonely so other people will feel sorry for her. Me? I'm different. I didn't want to be *dead* anymore. Especially after that gruesome car crash. That wasn't fair. Not at all."

"Why do you need me? Why would you try taking my powers?" He may have had a heartbreaking story, but the facts certainly weren't adding up.

"Why else? I was in the Death Field. Arica, I was *dead.* The only thing that's keeping me alive right now is the power you're radiating. As the Prophetic Child."

"I don't believe you," I stated firmly, but my hands trembled uncontrollably.

His eyebrows furrowed even more. "I'm a ghost, Arica. There's no denying that. But now you have to help me. I need some of your aura to stay alive; otherwise I'll die in a matter of minutes," he said, his voice becoming grave.

"I shouldn't help you. You *lied.* And you belong in the Death Field."

"Do I?" he asked innocently. "I deserve to live freely in the Sorcerers Underworld. Living or dead—does it really matter? Can't I live out life like I had before? That's where you come in. You help me, and I help you."

"Help me with what?" I shrilled immediately.

He paused, faint crinkles forming around his eyes. "I'm sorry, Arica. But it was me who took the King's Jewel. I stole it, in hopes that we could . . . exchange. You give me my life back, and I give you the Jewel. Is that so much to ask?"

"Stole? You *took* the Jewel? Are you crazy? Why would you—" My emotions spilled out of me helplessly. I finally

choked on the last word, too stunned to speak. My brain melted as if it had just been placed in the microwave.

"Arica, please. Just listen." He moved closer, placing his hand on my elbow. It felt like rubber, slowing fading. His touch became fainter by the second.

"I'm dying. Again. Slowly. But when I'm near you I'm alive. And I need you to help me. Please." He stared at me intensely. The rosy colour of his cheeks reappeared gradually, along with the familiar golden tone of his skin. "Let me finish the spell—I only meant to take some of your power, just enough to keep me alive. *Then* I'll give you the Jewel. I swear."

I choked back a million biting answers in hopes that Logan was telling the truth. But was he? I couldn't tell, with his handsome features arrayed so calmly.

Just as I mustered the courage to speak, a haunting voice crept out from the darkness: "Fool. Nothing but a bitter, bitter fool."

I spun around, my vision blurring. The Palace's lights flickered suddenly. I realized I had been away from Adam and my cousins for far too long. Had they reached the king's chamber already?

A resounding, creepy laugh echoed off the walls. I searched for the source of the noise, Logan's words still ringing in my ears. All except one of the lights flickered to their deaths: this one acted as the spotlight, posed right near the end of the hallway. At the bottom of the streaming candescence was a man, with a deep-set cloak shrouding his body like some sort of fabric barrier.

My lip trembled. The man's face, to my shock, was a familiar one. I'd seen him so long ago, when I'd first awoken at Head Quarters and met Adam's mom. I felt as though his name were being pounded into my head with a hammer, each hit representing another heartbeat.

It was . . . *Pedro.*

He sauntered forward, his cloak billowing behind him. His eyes were dark, like black holes, but they seemed to glint red ever so slightly.

I stood, frozen in position, as he raised his hand. A shocking blue-white light escaped his fingers and caught me in a trance. His grin grew larger.

At that moment, a nightmare suddenly encapsulated my thoughts. I was in a jail cell, far away, with a man controlling my every move . . . .

It was the nightmare I'd had when Ash had taken me to the Sorcerers Underworld without my knowledge. When that mark had appeared on my wrist. And, strangely enough, his reddish eyes perfectly matched those of the man in my nightmare. Was it true then? Was the man in my nightmare truly the Jail Guard, Pedro?

"Arica," he said, shooting a weak grin. He lowered his arm, allowing the throbbing blue light to fade from his fingers. "It's been quite a while, wouldn't you agree?"

I didn't dare move my lips. I was too stunned to speak. Logan, however, stepped forward, unfazed by Pedro's grand appearance.

"Fool," Pedro repeated.

"I'm not a—" I began.

"I'm not speaking to you, *Arica.* I meant the boy. You." Pedro gave Logan a long, piercing stare.

"M-me?" he said. "Why me?"

Pedro gave a deep chuckle. "One does not claim anything without the proper evidence. Surely you would have adduced it by now?"

"Uh . . . I have no clue what you're talking about." Logan seemed to shiver.

"Yes, I believe you do. You claim yourself the thief, do you? Show me the evidence. Where is the Jewel?"

"I . . . I don't have it," he admitted.

"You *don't have it*?" I questioned angrily. "What do you mean? We were going to trade! You said *your life*—"

"I said my life would disappear if you didn't help me, yes," Logan agreed. "And after those terms . . . I would have disappeared. Gone. Poof. I have no more business here."

"No *business*? You *stole* the Jewel!"

"No . . ." He swallowed. "No, Arica, I didn't."

I forced my emotions down. "Then who did?" My voice became gravelly, a mixture of anger and pity blending together.

Logan opened his mouth to speak, but instead, Pedro took his turn: "He didn't," Pedro said, a wry smile playing on his face, "because I did."

TWENTY-ONE: THE THIEF

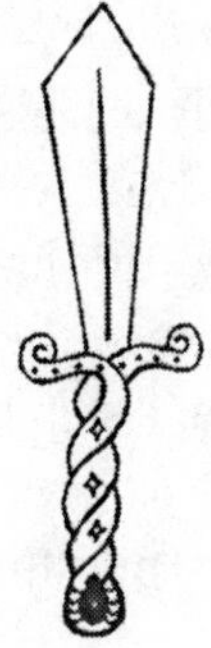

Even before I could register his words, Pedro threw his right arm forward and sent a torrent of blue light toward Logan. Logan, his skin nearly translucent, looked at Pedro with one last glance of horror before being knocked against the wall to the right. He collapsed beneath the staircase, stunned and unconscious.

Pedro then looked toward me; my eyes were glued to his involuntarily. He must've been using his power—the power to make people obey him—to make me stand forward, because at the moment I felt like I didn't have the stability to properly stand upright.

Then he removed something from the deep recesses of his cloak and placed it outward, as if handing me a peace offering. In his hand was a beautiful crown. It was gold, with several gems embedded horizontally along the front. The colours of the gems seemed to switch from purple, to white, to light pink, like a kaleidoscope. "Beautiful, isn't it?" Pedro inquired. He marvelled at the Jewel. "And it wasn't hard to steal, either. As soon as I made the scrambling chef obey me, he replaced his knife with the Jewel and handed it right to me."

"Lewis," I said, aghast.

"Ah, indeed. I recall the name," he said. He took another step forward, and then he sauntered toward a table to the side. It wasn't really a table, but rather just a large surface with a mirror attached. Pedro stared into the mirror inquisitively, and then set the Jewel on the dark surface. As soon as the crown touched the table, it began to shake uncontrollably. Pedro took a step back and observed as the crown rose into the air. The Jewel began to glow, golden light seeping from its exterior, until I could barely handle looking at it.

Pedro laughed, seeming amused by who-knows-what. He clenched his fists into a ball and gave a thin, sinister smile.

My memory suddenly shot back to the strange nightmare I'd had about the cloaked man. I had had that nightmare once in Hill Valley, and once on the Train, when I'd seen Violet's face. But Violet wasn't actually the cloaked person, then—it was Pedro. It only made sense. He was the Jail Guard, which was probably why I was in a prison in the nightmare, and *he* had the power to make people obey him. He was also the thief—it all clicked into place.

Pedro's amusement was still evident. "I do hope you received that note I sent you on the Train. *I am darkest when the sky is bright.*" Another chuckle. It made sense—shadows appear in brightness, and Pedro was a Shadower.

A voice suddenly produced itself from the door to the Hall. "Stop!"

I turned and almost collapsed at the sight of Janine and Jessica. Their identical cherry-red hair flew behind them as they strode toward me. "Stop!" Jess called. "That's the Jewel!"

"Yes, I am aware," Pedro said with a laugh. "And it belongs to me now. As soon as the process is complete . . . ."

"Process?!" Janine asked. "This is no *process.* That rattling is going to cause the building to collapse. Oh, dear," she continued in bewilderment, hands on both sides of her head.

"Where's my father?!" Adam stormed out of the Hall, looking frantic, Joseph just behind him. "Where did you take him?"

"I didn't take him anywhere," Pedro said, admiring his cloak. "However, I *did* take something of his . . ."

"The Jewel. We want it back," Joseph said calmly, placing his right hand out as if gesturing him to come closer. "Now."

"You think I'm just going to give this up? This Jewel is mine now! I have worked tirelessly for years, planning for this day. And now I have it!

"Do you know how long I've been preparing this for? This theft? Over fourteen years! I've been waiting for too long. Too long to steal the Jewel. Become the new king!"

"What?" I cried. "You think that you can just take a crown and call yourself a king? You're nothing but a sham. A fake. A liar!"

"Shut your mouth!" he demanded. "I will become the new king. That's no way to talk to your future leader."

"No," a voice claimed behind us. I turned around. It was Joseph. He was shaking his head from side to side, looking down at his feet. "No," he whispered again. "What makes you think you'll be our leader? You belong to the evil side. With the Shadowers."

"Not all Shadowers are evil, unfortunately," Pedro said, examining his finger nails. "There's Andrae. And Teal . . ." His voice choked on the last name.

"They're good because we put them in order. Now they work for us," Prince Adam stated, a hint of anger in his voice.

"Now, now," Pedro said. "Settle down, feisty one. No need to get all worked up." He grinned.

"There has to be more to it," I said disconcertedly, partly trying to convince myself. "More reason to why you took the Jewel. Becoming the king doesn't seem like your only interest," I said, giving his Shadowers tattoo a sharp glance.

"You are a clever girl. I guess that's why they call *you* the Prophetic Child, am I right?" He laughed again, and then cleared his throat quickly. "Yes . . . the Wishing Knife is the only object that is able to detach a gem from King Thoven's crown. Which is exactly why I *need* it."

Adam gripped the Knife in his right hand, his face awash with fear.

A blanket of perspiration wrapped my palm. "Why would you need it?" I retaliated, trying to compose my strength.

"There is a very special ruby on the crown that contains a powerful potion . . . one that is too rare to be found anywhere else in the Sorcerers Underworld. The final ingredient to the Shadowers potion—one that will cause the drinker to become immortal. An immortal Shadower."

"Immortality is impossible. Not even that ruby could contain something so powerful that it would make a person live forever," Joseph informed.

"There is no time to debate, if you haven't already realized," Pedro retaliated, his fingers dancing with anticipation. I could almost feel him summoning his power from here. "If you trade me the Wishing Knife, Arica, I promise to hand you the Jewel as it was—after I've retrieved my special ingredient, of course."

"I'd never give someone the chance to live forever. You deserve to be in the very place you've overlooked for so long—"

My throat suddenly became very dry. A throbbing pain enveloped my mind, followed by the sudden urge to lower my head. I tried to fight the mysterious desire, but it was as if someone was forcing me to do it.

"Very good. I see you know how to follow requests." Pedro gave a dry laugh that was echoed. It sounded as if a whole sinister crowd were behind him, laughing along with the joke.

And, to my horror, there was a crowd. I had barely noticed their entrances in the darkness, but several figures were now standing behind Pedro. To my horror, Ash was there, her hair as fiery as her eyes. There, too, was Rowen. I couldn't exactly make out his eye colour, but just the sight of him made me tempted to run toward him. To save him from the wretched Sapphires who had entrapped him in the first place.

"And who would we be without a noble leader, Pedro?" Ash said. Her words chilled me. I realized I hadn't heard her voice in a long time, but they still cut through me with the same effect they had on the night of the campfire.

"A noble leader indeed." He cleared his throat. "Co-leader, to be specific. Vina?"

My knees nearly buckled. The headmistress came sauntering in from the Hall, her hair tied up in a tight bun, eyes sinister. The emerald cloak she'd been wearing the last time I'd seen her was on her back now.

"Vina," I said, my voice filled with distaste.

"Arica. Lovely transition we've made." She grinned, licking her teeth. "We can battle right here, amid real magic, instead of that ratty old school." She pressed her lips together firmly. "Pedro here has his own desires with the Jewel, and as do I." Vina chuckled when she saw the twins' pale faces. "Oh, Janine, Jessica, why so pale? Surely you would expect the Sorceress Wife to come back with vengeance? To get what I truly deserve."

"You don't deserve anything," I spat.

Vina smirked. "The tables have turned. It looks as if we now have a possession that *you* need."

I swallowed, her observation running through my mind. Clearly she was right—and she'd come here with more than the Sapphires. She had Pedro, and with his abilities, nothing could turn out in our favour.

Geoff, Rein, and Cale's figures stood out more prominently as they drifted forward. A knot in my stomach grew larger, and I felt even more light-headed than before. Geoff and Rein standing beside each other was strange, like a torrent of fire and ice colliding, both diminishing and complementing each other still.

Jess stepped forward, her lips pressed together, looking as if she might throw up. I assumed it was the tremendous amount of evil that she sensed, swelling up inside her, overriding her other senses. Lembrose (calling her Vina was still strange) matched Jess's footsteps and advanced toward us formidably, her feet dragging across the bright, golden-tiled floor. Her heels clicked until she was finally just a few inches from Jessica's face. Vina let her fingers touch Jessica's chin for a moment, and she flinched. "Oh, dear Jessica," Vina said, as she leveled her face with Jess's, "you know you can't beat *us.* Not this time. Not with Pedro.

He can make you all obey with a single snap of his fingers. He can make everyone obey. Everyone in the entirety of the Sorcerers Underworld."

"We can stop him," Jess said while turning her head toward me. "We've got the Prophetic Child *and* the prince. We're unbeatable."

Vina took a moment to contemplate this, eyes down, fingers caressing her own chin now. Although the gemstones were not in her possession, she still looked and felt like a powerful, sinister villain, especially when placed beside Pedro. I won't deny it—a drop of fear slid down my back like sweat, and I shivered just thinking back to the night of the battle on Halloween. Would another dramatic event like that occur now?

"Unbeatable?" I wasn't sure if it was Pedro or Rein who had spoken, because both their voices had the same deep resonance. When Rein stepped out of the darkness, I realized it was him who had spoken the four syllables. His appearance clearly had not changed, save for the slight ruggedness of his dark black hair. Ice was now coating his hands, and his eyes flashed emerald-green. "We may have lost once, but it won't happen again now. We've got Pedro, and this time, your powers won't stand a chance." His voice still seemed to have the same casualness it had back in school, but now there was a pronounced wickedness.

The air turned moist. I wasn't sure if someone had turned up the temperature, but I felt just like I had on the beach in Miami. My clothes stuck to my skin, clinging to the perspiration.

Geoff was laughing, along with the rest of the Sapphires, but the heat was beginning to numb out my senses. I didn't see any fire on Geoff's hands, which meant he'd discovered some other way to emit his powers without having to turn his hands into a fireplace. Maybe the Sapphires had been learning and doing more on the Water Train than I'd thought.

Rowen stepped forward, almost as if in a trance, and I was sure his Sleeplock symptoms were kicking in. He moved scarily fast, and Lembrose caught his shoulder and reeled him back. "Oh, dear, Rowen," she said, and I struggled to remember that Vina was his great-grandmother, shuddering, "still not too well, I see. He'll see whose side he truly belongs to in good time," she said, and Rowen nodded. He gave me a long glance, and I felt my thoughts disperse. I clutched my forehead in agony, a sharp pain cutting through me like a knife, but the pain was only momentary. Soon I felt like my thoughts weren't dispersing, but rather coming together. Words, I noticed, came together to form a certain sentence:

I'll be better soon.

I couldn't believe my own mind. Had I formed that thought? Or had Rowen somehow learned how to implant the thought within me?

The possibility of that felt slim. But who else would have said that phrase other than Rowen? He was obviously trying to send a message. He would be better, and he would join our side.

There was still hope.

"Stand straight!" Pedro yelled, and then flicked his hand upward. I felt my back straighten involuntarily. Pedro was looking at me with a dazzling fire in his eyes, smiling evilly to himself, until a ball of ice hurled toward him. Pedro ducked, wheezed, and then eyed us with his jaw hung. I turned to Adam and saw him smirking. He spun his eyes toward me, and I grinned, gracious that he'd delayed Pedro's power for the moment.

Pedro reacted immediately. He summoned both hands and caught Adam in a trance, and Adam's knees began to buckle. Joseph mustered a bright light and threw Pedro off balance. Pedro stumbled slightly, but I didn't have time to see if he recovered. Joseph had just entered the corner of my vision. He was muttering something that looked like *effisate* but I soon realized he was saying *levitate.*

Joseph then turned toward the Jewel, and I realized what he'd meant. Levitate the Jewel. Capture it, without anyone else noticing. The thing was, it would be difficult to do with everyone's attention on the crown in the first place.

I turned to the twins, who were both crouched in running stance against the Sapphires. Cale was levitating an abstract piece of metal—some sort of weapon—and threw it across the wall. I wasn't sure what he was aiming for, but he'd caused the room to shake furiously. I fell to the ground, seeing bits of dust falling over me like a smoke screen. Finally, once it had dissipated, I lifted myself and the twins from the ground. Geoff appeared suddenly from the shroud, his hands covered in green fire. To my shock, he threw the fire just over our heads. I realized he was aiming for the banister above us. The railing circled just over our heads, so the fire trailed along the path and created a ring of emerald fire above us.

"The railing's going to crumble on us!" Janine noted, her voice ironed with anxiety. Jess was gripping her sister's arm.

"Quick! Get the Jewel!" Joseph called. Amid the green fire that was billowing above us, I realized that Joseph was still mustering a strong yellow-white light. Pedro, however, was battling back, causing a lightning-shaped blue-white energy to escape his hands and collide with Joseph's beam of light.

I turned my attention to the Jewel and thrust my hands outward. The crown began to rise shakily and, with overconfidence, I smiled. I brought the crown toward me, the gems embedded on the front glittering. It hovered there for a moment before it was suddenly whisked away. Cale was in control of it now, his hands caressing the invisible air.

How was it possible for Cale to control the Jewel when it wasn't even made of metal? Or was he now able to control different elements, too?

I didn't hesitate to fight back. The Jewel looked as if it was in the middle of a game of tug-of-war, moving back and forth, acting indecisive. A long line of golden light produced itself from Adam's Wishing Knife, aimed directly for the Jewel, so that the crown was now in his possession. The Jewel dragged closer toward him, moving eagerly . . .

"Stop him!" Ash cried. Adam's concentration broke, and the Jewel fell to the ground. Cale summoned the Jewel to him before I could even raise my arm.

The floor quaked angrily. I could feel Ash's Underworlder powers beginning to build, and at that moment, my thoughts flooded to Violet. My hands lowered, and I breathed heavily. A million thoughts trickled in at once. Violet, Ash's sister, had the same power as Ash, which meant that she could still travel between worlds even if she was dead at this very moment.

Ash's mouth was twisted up to the right in a sort of smirk. I suppose I had said Violet's name aloud, for she was laughing and saying something that I couldn't exactly hear over the lightning crackles of energy that Pedro was creating. Joseph was beginning to look weary.

Adam lunged forward, as if about to capture the Jewel, but Ash managed to get there first. I wasn't sure if I'd been seeing things incorrectly, but did Ash just *teleport* to Adam's place? She had appeared in a flash, unless she'd somehow travelled to the Sorcerers Underworld and back in a split second.

Ash gripped the Jewel before Adam could take it. Adam lunged again, but Ash grabbed his wrist. Adam cried out in pain, and I could see the Sorcerers Underworld insignia being burned upon his inner wrist. In a few seconds, Adam looked up in recovery fairly quickly. He swung his Knife toward her torso, but Ash just disappeared as she had before. After a second, she appeared behind Adam, now firmly holding his shoulder, her eyes filled with malice.

"No!" I cried. I felt my legs burn as I ran toward him. Ash wore an evil smile, and looked as if she was waiting for the perfect moment to teleport. Adam began to look blurry. I knew he was being taken at that moment, about to be transported someplace in the Sorcerers Underworld, just like I had on Halloween night.

I wanted to grab Adam's hand before he could disappear, but it was too late. He disappeared, along with Ash, leaving nothing but a thin white vapour and a knife.

A knife?

No—Adam had left the Wishing Knife in his place. But why?

Clearly he needed me to end this, and his Knife would do it. I picked it up hastily and then stood unsteadily, feeling woozy for some reason. The Wishing Knife felt as if it weighed a hundred pounds. Janine and Jess both steadied me, and then asked what had happened. There was, unfortunately, no time to explain. I had the Wishing Knife now, and I knew Adam would take care of Ash to prohibit her from reappearing back in the Palace. It was just me and my cousins now.

"It's just us Millers," I said finally. I turned back to Pedro, defiance taking over me. Pedro took a longing glance at the Knife and lowered his arms. Joseph, who had been working tirelessly to produce that light, fell back to the ground, heaving. Beads of sweat layered his body. Janine and Jess rushed to his side and fanned his weary face.

"The Knife," Pedro said, and abruptly threw up his arm as if to tell the other Sapphires to stop what they were doing. "The Knife is all I need, Arica. Give it, and we both win. I'll give you the Jewel."

Pedro summoned Cale to hand him the Jewel, and then he held it out to show its validity. "Come on, now. It's real. Just let me get what I want and I'll give you the same." Now he spoke with a strange innocence that was deeply rooted within him. His goal to retrieve the Jewel and get this last ingredient for his immortal Shadower potion truly was all he'd wanted for *years* on end. That was probably why he'd turned himself in to the Royals in the first place: so he could get a job and then, after years of calculation, steal what he needed most.

I stood there, stealing quick glances at my cousins, and felt, not for the first time, afraid. Afraid of what would happen if I did give the Knife, and afraid of what would happen if I didn't. The possibilities were endless with magic.

At that moment, I felt the Wishing Knife beginning to change form in my hand. It was evolving to take on a golden colour instead of silver, and the gems on the hilt glinted sapphire blue. The blade, too, became gold, and I caught my reflection on the surface. The spider image had changed into one of a sparrow, and I could almost hear its melodic chirps from within the hilt.

"Well?" Lembrose asked eagerly. Clearly she hadn't noticed the change of the Knife. What did this mean? Adam's father had passed on this possession to him, as did his father, and each generation the image on the hilt would change to the form that the Knife could take. If there was a sparrow on the hilt now, did that mean that it could change into that form? My heart raced at the possibility. But what exactly would a bird do for me now?

With no other options, I formulated a plan. Janine, Jess, and Joseph clearly wouldn't know my idea, but I counted on them to follow my act.

"And what happens after I give you the Jewel? After I've told the king who the real thief is?"

Pedro's jaw became slack. He cleared his throat. "T-turn me in, you mean?" Clearly he hadn't thought this through.

"Yes, exactly," I said. I gave Janine and Jess a wink, and they looked slightly confused. "What happens then? Surely the Royals want their thief incarcerated."

"I shall never be incarcerated. The closest I'll ever get to those jail cells is through my *former* job as a Jail Guard."

Janine stood reflexively, and then returned my wink surreptitiously. "Oh, no!" she said, feigning distress. She held one hand to her right temple, the other holding her gemstone. "The Royals . . . they're coming . . . they'll take you!"

"A Visioner?" Pedro asked, looking fearful now.

"She's lying," Cale said definitively.

"I'm not," Janine said, her voice barely quivering. "They're coming to take him. I swear."

Pedro looked furious now. He threw up his arms, and a tube of light flooded toward her. Janine was caught in his gaze. "Tell me the truth," he demanded.

Janine struggled to look away, but his power was too dominating. She would give in and obey any second now. "You . . . you . . ." she said.

I had to stop Janine from telling the truth. Before she could utter another word, I threw the Knife straight through the beam of light with archery precision and, to my surprise, it broke the blue light Pedro was producing. To his misfortune, however, the Knife grazed his hand and left a bloody gash on his palm. Pedro seethed, his wrist upturned, as blood began to escape his hand.

I looked away and observed as the Knife, in midair, transformed into a golden sparrow. The sparrow soared upward, chirping, and spread its small but precious golden wings. It seemed to radiate golden light, even brighter than the light that the Jewel created, and caught everyone in a trance. As everyone was staring upward, I pressed one hand against my gemstone and levitated the Jewel toward me. The crown flew into my hands safely, and in that moment, I felt triumphant.

Then the unexpected happened. The bird chirped again, but this time its chirp sounded almost sonic, a sound that someone could hear from miles away. The sound pierced my eardrums. I reflexively brought my hands to my ears, still clinging to the Jewel. Everyone followed.

After the sound of the chirps, the doors to the Sorcerer Palace swung open. An angry wave of water stormed inside, swallowing everything it its path. I felt like I was in the flood in Majestorium Square all over again.

The water ascended with tremendous speed, and this time I clung to my gemstone ferociously. If my gemstone flooded away again, I would never be able to forgive myself.

I struggled to hold the gemstone and the Jewel against my chest. I looked up for an infinitesimal moment, noticing the sparrow was gone. I began to feel something formulate in my palm, and with quick realization, I noticed it was the Wishing Knife. I released my palms from my ears, and, in my haste, I accidently jabbed the Knife toward the crown. The sharp blade connected with an emerald hidden on the back of the crown. The emerald flew off the crown and into the air. I knew the Knife was the only thing able to detach a gem from the crown, but I hadn't known how easily it could do so.

I looked at the empty spot on the back of the crown. The emerald couldn't have been that important, could it?

I was very wrong.

I sucked in a breath, and then the water rushed over us. The sound of the water blocked my ears. Janine and Jess were swimming nearby, but bright slivers of light shining through the water distorted my vision. Finally, the water began to lower, as if the floor was a giant sponge sucking up all the water. I tried standing in the water once it was wading just below my hips, and moved sluggishly to my cousins. The Jewel was still in my hands, but now something felt different. An emerald had clearly come off, and Pedro had noticed.

Pedro stirred nervously. "The emerald . . . it's gone," he said, aghast. Then he stared, fury filling his eyes. "You don't know what you've started."

I had no idea what he was talking about, but at the moment, I didn't have time to think about it. The water began rising again, but this time in a torrent, carrying me and my cousins up with it. Vina and the Sapphires, all damp with water, looked weary and small below us.

"It is only the beginning, Arica!" Pedro called from below. He said more, but his words drowned away. The water was closing in on us. I shivered once more, and then the twins and Joseph clung onto each other. We grouped in a tight circle, the Jewel hovering between us, as water rushed over our heads once more.

And then everything became black.

TWENTY-TWO:
AN UNEXPECTED RELATIVE

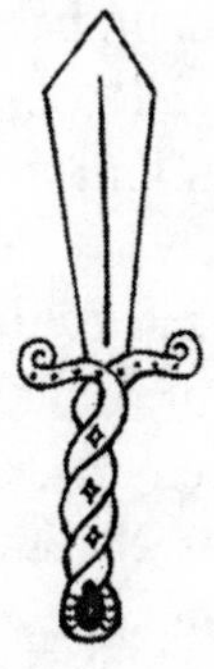

The first thing I noticed was the ceiling. A plain, white ceiling, but a familiar one. By the time I'd registered the mattress beneath me, I'd realized where I was.

Home.

Faint, melodic bird chirping sounded from my window. I turned my head, scanning for the source, when finally I spotted a beautiful golden sparrow nested in the very corner. It hopped a few times, chirping some more, as if trying to catch my attention.

I stood up roughly and walked, entranced, toward the window. Moonlight poured through the glass, casting an eerie light through the room. My hands seemed to move robotically toward the golden sparrow. It didn't look very real—more like something I would see in a dream, or some surreal image. I inched my fingers closer, about to touch it to verify that it was real, but then the bird puffed into a ball of feathers. A wisp of vapour rose from the feathers, slowly forming a wavering knife—the Wishing Knife.

I gripped the Knife, the gems engraving faint shapes on my palm. A pretty depiction of a bird was engraved on the hilt, just as a spider had been engraved on it when Adam owned the Knife. I examined my reflection in the blade and then realized how long it'd been since I'd last looked in a mirror. On the Water Train, probably. I felt as if I hadn't been on the Water Train in ages. Raven, Drake, Summer—even Violet—all seemed like distant images in my mind. With the recent battle, my mind was already seared with facts and worries. Pedro hadn't gotten to detach the ruby from the Jewel like he'd wanted, but something else had happened. Something to do with an emerald? Pedro had looked pretty shaken up the last time I'd seen him. And his final words—*It is only the beginning*—were not comforting, either.

Luckily, the Jewel was in our possession. I'd seen it disappear with the twins and Joseph, so they must've had it. We'd accomplished our goal—to retrieve the gemstones and the King's Jewel—but what about our new enemy, Pedro? The Sapphires and Lembrose were only stronger with him at their side, even if he was no longer in possession of the Jewel. A strong, calming smell overcame my senses. It smelt like tea, or coffee, something Mom would make.

I felt as if an iron fist gripped my heart for a moment before releasing itself again. *Mom.*

I grabbed the Wishing Knife, tore down the staircase, and ran into the kitchen. Mom, whose back had been facing me, had now twisted her torso. One hand rested on a teapot, the other holding a few dangling tea bags.

"Mom . . . oh, Mom!" I ran to her and gave her a long hug. She fumbled a bit with her tea bags, but finally returned the hug.

"Arica," she said smoothly. I looked toward her and noticed that her forehead was covered in worry lines. She looked back at the teapot sternly with her eyebrows furrowed together.

"Mom, I'm sorry I couldn't really talk to you before, but with my gemstone missing, and the Jewel—"

"I know, honey." She rested her hands against the table, and then spun her sea-blue eyes toward me. "But we've got a visitor over right now. Can't really talk much. And did you even brush your hair, sweetheart?" She gave my head a pat. "Speaking of which, how did you come in the house?"

I huffed, smiling. "I'll explain later. There's a lot I have to tell you—I mean *a lot*."

"Save it for tea time," Mom said. She placed the teapot on a tray and then lifted it gingerly. "Coming?" she asked.

"Is Aunt Liz over?" I questioned. I wondered why Mom would be making tea so late at night, unless it was some sort of special occasion.

Mom glanced down darkly. "No. Someone else. Come." She spoke in clipped tones, as if she had a lot on her mind. Suddenly Mom didn't really seem like Mom anymore.

I followed her out the kitchen door and into the living room. On the couch there sat a man, his back faced toward me. He had stiff brown-black hair, wore a trench coat, and was hunched over as if deeply concentrating on the Canucks game on the television screen.

When he turned, my heart completely stopped.

His electric gray eyes were speculative, surrounded by strangely ordinary square glasses. His face seemed less rough—more of a business-man sort of complexion. He stood up, and then held out his hand gingerly, palm outward, for a handshake.

That was when I noticed the scar.

Among the many lines engraved on his hand, one seemed to be more prominent than the others. A sort of snake-like line, one that must've come from a knife accident. Perhaps an accident in the kitchen, or an accident at work . . .

Or an accident in battle.

He noticed me staring down at his palm and slowly closed it into a fist. He then placed his hand back at his side, still curled in a ball. "That's all right," he said, seeming deflated. "My usual response when I try to give people handshakes. One of the many reasons I'm not on Wall Street."

Mom laughed quizzically. "You look so much like Aaron," she commented, which only caused my rage to increase. I felt as if I wanted to scream. There was no reason for this man to be inside my house—especially after a long, arduous battle involving the matter of the King's Jewel.

"Pedro, would you like some green tea?" Mom asked.

"Yes, please," he answered. His response was strangely warm, unlike the steel-hard voice I had heard only minutes before. He sat on the couch and then took in the room. Just at that moment, I felt like lunging forward—grabbing him with fists clenched, uttering everything and anything I could possibly imagine . . . .

At that moment, I remembered the man in the blinding white suit, the one who could foretell the future. He'd said something about the thief . . . something that we shared. But it wasn't until now that I finally figured out what he had said. Finally come to *terms* with what he had said.

The word rang in my ears like an alarm: blood. Meaning we were related.

I turned to Mom, who was pasting a large smile on her face. Tears of happiness filled her eyes, and I couldn't understand why Mom would be so happy that Pedro was here. How could she be smiling when the thief of the Jewel was sitting right in our living room?

Mom turned to me and uttered one of the most horrible sentences I'd ever heard. One that would replay in my mind for the rest of my life.

Mom poured the tea, and then rubbed my shoulders from behind. "Arica," she said, and then inhaled deeply, "I'd like you to meet your uncle Pedro."

CPSIA information can be obtained at www.ICGtesting.com
Printed in the USA
LVOW11s1731111113

360878LV00001B/16/P